I0649041

The Red Planet

William J. Locke

Contents

THE RED PLANET

BY

William J. Locke

THE RED PLANET

BY

WILLIAM J. LOCKE
AUTHOR OF "THE WONDERFUL
YEAR," "JAFFERY," "THE BELOVED VAGABOND," ETC.

Not only over death strewn plains,
Fierce mid the cold white stars,
But over sheltered vales of home,
Hides the Red Planet Mars.

THE RED PLANET
CHAPTER I

"Lady Fenimore's compliments, sir, and will you be so kind as to step round to Sir Anthony at once?"

Heaven knows that never another step shall I take in this world again; but Sergeant Marigold has always ignored the fact. That is one of the many things I admire about Marigold. He does not throw my poor paralysed legs, so to speak, in my face. He accepts them as the normal equipment of an employer. I don't know what I should do without Marigold.... You see we were old comrades in the South African War, where we both got badly knocked to pieces. He was Sergeant in my battery, and the same Boer shell did for both of us. At times we join in cursing that shell heartily, but I am not sure that we do not hold it in sneaking affection. It initiated us into the brotherhood of death. Shortly afterwards when we had crossed the border-line back into life, we exchanged, as tokens, bits of the shrapnel which they had extracted from our respective carcases. I have not enquired what he did with his bit; but I keep mine in a certain locked drawer.... There were only the two of us left on the gun when we were knocked out.... I should like to tell you the whole story, but you wouldn't listen to me. And no wonder. In comparison with the present world convulsion in which the slaughtered are reckoned by millions, the Boer War seems a trumpery affair of bows and arrows. I am a back-number. Still, back-numbers have their feelings--and their memories.

I sometimes wonder, as I sit in this wheel-chair, with my abominable legs dangling down helplessly, what Sergeant Marigold thinks of me. I know what I think of Marigold. I think him the ugliest devil that God ever created and further marred after creating him. He is a long, bony creature like a knobbly ram-rod, and his face is about the colour and shape of a damp, mildewed walnut. To hide a bald head into which a silver plate has been fixed, he wears a luxuriant curly brown wig, like those that used to adorn waxen gentlemen in hair-dressing windows. His is one of those unhappy moustaches that stick out straight and scanty like a cat's. He has the slit of a letter-box mouth of the Irishman in caricature, and only half a dozen teeth spaced like a skeleton company. Nothing will induce him to procure false ones. It is a matter of principle. Between the wearing of false hair and the wearing of false teeth he makes a distinction of unfathomable subtlety. He is an obstinate beast. If he wasn't he would not, with four fingers of his right hand shot away, have remained with me on that gun. In the same way, neither tears nor entreaties nor abuse have induced him to wear a glass eye. On high days and holidays, whenever he desires to look smart and dashing, he covers the unpleasing orifice with a black shade. In ordinary workaday life he cares not how much he offends the aesthetic sense. But the other eye, the sound left eye, is a wonder--the precious jewel set in the head of the ugly toad. It is large, of ultra-marine blue, steady, fearless, humorous, tender--everything heroic and beautiful and romantic you can imagine about eyes. Let him clap a hand over that eye and you will hold him the most dreadful ogre that ever escaped out of a fairy tale. Let him clap a hand over the other eye and look full at you out of the good one and you will think him the Knightliest man that ever was--and in my poor opinion, you would not be far wrong.

So, out of this nightmare of a face, the one beautiful eye of Sergeant Marigold was bent on me, as he delivered his message.

I thrust back my chair from the writing-table.

"Is Sir Anthony ill?"

"He rode by the gate an hour ago looking as well as either you or me, sir."

"That's not very reassuring," said I.

Marigold did not take up the argument. "They've sent the car for you, sir."

"In that case," said I, "I'll start immediately."

Marigold wheeled my chair out of the room and down the passage to the hall, where he fitted me with greatcoat and hat. Then, having trundled me to the front gate, he picked me up--luckily I have always been a small spare man--and deposited me in the car. I am always nervous of anyone but Marigold trying to carry me. They seem to stagger and fumble and bungle. Marigold's arms close round me like an iron clamp and they lift me with the mechanical certainty of a crane.

He jumped up beside the chauffeur and we drove off.

Perhaps when I get on a little further I may acquire the trick of telling a story. At present I am baffled by the many things that clamour for prior record. Before bringing Sir Anthony on the scene, I feel I ought to say something more about myself, to explain why Lady Fenimore should have sent for me in so peremptory a fashion. Following the model of my favourite author Balzac--you need the awful leisure that has been mine to appreciate him--I ought to describe the house in which I live, my establishment--well, I have begun with Sergeant Marigold--and the little country town which is practically the scene of the drama in which were involved so many bound to me by close ties of friendship and affection.

I ought to explain how I come to be writing this at all.

Well, to fill in my time, I first started by a diary--a sort of War Diary of Wellingsford, the little country town in question. Then things happened with which my diary was inadequate to cope. Everyone came and told me his or her side of the story. All through, I found thrust upon me the parts of father-confessor, intermediary, judge, advocate, and conspirator.... For look you, what kind of a life can a man lead situated as I am? The crowning glory of my days, my wife, is dead. I have neither chick nor child. No brothers or sisters, dead or alive. The Bon Dieu and Sergeant Marigold (the latter assisted by his wife and a maid or two) look after my creature comforts. What have I in the world to do that is worth doing save concern myself with my country and my friends?

With regard to my country, in these days of war, I do what I can. Until finally flattened out by the War Office, I pestered them for such employment as a cripple might undertake. As an instance of what a paralytic was capable I quoted Couthon, member of the National Convention and the Committee of Public Safety. You can see his chair, not very unlike mine, in the Musee Carnavalet in Paris. Perhaps that is where I blundered. The idea of a shrieking revolutionary in Whitehall must have sent a cold shiver down their spines. In the meanwhile, I serve on as many War Committees in Wellingsford as is physically possible for Sergeant Marigold to get me into. I address recruiting meetings. I have taken earnest young Territorial artillery officers in courses of gunnery. You know they work with my own beloved old fifteen pounders, brought up to date with new breeches, recoils, shields, and limbers. For months there was a brigade in Wellings Park, and I used to watch their drill. I was like an old actor coming once again before the footlights.... Of course it was only in the mathematics of the business that I could be of any help, and doubtless if the War Office had heard of the goings on in my study, they would have dropped severely on all of us. Still, I taught them lots of things about parabolas that they did not know and did not know were to be known--things that, considering the shells they fired went in parabolas, ought certainly to be known by artillery officers; so I think, in this way, I have done a little bit for my country.

With regard to my friends, God has given me many in this quiet market town--once a Sleepy Hollow awakened only on Thursdays by bleating sheep and lowing cattle and red-faced men in gaiters and hard felt hats; its life flowing on drowsily as the gaudily painted barges that are towed on the canal towards which, in scattered buildings, it drifts aimlessly; a Sleepy Hollow with one broad High Street, melting gradually at each end through shops, villas, cottages, into the King's Highway, yet boasting in its central heart a hundred yards or so of splendour, where the truculent new red brick Post Office sneers across the flagged market square at the new Portland-stone Town Hall, while the old thatched corn-market sleeps in the middle and the Early English spire of the Norman church dreams calmly above them. Once, I say, a Sleepy Hollow, but now alive with the tramp of soldiers and the rumble of artillery and transport; for Wellingsford is the centre of a district occupied by a division, which means twenty thousand men of all arms, and the streets and roads swarm with men in khaki, and troops are billeted in all the houses. The War has changed many aspects, but not my old friendships. I had made a home here during my soldiering days, long before the South African War, my wife being a kinswoman of Sir Anthony, and so I have grown into the intimacy of many folks around. And, as they have been more than good to me, surely I must give them of my best in the way of sympathy and counsel. So it is in no spirit of curiosity that I have pried into my friends' affairs. They have become my own, very vitally my own; and this book is a record of things as I know them to have happened.

My name is Meredyth, with a "Y," as my poor mother used proudly to say, though what advantage a "Y" has over an "I," save that of a swaggering tail, I have always been at a loss to determine; Major Duncan Meredyth, late R.F.A., aged forty-seven; and I live in a comfortable little house at the extreme north end of the High Street, standing some way back from the road; so that in fine weather I can sit in my front garden and watch everybody going into the town. And whenever any of my friends pass by, it is their kindly habit to cast an eye towards my gate, and, if I am visible, to pass the time of day with me for such time as they can spare.

Years ago, when first I realised what would be my fate for the rest of my life, I nearly broke my heart. But afterwards, whether owing to the power of human adaptability or to the theory of compensation, I grew to disregard my infirmity. By building a series of two or three rooms on to the ground floor of the house, so that I could live in it without the need of being carried up and down stairs, and by acquiring skill in the manipulation of my tricycle chair, I can get about the place pretty much as I choose. And Marigold is my second self. So, in spite of the sorrow and grief incident to humanity of which God has given me my share, I feel that my lot is cast in pleasant places and I am thankful.

The High Street, towards its southern extremity, takes a sudden bend, forming what the French stage directions call a pan coupe. On the inner angle are the gates of Wellings Park, the residence of Sir Anthony Fenimore, third baronet, and the most considerable man in our little community. Through these gates the car took me and down the long avenue of chestnut trees, the pride of a district braggart of its chestnuts and its beeches, but now leafless and dreary, spreading out an infinite tracery of branch and twig against a grey February sky. Thence we emerged into the open of rolling pasture and meadow on the highest ground of which the white

Georgian house was situated. As we neared the house I shivered, not only with the cold, but with a premonition of disaster. For why should Lady Fenimore have sent for me to see Sir Anthony, when he, strong and hearty, could have sent for me himself, or, for the matter of that, could have visited me at my own home? The house looked stark and desolate. And when we drew up at the front door and Pardoe, the elderly butler, appeared, his face too looked stark and desolate.

Marigold lifted me out and carried me up the steps and put me into a chair like my own which the Fenimores have the goodness to keep in a hall cupboard for my use.

"What's the matter, Pardoe?" I asked.

"Sir Anthony and her ladyship will tell you, sir. They're in the morning room."

So I was shewn into the morning room--a noble square room with French windows, looking on to the wintry garden, and with a log fire roaring up a great chimney. On one side of the fire sat Sir Anthony, and on the other, Lady Fenimore. And both were crying. He rose as he saw me--a short, crop-haired, clean-shaven, ruddy, jockey-faced man of fifty-five, the corners of his thin lips, usually curled up in a cheery smile, now piteously drawn down, and his bright little eyes now dim like those of a dead bird. She, buxom, dark, without a grey hair in her head, a fine woman defying her years, buried her face in her hands and sobbed afresh.

"It's good of you to come, old man," said Sir Anthony, "but you're in it with us."

He handed me a telegram. I knew, before reading it, what message it contained. I had known, all along, but dared not confess it to myself.

"I deeply regret to inform you that your son, Lieutenant Oswald Fenimore, was killed in action yesterday while leading his men with the utmost gallantry."

I had known him since he was a child. By reason of my wife's kinship, I was "Uncle Duncan." He was just one and twenty, but a couple of years out of Sandhurst. Only a week before I had received an exuberant letter from him extolling his men as "super-devil-angels," and imploring me if I loved him and desired to establish the supremacy of British arms, to send him some of Mrs. Marigold's potted shrimp.

And now, there he was dead; and, if lucky, buried with a little wooden cross with his name rudely inscribed, marking his grave.

I reached out my hand.

"My poor old Anthony!"

He jerked his head and glance towards his wife and wheeled me to her side, so that I could put my hand on her shoulder.

"It's bitter hard, Edith, but--"

"I know, I know. But all the same--"

"Well, damn it all!" cried Sir Anthony, in a quavering voice, "he died like a man and there's nothing more to be said."

Presently he looked at his watch.

"By George," said he, "I've only just time to get to my Committee."

"What Committee?" I asked.

"The Lord Lieutenant's. I promised to take the chair."

For the first time Lady Fenimore lifted her stricken face.

"Are you going, Anthony?"

"The boy didn't shirk his duty. Why should I?"

She looked at him squarely and the most poignant simulacrum of a smile I have ever seen flitted over her lips.

"Why not, darling? Duncan will keep me company till you come back."

He kissed his wife, a trifle more demonstratively than he had ever done in alien presence, and with a nod at me, went out of the room.

And suddenly she burst into sobbing again.

"I know it's wrong and wicked and foolish," she said brokenly. "But I can't help it. Oh, God! I can't help it."

Then, like an ass, I began to cry, too; for I loved the boy, and that perhaps helped her on a bit.

CHAPTER II

Dulce et decorum est pro patria mori. The tag has been all but outworn during these unending days of death; it has become almost a cant phrase which the judicious shrink from using. Yet to hundreds of thousands of mourning men and women there has been nothing but its truth to bring consolation. They are conscious of the supreme sacrifice and thereby are ennobled. The cause in which they made it becomes more sacred. The community of grief raises human dignity. In England, at any rate, there are no widows of Ashur. All are silent in their lamentations. You see little black worn in the public ways. The Fenimores mourned for their only son, the idol of their hearts; but the manifestation of their grief was stoical compared with their unconcealed desolation on the occasion of a tragedy that occurred the year before.

Towards the end of the preceding June their only daughter, Althea, had been drowned in the canal. Here was a tragedy unrelieved, stupid, useless. Here was no consoling knowledge of glorious sacrifice; no dying for one's country. There was no dismissing it with a heroic word that caught in the throat.

I have not started out to write this little chronicle of Wellingsford in order to weep over the pain of the world. God knows there is in it an infinity of beauty, fresh revelations of which are being every day unfolded before my eyes.

If I did not believe with all my soul that out of Darkness cometh Light, I would take my old service revolver from its holster and blow out my brains this very minute. The eternal laughter of the earth has ever since its creation pierced through the mist of tears in which at times it has been shrouded. What has been will be. Nay, more, what has been shall be. It is the Law of what I believe to be God.... As a concrete instance, where do you find a fuller expression of the divine gaiety of the human spirit than in the Houses of Pain, strewn the length and breadth of the land, filled with maimed and shattered men who have looked into the jaws of Hell? If it comes to that, I have looked into them myself, and have heard the heroic jests of men who looked with me.

For some years up to the outbreak of the war which has knocked all so-called modern values silly, my young friends, with a certain respectful superciliousness, regarded me as an amiable person hopelessly out of date. Now that we are at grip with elementals, I find myself, if anything, in advance of the fashion. This, however, by the way. What I am clumsily trying to explain is that if I am to make this story intelligible I must start from the darkness where its roots lie hidden. And that darkness is the black depths of the canal by the lock gates where Althea Fenimore's body was found.

It was high June, in leafy England, in a world at peace. Can one picture it? With such a wrench of memory does one recall scenes of tender childhood. In the shelter of a stately house lived Althea Fenimore. She was twenty-one; pretty, buxom, like her mother, modern, with (to me) a pathetic touch of mid-Victorian softness and sentimentality; independent in outward action, what we call "open-air"; yet an anomaly, fond at once of games and babies. I have seen her in the morning tearing away across country by the side of her father, the most passionate and reckless rider to hounds in the county, and in the evening I have come across her, a pretty mass of pink flesh and muslin--no, it can't be muslin--say chiffon--anyhow, something white and filmy and girlish--curled up on a sofa and absorbed in a novel of Mrs. Henry Wood, borrowed, if one could judge by the state of its greasy brown paper cover, from the servants' hall. I confess that, though to her as to her brother I was "Uncle Duncan," and loved her as a dear, sweet English girl, I found her lacking in spirituality, in intellectual grasp, in emotional distinction. I should have said that she was sealed by God to be the chaste, healthy, placid mother of men. She was forever laughing--just the spontaneous laughter of the gladness of life.

On the last afternoon of her existence she came to see me, bringing me a basket of giant strawberries from her own particular bed. We had tea in the garden, and with her young appetite she consumed half the fruit she had brought. At the time I did not notice an unusual touch of depression. I remember her holding by its stalk a great half-eaten strawberry and asking me whether sometimes I didn't find life rather rotten. I said idly:

"You can't expect the world to be a peach without a speck on it. Of such is the Kingdom of Heaven. The wise person avoids the specks."

"But suppose you've bitten a specky bit by accident?"

"Spit it out," said I.

She laughed. "You think you're like the wise Uncle in the Sunday School books, don't you?"

"I know I am," I said.

Whereupon she laughed again, finished the strawberry, and changed the conversation.

There seemed to be no foreshadowing of tragedy in that. I had known her (like many of her kind) to proclaim the rottenness of the Universe when she was off her stroke at golf, or when a favourite young man did not appear at a dance. I attributed no importance to it. But the next day I remembered. What was she doing after half-past ten o'clock, when she had bidden her father and mother goodnight, on the steep and lonely bank of the canal, about a mile and a half away? No one had seen her leave the house. No one, apparently, had seen her walking through the town. Nothing was known of her until dawn when they found her body by the lock gate. She had been dead some hours. It was a mysterious affair, upon which no light was thrown at the inquest. No one save myself had observed any sign of depression, and her half-bantering talk with me was trivial enough. No one could adduce a reason for her midnight walk on the tow-path. The obvious question arose. Whom had she gone forth to meet? What man? There was not a man in the neighbourhood with whom her name could be particularly associated. Generally, it could be associated with a score or so. The modern young girl of her position and upbringing has a drove of young male intimates. With one she rides, with another she golfs, with another she dances a two-step, with another she Bostons; she will let Tom read poetry to her, although, as she expresses it, "he bores her stiff," because her sex responds to the tribute; she plays lady patroness to Dick, and tries to intrigue him into a soft job; and as for Harry she goes on telling him month after month that unless he forswears sack and lives cleanly she will visit him with her high displeasure. Meanwhile, most of these satellites have affaires de coeur of their own, some respectable, others not; they regard the young lady with engaging frankness as a woman and a sister, they have the run of her father's house, and would feel insulted if anybody questioned the perfect correctness of their behaviour. Each man has, say, half a dozen houses where he is welcomed on the same understanding. Of course, when one particular young man and one particular young woman read lunatic things in each other's eyes, then the rest of the respective quasi-sisters and quasi-brothers have to go hang. (In parenthesis, I may state that the sisters are more ruthlessly sacrificed than the brothers.) At any rate, frankness is the saving quality of the modern note.

In the case of Althea, there had been no sign of such specialisation. She could not have gone forth, poor child, to meet the twenty with whom she was known to be on terms of careless comradeship. She had gone from her home, driven by God knows what impulse, to walk in the starlight--there was no moon--along the banks of the canal. In the darkness, had she missed her footing and stepped into nothingness and the black water? The Coroner's Jury decided the question in the affirmative. They brought in a verdict of death by misadventure. And up to the date on which I begin this little Chronicle of Wellingsford, namely that of the summons to Wellings Park, when I heard of the death of young Oswald Fenimore, that is all I knew of the matter.

Throughout July my friends were like dead people. There was nothing that could be said to them by way of consolation. The sun had gone out of their heaven. There was no light in the world. Having known Death as a familiar foe, and having fought against its terrors; having only by the grace of God been able to lift up a man's voice in my hour of awful bereavement, and cry, "O Death, where is thy sting, O Grave, thy Victory?" I could suffer with them and fear for their reason. They lived in a state of coma, unaware of life, performing, like automata, their daily tasks.

Then, in the early days of August, came the Trumpet of War, and they awakened. In my life have I seen nothing so marvellous. No broken spell of enchantment in an Arabian tale when dead warriors spring into life was ever more instant and complete. They arose in their full vigour; the colour came back to their cheeks and the purpose into their eyes. They laughed once more. Their days were filled with work and cheerfulness. In November Sir Anthony was elected Mayor. Being a practical, hard-headed little man, loved and respected by everybody, he drove a hitherto contentious Town Council into paths of high patriotism like a flock of sheep. And no less energy did Lady Fenimore exhibit in the sphere of her own activities.

A few days after the tidings came of Oswald's death, Sir Anthony was riding through the town and pulled up before Perkins' the fishmonger's. Perkins emerged from his shop and crossed the pavement.

"I hear you've had bad news."

"Yes, indeed, Sir Anthony."

"I'm sorry. He was a fine fellow. So was my boy. We're in the same boat, Perkins."

Perkins assented. "It sort of knocks one's life to bits, doesn't it?" said he. "We've nothing left."

"We have our country."

"Our country isn't our only son," said the other dully.

"No. She's our mother," said Sir Anthony.

"Isn't that a kind of abstraction?"

"Abstraction!" cried Sir Anthony, indignantly. "You must be imbibing the notions of that poisonous beast Gedge."

Gedge was a smug, socialistic, pacifist builder who did not hold with war--and with this one least of all, which he maintained was being waged for the exclusive benefit of the capitalist classes. In the eyes of the stalwarts of Wellingsford, he was a horrible fellow, capable of any stratagem or treason.

Perkins flushed. "I've always voted conservative, like my father before me, Sir Anthony, and like yourself I've given my boy to my country. I've no dealings with unpatriotic people like Gedge, as you know very well."

"Of course I do," cried Sir Anthony. "And that's why I ask you what the devil you mean by calling England an abstraction. For us, she's the only thing in the world. We're elderly chaps, you and I, Perkins, and the only thing we can do to help her is to keep our heads high. If people like you and me crumple up, the British Empire will crumple up."

"That's quite true," said Perkins.

Sir Anthony bent down and held out his hand.

"It's damned hard lines for us, and for the women. But we must keep our end up. It's doing our bit."

Perkins wrung his hand. "I wish to God," said he, "I was young enough--"

"By God! so do I!" said Sir Anthony.

This little conversation (which I afterwards verified) was reported to me by my arch-gossip, Sergeant Marigold.

"And I tell you what, sir," said he after the conclusion, "I'm of the same way of thinking and feeling."

"So am I."

"Besides, I'm not so old, sir. I'm only forty-two."

"The prime of life," said I.

"Then why won't they take me, sir?"

If there had been no age limit and no medical examination Marigold would have re-enlisted as John Smith, on the outbreak of war, without a moment's consideration of the position of his wife and myself. And Mrs. Marigold, a soldier's wife of twenty years' standing, would have taken it, just like myself, as a matter of course.

But as he could not re-enlist, he pestered the War Office (just as I did) and I pestered for him to give him military employment. And all in vain.

"Why don't they take me, sir? When I see these fellows with three stripes on their arms, and looking at them and wondering at them as if they were struck three stripes by lightning, and calling themselves Sergeants and swanking about and letting their men waddle up to their gun like cows--and when I see them, as I've done with your eyes--watch one of their men pass by an officer in the street without saluting, and don't kick the blighter to--to--to barracks--it fairly makes me sick. And I ask myself, sir, what I've done that I should be loafing here instead of serving my country."

"You've somehow mislaid an eye and a hand and gone and got a tin head. That's what you've done," said I. "And the War Office has a mark against you as a damned careless fellow."

"Tin head or no tin head," he grumbled, "I could teach those mother's darlings up there the difference between a battery of artillery and a skittle-ally."

"I believe you've mentioned the matter to them already," I observed softly.

Marigold met my eye for a second and then looked rather sheepish. I had heard of a certain wordy battle between him and a Territorial Sergeant whom he had set out to teach. Marigold encountered a cannonade of blasphemous profanity, new, up-to-date, scientific, against which the time-worn expletives in use during his service days were ineffectual. He was routed with heavy loss.

"This is a war of the young," I continued. "New men, new guns, new notions. Even a new language," I insinuated.

"I wish 'em joy of their language," said Marigold. Then seeing that I was mildly amusing myself at his expense, he asked me stiffly if there was anything more that he could do for me, and on my saying no, he replied "Thank you, sir," most correctly and left the room.

On the 3d of March Betty Fairfax came to tea.

Of all the young women of Wellingsford she was my particular favourite. She was so tall and straight, with a certain Rosalind boyishness about her that made for charm. I am not yet, thank goodness, one of the fossils who hold up horror-stricken hands at the independent ways of the modern young woman. If it were not for those same independent ways the mighty work that English women are doing in this war would be left undone. Betty Fairfax was breezily independent. She had a little money of her own and lived, when it suited her, with a well-to-do and comfortable aunt. She was two and twenty. I shall try to tell you more about her, as I go on.

As I have said, and as my diary tells me, she came to tea on the 3d of March. She was looking particularly attractive that afternoon. Shaded lamps and the firelight of a cosy room, with all their soft shadows, give a touch of mysterious charm to a pretty girl. Her jacket had a high sort of Medici collar edged with fur, which set off her shapely throat. The hair below her hat was soft and brown. Her brows were wide, her eyes brown and steady, nose and lips sensitive. She had a way of throwing back her head and pointing her chin fearlessly, as though in perpetual declaration that she cared not a hang either for black-beetles or Germans. And she was straight as a dart, with the figure of a young Diana--Diana before she began to worry her head about beauty competitions. A kind of dark hat stuck at a considerable angle on her head gave her the prettiest little swaggering air in the world.... Well, there was I, a small, brown, withered, grizzled, elderly, mustachioed monkey, chained to my wheel-chair; there were the brave logs blazing up the wide chimney; there was the tea table on my right with its array of silver and old china; and there, on the other side of it, attending to my wants, sat as brave and sweet a type of young English womanhood as you could find throughout the length and breadth of the land. Had I not been happy, I should have been an ungrateful dog.

We talked of the war, of local news, of the wounded at the hospital.

And here I must say that we are very proud of our Wellingsford Hospital. It is the largest and the wealthiest in the county. We owe it to the uneasy conscience of a Wellingsford man, a railway speculator in the forties, who, having robbed widows and orphans and, after trial at the Old Bailey, having escaped penal servitude by the skin of his teeth, died in the odour of sanctity, and the possessor of a colossal fortune in the year eighteen sixty-three. This worthy gentleman built the hospital and endowed it so generously that a wing of it has been turned into a military hospital with forty beds. I have the honour to serve on the Committee. Betty Fairfax entered as a Probationer early in September, and has worked there night and day ever since. That is why we chatted about the wounded. Having a day off, she had indulged in the luxury of pretty clothes. Of these I had duly expressed my admiration.

Tea over, she lit a cigarette for me and one for herself and drew her chair a trifle nearer the fire. After a little knitting of the brow, she said:--

"You haven't asked me why I invited myself to tea."

"I thought," said I, "it was for my beaux yeux."

"Not this time. I rather wanted you to be the first to receive a certain piece of information."

I glanced at her sharply. "You don't mean to say you're going to be married at last?"

In some astonishment she retorted:--

"How did you guess?"

"Holy simplicity!" said I. "You told me so yourself."

She laughed. Suddenly, on reflection, her face changed.

"Why did you say 'at last'?"

"Well--" said I, with a significant gesture.

She made a defiant announcement:--

"I am going to marry Willie Connor."

It was my turn to be astonished. "Captain Connor?" I echoed.

"Yes. What have you to say against him?"

"Nothing, my dear, nothing."

And I hadn't. He was an exemplary young fellow, a Captain in a Territorial regiment that had been in hard training in the neighbourhood since August. He was of decent family and upbringing, a barrister by profession, and a comely pink-faced boy with a fair moustache. He brought a letter or two of introduction, was billeted on Mrs. Fairfax, together with one of his subs, and was made welcome at various houses. Living under the same roof as Betty, it was natural that he should fall in love with her. But it was not at all natural that she should fall in love with him. She was not one of the kind that suffer fools gladly.... No; I had nothing against Willie Connor. He was merely a common-place, negative young man; patriotic, keen in his work, an excellent soldier, and, as far as I knew, of blameless life; but having met him two or three times in general company, I had found him a dull dog, a terribly dull dog,--the last man in the world for Betty Fairfax.

And then there was Leonard Boyce. I naturally had him in my head, when I used the words "at last."

"You don't seem very enthusiastic," said Betty.

"You've taken me by surprise," said I. "I'm not young enough to be familiar with these sudden jerks."

"You thought it was Major Boyce."

"I did, Betty. True, you've said nothing about it to me for ever so long, and when I have asked you for news of him your answers have shewed me that all was not well. But you've never told me, or anyone, that the engagement was broken off."

Her young face was set sternly as she looked into the fire.

"It's not broken off--in the formal sense. Leonard thought fit to let it dwindle, and it has dwindled until it has perished of inanition." She flashed round. "I'm not the sort to ask any man for explanations."

"Boyce went out with the first lot in August," I said. "He has had seven awful months. Mons and all the rest of it. You must excuse a man in the circumstances for not being aux petits soins des dames. And he seems to be doing magnificently-- twice mentioned in dispatches."

"I know all that," she said. "I'm not a fool. But the war has nothing to do with it. It started a month before the war broke out. Don't let us talk of it."

She threw the end of her cigarette into the fire and lit a fresh one. I accepted the action as symbolical. I dismissed Boyce, and said:--

"And so you're engaged to Captain Connor?"

"More than that," she laughed. "I'm going to marry him. He's going out next week. It's idiotic to have an engagement. So I'm going to marry him the day after to-morrow."

Now here was a piece of news, all flung at my head in a couple of minutes. The day after to-morrow! I asked for the reason of this disconcerting suddenness.

"He's going out next week."

"My dear," said I, "I have known you for a very long time--and I suppose it's because I'm such a very old friend that you've come to tell me all about it. So I can talk to you frankly. Have you considered the terrible chances of this war? Heaven knows what may happen. He may be killed."

"That's why I'm marrying him," she said.

There was a little pause. For the moment I had nothing to say, as I was busily searching for her point of view. Then, with pauses between each sentence, she went on:--

"He asked me two months ago, and again a month ago. I told him to put such ideas out of his head. Yesterday he told me they were off to the front and said what a wonderful help it would be to him if he could carry away some hope of my love. So I gave it to him."--She threw back her head and looked at me, with flushed cheeks. "The love, not the hope."

"I don't think it was right of him to press for an immediate marriage," said I, in a grandfatherly way--though God knows if I had been mad for a girl I should have done the same myself when I was young.

"He didn't" said Betty, coolly. "It was all my doing. I fixed it up there and then. Looked up Whitaker's Almanack for the necessary information, and sent him off to get a special license."

I nodded a non-committal head. It all seemed rather mad. Betty rose and from her graceful height gazed down on me.

"If you don't look more cheerful, Major, I shall cry. I've never done so yet, but I'm sure I've got it in me."

I stretched out my hand. She took it, and, still holding it, seated herself on a footstool close to my chair.

"There are such a lot of things that occur to me," I said. "Things that your poor mother, if she were alive, would be more fitted to touch on than myself."

"Such as--"

She knelt by me and gave me both her hands. It was a pretty way she had. She had begun it soon after her head overtopped mine in my eternal wheelbarrow. There was a little mockery in her eyes.

"Well--" said I. "You know what marriage means. There is the question of children."

She broke into frank laughter.

"My darling Majy--" That is the penalty one pays for admitting irresponsible modern young people into one's intimacy. They miscall one abominably. I thought she had outgrown this childish, though affectionate appellation of disrespect. "My darling Majy!" she said. "Children! How many do you think I'm going to have?"

I was taken aback. There was this pure, proud, laughing young face a foot away from me. I said in desperation:--

"You know very well what I mean, young woman. I want to put things clearly before you--" It is the most difficult thing in the world for a man--even without legs--to talk straight about the facts of life to a young girl. He has no idea how much she knows about them and how much she doesn't. To tear away veils and reveal frightening starkness is an act from which he shrinks with all the modesty of a (perhaps) deluded sex. I took courage. "I want," I repeated, "to put things clearly before you. You are marrying this young man. You will have a week's married life. He goes away like a gallant fellow to fight for his country. He may be killed in the course of the next few weeks. Like a brave girl you've got to face it. In the course of time a child may be born--without a father to look after him. It's a terrific responsibility."

She knelt upright and put both her hands on my shoulders, almost embracing me, and the laughter died away from her eyes, giving place to something which awakened memories of what I had seen once or twice in the eyes of the dearest of all women. She put her face very close to mine and whispered:

"Don't you see, dear, it's in some sort of way because of that? Don't you think it would be awful for a strong, clean, brave English life like his to go out without leaving behind him someone to--well, you know what I mean--to carry on the same traditions--to be the same clean brave Englishman in the future?"

I smiled and nodded. Quite a different kind of nod from the previous one.

"Thousands of girls are doing it, you dear old Early Victorian, and aren't ashamed to say so to those who really love and can understand them. And you do love and understand, don't you?"

She set me off at arm's length, and held me with her bright unflinching eyes.

"I do, my dear," said I. "But there's only one thing that troubles me. Marriage is a lifelong business. Captain Connor may win through to a green old age. I hope to God the gallant fellow will. Your present motives are beautiful and heroic. But do you care for him sufficiently to pass a lifetime with him--after the war--an ordinary, commonplace lifetime?"

With the same clear gaze full on me she said:--

"Didn't I tell you that I had given him my love?"

"You did."

"Then," she retorted with a smile, "my dear Major Didymus, what more do you want?"

"Nothing, my dear Betty."

I kissed her. She threw her arms round my neck and kissed me again. Sergeant Marigold entered on the sentimental scene and preserved a face of wood. Betty rose to her feet slowly and serenely and smiled at Marigold.

"Miss Fairfax's car," he announced.

"Marigold," said I, "Miss Fairfax is going to be married the day after to-morrow to Captain Connor of the--"

"I know, sir," interrupted my one-eyed ramrod. "I'm very glad, if I may be permitted to say so, Miss. I've made it my duty to inspect all the troops that have been quartered hereabouts during the last eight months. And Captain Connor is one of the few that really know their business. I shouldn't at all mind to serve under him. I can't say more, Miss. I wish you happiness."

She flushed and laughed and looked adorable, and held out her hand, which he enclosed in his great left fist.

"And you'll come to my wedding, Sergeant?"

"I will, Miss," said he. "With considerable pleasure."

CHAPTER III

When I want to shew how independent I am of everybody, I drive abroad in my donkey carriage. I am rather proud of my donkey, a lithe-limbed pathetically eager little beast, deep bay with white tips to his ears. Marigold bought him for me last spring, from some gipsies, when his predecessor, Dan, who had served me faithfully for some years, struck work and insisted on an old-age pension. He is called Hosea, a name bestowed on him, by way of clerical joke, and I am sure with a profane reminiscence of Jorrocks, by the Vicar, because he "came after Daniel." At first I thought it rather silly; but when I tried to pull him up I found that "Whoa-Hosea!" came in rather pat; so Hosea he has remained. He has quite a fast, stylish little trot, and I can square my elbows and cock my head on one side as I did in the days of my youth when the brief ownership of a tandem and a couple of thoroughbreds would have landed me in the bankruptcy court, had it not mercifully first landed me in the hospital.

The afternoon after Betty's visit, I took Hosea to Wellings Park. The Fenimores shewed me a letter they had received from Oswald's Colonel, full of praise of the gallant boy, and after discussing it, which they did with brave eyes and voices, Sir Anthony said:--

"I want your advice, Duncan, on a matter that has been worrying us both. Briefly it is this. When Oswald came of age I promised to allow him a thousand a year till I should be wiped out and he should come in. Now I'm only fifty-five and as strong as a horse. I can reasonably expect to live, say, another twenty years. If Oswald were alive I should owe him, in prospectu, twenty thousand pounds. He has given his life for his country. His country, therefore, is his heir, comes in for his assets, his twenty years' allowance--"

"And the whole of your estate at your death?" I interposed.

"No. Not at all," said he. "At my death, it would have been his to dispose of as he pleased. Up to my death, he would have had no more claim to deal with it than you have. Look at things from my point of view, and don't be idiotic. I am considering my debt to Oswald, and therefore, logically, my debt to the country. It is twenty thousand pounds. I'm going to pay it. The only question is--and the question has kept Edith and myself awake the last two nights--is what's the best thing to do with it? Of course I could give it to some fund,--or several funds,--but it's a lot of money and I should like it to be used to the best advantage. Now what do you say?"

"I say," said I, "that you Croesuses make a half-pay Major of Artillery's head reel. If I were like you, I should go into a shop and buy a super-dreadnought, and stick a card on it with a drawing pin, and send it to the Admiralty with my compliments."

"Duncan," said Lady Fenimore, severely, "don't be flippant."

Heaven knows I was in no flippant mood; but it was worth a foolish jest to bring a smile to Sir Anthony's face. Also this grave, conscientious proposition had its humorous side. It was so British. It reminded me of the story of Swift, who, when Gay and Pope visited him and refused to sup, totted up the cost of the meal and insisted on their accepting half-a-crown apiece. It reminded me too of the rugged old Lancashire commercial blood that was in him--blood that only shewed itself on the rarest and greatest of occasions--the blood of his grandfather, the Manchester cotton-spinner, who founded the fortunes of his house. Sir Anthony knew less about cotton than he did about ballistics and had never sat at a desk in a business office for an hour in his life; but now and again the inherited instinct to put high impulses on a scrupulously honest commercial basis asserted itself in the quaintest of fashions.

"There's some sense in what he says, Edith," remarked Sir Anthony. "It's only vanity that prompted us to ear-mark this sum for something special."

"Vanity!" cried Lady Fenimore. "You weren't by any chance thinking of advertising our gift or contribution or whatever you like to call it in the Daily Mail?"

"Heaven forbid, my dear," Sir Anthony replied warmly; and he stood, his hands under his coat-tails and his gaitered legs apart, regarding her with the air of a cock-sparrow accused of murdering his young, or a sensitive jockey repudiating a suggestion of crooked riding. "Heaven forbid!" he repeated. "Such an idea never entered my head."

"Then where does the vanity come in?" asked Lady Fenimore.

They had their little argument. I lit a cigarette and let them argue. In such cases, every married couple has its own queer and private and particular and idiosyncratic way of coming to an agreement. The third party who tries to foist on it his own suggestion of a way is an imbecile. The dispute on the point of vanity, charmingly conducted, ended by Sir Anthony saying triumphantly:--

"Well, my dear, don't you see I'm right?" and by his wife replying with a smile:--

"No, darling, I don't see at all. But since you feel like that, there's nothing more to be said."

I was mildly enjoying myself. Perhaps I'm a bit of a cynic. I broke in.

"I don't think it's vanity to see that you get your money's worth. There's lots of legitimate fun in spending twenty thousand pounds properly. It's too big to let other people manage or mis-manage. Suppose you decided on motor-ambulances or hospital trains, for instance, it would be your duty to see that you got the best and most up-to-date ambulances or trains, with the least possible profits, to contractors and middle-men."

"As far as that goes, I think I know my way about," said Sir Anthony.

"Of course. And as for publicity--or the reverse, hiding your light under a bushel--any fool can remain anonymous."

Sir Anthony nodded at me, rubbed his hands, and turned to his wife.

"That's just what I was saying, Edith."

"My dear, that is just what I was trying to make you understand."

Neither of the two dear things had said, or given the other to understand, anything of the kind. But you see they had come in their own quaint married way to an agreement and were now receptive of commonsense.

"The motor ambulance is a sound idea," said Sir Anthony, rubbing his chin between thumb and forefinger.

"So is the hospital train," said Lady Fenimore.

What an idiot I was to suggest these alternatives! I looked at my watch. It was getting late. Hosea, like a silly child, is afraid of the dark. He just stands still and shivers at the night, and the more he is belaboured the more he shivers, standing stock-still with ears thrown back and front legs thrown forward. As I can't get out and pull, I'm at the mercy of Hosea. And he knows it. Since the mount of Balaam, there was never such an intelligent idiot of an ass.

"What do you say?" asked Sir Anthony. "Ambulance or train?"

"Donkey carriage," said I. "This very moment minute."

I left them and trotted away homewards.

Just as I had turned a bend of the chestnut avenue near the Park gates, I came upon a couple of familiar figures--familiar, that is to say, individually, but startlingly unfamiliar in conjunction. They were a young man and girl, Randall Holmes and Phyllis Gedge. Randall had concluded a distinguished undergraduate career at Oxford last summer. He was a man of birth, position, and, to a certain extent, of fortune. Phyllis Gedge was the daughter, the pretty and attractive daughter, of Daniel Gedge, the socialistic builder who did not hold with war. What did young Randall mean by walking in the dark with his arm round Phyllis's waist? Of course as soon as he heard the click-clack of Hosea's hoofs he whipped his arm away; but I had already caught him. They tried to look mighty unconcerned as I pulled up. I took off my hat politely to the lady and held out my hand to the young man.

"Good evening, Randall," said I. "I haven't seen you for ages."

He was a tall, clean-limbed, clear-featured boy, with black hair, which though not long, yet lacked the military trimness befitting the heads of young men at the present moment. He murmured something about being busy.

"It will do you good to take a night off," I said; "drop in after dinner and smoke a pipe with an old friend."

I smiled, bowed again politely, whipped up Hosea and trotted off. I wondered whether he would come. He had said: "Delighted, I'm sure," but he had not looked delighted. Very possibly he regarded me as a meddlesome, gossiping old tom-cat. Perhaps for that reason he would deem it wise to adopt a propitiatory attitude. Perhaps also he retained a certain affectionate respect for me, seeing that I had known him as a tiny boy in a sailor suit, and had fed him at Harrow (as I did poor Oswald Fenimore at Wellington) with Mrs. Marigold's famous potted shrimp and other comestibles, and had put him up, during here and there holidays and later a vacation, when his mother and aunts, with whom he lived, had gone abroad to take inefficacious cures for the tedium of a futile life. Oxford, however, had set him a bit off my plane.

As an ordinary soldierman, trained in the elementary virtues of plain-speaking and direct dealing, love of country and the sacredness of duty, I have had no use for the metaphysician. I haven't the remotest notion what his jargon means. From Aristotle to William James, I have dipped into quite a lot of them--Descartes, Berkeley, Kant, Schopenhauer (the thrice besotted Teutonic ass who said that women weren't beautiful), for I hate to be thought an ignorant duffer--and I have never come across in them anything worth knowing, thinking, or doing that I was not taught at my mother's knee. And as for her, dear, simple soul, if you had asked her what was the Categorical Imperative (having explained beforehand the meaning of the words), she would have said, "The Sermon on the Mount."

Of course, please regard this as a criticism not of the metaphysicians and the philosophers, but of myself. All these great thinkers have their niches in the Temple of Fame, and I'm quite aware that the consensus of human judgment does not immortalise even such an ass as Schopenhauer, without sufficient reason. All I want to convey to you is that I am only a plain, ordinary God-fearing, law-abiding Englishman, and that when young Randall Holmes brought down from Oxford all sorts of highfalutin theories about everything, not only in God's Universe, but in the super-Universe that wasn't God's, and of every one of which he was cocksure, I found my homely self very considerably out of it.

Then--young Randall was a poet. He had won the Newdigate. The subject was Andrea del Sarto, one of my favourite painters--il pittore senza errore--and his prize poem--it had, of course, to be academic in form--was excellent. It said just the things about him which Browning somehow missed, and which I had always been impotently wanting to say. And a year or so afterwards--when I praised his poem--he would shrink in a more than deprecating attitude: I might just as well have extolled him for seducing the wife of his dearest friend. His later poems, of which he was immodestly proud--"Sensations Captured on the Wing," he defined them--left me cold and unsympathetic. So, for these reasons, the boy and I had drifted apart. Until I had caught him in flagrante delicto of walking with his arm round the waist of pretty Phyllis Gedge, I had not seen him to speak to for a couple of months.

He came, however, after dinner, looking very sleek and handsome and intellectual, and wearing a velvet dinner jacket which I did not like. After we had gossiped awhile:--

"You said you were very busy?" I remarked.

He flicked off his cigarette ash and nodded.

"What at?"

"War poetry," he replied. "I am trying to supply the real note. It is badly wanted. There are all kinds of stuff being written, but all indifferent and valueless. If it has a swing, it's merely vulgar, and what isn't vulgar is academic, commonplace. There's a crying need for the high level poetry that shall interpret with dignity and nobility the meaning of the war."

"Have you written much?"

"I have an ode every week in the Albemarle Review. I also write the political article. Didn't you know? Haven't you seen them?"

"I don't take in that periodical," said I. "The omniscience of the last copy I saw dismayed me. I couldn't understand why the Government were such insensate fools as not to move from Downing Street to their Editorial offices."

Randall, with a humouring smile, defended the Albemarle Review.

"It is run," said he, "by a little set of intellectuals--some men up with me at Oxford--who must naturally have a clearer vision than men who have been living for years in the yellow fog of party politics."

He expounded the godlike wisdom of young Oxford at some length, replying vividly to here and there a Socratic interpolation on my part. After a while I began to grow irritated. His talk, like his verse, seemed to deal with unrealities. It was a negation of everything, save the intellectual. If he and his friends had been in power, there would never have been a war; there never would have been a German menace; the lamb would have lain down in peace, outside the lion. He had an airy way of dismissing the ruder and more human aspects of the war. Said I:--

"Anyone can talk of what might have been. But that's all over and done with. We're up against the tough proposition of the present. What are you doing for it?"

He waved a hand. "That's just the point. The present doesn't matter--not in the wide conception of things. It is the past and the future that count. The present is mere fluidity."

"The poor devils up to their waists in water in the trenches would agree with you," said I.

"They would also agree with me," he retorted, "if they had time to go into the reconstruction of the future that we are contemplating."

At this juncture Marigold came in with the decanters and syphons. I noticed his one eye harden on the velvet dinner-jacket. He fidgeted about the room, threw a log on the fire, drew the curtains closer, always with an occasional malevolent glance at the jacket. Then Randall, like a silly young ass, said, from the depths of his easy chair, a very silly thing.

"I see you've not managed to get into khaki yet, Sergeant."

Marigold took a tactical pace or two to the door.

"Neither have you, sir," he said in a respectful tone, and went out.

Randall laughed, though I saw his dark cheek flush. "If Marigold had his way he would have us all in a barrack square."

"Preferably in those fluid trenches of the present," said I. "And he wouldn't be far wrong."

My eyes rested on him somewhat stonily. People have complained sometimes--defaulters, say, in the old days--that there can be a beastly, nasty look in them.

"What do you mean, Major?" he asked.

"Sergeant Marigold," said I, "is a brave, patriotic Englishman who has given his country all he can spare from the necessary physical equipment to carry on existence; and it's making him hang-dog miserable that he's not allowed to give the rest to-morrow. You must forgive his plain speaking," I continued, gathering warmth as I went on, "but he can't understand healthy young fellows like you not wanting to do the same. And, for the matter of that, my dear Randall, neither do I. Why aren't you serving your country?"

He started forward in his chair and threw out his arms, and his dark eyes flashed and a smile of conscious rectitude overspread his clear-cut features.

"My dear Major--serving my country? Why, I'm working night and day for it. You don't understand."

"I've already told you I don't."

The boy was my guest. I had not intended to hold a pistol to his head in one hand and dangle a suit of khaki before his eyes in the other. I had been ill at ease concerning him for months, but I had proposed to regain his confidence in a tactful, fatherly way. Instead of which I found myself regarding him with my beastly defaulter glare. The blood sometimes flies to one's head.

He condescended to explain.

"There are millions of what the Germans call 'cannon fodder' about. But there are few intellects--few men, shall I say?--of genius, scarcely a poet. And men like myself who can express--that's the whole vital point--who can EXPRESS the higher philosophy of the Empire, and can point the way to its realisation are surely more valuable than the yokel or factory hand, who, as the sum-total of his capabilities, can be trained merely into a sort of shooting machine. Just look at it, my dear Major, from a commonsense point of view--" He forgot, the amazing young idiot, that he was talking not to a maiden aunt, but to a hard-bitten old soldier. "What good would it serve to stick the comparatively rare man--I say it in all modesty--the comparatively rare man like myself in the trenches? It would be foolish waste. I assure you I'm putting all my talents at the disposal of the country." Seeing, I suppose, in my eyes, the maintained stoniness of non-conviction, he went on, "But, pay dear sir, be reasonable." ... Reasonable! I nearly choked. If I could have stood once more on my useless legs, I should have swung my left arm round and clouted him on the side of the head. Reasonable indeed! This well-fed, able-bodied, young Oxford prig to tell me, an honourable English officer and gentleman, to be reasonable, when the British Empire, in peril of its existence, was calling on all its manhood to defend it in arms! I glared at him. He continued:--

"Yes, be reasonable. Everyone has his place in this World conflict. We can't all be practical fighters. You wouldn't set Kitchener or Grey or Lord Crewe to bayonet Germans--"

"By God, sir," I cried, smiting one palm with the fist of the other hand. "By God, sir, I would, if they were three and twenty." I had completely lost my temper. "And if I saw them doing nothing, while the country was asking for MEN, but writing rotten doggerel and messing about with girls far beneath them in station, I should call them the damnedest skunks unskinned!"

He had the decency to rise. "Major Meredyth," said he, "you're under a terrible misapprehension. You're a military man and must look at everything from a military point of view. It would be useless to discuss the philosophy of the situation with you. We're on different planes."

Just what I said.

"You," said I, "seem to be hovering near Tophet and the Abyss."

"No, no," he answered with an indulgent smile. "You are quoting Carlyle. You must give him up."

"Damned pro-German, I should think I do," I cried. I had forgotten where my phrase came from.

"I'm glad to hear it. He's a back-number. I'm a modern. I represent equilibrium--" He made a little rocking gesture with his graceful hand. "I am out for Eternal Truth, which I think I perceive."

"In poor little Phyllis Gedge, I suppose?"

"Why not? Look. I am the son, grandson, great-grandson, of English Tories. She is the daughter of socialism, syndicalism, pacifism, internationalism--everything that is most apart from my traditions. But she brings to me beauty, innocence, the feminine solution of all intellectual concepts. She, the woman, is the soul of conflicting England. She is torn both ways. But as she has to breed men, some day, she is instinctively on our side. She is invaluable to me. She inspires my poems. You may not believe it, but she is at the back of my political articles. You must really be a little more broad-minded, Major, and look at these things from the right point of view. From the point of view of my work, she is merely a symbol."

"And you?" said I, wrathfully. "What are you to her? Do you suppose she takes you for a symbol? I wish to Heaven she did. A round cipher of naught, the symbol of inanity. She takes you for an honourable gentleman. I've known the child since she was born. As good a little girl as you could wish to meet."

He drew himself up. "That's the opinion of her I am endeavouring to express."

"Quite so. You win a good decent girl's affection,--if you hadn't, she would never have let you walk about with her at nightfall, with your arm round her waist,--and you have the cynical audacity to say that she's only a symbol."

"When you asked me to come in this evening," said he, "I naturally concluded you would broach this subject. I came prepared to give you a complete explanation of what I am ready to admit was a compromising situation."

"There is only one explanation," said I angrily. "What are your intentions regarding the girl?"

He smiled. "Quite honourable."

"You mean marriage?"

"Oh, no," said he, emphatically.

"Then the other thing? That's not honourable."

"Of course not. Certainly not the other thing. I'm not a blackguard."

"Then what on earth are you playing at?"

He sighed. "I'm afraid you will never understand."

"I'm afraid I won't," said I. "By your own confession you are neither a lusty blackguard nor an honourable gentleman. You're a sort of philanderer, somewhere in between. You neither mean to fight like a man nor love like a man. I'm sorry to say it, but I've no use for you. As I can't do it myself, will you kindly ring the bell?"

"Certainly," said he, white with anger, which I was glad to see, and pressed the electric button beside the mantelpiece. He turned on me, his head high. There was still some breeding left in him.

"I'm sorry we're at such cross-purposes, Major. All my life long I've owed you kindnesses I can't ever repay. But at present we're hopelessly out of sympathy!"

"It seems so," said I. "I had hoped your father's son would be a better man!"

"My father," said he, "was a successful stockbroker, without any ideas in his head save the making of money. I don't see what he has got to do with my well-considered attitude towards life."

"Your callow attitude towards life, my poor boy," said I, "is a matter of profound indifference to me. But I shall give orders that you are no longer admitted to this house except in uniform."

"That's absurd," said he.

"Not at all," said I.

In obedience to the summons of the bell Sergeant Marigold appeared and stood in his ramrod fashion by the door.

Randall came forward to my wheel-chair, with hand outstretched.

"I'm desperately sorry, Major, for this disastrous misunderstanding."

I thrust my hands beneath the light shawl that covered my legs.

"Don't be such a self-sufficient fool, Randall," I said, "as to think I don't understand. In the present position there are no subtleties and no complications. Good-night."

Marigold, with a wooden face, opened wide the door, and Randall, with a shrug of the shoulders, went out.

I stayed awake the whole of that livelong night.

When I learned the death of young Oswald Fenimore, whom I loved far more dearly than Randall Holmes, I went to bed and slept peacefully. A gallant lad died in battle; there is nothing more to be said, nothing more to be thought. The finality, heroically sublime, overwhelms the poor workings of the brain. But in the case of a fellow like Randall Holmes--well, as I have said, I did not get a wink of sleep the whole night long.

Someone, a few months ago, told me of a young university man--Oxford or Cambridge, I forget--who, when asked why he was not fighting, replied; "What has the war to do with me? I disapprove of this brawling."

Was that the attitude of Randall, whom I had known all his life long? I shivered, like a fool, all night. The only consolation I had was to bring commonsense to my aid and to meditate on the statistical fact that the Universities of Oxford and Cambridge were practically empty.

But my soul was sick for young Randall Holmes.

CHAPTER IV

On the wedding eve Betty brought the happy young man to dine with me. He was in that state of unaccustomed and somewhat embarrassed bliss in which a man would have dined happily with Beelzebub. A fresh-coloured boy, with fair crisply set hair and a little moustache a shade or two fairer, he kept on blushing radiantly, as if apologising in a gallant sort of fashion for his existence in the sphere of Betty's affection. As I had known him but casually and desired to make his closer acquaintance, I had asked no one to meet them, save Betty's aunt, whom a providential cold had prevented from facing the night air. So, in the comfortable little oak-panelled dining-room, hung round with my beloved collection of Delft, I had the pair all to myself, one on each side; and in this way I was able to read exchanges of glances whence I might form sage conclusions. Bella, spruce parlour-maid, waited deftly. Sergeant Marigold, when not occupied in the mild labour of filling glasses, stood like a guardian ramrod behind my chair--a self-assigned post to which he stuck grimly like a sentinel. As I always sat with my back to the fire there must have been times when, the blaze roaring more fiercely than usual up the chimney, he must have suffered martyrdom in his hinder parts.

As I talked--for the first time on such intimate footing--with young Connor, I revised my opinion of him and mentally took back much that I had said in his disparagement. He was by no means the dull dog that I had labelled him. By diligent and sympathetic enquiry I learned that he had been a Natural Science scholar at Trinity College, Cambridge, where he had taken a first-class degree--specialising in geology; that by profession (his father's) he was a mining-engineer, and, in pursuit of his vocation, had travelled in Galicia, Mexico and Japan; furthermore, that he had been one of the ardent little band who of recent years had made the Cambridge Officers Training Corps an effective school. Hitherto, when I had met him he had sat so agreeably smiling and modestly mumchance that I had accepted him at his face value.

I was amused to see how Betty, in order to bring confusion on me, led him to proclaim himself. And I loved the manner in which he did so. To hear him, one would have thought that he owed everything in the world to Betty--from his entrance scholarship at the University to the word of special commendation which his company had received from the General of his Division at last week's inspection. Yes, he was the modest, clean-bred, simple English gentleman who, without self-consciousness or self-seeking, does his daily task as well as it can be done, just because it is the thing that is set before him to do. And he was over head and ears in love with Betty.

I took it upon myself to dismiss her with a nod after she had smoked a cigarette over her coffee. Mrs. Marigold, as a soldier's wife, I announced, had a world of invaluable advice to give her. Willie Connor opened the door. On the threshold she said very prettily:

"Don't drink too much of Major Meredyth's old port. It has been known before now to separate husbands and wives for years and years."

He looked after her for a few seconds before he closed the door.

Oh, my God! I've looked like that, in my time, after one dear woman.... Humanity is very simple, after all. Every generation does exactly the same beautiful, foolish things as its forerunner. As he approached the table, I said with a smile:--

"You're only copying your great-great-grandfather."

"In what way, sir?" he asked, resuming his place.

I pushed the decanter of port. "He watched the disappearing skirt of your great-great-grandmother."

"She was doubtless a very venerable old lady," said he, flushing and helping himself to wine. "I never knew her, but she wasn't a patch on Betty!"

"But," said I, "when your great-great-grandfather opened the door for her to pass out, she wasn't venerable at all, but gloriously young."

"I suppose he was satisfied, poor old chap." He took a sip. "But those days did not produce Betty Fairfaxes." He laughed. "I'm jolly sorry for my ancestors."

Well--that is the way I like to hear a young man talk. It was the modern expression of the perfect gentle knight. In so far as went his heart's intention and his soul's strength to assure it, I had no fear for Betty's happiness. He gave it to her fully into her own hands; whether she would throw it away or otherwise misuse it was another matter.

Though I have ever loved women, en tout bien et tout honneur, their ways have never ceased from causing me mystification. I think I can size up a man, especially given such an opportunity as I had in the case of Willie Connor--I have been more or less trained in the business all my man's life; but Betty Fairfax, whom I had known intimately for as many years as she could remember, puzzled me exceedingly. I defy anyone to have picked a single fault in her demeanour towards her husband of to-morrow. She lit a cigarette for him in the most charming way in the world, and when he guided the hand that held the match, she touched his crisp hair lightly with the fingers of the other. She was all smiles. When we met in the drawing-room, she retailed with a spice of mischief much of Mrs. Marigold's advice. She had seated herself on the music stool. Swinging round, she quoted:

"'Even the best husband,' she said, 'will go on swelling himself up with vanity just because he's a man. A sensible woman, Miss, lets him go on priding of himself, poor creature. It sort of helps his dignity when the time comes for him to eat out of your hand, and makes him think he's doing you a favour.'"

"When are you going to eat out of my hand, Willie?" she asked.

"Haven't I been doing it for the past week?"

"Oh, they always do that before they're married--so Mrs. Marigold informed me. I mean afterwards."

"Don't you think, my dear," I interposed, "it depends on what your hands hold out for him to eat?"

Her eyes wavered a bit under mine.

"If he's good," she answered, "they'll be always full of nice things."

She sat, flushed, happy, triumphant, her arms straight down, her knuckles resting on the leathern seat, her silver-brocaded, slender feet, clear of the floor, peeping close together beneath her white frock.

"And if he isn't good?"

"They'll be full of nasty medicine."

She laughed and pivoted round and, after running over the keys of the piano for a second or two, began to play Gounod's "Death March of a Marionette." She played it remarkably well. When she had ended, Connor walked from the hearth, where he had been standing, to her side. I noticed a little puzzled look in his eyes.

"Delightful," said he. "But, Betty, what put that thing suddenly into your head?"

"We had been talking nonsense," she replied, picking out a chord or two, without looking al him. "And I thought we ought to give all past vanities and frivolities and lunacies a decent burial."

He put both hands very tenderly on her shoulders.

"Requiescat," said he.

She spread out her fingers and struck the two resonant chords of an "Amen," and then glanced up at him, laughing.

After a while, Marigold announced her car, or, rather, her aunt's car. They took their leave. I gave them my benediction. Presently, Betty, fur-coated, came running in alone. She flung herself down, in her impetuous way, beside my wheel-chair. No visit of Betty's would have been complete without this performance.

"I haven't had a word with you all the evening, Majy, dear. I've told Willie to discuss strategy with Sergeant Marigold in the hall, till I come. Well--you thought I was a damn little fool the other day, didn't you? What do you think now?"

"I think, my dear," said I, with a hand on her forehead, "that you are marrying a very gallant English gentleman of whose love any woman in the land might be proud."

She clutched me round the neck and brought her young face near mine--and looked at me--I hesitate to say it,--but so it seemed,--somewhat haggardly.

"I love to hear you say that, it means so much to me. Don't think I haven't a sense of proportion. I have. In all this universal slaughter and massacre, a woman's life counts as much as that of a mosquito." She freed an arm and snapped her fingers. "But to the woman herself, her own life can't help being of some value. Such as it is, I want to give it all, every bit of it, to Willie. He shall have everything, everything, everything that I can give him."

I looked into the young, drawn, pleading face long and earnestly. No longer was I mystified. I remembered her talk with me a couple of days before, and I read her riddle.

She had struck gold. She knew it. Gold of a man's love. Gold of a man's strength. Gold of a man's honour. Gold of a man's stainless past. Gold of a man's radiant future. And though she wore the mocking face and talked the mocking words of the woman who expected such a man to "eat out of her hand," she knew that never out of her hand would he eat save that which she should give him in honourable and wifely service. She knew that. She was exquisitely anxious that I should know it too. Floodgates of relief were expressed when she saw that I knew it. Not that I, personally, counted a scrap. What she craved was a decent human soul's justification of her doings. She craved recognition of her action in casting away base metal forever and taking the pure gold to her heart.

"Tell me that I am doing the right thing, dear," she said, "and to-morrow I'll be the happiest woman in the world."

And I told her, in the most fervent manner in my power.

"You quite understand?" she said, standing up, looking very young and princess-like, her white throat gleaming between her furs and up-turned chin.

"You will find, my dear," said I, "that the significance of your Dead March of a Marionette will increase every day of your married life."

She stiffened in a sudden stroke of passion, looking, for the instant, electrically beautiful.

"I wish," she cried, "someone had written the Dead March of a Devil."

She bent down, kissed me, and went out in a whirr of furs and draperies.

Of course, all I could do was to scratch my thin iron-grey hair and light a cigar and meditate in front of the fire. I knew all about it--or at any rate I thought I did, which, as far as my meditation in front of the fire is concerned, comes to the same thing.

Betty had cast out the base metal of her love for Leonard Boyce in order to accept the pure gold of the love of Willie Connor. So she thought, poor girl. She had been in love with Boyce. She had been engaged to Boyce. Boyce, for some reason or the other, had turned her down. Spretae injuria formae--she had cast Boyce aside. But for all her splendid surrender of her womanhood to Willie Connor, for the sake of her country, she still loved Leonard Boyce. Or, if she wasn't in love with him, she couldn't get him out of her head or her senses. Something like that, anyhow. I don't pretend to know exactly what goes on in the soul or nature, or whatever it is, of a young girl, who has given her heart to a man. I can only use the crude old phrase: she was still in love (in some sort of fashion) with Leonard Boyce, and she was going to marry, for the highest motives, somebody else.

"Confound the fellow," said I, with an irritable gesture and covered myself with cigar ash.

She had called Boyce a devil and implied a wish that he were dead. For myself I did not know what to make of him, for reasons which I will state. I never approved of the engagement. As a matter of fact, I knew--and was one of the very few who knew--of a black mark against him--the very blackest mark that could be put against a soldier's name. It was a puzzling business. And when I say I knew of the mark, I must be candid and confess that its awful justification lies in the conscience of one man living in the world to-day--if indeed he be still alive.

Boyce was a great bronzed, bull-necked man, with an overpowering personality. People called him the very model of a soldier. He was always admired and feared by his men. His fierce eye and deep, resonant voice, and a suggestion of hidden strength, even of brutality, commanded implicit obedience. But both glance and voice would soften caressingly and his manner convey a charm which made him popular with men--brother officers and private soldiers alike--and with women. With regard to the latter--to put things crudely--they saw in him the essential, elemental male. Of that I am convinced. It was the open secret of his many successes. And he had a buoyant, boyish, disarming, chivalrous way with him. If he desired a woman's lips he would always begin by kissing the hem of her skirt.

Had I not known what I did, I, an easy-going sort of Christian temperamentally inclined to see the best in my fellow-creatures, and, as I boastingly said a little while ago, a trained judge of men, should doubtless have fallen, like most other people, under the spell of his fascination. But whenever I met him, I used to look at him and say to myself: "What's at the back of you anyway? What about that business at Vilboek's Farm?"

Now this is what I knew--with the reservation I have made above--and to this day he is not aware of my knowledge.

It was towards the end of the Boer War. Boyce had come out rather late; for which, of course, he was not responsible. A soldier has to go when he is told. After a period of humdrum service he was sent off with a section of mounted infantry to round up a certain farm-house suspected of harbouring Boer combatants. The excursion was a mere matter of routine--of humdrum commonplace. As usual it was made at night, but this was a night of full dazzling moon. The farm lay in a hollow of the veldt, first seen from the crest of a kopje. There it lay below, ramshackle and desolate, a rough wall around; flanked by outbuildings--barn and cowsheds. The section rode down. The stoep led to a shuttered front. There was no sign of life. The moonlight blazed full on it. They dismounted, tethered their horses behind the wall, and entered the yard. The place was deserted, derelict--not even a cat.

Suddenly a shot rang out from somewhere in the main building, and the Sergeant, the next man to Boyce, fell dead, shot through the brain. The men looked at Boyce for command and saw a hulking idiot paralysed by fear.

"His mouth hung open and his eyes were like a silly servant girl's looking at a ghost." So said my informant.

Two more shots and two men fell. Boyce still stood white and gasping, unable to move a muscle or utter a sound. His face looked ghastly in the moonlight. A shot pierced his helmet, and the shock caused him to stagger and lose his legs. A corporal rushed up, thinking he was hit, and, finding him whole, rose, in order to leave him there, and, in rising, got a bullet through the neck. Thus there were four men killed, and the Commanding Officer, of his own accord, put out of action. It all happened in a few confused moments. Then the remaining men did what Boyce should have commanded as soon as the first shot was fired--they rushed the house.

It contained one solitary inmate, an old man with a couple of Mauser rifles, whom they had to shoot in self-defence.

Meanwhile Boyce, white and haggard-eyed, had picked himself up; revolver in hand he stood on the stoep. His men came out, cursed him to his face while giving him their contemptuous reports brought the dead bodies of their comrades into the house and laid them out decently, together with the body of the white-bearded Boer. After that they mounted their horses without a word to him and rode off. And he let them ride; for his authority was gone; and he knew that they justly laid the deaths of their comrades at the door of his cowardice.

What he did during the next few awful hours is known only to God and to Boyce himself. The four dead men, his companions, have told no tales. But at last, one of his men--Somers was his name--came riding back at break-neck speed. When he had left the moon rode high in the heavens; when he returned it was dawn--and he had a bloody tunic and the face of a man who had escaped from hell. He threw himself from his horse and found Boyce, sitting on the stoep with his head in his hands. He shook him by the shoulder. Boyce started to his feet. At first he did not recognise Somers. Then he did and read black tidings in the man's eyes.

"What's the matter?"

"They're all wiped out, sir. The whole blooming lot."

He told a tale of heroic disaster. The remnant of the section had ridden off in hot indignation and had missed their way. They had gone in a direction opposite to safety, and after a couple of hours had fallen in with a straggling portion of a Boer Commando. Refusing to surrender, they had all been killed save Somers, who, with a bullet through his shoulder, had prudently turned bridle and fled hell for leather.

Boyce put his hands up to his head and walked about the yard for a few moments. Then he turned abruptly and stood toweringly over the scared survivor--a tough, wizened little Cockney of five foot six.

"Well, what's going to happen now?" he asked, in his soft, dangerous voice.

Somers replied, "I must leave that to you, sir."

Boyce regarded him glitteringly for a long time. A scheme of salvation was taking vivid shape in his mind....

"My report of this occurrence will be that as soon as, say, three men dropped here, the rest of the troop got into a panic and made a bolt of it. Say the Sergeant and myself remained. We broke into the house and did for the old Boer, who, however, unfortunately did for the Sergeant. Then I alone went out in search of my men and following their track found they had gone in a wrong direction, and eventually scented danger, which was confirmed by my meeting you, with your bloody tunic and your bloody tale."

"But good God! sir," cried the man, "You'd be having me shot for running away. I could tell a damned different story, Captain Boyce."

"Who would believe you?"

The Cockney intelligence immediately appreciated the situation. It also was ready for the alternative it guessed at the back of Boyce's mind.

"I know it's a mess, sir," he replied, with a straight look at Boyce. "A mess for both of us, and, as I have said, I'll leave it to you, sir."

"Very well," said Boyce. "It's the simplest thing in the world. There were four killed at once, including Sergeant Oldham. You remained faithful when the others bolted. You and I tackled the old Boer and you got wounded. You and I went on trek for the rest of the troop. We got within breathing distance of the Commando-

-how many strong?"

"About a couple of hundred, sir."

"And of course we bolted back without knowing anything about the troop, except that we are sure that, dead or alive, the Boers have accounted for them. If you'll agree to this report, we can ride back to Headquarters and I think I can promise you sergeant's stripes in a very short time!"

"I agree to the report, sir," said Somers, "because I don't see that I can do anything else. But to hell with the stripes under false pretences and don't you try playing that sort of thing off on me."

"As you like," replied Boyce, unruffled. "Provided we understand each other on the main point."

So they left the farm and rode to Headquarters and Boyce made his report, and as all save one of his troop were dead, there were none, save that one, to gainsay him. On his story no doubt was cast; but an officer who loses his whole troop in the military operation of storming a farm-house garrisoned by one old man does not find peculiar favour in the eyes of his Colonel. Boyce took a speedy opportunity of transference, and got into the thick of some fighting. Then he served with distinction and actually got mentioned in dispatches for pluckily rescuing a wounded man under fire.

For a long time Somers kept his mouth shut; but at last he began to talk. The ugly rumour spread. It even reached my battery which was a hundred miles away; for Johnny Dacre, one of my subs, had a brother in Boyce's old regiment. For my own part I scouted the story as soon as I heard it, and I withered up young Dacre for daring to bring such abominable slander within my Rhadamanthine sphere. I dismissed the calumny from my mind. Providentially, (as I heard later), the news came of Boyce's "mention," and Somers was set down as a liar. The poor devil was had up before the Colonel and being an imaginative and nervous man denied the truth of the rumour and by dexterous wriggling managed to exculpate himself from the charge of being its originator.

I must, parenthetically, crave indulgence for these apparently irrelevant details. But as, in this chronicle, I am mainly concerned with the career of Leonard Boyce, I have no option but to give them. They are necessary for a conception of the character of a remarkable man to whom I have every reason and every honourable desire to render justice. It is necessary, too, that I should state clearly the manner in which I happened to learn the facts of the affair at Vilboek's Farm, for I should not like you to think that I have given a credulous ear to idle slander.

It was in Cape Town, whither I had been despatched, on a false alarm of enteric. I was walking with Johnny Dacre up Adderley Street, dun with kahki, when he met his brother Reginald, who was promptly introduced to Johnny's second in command. Reggie was off to hospital to see one of his men who had been badly hurt.

"It's the chap," he said to his brother, "who was with Boyce through that shady affair at Vilboek's Farm."

"I don't know why you call it a shady affair," said I, somewhat acidly. "I know Captain Boyce--he is a near neighbour of mine at home--and he has proved himself to be a gallant officer and a brave man."

The young fellow reddened. "I'm awfully sorry, sir. I withdraw the word 'shady.' But this poor chap has something on his mind, and everyone has a down on him. He led a dog's life till he was knocked out, and he has been leading a worse one since. I don't call it fair." He looked at me squarely out of his young blue eyes--the lucky devil, he is commanding his regiment now in Flanders, with the D.S.O. ribbon on his tunic. "Will you come with me and see him, sir?"

"Certainly," said I, for I had nothing to do, and the boy's earnestness impressed me.

On our way he told me of such mixture of rumour and fact as he was acquainted with. It was then that I heard the man Somers's name for the first time. We entered the hospital, sat by the side of the man's bed, and he told us the story of Vilboek's Farm which I have, in bald terms, just related. Shortly afterwards I returned to the front, where the famous shell knocked me out of the Army forever.

What has happened to Somers I don't know. He was, I learned, soon afterwards discharged from the Army. He either died or disappeared in the full current of English life. Perhaps he is with our armies now. It does not matter. What matters is my memory of his nervous, sallow, Cockney face, its earnestness, its imprint of veracity, and the damning lucidity of his narrative.

I exacted from my young friends a promise to keep the unsavoury tale to themselves. No good would arise from a publicity which would stain the honour of the army. Besides, Boyce had made good. They have kept their promise like honest gentlemen. I have never, personally, heard further reference to the affair, and of course I have never mentioned it to anyone.

Now, it is right for me to mention that, for many years, I lived in a horrible state of dubiety with regard to Boyce. There is no doubt that, after the Vilboek business, he acted in an exemplary manner; there is no doubt that he performed the gallant deed for which he got his mention. But what about Somers's story? I tried to disbelieve it as incredible. That an English officer--not a nervous wisp of a man like Somers, but a great, hulking, bull-necked gladiator--should have been paralysed with fear by one shot coming out of a Boer farm, and thereby demoralised and incapacitated from taking command of a handful of men; that, instead of blowing his brains out, he should have imposed his Mephistophelian compact upon the unhappy Somers and carried off the knavish business successfully--I could not believe it. On the other hand, there was the British private. I have known him all my life, God bless him! Thank God, it is my privilege to know him now, as he lies knocked to bits, cheerily, in our hospital. It was inconceivable that out of sheer funk he could abandon a popular officer. And his was not even a scratch crowd, but a hard-bitten regiment with all sorts of glorious names embroidered on its colours....

I hope you see my difficulty in regard to my Betty's love affairs. I had nothing against Boyce, save this ghastly story, which might or might not be true. Officially, he had made an unholy mess of such a simple military operation as rounding up a Boer farm, and the prize of one dead old Boer had covered him with ridicule; but officially, also, he had retrieved his position by distinguished service. After all, it was not his fault that his men had run away. On the other hand...well, you cannot but appreciate the vicious circle of my thoughts, when Betty, in her frank way, came and told me of her engagement to him. What could I say? It would have been damnable of me to hint at scandal of years gone by. I received them both and gave them my paralytic blessing, and Leonard Boyce accepted it with the air of a man who might have been blessed, without a qualm of conscience, by the Third Person of the Trinity in Person.

This was in April, 1914. He had retired from the Army some years before with the rank of Major, and lived with his mother--he was a man of means--in Wellingsford. In the June of that year he went off salmon fishing in Norway. On the outbreak of war he returned to England and luckily got his job at once. He did not come back to Wellingsford. His mother went to London and stayed there until he was ordered out to the front. I had not seen him since that June. And, as far as I am aware, my dear Betty had not seen him either.

Marigold entered.

"Well?" said I.

"I thought you rang, sir."

"You didn't," I said. "You thought I ought to have rung, But you were mistaken."

I have on my mantelpiece a tiny, corroded, wooden Egyptian bust, of so little value that Mr. Hatoun of Cairo (and every visitor to Cairo knows Hatoun) gave it me as Baksheesh; it is, however, a genuine bit from a poor humble devil's tomb of about five thousand years ago. And it has only one positive eye and no expression.

Marigold was the living replica of it--with his absurd wig.

"In a quarter of an hour," said I, "I shall have rung."

"Very good, sir," said Marigold.

But he had disturbed the harmonical progression of my reflections. They all went anyhow. When he returned, all I could say was:

"It's Miss Betty's wedding to-morrow. I suppose I've got a morning coat and a top hat."

"You have a morning coat, sir," said Marigold. "But your last silk hat you gave to Miss Althea, sir, to make a work-bag out of the outside."

"So I did," said I.

It was an unpleasant reminiscence. A hat is about as symbolical a garment as you may be pleased to imagine. I wanted to wear at the live Betty's wedding the ceremonious thing which I had given, for purposes of vanity, to the dead Althea. I was cross with Marigold.

"Why did you let me do such a silly thing? You might have known that I should want it some day or other. Why didn't you foresee such a contingency?"

"Why," asked Marigold woodenly, "didn't you or I, sir, or many wiser than us, foresee the war?"

"Because we were all damned fools," said I.

Marigold approached my chair with his great inexorable tentacles of arms. It was bed time.

"I'm sorry about the hat, sir," said he.

CHAPTER V

In due course Captain Connor's regiment went off to France; not with drums beating and colours flying--I wish to Heaven it had; if there had been more pomp and circumstance in England, the popular imagination would not have remained untouched for so long a time--but in the cold silent hours of the night, like a gang of marauders. Betty did not go to bed after he had left, but sat by the fire till morning. Then she dressed in uniform and resumed her duties at the hospital. Many a soldier's bride was doing much the same. And her days went on just as they did before her marriage. She presented a smiling face to the world; she said:

"If I'm as happy as can be expected in the circumstances, I think it my duty to look happier."

It was a valiant philosophy.

The falling of a chimney-stack brought me up against Daniel Gedge, who before the war did all my little repairs. The chimney I put into the hands of Day & Higgins, another firm of builders.

A day or two afterwards Hosea shied at something and I discovered it was Gedge, who had advanced into the roadway expressing a desire to have a word with me. I quieted the patriotic Hosea and drew up by the kerb. Gedge was a lean foxy-faced man with a long, reddish nose and a long blunt chin from which a grizzled beard sprouted aggressively forwards. He had hard, stupid grey eyes.

"I hope you 'll excuse the liberty I take in stopping you, sir," he said, civilly.

"That's all right," said I. "What's the matter?"

"I thought I had given you satisfaction these last twenty years."

I assented. "Quite correct," said I.

"Then, may I ask, sir, without offence, why you've called in Day & Higgins?"

"You may," said I, "and, with or without offence, I'll answer your question. I've called them in because they're good loyal people. Higgins has joined the army, and so has Day's eldest boy, while you have been going on like a confounded pro-

German."

"You've no right to say that, Major Meredyth."

"Not when you go over to Godbury"--the surging metropolis of the County some fifteen miles off--"and tell a pack of fools to strike because this is a capitalists' war? Not when you go round the mills here, and do your best to stop young fellows from fighting for their country? God bless my soul, in whose interests are you acting, if not Germany's?"

He put on his best platform manner. "I'm acting in the best interests of the people of this country. The war is wrong and incredibly foolish and can bring no advantage to the working man. Why should he go and be killed or maimed for life? Will it put an extra penny in his pocket or his widow's? No. Oh!"--he checked my retort--"I know everything you would say. I see the arguments every day in all your great newspapers. But the fact remains that I don't see eye to eye with you, or those you represent. You think one way, I think another. We agree to differ."

"We don't," said I. "I don't agree at all."

"At any rate," he said, "I can't see how a difference of political opinion can affect my ability now to put a new chimney-stack in your house, any more than it has done in the past."

"In the past," said I, "political differences were parochial squabbles in comparison with things nowadays. You're either for England, or against her."

He smiled wryly. "I'm for England. We both are. You think her salvation lies one way. I think another. This is a free country in which every man has a right to his own opinion."

"Exactly so," said I. "Therefore you'll admit that I've a right to the opinion that you ought to be locked up either in a gaol or a lunatic asylum as a danger to the state, and that, having that rightful opinion, I'm justified in not entrusting the safety of my house to one who, in my aforesaid opinion, is either a criminal or a lunatic."

Dialectically, I had him there. It afforded me keen enjoyment. Besides being a John Bull Englishman, I am a cripple and therefore ever so little malicious.

"It's all very well for you to talk, Major Meredyth," said he, "but your opinions cost you nothing--mine are costing me my livelihood. It isn't fair."

"You might as well say," I replied, "that I, who have never dared to steal anything in my life, live in ease and comfort, whereas poor Bill Sykes, who has devoted all his days to burglary, has seven years' penal servitude. No, Gedge," said I, gathering up the reins, "it can't be done. You can't have it both ways."

He put a detaining hand on Hosea's bridle and an evil flash came into his hard grey eyes.

"I'll have it some other way, then," he said. "A way you've no idea of. A way that'll knock all you great people of Wellingsford off your high horses. If you drive me to it, you'll see. I'll bide my time and I don't care whether it breaks me."

He stamped his foot and tugged at the bridle. Two or three passers-by halted wonderingly and Prettilove, the hairdresser, moved across the pavement from his shop door where he had been taking the air.

"My good fellow," said I, "you have lost your temper and are talking drivel. Kindly unhand my donkey."

Prettilove, who has a sycophantic sense of humour, burst into a loud guffaw. Gedge swung angrily away, and Hosea and I continued our interrupted progress down the High Street. Although I had called his dark menaces drivel, I could not help wondering what it meant. Was he going to guide a German Army to Wellingsford? Was he, a modern Guy Fawkes, plotting to blow up the Town Hall while Mayor and Corporation sat in council? He was not the man to utter purely idle threats. What the dickens was he going to do? Something mean and dirty and underhand. I knew his ways, He was always getting the better of somebody. The wise never let him put in a pane of glass without a specification and estimate, and if he had not been by far the most competent builder in the town--perhaps the only one who thoroughly knew his business in all its branches--no one would have employed him.

When I next saw Betty, it was in one of the corridors of the hospital, after a committee meeting; she stopped by my chair to pass the time of day. Through the open doorway of a ward I perceived a well-known figure in nurse's uniform.

"Why," said I, "there's Phyllis Gedge."

Betty nodded. "She has just come in as a probationer."

"I thought her father wouldn't let her. I've heard--Heaven knows whether it's true, but it sounds likely--that he said if men were such fools as to get shot he didn't see why his daughter should help to mend them."

"He has consented now," said Betty, "and Phyllis is delighted."

"No doubt it's a bid for popular favour," said I. And I told her of his dwindling business and of my encounter with him. When I came to his threat Betty's brows darkened.

"I don't like that at all," she said.

"Why? What do you think he means?"

"Mischief." She lowered her voice, for, it being visiting day at the hospital, people were passing up and down the corridor. "Suppose he has some of the people here in his power?"

"Blackmail--?" I glanced up at her sharply. "What do you know about it?"

"Nothing," she replied abruptly. Then she looked down and fingered her wedding-ring. "I only said 'suppose.'"

A Sister appeared at the door of the ward and seeing us together paused hoveringly.

"I rather think you're wanted," said I.

I left the hospital somewhat disturbed in mind. Summons to duty had cut our conversation short; but I knew that no matter how long I had cross-questioned Betty I should have got nothing further out of her. She was a remarkably outspoken young woman. What she said she meant, and what she didn't want to say all the cripples in the British Army could not have dragged out of her.

I tried her again a few days later. A slight cold, aided and abetted by a dear exaggerating idiot of a tyrannical doctor, confined me to the house and she came flying in, expecting to find me in extremis. When she saw me clothed and in my right mind and smoking a big cigar, she called me a fraud.

"Look here," said I, after a while. "About Gedge--" again her brow darkened and her lips set stiffly--"do you think he has his knife into young Randall Holmes?"

I had worried about the boy. Naturally, if Gedge found the relations between his daughter and Randall unsatisfactory, no one could blame him for any outbreak of parental indignation. But he ought to break out openly, while there was yet time--before any harm was done--not nurse some diabolical scheme of subterraneous vengeance. Betty's brow cleared, and she laughed. I saw at once that I was on a wrong track.

"Why should he have his knife into Randall? I suppose you've got Phyllis in your mind."

"I have. How did you guess?"

She laughed again.

"What other reason could he have? But how did you come to hear of Randall and Phyllis?"

"Never mind," said I, "I did. And if Gedge is angry, I can to some extent sympathize with him."

"But he's not. Not the least little bit in the world," she declared, lighting a cigarette. "Gedge and Randall are as thick as thieves, and Phyllis won't have anything to do with either of them."

"Now, my dear," said I. "Now that you're married, become a real womanly woman and fill my empty soul with gossip."

"There's no gossip at all about it," she replied serenely. "It's all sordid and romantic fact. The two men hold long discussions together at Gedge's house, Gedge talking anti-patriotism and Randall talking rot which he calls philosophy. You can hear them, can't you? Their meeting-ground is the absurdity of Randall joining the army."

"And Phyllis?"

"She is a loyal little soul and as miserable as can be. She's deplorably in love with Randall. She has told me so. And because she's in love with a man whom she knows to be a slacker she's eaten up with shame. Now she won't speak to him To avoid meeting him she lives entirely at the hospital--a paying probationer."

"That must be since the last Committee Meeting," I said.

"Yes."

"And Daniel Gedge pays a guinea a week?"

"He doesn't," said Betty. "I do."

I accepted the information with a motion of the head. She went on after a minute or so. "I have always been fond of the child"--there were only three or four years difference between them!--"and so I want to protect her. The time may come when she'll need protection. She has told me things--not now--but long ago--which frightened her. She came to me for advice. Since then I've kept an eye on her--as far as I could. Her coming into the hospital helps me considerably."

"When you say 'things which frightened her,' do you mean in connection with her father?"

Again the dark look in Betty's eyes.

"Yes," she said. "He's an evil, dangerous man."

That was all I could get out of her. If she had meant me to know the character of Gedge's turpitude, she would have told me of her own accord. But in our talk at the hospital she had hinted at blackmail--and blackmailers are evil, dangerous men.

I went to see Sir Anthony about it. Beyond calling him a damned scoundrel, a term which he applied to all pro-Germans, pacifists and half the Cabinet, he did not concern himself about Gedge. Young Randall Holmes's intimacy with the scoundrel seemed to him a matter of far greater importance. He strode up and down his library, choleric and gesticulating.

"A gentleman and a scholar to hob-nob with a traitorous beast like that! I know that he writes for a filthy weekly paper. Somebody sent me a copy a few days ago. It's rot--but not actually poisonous like that he must hear from Gedge. That's the reason, I suppose, he's not in the King's uniform. I've had my eye on him for some time. That's why I've not asked him to the house."

I told Sir Anthony of my interview with the young man. He waxed wroth. In a country with a backbone every Randall Holmes in the land would have been chucked willy-nilly into the army. But the country had spinal disorders. It had locomotor ataxy. The result of sloth and self-indulgence. We had the Government we deserved ... I need not quote further. You can imagine a fine old fox-hunting Tory gentleman, with England filling all the spaces of his soul, blowing off the steam of his indignation.

When he had ended, "What," said I, "is to be done?"

"I'll lay my horsewhip across the young beggar's shoulders the next time I meet him."

"Capital," said I. "If I were you I should never ride abroad except in my mayor's gown and chain, so that you can give an official character to the thrashing."

He glanced swiftly at me in his bird-like fashion, his brow creased into a thousand tiny horizontal lines--it always took him a fraction of a second to get clear of the literal significance of words--and then he laughed. Personal violence was out of the question. Why, the young beggar might summon him for assault. No; he had a better idea. He would put in a word at the proper quarter, so that every recruiting sergeant in the district should have orders to stop him at every opportunity.

"I shouldn't do that," said I.

"Then, I don't know what the deuce I can do," said Sir Anthony.

As I didn't know, either, our colloquy was fruitless. Eventually Sir Anthony said:

"Perhaps it's likely, after all, that Gedge may offend young Oxford's fastidiousness. It can't be long before he discovers Gedge to be nothing but a vulgar, blatant wind-bag; and then he may undergo some reaction."

I agreed. It seemed to be the most sensible thing he had said. Give Gedge enough rope and he would hang himself. So we parted.

I have said before that when I want to shew how independent I am of everybody I drive abroad in my donkey carriage. But there are times when I have to be dependent on Marigold for carrying me into the houses I enter; on these helpless occasions I am driven about by Marigold in a little two-seater car. That is how I visited Wellings Park and that is how I set off a day or two later to call on Mrs. Boyce.

As she took little interest in anything foreign to her own inside, she was not to most people an exhilarating companion. She even discussed the war in terms of her digestion. But we were old friends. Being a bit of a practical philosopher I could always derive some entertainment from her serial romance of a Gastric Juice, and besides, she was the only person in Wellingsford whom I did not shrink from boring with the song of my own ailments. Rather than worry the Fenimores or Betty or Mrs. Holmes with my aches and pains I would have hung on, like the idiot boy of Sparta with the fox, until my vitals were gnawed out--parenthetically, it has always worried me to conjecture why a boy should steal a fox, why it should have been so valuable to the owner, and to what use he put it. In the case of all my other friends I regarded myself as too much of an obvious nuisance, as it was, for me to work on their sympathy for infirmities that I could hide; but with Mrs. Boyce it was different. The more I chanted antistrophe to her strophe of lamentation the more was I welcome in her drawing-room. I had not seen her for some weeks. Perhaps I had been feeling remarkably well with nothing in the world to complain about, and therefore unequipped with a topic of conversation. However, hearty or not, it was time for me to pay her a visit. So I ordered the car.

Mrs. Boyce lived in a comfortable old house half a mile or so beyond the other end of the town, standing in half a dozen well-wooded acres. It was a fair April afternoon, all pale sunshine and tenderness. A dream of fairy green and delicate pink and shy blue sky melting into pearl. The air smelt sweet. It was good to be in it, among the trees and the flowers and the birds.

Others must have also felt the calls of the spring, for as we were driving up to the house, I caught a glimpse of the lawn and of two figures strolling in affectionate attitude. One was that of Mrs. Boyce; the other, khaki-clad and towering above her, had his arm round her waist. The car pulled up at the front door. Before we had time to ring, a trim parlour-maid appeared.

"Mrs. Boyce is not at home, sir."

Marigold, who, when my convenience was in question, swept away social conventions like cobwebs, fixed her with his one eye, and before I could interfere, said:

"I'm afraid you're mistaken. I've just seen Major Boyce and Madam on the lawn."

The maid reddened and looked at me appealingly.

"My orders were to say not at home, sir."

"I quite understand, Mary," said I. "Major Boyce is home on short leave, and they don't want to be disturbed. Isn't that it?"

"Yes, sir."

"Marigold," said I. "Right about turn."

Marigold, who had stopped the car, got out unwillingly and went to the starting-handle. That I should be refused admittance to a house which I had deigned to honour with my presence he regarded as an intolerable insult. He also loved to have tea, as a pampered guest, in other folks' houses. When he got home Mrs. Marigold, as like as not, would give him plain slabs of bread buttered by her economical self. I knew my Marigold. He gave a vicious and ineffectual turn or two and then stuck his head in the bonnet.

The situation was saved by the appearance from the garden of Mrs. Boyce herself, a handsome, erect, elegantly dressed old lady in the late sixties, pink and white like a Dresden figure and in her usual condition of resplendent health. She held out her hand.

"I couldn't let you go without telling you that Leonard is back. I don't want the whole town to know. If it did, I should see nothing of him, his leave is so short. That's why I told Mary to say 'not at home.' But an old friend like you--Would you like to see him?"

Marigold closed the bonnet and stood up with a grimace which passed for a happy smile.

"I should, of course," said I, politely. "But I quite understand. You have everything to say to each other. No. I won't stay"--Marigold's smile faded into woodenness--"I only turned in idly to see how you were getting on. But just tell me. How is Leonard? Fit, I hope?"

"He's wonderful," she said.

I motioned Marigold to start the car.

"Give him my kind regards," said I. "No, indeed. He doesn't want to see an old crock like me." The engine rattled. "I hope he's pleased at finding his mother looking so bonny."

"It's only excitement at having Leonard," she explained earnestly. "In reality I'm far from well. But I wouldn't tell him for worlds."

"What's that you wouldn't tell, mother?" cried a soft, cheery voice, and Leonard, the fine flower of English soldiery, turned the corner of the house.

There he stood, tall, deep-chested, clear-eyed, bronzed, his heavy chin in the air, his bull-neck not detracting from his physical handsomeness, but giving it a seal of enormous strength.

"My dear fellow," he cried, grasping my hand heartily, "how glad I am to see you. Come along in and let mother give you some tea. Nonsense!" he waved away my protest. "Marigold, stop that engine and bring in the Major. I've got lots of things to tell you. That's right."

He strode boyishly to the front door, which he threw open wide to admit Marigold and myself and followed us with Mrs. Boyce into the drawing-room, talking all the while. I must confess that I was just a little puzzled by his exuberant welcome. And, to judge by the blank expression that flitted momentarily over her face, so was his mother. If he were so delighted by my visit, why had he not crossed the lawn at once as soon as he saw the car? Why had he sent his mother on ahead? I was haunted by an exchange of words overheard in imagination:

"Confound the fellow! What has he come here for?"

"Mary will say 'not at home.'"

"But he has spotted us. Do go and get rid of him."

"Such an old friend, dear."

"We haven't time for old fossils. Tell him to go and bury himself."

And (in my sensitive fancy) she had delivered the import of the message. I had gathered that my visit was ill-timed. I was preparing to cut it short, when Leonard himself came up and whisked me against my will to the tea-table. If my hypothesis were correct he had evidently changed his mind as to the desirability of getting rid, in so summary a fashion, of what he may have considered to be an impertinent and malicious little factor in Wellingsford gossip.

At any rate, if he was playing a part, he played it very well. It was not in the power of man to be more cordial and gracious. He gave me a vivid account of the campaign. He had been through everything, the retreat from Mons, the Battle of the Aisne, the great rush north, and the Battle of Neuve Chapelle on the 17th of March. I listened, fascinated, to his tale, which he told with a true soldier's impersonal modesty.

"I was glad," said I, after a while, "to see you twice mentioned in dispatches."

Mrs. Boyce turned on me triumphantly. "He is going to get his D. S. O."

"By Jove!" said I.

Leonard laughed, threw one gaitered leg over the other and held up his hands at her.

"Oh, you feminine person!" He smiled at me. "I told my dear old mother as a dead and solemn secret."

"But it will be gazetted in a few days, dear."

"One can never be absolutely sure of these things until they're in black and white. A pretty ass I'd look if there was a hitch--say through some fool of a copying clerk--and I didn't get it after all. It's only dear, silly understanding things like mothers that would understand. Other people wouldn't. Don't you think I'm right, Meredyth?"

Of course he was. I have known, in my time, of many disappointments. It is not every recommendation for honours that becomes effective. I congratulated him, however, and swore to secrecy.

"It's all luck," said he. "Just because a man happens to be spotted. If my regiment got its deserts, every Jack man would walk about in a suit of armour made of Victoria Crosses. Give me some more tea, mother."

"The thing I shall never understand, dear," she said, artlessly, looking up at him, while she handed him his cup, "is when you see a lot of murderous Germans rushing at you with guns and shells and bayonets, how you are not afraid."

He threw back his head and laughed in his debonair fashion; but I watched him narrowly and I saw the corners of his mouth twitch for the infinitesimal fraction of a second.

"Oh, sometimes we're in an awful funk, I assure you," he replied gaily. "Ask Meredyth."

"We may be," said I, "but we daren't shew it--I'm speaking of officers. If an officer funks he's generally responsible for the death of goodness knows how many men. And if the men funk they're liable to be shot for cowardice in the face of the enemy."

"And what happens to officers who are afraid?"

"If it's known, they get broke," said I.

Boyce swallowed his tea at a gulp, set down the cup, and strode to the window. There was a short pause. Presently he turned.

"Physical fear is a very curious thing," he said in a voice unnecessarily loud. "I've seen it take hold of men of proved courage and paralyse them. It's just like an epileptic fit--beyond a man's control. I've known a fellow--the most reckless, hare-brained daredevil you can imagine--to stand petrified with fear on the bank of a river, and let a wounded comrade drown before his eyes. And he was a good swimmer too."

"What happened to him?" I asked.

He met my gaze for a moment, looked away, and then met it again--it seemed defiantly.

"What happened to him? Well--" there was the tiniest possible pause--a pause that only an uneasy, suspicious repository of the abominable story of Vilboek's Farm could have noticed--"Well, as he stood there he got plugged--and that was the end of him. But what I--"

"Was he an officer, dear?"

"No, no, mother, a sergeant," he answered abruptly, and in the same breath continued. "What I was going to say is this. No one as far as I know has ever bothered to work out the psychology of fear. Especially the sudden thing that hits a man's heart and makes him stand stock-still like a living corpse--unable to move a muscle--all his willpower out of gear--just as a motor is out of gear. I've seen a lot of it. Those men oughtn't to be called cowards. It's as much a fit, say, as epilepsy. Allowances ought to made for them."

It was a warm day, the windows were closed, my valetudinarian hostess having a horror of draughts, and a cheery fire was blazing up the chimney. Boyce took out a handkerchief and mopped his forehead.

"Dear old mother," said he, "you keep this room like an oven."

"It is you who have got so excited talking, dear," said Mrs. Boyce. "I'm sure it can't be good for your heart. It is just the same with me. I remember I had to speak quite severely to Mary a week--no, to-day's Tuesday--ten days ago, and I had dreadful palpitations afterwards and broke out into a profuse perspiration and had to send for Doctor Miles."

"Now, that's funny," said I. "When I'm excited about anything I grow quite cold."

Boyce lit a cigarette and laughed. "I don't see where the excitement in the present case comes in. Mother started an interesting hare, and I followed it up. Anyhow--" he threw himself on the sofa, blew a kiss to his mother in the most charming way in the world, and smiled on me--"anyhow, to see you two in this dearest bit of dear old England is like a dream. And I'm not going to think of the waking up. I want all the cushions and the lavender and the neat maid's caps and aprons--I said to Mary this morning when she drew my curtains: 'Stay just there and let me look at you so that I can realise I'm at home and not in my little grey trench in West Flanders'--she got red and no doubt thought me a lunatic and felt inclined to squawk--but she stayed and looked jolly pretty and refreshing--only for a minute or two, after which I dismissed her--yes, my dears, I want everything that the old life means, the white table linen, the spring flowers, the scent of the air which has never known the taint of death, and all that this beautiful mother of England, with her knitting needles, stands for. I want to have a debauch of sweet and beautiful things."

"As far as I can give them you shall have them. My dear--" she dropped her knitting in her lap and looked over at him tragically--"I quite forgot to ask. Did Mary put bath-salts, as I ordered, into your bath this morning?"

Leonard threw away his cigarette and slapped his leg.

"By George!" he cried. "That explains it. I was wondering where the Dickens that smell of ammonia came from."

"If you use it every day it makes your skin so nice and soft," remarked Mrs. Boyce.

He laughed, and made the obvious jest on the use of bath-salts in the trenches.

"I wonder, mother, whether you have any idea of what trenches and dug-outs look like."

He told her, very picturesquely, and went on to a general sketch of life at the front. He entertained me with interesting talk for the rest of my visit. I have already said that he was a man of great personal charm.

He accompanied me to the car and saw me comfortably tucked in.

"You won't give me away, will you?" he said, shaking hands.

"How?" I asked.

"By telling any one I'm here."

I promised and drove off. Marigold, full of the tea that is given to a guest, strove cheerfully to engage me in conversation. I hate to snub Marigold, excellent and devoted fellow, so I let him talk; but my mind was occupied with worrying problems.

CHAPTER VI

Leonard Boyce had received me on sufferance. I had come upon him while he was imprudently exposing himself to view. There had been no way out of it. But he made it clear that he desired no other Wellingsfordian to invade his privacy. Secretly he had come to see his mother and secretly he intended to go. I remembered that before he went to the front he had not come home, but his mother had met him in London. He had asked me for no local news. He had inquired after the welfare of none of his old friends. Never an allusion to poor Oswald Fenimore's gallant death--he used to run in and out of Wellings Park as if it were his own house. What had he against the place which for so many years had been his home?

With regard to Betty Fairfax, he had loved and ridden away, it is true, leaving her disconsolate. But though everyone knew of the engagement, no one had suspected the defection. Betty was a young woman who could keep her own counsel and baffle any curiosity-monger or purveyor of gossip in the country. So when she married Captain Connor, a little gasp went round the neighbourhood, which for the first time remembered Leonard Boyce. There were some who blamed her for callous treatment of Boyce, away and forgotten at the front. The majority, however, took the matter calmly, as we have had to take far more amazing social convulsions. The fact remained that Betty was married, and there was no reason whatever, on the score of the old engagement, for Boyce to manifest such exaggerated shyness with regard to Wellingsford society.

If it had been any other man than Boyce, I should not have worried about the matter at all. Save that I was deeply attached to Betty, what had her discarded lover's attitude to do with me? But Boyce was Boyce, the man of the damnable story of Vilboek's Farm. And he, of his own accord, had revived in my mind that story in all its intensity. A chance foolish question, such as thousands of gentle, sheltered women have put to their suddenly, uncomprehended, suddenly deified sons and husbands, had obviously disturbed his nervous equilibrium. That little reflex twitch at the corner of his lips--I have seen it often in the old times. I should like to have had him stripped to the waist so that I could have seen his heart--the infallible test. At moments of mighty moral strain men can keep steady eyes and nostrils and mouth and speech; but they cannot control that tell-tale diaphragm of flesh over the heart. I have known it to cause the death of many a Kaffir spy.... But, at any rate, there was the twitch of the lips ... I deliberately threw weight into the scale of Mrs. Boyce's foolish question. If he had not lost his balance, why should he have launched into an almost passionate defence of the physical coward?

My memory went back to the narrative of the poor devil in the Cape Town hospital. Boyce's description of the general phenomenon was a deadly corroboration of Somers's account of the individual case. They had used the same word-- "paralysed." Boyce had made a fierce and definite apologia for the very act of which

Somers had accused him. He put it down to the sudden epilepsy of fear for which a man was irresponsible. Somers's story had never seemed so convincing--the first part of it, at least--the part relating to the paralysis of terror. But the second part--the account of the diabolical ingenuity by means of which Boyce rehabilitated himself--instead of blowing his brains out like a gentleman--still hammered at the gates of my credulity.

Well--granted the whole thing was true--why revive it after fifteen years' dead silence, and all of a sudden, just on account of an idle question? Even in South Africa, his "mention" had proved his courage. Now, with the D. S. O. a mere matter of gazetting, it was established beyond dispute.

On the other hand, if the Vilboek story, more especially the second part, was true, what reparation could he make in the eyes of honourable men?--in his own eyes, if he himself had succeeded to the status of an honourable man? Would not any decent soldier smite him across the face instead of grasping him by the hand? I was profoundly worried.

Moreover Betty, level-headed Betty, had called him a devil. Why?

If the second part of Somers's story were true, he had acted like a devil. There is no other word for it. Now, what concrete diabolical facts did Betty know? Or had her instinctive feminine insight pierced through the man's outer charm and merely perceived horns, tail, and cloven hoof cast like a shadow over his soul?

How was I to know?

She came to dine with me the next evening: a dear way she had of coming uninvited, and God knows how a lonely cripple valued it. She was in uniform, being too busy to change, and looked remarkably pretty. She brought with her a cheery letter from her husband, received that morning, and read me such bits as the profane might hear, her eyes brightening as she glanced over the sections that she skipped. Beyond doubt her marriage had brought her pleasure and pride. The pride she would have felt to some extent, I think, if she had married a grampus; for when a woman has a husband at the front she feels that she is taking her part in the campaign and exposing herself vicariously to hardship and shrapnel; and in the eyes of the world she gains thereby a little in stature, a thing dear to every right-minded woman. But Betty's husband was not a grampus, but a very fine fellow, a mate to be wholly proud of: and he loved her devotedly and expressed his love beautifully loverwise, as her tell-tale face informed me. Gratefully and sturdily she had set herself out to be happy. She was succeeding.... Lord bless you! Millions of women who have married, not the wretch they loved, but the other man, have lived happy ever after. No: I had no fear for Betty now. I could not see that she had any fear for herself.

After dinner she sat on the floor by my side and smoked cigarettes in great content. She had done a hard day's work at the hospital; her husband had done a hard day's work--probably was still doing it--in Flanders. Both deserved well of their country and their consciences. She was giving a poor lonely paralytic, who had given his legs years ago to the aforesaid country, a delightful evening. ... No, I'm quite sure such a patronising thought never entered my Betty's head. After all, my upper half is sound, and I can talk sense or nonsense with anybody. What have one's legs to do with a pleasant after-dinner conversation? Years ago I swore a great oath that I would see them damned before they got in the way of my intelligence.

We were getting on famously. We had put both war and Wellingsford behind us, and talked of books. I found to my dismay that this fair and fearless high product of modernity had far less acquaintance with Matthew Arnold than with the Evangelist of the same praenomen. She had never heard of "The Forsaken Merman," one of the most haunting romantic poems in the English language. I pointed to a bookcase and bade her fetch the volume. She brought it and settled down again by my chair, and, as a punishment of ignorance, and for the good of her soul, I began to read aloud. She is an impressionable young person and yet one of remarkable candour. If she had not been held by the sea-music of the poem, she would not have kept her deep, steady brown eyes fixed on me. I have no hesitation in repeating that we were getting on famously and enjoying ourselves immensely. I got nearly to the end:

"... Here came a mortal, But faithless was she, And alone dwell forever The Kings of the sea. But, children at midnight--"

The door opened wide. Topping his long stiff body, Marigold's ugly one-eyed head appeared, and, as if he was tremendously proud of himself, he announced:

"Major Boyce."

Boyce strode quickly past him and, suddenly aware of Betty by my side, stopped short, like a private suddenly summoned to attention. Marigold, unconscious of the blackest curses that had ever fallen upon him during his long and blundering life, made a perfect and self-satisfied exit. Betty sprang to her feet, held her tall figure very erect, and faced the untimely visitor, her cheeks flushing deep red. For an appreciable time, say, thirty seconds, Boyce stood stock still, looking at her from under heavy contracted brows. Then he recovered himself, smiled, and advanced to her with outstretched hand, But, on his movement, she had been quick to turn and bend down in order to pick up the book that had fallen from my fingers on the further side of my chair. So, swiftly he wheeled to me with his handshake. It was very deft manoeuvring on both sides.

"The faithful Marigold didn't tell me that you weren't alone, Meredyth," he said in his cordial, charming way. "Otherwise I shouldn't have intruded. But my dear old mother had an attack of something and went to bed immediately after dinner, and I thought I'd come round and have a smoke and a drink in your company."

Betty, who had occupied herself by replacing Matthew Arnold's poems in the bookcase, caught up the box of cigars that lay on the brass tray table by my side, and offered it to him.

"Here is the smoke," she said.

And when, after a swift, covert glance at her, he had selected a cigar, she went to the bell-push by the mantelpiece.

"The drinks will be here in a minute."

In order to do something to save this absurd situation, I drew from my waist-coat pocket a little cigar-cutter attached to my watch-chain, and clipped the end of his cigar. I also lit a match from my box and handed it up to him. When he had finished with the match he threw it into the fireplace and turned to Betty.

"My congratulations are a bit late, but I hope I may offer them."

She said, "Thank you." Waved a hand. "Won't you sit down?"

"Wasn't it rather sudden?" he asked.

"Everything in war time is sudden--except the action of the British Government. Your own appearance to-night is sudden."

He laughed at her jest and explained, much as he had done to me, his reasons for wishing to keep his visit to Wellingsford a secret. Meanwhile Marigold had brought in decanters and syphons. Betty attended to Boyce's needs with a provoking air of nonchalance. If a notorious German imbrued in the blood of babes had chanced to be in her hospital, she would have given him his medicine with just the same air. Although no one could have specified a lack of courtesy towards a guest--for in my house she played hostess--there was an indefinable touch of cold contumely in her attitude. Whether he felt the hostility as acutely as I did, I cannot say; but he carried it off with a swaggering grace. He bowed to her over his glass.

"Here's to the fortunate and gallant fellow over there."

I saw her knuckles whiten as, with an inclination of the head, she acknowledged the toast.

"By the way," said he, "what's his regiment? My good mother told me his name. Captain Connor, isn't it? But for the rest she is vague. She's the vaguest old dear in the world. I found out to-day that she thought there was a long row of cannons, hundreds of them, all in a line, in front of the English Army, and a long row in front of the German Army, and, when there was a battle, that they all blazed away. So when I asked her whether your husband was in the Life Guards or the Army Service Corps, she said cheerfully that it was either one or the other but she wasn't quite sure. So do give me some reliable information."

"My husband is in the 10th Wessex Fusiliers, a Territorial battalion," she replied coldly.

"I hope some day to have the pleasure of making his acquaintance."

"Stranger things have happened," said Betty. She glanced at the clock and rose abruptly. "It's time I was getting back to the hospital."

Boyce rose too. "How are you going?" he asked.

"I'm walking."

He advanced a step towards her. "Won't you let me run you round in the car?"

"I prefer to walk."

Her tone was final. She took affectionate leave of me and went to the door, which Boyce held open.

"Good-night," she said, without proffering her hand.

He followed her out into the hall.

"Betty," he said in a low voice, "won't you ever forgive me?"

"I have no feelings towards you either of forgiveness or resentment," she replied.

They did not mean to be overheard, but my hearing is unusually acute, and I could not help catching their conversation.

"I know I seem to have behaved badly to you."

"You have behaved worse to others," said Betty. "I don't wonder at your shrinking from showing your face here." Then, louder, for my benefit. "Good-night, Major Boyce. I really can walk up to the hospital by myself."

Evidently she walked away and Boyce after her, for I heard him say:

"You shan't go till you've told me what you mean."

What she replied I don't know. To judge by the slam of the front door it must have been something defiant. Presently he entered debonair, with a smile on his lips.

"I'm afraid I've left you in a draught," he said, shutting the door. "I couldn't resist having a word with her and wishing her happiness and the rest of it. We were engaged once upon a time."

"I know," said I.

"I hope you don't think I did wrong in releasing her from the engagement. I don't consider a man has a right to go on active service--especially on such service as the present war--and keep a girl bound at home. Still less has he a right to marry her. What happens in so many cases? A fortnight's married life. The man goes to the front. Then ping! or whizz-bang! and that's the end of him, and so the girl is left."

"On the other hand," said I, "you must remember that the girl may hold very strong opinions and take pings and whizz-bangs very deliberately into account."

Boyce helped himself to another whisky and soda. "It's a matter for the individual conscience. I decided one way. Connor obviously decided another, and, like a lucky fellow, found Betty of his way of thinking. Perhaps I have old-fashioned notions." He took a long pull at his drink. "Well, it can't be helped," he said with a smile. "The other fellow has won, and I must take it gracefully. ... By George! wasn't she looking stunning to-night--in that kit? ... I hope you didn't mind my bursting in on you--"

"Of course not," said I, politely.

He drained his glass. "The fact is," said he, "this war is a nerve-racking business. I never dreamed I was so jumpy until I came home. I hate being by myself. I've kept my poor devoted mother up till one o'clock in the morning. To-night she struck, small blame to her; but, after five minutes on my lones, I felt as if I should go off my head. So I routed out the car and came along. But of course I didn't expect to see Betty. The sight of Betty in the flesh as a married woman nearly bowled me over. May I help myself again?" He poured out a very much stiffer drink than before, and poured half of it down his throat. "It's not a joyous thing to see the woman one has been crazy over the wife of another fellow."

"I suppose it isn't," said I.

Of course I might have made some subtle and cunning remark, suavely put a leading question which would have led him on, in his unbalanced mood, to confidential revelations. But the man was a distinguished soldier and my guest. To what he chose to tell me voluntarily I could listen. I could do no more. He did not reply to my last unimportant remark, but lay back in his armchair watching the blue spirals of smoke from the end of his cigar. There was a fairly long silence.

I was worried by the talk I had overheard through the open door. "You have behaved worse to others. I don't wonder at your shrinking from showing your face here." Betty had, weeks ago, called him a devil. She had treated him to-night in a manner which, if not justified, was abominable. I was forced to the conclusion that Betty was fully aware of some discreditable chapter in the man's life which had nothing to do with the affair at Vilboek's Farm, which, indeed, had to do with another woman and this humdrum little town of Wellingsford. Otherwise why did she taunt him with hiding from the light of Wellingsfordian day?

Now, please don't think me little-minded. Or, if you do think so, please remember the conditions under which I have lived for so many years and grant me your kind indulgence for a confession I have to make. Besides being worried, I felt annoyed. Wellingsford was my little world. I knew everybody in it. I had grown to regard myself as the repository of all its gossip. The fraction of it that I retailed was a matter of calculated discretion. I made a little hobby--it was a foible, a vanity, what you will--of my omniscience. I knew months ahead the dates of the arrivals of young Wellingsfordians in this world of pain and plenitude. I knew of maidens who were wronged and youths who were jilted; of wives who led their husbands a deuce of a dance, and of wives who kept their husbands out of the bankruptcy court. When young Trexham, the son of the Lord Lieutenant of the county, married a minor light of musical comedy at a registrar's office, I was the first person in the place to be told; and I flatter myself that I was instrumental in inducing a pig-headed old idiot to receive an exceedingly charming daughter-in-law. I loved to look upon Wellingsford as an open book. Can you blame me for my resentment at coming across, so to speak, a couple of pages glued together? The only logical inference from Betty's remark was that Boyce had behaved abominably and even notoriously to a woman in Wellingsford. To do him justice, I declare I had never heard his name associated with any woman or girl in the place save Betty herself. I felt that, in some crooked fashion, or the other, I had been done out of my rights.

And there, placidly smoking his cigar and watching the wreaths of blue smoke with the air of an idle seraph contemplating a wisp of cirrus in Heaven's firmament, sat the man who could have given me the word of the enigma.

He broke the silence by saying:

"Have you ever seriously considered the real problems of the Balkans?"

Now what on earth had the Balkans to do with the thoughts that must have been rolling at the back of the man's mind? I was both disappointed and relieved. I expected him to resume the personal talk, and I dreaded lest he should entrust me with embarrassing confidences. After three strong whiskies and sodas a man is apt to relax hold of his discretion.... Anyhow, he jerked me back to my position of host. I made some sort of polite reply. He smiled.

"You, my dear Meredyth, like the rest of the country, are half asleep. In a few months' time you'll get the awakening of your life."

He began to discourse on the diplomatic situation. Months afterwards I remembered what he had said that night and how accurate had been his forecast. He talked brilliantly for over an hour, during which, keenly interested in his arguments, I lost the puzzle of the man in admiration of the fine soldier and clear and daring thinker. It was only when he had gone that I began to worry again.

And before I went to sleep I had fresh cause for anxious speculation.

"Marigold," said I, when he came in as usual to carry me to bed, "didn't I tell you that Major Boyce particularly wanted no one to know that he was in the town?"

"Yes, sir," said Marigold. "I've told nobody."

"And yet you showed him in without informing him that Mrs. Connor was here. Really you ought to have had more tact."

Marigold received his reprimand with the stolidity of the old soldier. I have known men who have been informed that they would be court-martialled and most certainly shot, make the same reply.

"Very good, sir," said he.

I softened. I was not Marigold's commanding officer, but his very grateful friend. "You see," said I, "they were engaged before Mrs. Connor married--I needn't tell you that; it was common knowledge--and so their sudden meeting was awkward."

"Mrs. Marigold has already explained, sir," said he.

I chuckled inwardly all the way to my bedroom.

"All the same, sir," said he, aiding me in my toilet, which he did with stiff military precision, "I don't think the Major is as incognighto" (the spelling is phonetic) "as he would like. Prettilove was shaving me this morning and told me the Major was here. As I considered it my duty, I told him he was a liar, and he was so upset that he nicked my Adam's apple and I was that covered with blood that I accused him of trying to cut my throat, and I went out and finished shaving myself at home, which is unsatisfactory when you only have a thumb on your right hand to work the razor."

I laughed, picturing the scene. Prettilove is an inoffensive little rabbit of a man. Marigold might sit for the model of a war-scarred mercenary of the middle ages, and when he called a man a liar he did it with accentuaton and vehemence. No wonder Prettilove jumped.

"And then again this evening, sir," continued Marigold, slipping me into my pyjama jacket, "as I was starting the Major's car, who should be waiting there for him but Mr. Gedge."

"Gedge?" I cried.

"Yes, sir. Waiting by the side of the car. 'Can I have a word with you, Major Boyce?' says he. 'No, you can't,' says the Major. 'I think it's advisable,' says he. 'Those repairs are very pressing.' 'All right,' says the Major, 'jump in.' Then he says: 'That'll do, Marigold. Good-night.' And he drives off with Mr. Gedge. Well, if Mr. Gedge and Prettilove know he's here, then everyone knows it."

"Was Gedge inside the drive?" I asked. The drive was a small semicircular sort of affair, between gate and gate.

"He was standing by the car waiting," said Marigold. "Now, sir." He lifted me with his usual cast-iron tenderness into bed and pulled the coverings over me. "It's a funny time to talk about house repairs at eleven o'clock, at night," he remarked.

"Nothing is funny in war-time," said I.

"Either nothing or everything," said Marigold. He fussed methodically about the room, picked up an armful of clothes, and paused by the door, his hand on the switch.

"Anything more, sir?"

"Nothing, thank you, Marigold."

"Good-night, sir."

The room was in darkness. Marigold shut the door. I was alone.

What the deuce was the meaning of this waylaying of Boyce by Daniel Gedge?

CHAPTER VII

"Major Boyce has gone, sir," said Marigold, the next morning, as I was tapping my breakfast egg.

"Gone?" I echoed. Boyce had made no reference the night before to so speedy a departure.

"By the 8.30 train, sir."

Every train known by a scheduled time at Wellingsford goes to London. There may be other trains proceeding from the station in the opposite direction but nobody heeds them. Boyce had taken train to London. I asked my omniscient sergeant:

"How did you find that out?"

It appeared it was the driver of the Railway Delivery Van. I smiled at Boyce's ostrich-like faith in the invisibility of his hinder bulk. What could occur in Wellingsford without it being known at once to vanmen and postmen and barbers and servants and masters and mistresses? How could a man hope to conceal his goings and comings and secret actions? He might just as well expect to take a secluded noontide bath in the fountain in Piccadilly Circus.

"Perhaps that's why the matter of those repairs was so pressing, sir," said Marigold.

"No doubt of it," said I.

Marigold hung about, his finger-tips pushing towards me mustard and apples and tulips and everything that one does not eat with egg. But it was no use. I had no desire to pursue the conversation. I continued my breakfast stolidly and read the newspaper propped up against the coffee-pot. So many circumstances connected with Boyce's visit were of a nature that precluded confidential discussion with Marigold,--that precluded, indeed, confidential discussion with anyone else. The suddenness of his departure I learned that afternoon from Mrs. Boyce, who sent me by hand a miserable letter characteristically rambling. From it I gathered certain facts. Leonard had come into her bedroom at seven o'clock, awakening her from the first half-hour's sleep she had enjoyed all night, with the news that he had been unexpectedly summoned back. When she came to think of it, she couldn't imagine how he got the news, for the post did not arrive till eight o'clock, and Mary said no telegram had been delivered and there had been no call on the telephone. But she supposed the War Office had secret ways of communicating with officers which it would not be well to make known. The whole of this war, with its killing off of the sons of the best families in the land, and the sleeping in the mud with one's boots on, to say nothing of not being able to change for dinner, and the way in which they knew when to shoot and when not to shoot, was all so mysterious that she had long ago given up hope of understanding any of its details. All she could do was to pray God that her dear boy should be spared. At any rate, she knew the duty of an English mother when the country was in danger; so she had sent him away with a brave face and her blessing, as she had done before. But, although English mothers could show themselves Spartans--(she spelt it "Spartians," dear lady, but no matter)--yet they were women and had to sit at home and weep. In the meanwhile, her palpitations had come on dreadfully bad, and so had her neuritis, and she had suffered dreadfully after eating some fish at dinner which she was sure Pennideath, the fishmonger--she always felt that man was an anarchist in disguise--had bought out of the condemned stock at Billingsgate, and none of the doctor's medicines were of the slightest good to her, and she was heartbroken at having to part so suddenly from Leonard, and would I spare half an hour to comfort an old woman who had sent her only son to die for his country and was ready, when it pleased God, if not sooner, to die in the same sacred cause?

So of course I went. The old lady, propped on pillows in an overheated room, gave me tea and poured into my ear all the anguish of her simple heart. In an abstracted, anxious way, she ate a couple of crumpets and a wedge of cake with almond icing, and was comforted.

We continued our discussion of the war--or rather Leonard, for with her Leonard seemed to be the war. She made some remark deliciously inept--I wish I could remember it. I made a sly rejoinder. She sat bolt upright and a flush came into her Dresden-china cheek and her old eyes flashed.

"You may think I'm a silly old woman, Duncan. I dare say I am. I can't take in things as I used to do when I was young. But if Leonard should be killed in the war--I think of it night and day--what I should like to do would be to drive to the Market Square of Wellingsford and wave a Union Jack round and round and fall down dead."

I made some sort of sympathetic gesture.

"And I certainly should," she added.

"My dear friend," said I, "if I could move from this confounded chair, I would kiss your brave hands."

And how many brave hands of English mothers, white and delicate, coarse and toil-worn, do not demand the wondering, heart-full homage of us all?

And hundreds of thousands of them don't know why we are fighting. Hundreds of thousands of them have never read a newspaper in their lives. I doubt whether they would understand one if they tried, I doubt whether all could read one in the literal sense of the word. We have had--we have still--the most expensive and rottenest system of primary education in the world, the worst that squabbling sectarians can devise. Arab children squatting round the courtyard of a Mosque and swaying backwards and forwards as they get by heart meaningless bits of the Koran, are not sent out into life more inadequately armed with elementary educational weapons than are English children. Our state of education has nominally been systematised for forty-five years, and yet now in our hospitals we have splendid young fellows in their early twenties who can neither read nor write. I have talked with them. I have read to them. I have written letters for them. Clean-cut, decent, brave, honourable Englishmen--not gutter-bred Hooligans dragged from the abyss by the recruiting sergeant, but men who have thrown up good employment because something noble inside them responded to the Great Call. And to the eternal disgrace of governments in this disastrously politician-ridden land such men have not been taught to read and write. It is of no use anyone saying to me that it is not so. I know of my own certain intimate knowledge that it is so.

Even among those who technically have "the Three R's," I have met scores of men in our Wellingsford Hospital who, bedridden for months, would give all they possess to be able to enjoy a novel--say a volume of W. W. Jacobs, the writer who above all others has conferred the precious boon of laughter on our wounded--but to whom the intellectual strain of following the significance of consecutive words is far too great. Thousands and thousands of men have lain in our hospitals deprived, by the criminal insanity of party politicians, of the infinite consolation of books.

Christ, whom all these politicians sanctimoniously pretend to make such a fuss of, once said that a house divided against itself cannot stand. And yet we regard this internecine conflict between our precious political parties as a sacred institution. By Allah, we are a funny people!

Of course your officials at the Board of Education--that beautiful timber-headed, timber-hearted, timber-souled structure--could come down on me with an avalanche of statistics. "Look at our results," they cry. I look. There are certain brains that even our educational system cannot benumb. A few clever ones, at the cost of enormously expensive machinery, are sent to the universities, where they learn how to teach others the important things whereby they achieved their own unimportant success. The shining lights are those whom we turn out as syndicalist leaders and other kinds of anti-patriotic demagogues. We systematically deny them the wine of thought, but give them the dregs. But in the past we did not care; they were vastly clever people, a credit to our national system. It gave them chances which they took. We were devilish proud of them.

On the other hand, the vast mass are sent away with the intellectual equipment of a public school-boy of twelve, and, as I have declared, a large remnant have not been taught even how to read and write. The storm of political controversy on educational matters has centred round such questions as whether the story of Joseph and his Brethren and the Parable of the Prodigal Son should be taught to little Baptists by a Church of England teacher, and what proportion of rates paid by Church of England ratepayers should go to giving little Baptists a Baptistical training. If there was a Christ who could come down among us, with what scorching sarcasm would he not shrivel up the Scribes and Pharisees, hypocrites, who in His Name have prevented the People from learning how to read and write.

Look through Hansard. There never has been a Debate in the House of Commons devoted to the question of Education itself. If the War can teach us any lessons, as a nation--and sometimes I doubt whether it will--it ought at least to teach us the essential vicious rottenness of our present educational system.

This tirade may seem a far cry from Mrs. Boyce and her sister mothers. It is not. I started by saying that there are hundreds of thousands of British mothers, with sons in the Army, who have never read a line of print dealing with the war, who have the haziest notion of what it is all about. All they know is that we are fighting Germans, who for some incomprehensible reason have declared themselves to be our enemies; that the Germans, by hearsay accounts, are dreadful people who stick babies on bayonets and drop bombs on women and children. They really know little more. But that is enough. They know that it is the part of a man to fight for his country. They would not have their sons be called cowards. They themselves have the blind, instinctive, and therefore sacred love of country, which is named patriotism--and they send forth their sons to fight.

I stand up to kiss the white and delicate hand of the gentlewoman who sends her boy to the war, for its owner knows as well as I do (or ought to) all that is involved in this colossal struggle. But to the toil-worn, coarse-handed mother I go on bended knees; nothing intellectual comes within the range of her ideas. Her boy is fighting for England. She would be ashamed if he were not. Were she a man she would fight too. He has gone "with a good 'eart"--the stereotyped phrase with which every English private soldier, tongue-tied, hides the expression of his unconquerable soul. How many times have I not heard it from wounded men healed of their wounds? I have never heard anything else. "The man who says he WANTS to go back is a liar. But if they send me, I'll go WITH A GOOD 'EART"--The phrase which ought to be immortalized on every grave in Flanders and France and Gallipoli and Mesopotamia.

    17735 P'V'TE THOMAS ATKINS 1ST GOD'S OWN REG'T
    HE DIED WITH A GOOD 'EART

So, you see, I looked at this rather silly malade imaginaire of an old lady with whom I was taking tea, and suddenly conceived for her a vast respect--even veneration. I say "rather silly." I had many a time qualified the adjective much more forcibly. I took her to have the intellectual endowment of a hen. But then she flashed out suddenly before me an elderly Jeanne d'Arc. That to me Leonard Boyce was suspect did not enter at all into the question. To her--and that was all that mattered--he was Sir Galahad, Lancelot, King Arthur, Bayard, St. George, Hector, Lysander, Miltiades, all rolled into one. The passion of her life was spent on him. To do him justice, he had never failed to display to her the most tender affection. In her eyes he was perfection. His death would mean the wiping out of everything between Earth and Heaven. And yet, paramount in her envisagement of such a tragedy was the idea of a public proclamation of the cause of England in which he died.

In this war the women of England--the women of Great Britain and Ireland--the women of the far-flung regions of the British Empire, have their part.

Now and then mild business matters call me up to London. On these occasions Marigold gets himself up in a kind of yachting kit which he imagines will differentiate him from the ordinary chauffeur and at the same time proclaim the dignity of the Meredyth-Marigold establishment. He loves to swagger up the steps of my Service Club and announce my arrival to the Hall Porter, who already, warned by telephone of my advent, has my little wicker-work tricycle chair in readiness. I think he feels, dear fellow, that he and I are keeping our end up; that, although there are only bits of us left, we are there by inalienable right as part and parcel of the British Army--none of your Territorials or Kitcheners, but the old original British Army whose prestige and honour were those of his own straight soul. The Hall Porter is an ex-Sergeant-Major, and he and Marigold are old acquaintances, and the meeting of the two warriors is acknowledged by a wink and a military jerk of the head. I think it is Marigold that impresses Bunworthy with a respect for me, for that august functionary never fails to descend the steps and cross the pavement to my modest little two-seater; an act of graciousness which (so I am given to understand by my friends) he will only perform in the case of Royalty Itself. A mere Field-marshal has to mount the steps unattended like any subaltern.

These red-letter days when I drive through the familiar (and now exciting) hubbub of London, I love (strange taste!) every motor omnibus, every pretty woman, every sandwich-man, every fine young fellow in khaki, every car-load of men in blue hospital uniform. I love the smell of London, the cinematographic picture of London, the thrill of London. To understand what I mean you have only got to get rid of your legs and keep your heart and nerves and memories, and live in a little country town.

Yes, my visits to London are red-letter days. To get there with any enjoyment to myself involves such a fussification, and such an unauthorised claim on the services of other people, that my visits are few and far between.

A couple of hours in a club smoking-room--to the normal man a mere putting in of time, a vain surcease from boredom, a vacuous habit--is to me, a strange wonder and delight. After Wellingsford the place is resonant with actualities. I hear all sorts of things; mostly lies, I know; but what matter? When a man tells me that his cousin knows a man attached as liaison officer to the staff of General Joffre, who has given out confidentially that such and such a thing is going to happen I am all ears. I feel that I am sucked into the great whirlpool of Vast Events. I don't care a bit about being disillusioned afterwards. The experience has done me good, made a man of me and sent me back to Wellingsford as an oracle. And if you bring me a man who declares that he does not like being an oracle, I will say to his face that he is an unblushing liar.

All this is by way of preface to the statement that on the third of May (vide diary) I went to the club. It was just after lunch and the great smoking-room was full of men in khaki and men in blue and gold, with a sprinkling of men, mostly elderly, in mufti; and from their gilt frames the full-length portraits of departed men of war in gorgeous uniforms looked down superciliously on their more sadly attired descendants. I got into a corner by the door, so as to be out of the way, for I knew by experience that should there be in the room a choleric general, he would inevitably trip over the casually extended front wheel of my chair, greatly to the scandal of modest ears and to my own physical discomfiture.

Various seniors came up and passed the time of the day with me--one or two were bald-headed retired colonels of sixty, dressed in khaki, with belts like equators on a terrestrial globe and with a captain's three stars on their sleeves. Gallant old boys, full of gout and softness, they had sunk their rank and taken whatever dull jobs, such as guarding internment camps or railway bridges, the War Office condescendingly thought fit to give them. They listened sympathetically to my griev-ances, for they had grievances of their own. When soldiers have no grievances the Army will perish of smug content.

"Why can't they give me a billet in the Army Pay and let me release a man sounder of wind and limb?" I asked. "What's the good of legs to a man who sits on his hunkers all day in an office and fills up Army forms? I hate seeing you lucky fellows in uniform."

"We're not a pretty sight," said the most rotund, who was a wag in his way.

Then we discussed what we knew and what we didn't know of the Battle of Ypres, and the withdrawal of our Second Army, and shook our heads dolorously over the casualty lists, every one of which in those days contained the names of old comrades and of old comrades' boys. And when they had finished their coffee and mild cigars they went off well contented to their dull jobs and the room began to thin. Other acquaintances on their way out paused for a handshake and a word, and I gathered scraps of information that had come "straight from Kitchener," and felt wonderfully wise and cheerful.

I had been sitting alone for a few minutes when a man rose from a far corner, a tall soldierly figure, his arm in a sling, and came straight towards me with that supple, easy stride that only years of confident command can give. He had keen blue eyes and a pleasant bronzed face which I knew that I had seem somewhere before. I noticed on his sleeve the crown and star of a lieutenant-colonel. He said pleasantly:

"You're Major Meredyth, aren't you?"

"Yes," said I.

"You don't remember me. No reason why you should. But my name's Dacre-- Reggie Dacre, brother of Johnnie Dacre in your battery. We met in Cape Town."

I held out my hand.

"Of course," said I. "You took me to a hospital. Do sit down for a bit. You a member here?"

"No. I belong to the Naval and Military. Lunching with old General Donovan, a sort of god-father of mine. He told me who you were. I haven't seen you since that day in South Africa."

I asked for news of Johnnie, who had been lost to my ken for years. Johnnie had been in India, and was now doing splendidly with his battery somewhere near La Bassee. I pointed to the sling. Badly hurt? No, a bit of flesh torn by shrapnel. Bone, thank God, not touched. It was only horny-headed idiots like the British R. A. M. C. that would send a man home for such a trifle. It was devilish hard lines to be hoofed away from the regiment practically just after he had got his command. However, he would be back in a week or two. He laughed.

"Lucky to be alive at all."

"Or not done in for ever like myself," said I.

"I didn't like to ask--" he said. Men would rather die than commit the indelicacy of appearing to notice my infirmity.

"You haven't been out there?"

"No such luck," said I. "I got this little lot about a fortnight after I saw you. Johnnie was still on sick leave and so was out of that scrap."

He commiserated with me on my ill-fortune, and handed me his cigarette case. We smoked.

"You've been on my mind for months," he said abruptly.

"I?"

He nodded. "I thought I recognised you. I asked the General who you were. He said 'Meredyth of the Gunners.' So I knew I was right and made a bee line for you. Do you remember the story of that man in the hospital?"

"Perfectly," said I.

"About Boyce of the King's Watch?"

"Yes," said I. "I saw Boyce, home on leave, about a fortnight ago. I suppose you saw his D.S.O. gazetted?"

"I did. And he deserves a jolly sight more," he exclaimed heartily. "I've come to the conclusion that that fellow in the hospital--I forget the brute's name--"

"Somers," said I.

"Yes, Somers. I've come to the conclusion that he was the damn'dest, filthiest, lyingest hound that ever was pupped."

"I'm glad to hear it," said I. "It was a horrible story. I remember making your brother and yourself vow eternal secrecy."

"You can take it from me that we haven't breathed a word to anybody. As a matter of fact, the whole damn thing had gone out of my head for years. Then I begin to hear of a fellow called Boyce of the Rifles doing the most crazy magnificent things. I make enquiries and find it's the same Leonard Boyce of the Vilboek Farm story. We're in the same Brigade.

"You don't often hear of individual men out there--your mind's too jolly well concentrated on your own tiny show. But Boyce has sort of burst out beyond his own regiment and, with just one or two others, is beginning to be legendary. He has done the maddest things and won the V.C. twenty times over. So that blighter Somers, accusing him of cowardice, was a ghastly liar. And then I remembered taking you up to hear that damnable slander, and I felt that I had a share in it, as far as you were concerned, and I longed to get at you somehow and tell you about it. I wanted to get it off my chest. And now," said he with a breath of relief, "thank God, I've been able to do so."

"I wish you would tell me of an incident or two," said I.

"He has got a life-preserver that looks like an ordinary cane--had it specially made. It's quite famous. Men tell me that the knob is a rich, deep, polished vermilion. He'll take on any number of Boches with it single-handed. If there's any sign of wire-cutting, he'll not let the men fire, but will take it on himself, and creep like a Gurkha and do the devils in. One night he got a whole listening post like that. He does a lot of things a second in command hasn't any business to do, but his men would follow him anywhere. He bears a charmed life. I could tell you lots of things--but I see my old General's getting restive." He rose, stretched out his hand. "At any rate, take my word for it--if there's a man in the British Army who doesn't know what fear is, that man is Leonard Boyce."

He nodded in his frank way and rejoined his old General. As I had had enough exciting information for one visit to town, I motored back to Wellingsford.

CHAPTER VIII

My house, as I have already mentioned, is situated at the extreme end of the town on the main road, already called the Rowdon Road, which is an extension of the High Street. It stands a little way back to allow room for a semicircular drive, at each end of which is a broad gate. The semicircle encloses a smooth-shaven lawn of which I am vastly proud. In the spandrels by the side of the house are laburnums and lilacs and laurels. From gate to gate stretch iron railings, planted in a low stone parapet and unencumbered with vegetation, so that the view from road to lawn and from lawn to road is unrestricted. Thus I can take up my position on my lawn near the railings and greet all passers-by.

It was a lovely May morning. My laburnums and lilacs were in flower. On the other side of the way the hedge of white-thorn screening the grounds of a large preparatory school was in flower also, and deliciously scented the air. I sat in my accustomed spot, a table with writing materials, tobacco, and books by my side, and a mass of newspapers at my feet. There was going to be a coalition Government. Great statesmen were going to forget that there was such a thing as party politics, except in the distribution of minor offices, when the claims of good and faithful jackals on either side would have to be considered. And my heart grew sick within me, and I longed for a Man to arise who, with a snap of his strong fingers, would snuff out the Little Parish-Pump Folk who have misruled England this many a year with their limited vision and sordid aspirations, and would take the great, unshakable, triumphant command of a mighty Empire passionately yearning to do his bidding... I could read no more newspapers. They disgusted me. One faction seemed doggedly opposed to any proposition for the amelioration of the present disastrous state of affairs. The salvation of wrecked political theories loomed far more important in their darkened minds than the salvation, by hook or crook, of the British Empire. The other faction, more patriotic in theory, cried aloud stinking fish, and by scurrilous over-statement defeated their own ends. In the general ignoble screech the pronouncements of the one or two dignified and thoughtful London newspapers passed unheeded....

I drew what comfort I could from the sight of the continually passing troops; a platoon off to musketry training; a battalion, brown and dusty, on a route march with full equipment, whistling "Tipperary"; sections of an Army Service train cursing good-humouredly at their mules; a battery of artillery thundering along at a clean, rhythmical trot which, considering what they were like in their slovenly jogging and bumping three months ago, afforded me prodigious pleasure. On the passing of these last-mentioned I felt inclined to clap my hands and generally proclaim my appreciation. Indeed, I did arrest a fresh-faced subaltern bringing up the rear of the battery who, having acquaintance with me, saluted, and I shouted:

"They're magnificent!"

He reared up his horse and flushed with pleasure.

"We've done our best, sir," said he. "We had news last week that we should be sent out quite soon, and that has bucked them up enormously."

He saluted again and rode off, and my heart went with him. What a joy it would be to clatter down a road once again with the guns!

And other people passed. Townsfolk who gave me a kindly "Morning, Major!" and went on, and others who paused awhile and gave me the gossip of the day. And presently young Randall Holmes went by on a motor bicycle. He caught sight of me, disappeared, and then suddenly reappeared, wheeling his machine. He rested it by the kerb of the sidewalk and approached the railings. He was within a yard of me.

"Would you let me speak to you for half a minute, Major?"

"Certainly," said I. "Come in."

He swung through the gate and crossed the lawn.

"You said very hard things to me some time ago."

"I did," said I, "and I don't think they were undeserved."

"Up to a certain point I agree with you," he replied.

He looked extraordinarily robust and athletic in his canvas kit. Why should he be tearing about aimlessly on a motor bicycle this May morning when he ought to be in France?

"I wish you agreed with me all along the line," said I.

He found a little iron garden seat and sat down by my side.

"I don't want to enter into controversial questions," he said.

Confound him! He might have been fifty instead of four-and-twenty. Controversial questions! His assured young Oxford voice irritated me.

"What do you want to enter into?" I asked.

"A question of honour," he answered calmly. "I have been wanting to speak to you, but I didn't like to. Passing you by, just now, I made a sudden resolution. You have thought badly of me on account of my attitude towards Phyllis Gedge. I want to tell you that you were quite right. My attitude was illogical and absurd."

"You have discovered," said I, "that she is not the inspiration you thought she was, and like an honest man have decided to let her alone."

"On the contrary," said he. "I'd give the eyes out of my head to marry her."

"Why?"

He met my gaze very frankly. "For the simple reason, Major Meredyth, that I love her."

All this natural, matter-of-fact simplicity coming from so artificial a product of Balliol as Randall Holmes, was a bit upsetting. After a pause, I said:

"If that is so, why don't you marry her?"

"She'll have nothing to do with me."

"Have you asked her?"

"I have, in writing. There's no mistake about it. I'm in earnest."

"I'm exceedingly glad to hear it," said I.

And I was. An honest lover I can understand, and a Don Juan I can understand. But the tepid philanderer has always made my toes tingle. And I was glad, too, to hear that little Phyllis Gedge had so much dignity and commonsense. Not many small builders' daughters would have sent packing a brilliant young gentleman like Randall Holmes, especially if they happened to be in love with him. As I did not particularly wish to be the confidant of this love-lorn shepherd, I said nothing more. Randall lit a cigarette.

"I hope I'm not boring you," he said.

"Not a bit."

"Well--what complicates the matter is that her father's the most infernal swine unhung." I started, remembering what Betty had told me.

"I thought," said I, "that you were fast friends."

"Who told you so?" he asked.

"All the birds of Wellingsford."

"I did go to see him now and then," he admitted. "I thought he was much maligned. A man with sincere opinions, even though they're wrong, is deserving of some respect, especially when the expression of them involves considerable courage and sacrifice. I wanted to get to the bottom of his point of view."

"If you used such a metaphor in the Albemarle," I interrupted, "I'm afraid you would be sacrificed by your friends."

He had the grace to laugh. "You know what I mean."

"And did you get to the bottom of it?"

"I think so."

"And what did you find?"

"Crass ignorance and malevolent hatred of everyone better born, better educated, better off, better dressed, better spoken than himself."

"Still," said I, "a human being can have those disabilities and yet not deserve to be qualified as the most infernal swine unhung."

"That's a different matter," said he, unbuttoning his canvas jacket, for the morning was warm. "I can talk patiently to a fool--to be able to do so is an elementary equipment for a life among men and women--" Why the deuce, thought I, wasn't he expending this precious acquirement on a platoon of agricultural recruits? The officer who suffers such gladly has his name inscribed on the Golden Legend (unfortunately unpublished) of the British Army--"but when it comes," he went on, "to low-down lying knavery, then I'm done. I don't know how to tackle it. All I can do is to get out of the knave's way. I've found Gedge to be a beast, and I'm very honourably in love with Gedge's daughter, and I've asked her to marry me. I attach some value, Major, to your opinion of me, and I want you, to know these two facts."

I again expressed my gratification at learning his honourable intentions towards Phyllis, and I commended his discovery of Gedge's fundamental turpitude. I cannot say that I was cordial. At this period, the unmilitary youth of England were not affectionately coddled by their friends. Still, I was curious to see whether Gedge's depravity extended beyond a purely political scope. I questioned my young visitor.

"Oh, it's nothing to do with abstract opinions," said he, thinning away the butt-end of his cigarette. "And nothing to do with treason, or anything of that kind. He has got hold of a horrible story--told me all about it when he was foully drunk--that in itself would have made me break with him, for I loathe drunken men--and gloats over the fact that he is holding it over somebody's head. Oh, a ghastly story!"

I bent my brows on him. "Anything to do with South Africa?"

"South Africa--? No. Why?"

The puzzled look on his face showed that I was entirely on the wrong track. I was disappointed at the faultiness of my acumen. You see, I argued thus: Gedge goes off on a mysterious jaunt with Boyce. Boyce retreats precipitately to London. Gedge in his cups tells a horrible scandal with a suggestion of blackmail to Randall Holmes. What else could he have divulged save the Vilboek Farm affair? My nimble wit had led me a Jack o' Lantern dance to nowhere.

"Why South Africa?" he repeated.

I replied with Macchiavellian astuteness, so as to put him on a false scent: "A stupid slander about illicit diamond buying in connection with a man, now dead, who used to live here some years ago."

"Oh, no," said Randall, with a superior smile "Nothing of that sort."

"Well, what is it?" I asked.

He helped himself to another cigarette. "That," said he, "I can't tell you. In the first place I gave my word of honour as to secrecy before he told me, and, in the next, even if I hadn't given my word, I would not be a party to such a slander by repeating it to any living man." He bent forward and looked me straight in the eyes. "Even to you, Major, who have been a second father to me."

"A man," said I, "has a priceless possession that he should always keep--his own counsel."

"I've only told you as much as I have done," said Randall, "because I want to make clear to you my position with regard both to Phyllis and her father."

"May I ask," said I, "what is Phyllis's attitude towards her father?" I knew well enough from Betty; but I wanted to see how much Randall knew about it.

"She is so much out of sympathy with his opinions that she has gone to live at the hospital."

"Perhaps she thinks you share those opinions, and for that reason won't marry you?"

"That may have something to do with it, although I have done my best to convince her that I hold diametrically opposite views, But you can't expect a woman to reason."

"The unexpected sometimes happens," I remarked. "And then comes catastrophe; in this case not to the woman." I cannot say that my tone was sympathetic. I had cause for interest in his artless tale, but it was cold and dispassionate. "Tell me," I continued, "when did you discover the diabolical nature of the man Gedge?"

"Last night."

"And when did you ask Phyllis to marry you?"

"A week ago."

"What's going to happen now?" I asked.

"I'm hanged if I know," said he, gloomily.

I was in no mood to offer the young man any advice. The poor little wretch at the hospital--so Betty had told me--was crying her eyes out for him; but it was not for his soul's good that he should know it.

"In heroic days," said I, "a hopeless lover always found a sovereign remedy against an obdurate mistress."

He rose and buttoned up his canvas jacket.

"I know what you mean," he said. "And I didn't come to discuss it--if you'll excuse my apparent rudeness in saying so."

"Then things are as they were between us."

"Not quite, I hope," he replied in a dignified way. "When last you spoke to me about Phyllis Gedge, I really didn't know my own mind. I am not a cad and the thought of--of anything wrong never entered my head. On the other hand, marriage seemed out of the question."

"I remember," said I, "you talked some blithering rot about her being a symbol."

"I am quite willing to confess I was a fool," he admitted gracefully. "And I merited your strictures."

His reversion to artificiality annoyed me. I'm far from being of an angelic disposition.

"My dear boy," I cried. "Do, for God's sake, talk human English, and not the New Oxford Dictionary."

He flushed angrily, snapped an impatient finger and thumb, and marched away to the gravel path. I sang out sharply:

"Randall!"

He turned. I cried:

"Come here at once."

He came with sullen reluctance. Afterwards I was rather tickled at realizing that the lame old war-dog had so much authority left. If he had gone defiantly off, I should have felt rather a fool.

"My dear boy," I said, "I didn't mean to insult you. But can't a clever fellow like you understand that all the pretty frills and preciousness of a year ago are as dead as last year's Brussels sprouts? We're up against elemental things and can only get at them with elemental ideas expressed in elemental language."

"I'd have you to know," said Randall, "that I spoke classical English."

"Quite so," said I. "But the men of to-day speak Saxon English, Cockney English, slang English, any damned sort of English that is virile and spontaneous. As I say, you're a clever fellow. Can't you see my point? Speech is an index of mental attitude. I bet you what you like Phyllis Gedge would see it at once. Just imagine a subaltern at the front after a bad quarter of an hour with his Colonel--'I've merited your strictures, sir!' If there was a bomb handy, the Colonel would catch it up and slay him on the spot."

"But I don't happen to be at the front, Major," said Randall.

"Then you damned well ought to be," said I, in sudden wrath.

I couldn't help it. He asked for it. He got it.

He went away, mounted his motor bicycle, and rode off.

I was sorry. The boy evidently was in a chastened mood. If I had handled him gently and diplomatically, I might have done something with him. I suppose I'm an irritable, nasty-tempered beast. It is easy to lay the blame on my helpless legs. It isn't my legs. I've conquered my damned legs. It isn't my legs. Its ME.

I was ashamed of myself. And when, later, Marigold enquired whether the doors were still shut against Mr. Holmes, I asked him what the blazes he meant by not minding his own business. And Marigold said: "Very good, sir."

CHAPTER IX

For a week or two the sluggish stream of Wellingsfordian life flowed on undisturbed. The chief incident was a recruiting meeting held on the Common. Sir Anthony Fenimore in his civic capacity, a staff-officer with red tabs, a wounded soldier, an elderly, eloquent gentleman from recruiting headquarters in London, and one or two nondescripts, including myself, were on the platform. A company of a County Territorial Battalion and the O.T.C. of the Godbury Grammar School gave a semblance of military display. The Town Band, in a sort of Hungarian uniform, discoursed martial music. Old men and maidens, mothers and children, and contented young fellows in khaki belonging to all kinds of arms, formed a most respectable crowd. The flower of Wellingsfordian youth was noticeably absent. They were having too excellent a time to be drawn into the temptation of a recruiting meeting, in spite of the band and the fine afternoon and the promiscuity of attractive damsels. They were making unheard-of money at the circumjacent factories; their mothers were waxing fat on billeting-money. They never had so much money to spend on moving-picture-palaces and cheap jewellery for their inamoratas in their lives. As our beautiful Educational system had most scrupulously excluded from their school curriculum any reference to patriotism, any rudimentary conception of England as their sacred heritage, and as they had been afforded no opportunity since they left school of thinking of anything save their material welfare and grosser material appetites, the vague talk of peril to the British Empire left them unmoved. They were quite content to let others go and fight. They had their own comfortable theories about it. Some fellows liked that sort of thing. They themselves didn't. In ordinary times, it amused that kind of fellow to belong to a Harriers Club, and clad in shorts and zephyrs, go on Sundays for twenty-mile runs. It didn't amuse them. A cigarette, a girl, and a stile formed their ideal of Sunday enjoyment. They had no quarrel with the harrier fellow or the soldier fellow for following his bent. They were most broad-minded. But they flattered themselves that they were fellows of a superior and more intelligent breed. They were making money and living warm, the only ideal of existence of which they had ever heard, and what did anything else matter?

If a man has never been taught that he has a country, how the deuce do you expect him to love her--still less to defend her with his blood? Our more than damnable governments for the last thirty years have done everything in their power to crush in English hearts the national spirit of England. God knows I have no quarrel with Scotland, Ireland, and Wales. I speak in no disparagement of them. Quite the reverse. In this war they have given freely of their blood. I only speak as an Englishman of England, the great Mother of the Empire. Scot, Irishman, Welshman, Canadian, Australian are filled with the pride of their nationality. It is part of their being. Wisely they have been trained to it from infancy. England, who is far bigger, far more powerful than the whole lot of them put together--it's a statistical fact--has deliberately sunk herself in her own esteem, in her own pride. Only one great man has stood for England, as England, the great Mother, for the last thirty years. And that man is Rudyard Kipling. And the Little Folk in authority in England have spent their souls in rendering nugatory his inspired message.

This criminal self-effacement of England is at the root of the peril of the British Empire during this war.

I told you at the beginning that I did not know how to write a story. You must forgive me for being led away into divagations which seem to be irrelevant to the dramatic sequence. But when I remember that the result of all the pomp and circumstance of that meeting was seven recruits, of whom three were rejected as being physically unfit, my pen runs away with my discretion, and my conjecturing as to artistic fitness.

Yes, the Major spoke. Sir Anthony is a peppery little person and the audience enjoyed the cayenne piquancy of his remarks. The red-tabbed Lieutenant-Colonel spoke. He was a bit dull. The elderly orator from London roused enthusiastic cheers. The wounded sergeant, on crutches, displaying a foot like a bandaged mop, brought tears into the eyes of many women and evoked hoarse cheers from the old men. I spoke from my infernal chair, and I think I was quite a success with the good fellows in khaki. But the only men we wanted to appeal to had studiously refrained from being present. The whole affair was a fiasco.

When we got home, Marigold, who had stood behind my chair during the proceedings, said to me:

"I think I know personally about thirty slackers in this town, sir, and I'm more than a match for any three of them put together. Suppose I was to go the rounds, so to speak, and say to each of them, 'You young blighter, if you don't come with me and enlist, I 'll knock hell out of you!'--and, if he didn't come, I did knock hell out of him--what exactly would happen, sir?"

"You would be summoned," said I, "for thirty separate cases of assault and battery. Reckoning the penalty at six months each, you would have to go to prison for fifteen years."

Marigold's one eye grew pensive and sad.

"And they call this," said he, "a free country!"

I began this chapter by remarking that for a week or two after my second interview with Randall Holmes, nothing particular happened. Then one afternoon came Sir Anthony Fenimore to see me, and with a view to obtaining either my advice or my sympathy, reopened the story of his daughter Althea found drowned in the canal eleven months before.

What he considered a most disconcerting light had just been cast on the tragedy by Maria Beccles. This lady was Lady Fenimore's sister. A deadly feud, entirely of Miss Beccles' initiating and nourishing, had existed between them for years. They had been neither on speaking nor on writing terms. Miss Beccles, ten years Lady Fenimore's senior, was, from all I had heard, a most disagreeable and ill-conditioned person, as different from my charming friend Edith Fenimore as the ugly old sisters were from Cinderella. Although she belonged to a good old South of England family, she had joined, for reasons known only to herself, the old Free Kirk of Scotland, found a congenial Calvinistic centre in Galloway, and after insulting her English relations and friends in the most unconscionable way, cut herself adrift from them for ever. "Mad as a hatter," Sir Anthony used to say, and, never having met the lady, I agreed with him. She loathed her sister, she detested Anthony, and she appeared to be coldly indifferent to the fact of the existence of her nephew Oswald. But for Althea, and for Althea alone, she entertained a curious, indulgent affection, and every now and then Althea went to spend a week or so in Galloway, where she contrived to obtain considerable amusement. Aunt Maria did both herself and her visitors very well, said Althea, who had an appreciative eye for the material blessings of life. Althea walked over the moors and fished and took Aunt Maria's cars out for exercise and, except whistle on the Sabbath, seemed to do exactly what she liked.

Now, in January 1914, Althea announced to her parents that Aunt Maria had summoned her for a week to Galloway. Sir Anthony stuffed her handbag with five-pound notes, and at an early hour of the morning sent her up in the car to London in charge of the chauffeur. The chauffeur returned saying that he had bought Miss Althea's ticket at Euston and seen her start off comfortably on her journey. A letter or two had been received by the Fenimores from Galloway, and letters they had written to Galloway had been acknowledged by Althea. She returned to Wellingsford in due course, with bonny cheeks and wind-swept eyes, and told us all funny little stories about Aunt Maria. No one thought anything more about it until one fine afternoon in May, 1915, when Maria Beccles walked unexpectedly into the drawing-room of Wellings Park, while Sir Anthony and Lady Fenimore were at tea.

"My dear Edith," she said to her astounded hostess, who had not seen her for fifteen years. "In this orgy of hatred and strife that is going on in the world, it seems ridiculous to go on hating and fighting one's own family. We must combine against the Germans and hate them. Let us be friends."

"Mad as Crazy Jane," said Sir Anthony, telling me the story. But I, who had never heard Aunt Maria's side of the dispute, thought it very high-spirited of the old lady to come and hold out the olive-branch in so uncompromising a fashion.

Lady Fenimore then said that she had never wished to quarrel with Maria, and Sir Anthony declared that her patriotic sentiments did her credit, and that he was proud to receive her under his roof, and in a few minutes Maria was drinking tea and discussing the war in the most contented way in the world.

"I didn't write to you on the occasion of the death of your two children because you knew I didn't like you," said this outspoken lady. "I hate hypocrisy. Also I thought that tribulation might chasten you in the eyes of the Lord. I've discussed it with our Minister, a poor body, but a courageous man. He told me I was unchristian. Now, what with all this universal massacre going on and my unregenerate longing, old woman as I am, to wade knee-deep in German blood, I don't know what the devil I am."

The more Anthony told me of Aunt Maria, the more I liked her.

"Can't I come round and make her acquaintance?" I cried. "She's the sort of knotty, solid human thing that I should love. No wonder Althea was fond of her."

"This happened a week ago. She only stayed a night," replied Sir Anthony. "I wish to God we had never seen her or heard of her."

And then the good, heart-wrung little man, who had been beating about the bush for half an hour, came straight to the point.

"You remember Althea's visit to Scotland in January last year?"

"Perfectly," said I.

He rose from his chair and looked at me in wrinkled anguish.

"She never went there," he said.

That was what he had come to tell me. A natural reference to the last visit of

Althea to her aunt had established the stupefying fact.

"Althea's last visit was in October, 1913," said Miss Beccles.

"But we have letters from your house to prove she was with you in January," said Sir Anthony.

Most methodical and correspondence-docketing of men, he went to his library and returned with a couple of letters.

The old lady looked them through grimly.

"Pretty vague. No details. Read 'em again, Anthony."

When he had done so, she said: "Well?"

Lady Fenimore objected: "But Althea did stay with you. She must have stayed with you."

"All right, Edith," said Maria, sitting bolt upright. "Call me a liar, and have done with it. I've come here at considerable dislocation of myself and my principles, to bury the hatchet for the sake of unity against the enemy, and this is how I'm treated. I can only go back to Scotland at once."

Sir Anthony succeeded in pacifying her. The letters were evidence that Edith and himself believed that Althea was in Galloway at the time. Maria's denial had come upon them like a thunderclap, bewildering, stunning. If Althea was not in Galloway, where was she?

Maria Beccles did not reply for some time to the question. Then she took the pins out of her hat and threw it on a chair, thus symbolising the renunciation of her intention of returning forthwith to Scotland.

"Yes, Maria," said Lady Fenimore, with fear in her dark eyes, "we don't doubt your word--but, as Anthony has said, if she wasn't with you, where was she?"

"How do I know?"

Maria Beccles pointed a lean finger--she was a dark and shrivelled, gipsy-like creature. "You might as well ask the canal in which she drowned herself."

"But, my God, Anthony!" I cried, when he had got thus far, "What did you think? What did you say?"

I realised that the old lady had her social disqualifications. Plain-dealing is undoubtedly a virtue. But there are several virtues which the better class of angel keeps chained up in a dog-kennel. Of course she was acute. A mind trained in the acrobatics of Calvinistic Theology is, within a narrow compass, surprisingly agile. It jumped at one bound from the missing week in Althea's life into the black water of the canal. It was incapable, however, of appreciating the awful horror in the minds of the beholders.

"I don't know what I said," replied Sir Anthony, walking restlessly about my library. "We were struck all of a heap. As you know, we never had reason to think that the poor dear child's death was anything but an accident. We were not narrow-minded old idiots. She was a dear good girl. In a modern way she claimed her little independence. We let her have it. We trusted her. We took it for granted--you know it, Duncan, as well as I do--that, a hot night in June--not able to sleep--she had stuck on a hat and wandered about the grounds, as she had often done before, and a spirit of childish adventure had tempted her, that night, to walk round the back of the town and--and--well, until in the dark, she stepped off the tow-path by the lock gates, into nothing--and found the canal. It was an accident," he continued, with a hand on my shoulder, looking down on me in my chair. "The inquest proved that. I accepted it, as you know, as a visitation of God. Edith and I sorrowed for her like cowards. It took the war to bring us to our senses. But, now, this damned old woman comes and upsets the whole thing."

"But," said I, "after all, it was only a bow at a venture on the part of the old lady."

"I wish it were," said he, and he handed me a letter which Maria had written to him the day after her return to Scotland.

The letter contained a pretty piece of information. She had summarily discharged Elspeth Macrae, her confidential maid of five-and-twenty years' standing. Elspeth Macrae, on her own confession, had, out of love for Althea, performed the time-honoured jugglery with correspondence. She had posted in Galloway letters which she had received, under cover, from Althea, and had forwarded letters that had arrived addressed to Althea to an accommodation address in Carlisle. So have sentimental serving-maids done since the world began.

"What do you make of it?" asked Sir Anthony.

What else could I make of it but the one sorry theory? What woman employs all this subterfuge in order to obtain a weeks liberty for any other purpose than the one elementary purpose of young humanity?

We read the inevitable conclusion in each other's eyes.

"Who is the man, Duncan?"

"I suppose you have searched her desk and things?"

"Last year. Everything most carefully. It was awful--but we had to. Not a scrap of paper that wasn't innocence itself."

"It can't be anyone here," said I. "You know what the place is. The slightest spark sends gossip aflame like the fumes of petrol."

He sat down by my side and rubbed his close-cropped grey head.

"It couldn't have been young Holmes?"

The little man had a brave directness that sometimes disconcerted me. I knew the ghastly stab that every word cost him.

"She used to make mock of Randall," said I. "Don't you remember she used to call him 'the gilded poet'? Once she said he was the most lady-like young man of her acquaintance. I don't admire our young friend, but I think you're on the wrong track, Anthony."

"I don't see it," said he. "That sort of flippancy goes for nothing. Women use it as a sort of quickset hedge of protection." He bent forward and tapped me on my senseless knee. "Young Holmes always used to be in and out of the house. They had known each other from childhood. He had a distinguished Oxford career. When he won the Newdigate, she came running to me with the news, as pleased as Punch. I gave him a dinner in honour of it, if you remember."

"I remember," said I.

I did not remind him that he had made a speech which sent cold shivers down the spine of our young Apollo; that, in a fine rhetorical flourish--dear old fox-hunting ignoramus--he declared that the winner of the Newdigate carried the bays of the Laureate in his knapsack; that Randall, white-lipped with horror, murmured to Betty Fairfax, his neighbour at the table: "My God! The Poet-Laureate's unhallowed grave! I must burn the knapsack and take to a hod!" It was too tragical a conversation for light allusion.

"The poor dear child--Edith and I have sized it up--was all over him that evening."

"What more youthfully natural," said I, "than that she should carry off the hero of the occasion--her childhood's playfellow?"

"All sorts of apparently insignificant details, Duncan, taken together--especially if they fit in--very often make up a whole case for prosecution."

"You're a Chairman of Quarter Sessions," I admitted, "and so you ought to know."

"I know this," said he, "that Holmes only spent part of that Christmas vacation with his mother, and went off somewhere or the other early in January." I cudgelled back my memory into confirmation of his statement. To remember trivial incidents before the war takes a lot of cudgelling. Yes. I distinctly recollected the young man's telling me that Oxford being an intellectual hothouse and Wellingsford an intellectual Arabia Petrea, he was compelled, for the sake of his mental health, to find a period of repose in the intellectual Nature of London. I mentioned this to Sir Anthony.

"Yet," I said, "I don't think he had anything to do with it."

"Why?"

"It would have been far too much moral exertion--"

"You call it moral?" Sir Anthony burst out angrily.

I pacified him with an analysis, from my point of view, of Randall's character. Centripetal forces were too strong for the young man. I dissertated on his amours with Phyllis Gedge.

"No, my dear old friend," said I, in conclusion, "I don't think it was Randall Holmes."

Sir Anthony rose and shook his fist in my face. As I knew he meant me no bodily harm, I did not blench.

"Who was it, then?"

"Althea," said I, "often used to stay in town with your sister. Lady Greatorex has a wide circle of acquaintances. Do you know anything of the men Althea used to meet at her house?"

"Of course I don't," replied Sir Anthony. Then he sat down again with a gesture of despair. "After all, what does it matter? Perhaps it's as well I don't know who the man was, for if I did, I'd kill him!"

He set his teeth and glowered at nothing and smote his left palm with his right fist, and there was a long silence. Presently he repeated:

"I'd kill him!"

We fell to discussing the whole matter over again. Why, I asked, should we assume that the poor child was led astray by a villain? Might there not have been a romantic marriage which, for some reason we could not guess, she desired to keep secret for a tune? Had she not been bright and happy from January to June? And that night of tragedy... What more likely than that she had gone forth to keep tryst with her husband and accidentally met her death? "He arrives," said I, "waits for her. She never comes. He goes away. The next day he learns from local gossip or from newspapers what has happened. He thinks it best to keep silent and let her fair name be untouched...What have you to say against that theory?"

"Possible," he replied. "Anything conceivable within the limits of physical possibility is possible. But it isn't probable. I have an intuitive feeling that there was villainy about--and if ever I get hold of that man--God help him!"

So there was nothing more to be said.

CHAPTER X

I haven't that universal sympathy which is the most irritating attribute of saints and other pacifists. When, for instance, anyone of the fraternity arguing from the Sermon on the Mount tells me that I ought to love Germans, either I admit the obligation and declare that, as I am a miserable sinner, I have no compunction in breaking it, or, if he is a very sanctimonious saint, I remind him that, such creatures as modern Germans not having been invented on or about the year A.D. 30, the rule about loving your enemies could not possibly apply. At least I imagine I do one of these two things (sometimes, indeed, I dream gloatfully over acts of physical violence) when I read the pronouncements of such a person; for I have to my great good fortune never met him in the flesh. If there are any saintly pacifists in Wellingsford, they keep sedulously out of my way, and they certainly do not haunt my Service Club. And these are the only two places in which I have my being. Even Gedge doesn't talk of loving Germans. He just lumps all the belligerents together in one conglomerate hatred, for upsetting his comfortable social scheme.

As I say, I lack the universal sympathy of the saint. I can't like people I don't like. Some people I love very deeply; others, being of a kindly disposition, I tolerate; others again I simply detest. Now Wellingsford, like every little country town in England, is drab with elderly gentlewomen. As I am a funny old tabby myself, I have to mix with them. If I refuse invitations to take tea with them, they invite themselves to tea with me. "The poor Major," they say, "is so lonely." And they bait their little hooks and angle for gossip of which I am supposed--Heaven knows why--to be a sort of stocked pond. They don't carry home much of a catch, I assure you.... Well, of some of them I am quite fond. Mrs. Boyce, for all her shortcomings, is an old crony for whom I entertain a sincere affection. Towards Betty's aunt, Miss Fairfax, a harmless lady with a passion for ecclesiastical embroidery, I maintain an attitude of benevolent neutrality. But Mrs. Holmes, Randall's mother, and her sisters, the daughters of an eminent publicist who seems to have reared his eminence on bones of talk flung at him by Carlisle, George Eliot, Lewes, Monckton Milnes, and is now, doubtless, recording their toe-prints on the banks of Acheron, I never could and never can abide. My angel of a wife saw good in them, and she loved the tiny Randall, of whom I too was fond; so, for her sake, I always treated them with courtesy and kindness. Also for Randall's father's sake. He was a bluff, honest, stock-broking Briton who fancied pigeons and bred greyhounds for coursing, and cared less for literature and art than does the equally honest Mrs. Marigold in my kitchen. But his wife and her sisters led what they called the intellectual life. They regarded it as a heritage from their pompous ass of a father. Of course they were not eighteen-sixty, or even eighteen-eighty. They prided themselves on developing the hereditary tradition of culture to its extreme modern expression. They were of the semi-intellectual type of idiot--and, if it destroys it, the great war will have some justification--which professes to find in the dull analysis of the drab adultery and suicide of a German or Scandinavian rabbit-picker a supreme expression of human existence. All their talk was of Hauptmann and Sudermann (they dropped them patriotically, I must say, as outrageous fellows, on the outbreak of war), Strindberg, Dostoievsky--though I found they had never read either "Crime and Punishment" or "The Brothers Karamazoff"--Tolstoi, whom they didn't understand; and in art-- God save the mark!--the Cubist school. That is how my poor young friend, Randall, was trained to get the worst of the frothy scum of intelligent Oxford. But even he sometimes winced at the pretentiousness of his mother and his aunts. He was a clever fellow and his knowledge was based on sound foundations. I need not say that the ladies were rather feared than loved in Wellingsford.

All this to explain why it was that when Marigold woke me from an afternoon nap with the information that Mrs. Holmes desired to see me, I scowled on him.

"Why didn't you say I was dead?"

"I told Mrs. Holmes you were asleep, sir, and she said: 'Will you be so kind as to wake him?' So what could I do, sir?"

I have never met with an idiot so helpless in the presence of a woman. He would have defended my slumbers before a charge of cavalry; but one elderly lady shoo'd him aside like a chicken.

Mrs. Holmes was shewn in, a tall, dark, thin, nervous woman wearing pince-nez and an austere sad-coloured garment.

She apologised for disturbing me.

"But," she said, sitting down on the couch, "I am in such great trouble and I could think of no one but you to advise me."

"What's the matter?" I asked.

"It's Randall. He left the house the day before yesterday, without telling any of us good-bye, and he hasn't written, and I don't know what on earth has become of him."

"Did he take any luggage?"

"Just a small suit-case. He even packed it himself, a thing he has never done at home in his life before."

This was news. The proceedings were unlike Randall, who in his goings and comings loved the domestic brass-band. To leave his home without valedictory music and vanish into the unknown, betokened some unusual perturbation of mind.

I asked whether she knew of any reason for such perturbation.

"He was greatly upset," she replied, "by the stoppage of The Albemarle Review for which he did such fine work."

I strove politely to hide my inability to condole and wagged my head sadly:

"I'm afraid there was no room for it in a be-bombed and be-shrapnelled world."

"I suppose the still small voice of reason would not be heard amid the din," she sighed. "And no other papers--except the impossible ones--would print Randall's poems and articles."

More news. This time excellent news. A publicist denied publicity is as useful as a German Field Marshal on a desert island. I asked what The Albemarle died of.

"Practically all the staff deserted what Randall called the Cause and dribbled away into the army," she replied mournfully.

As to what this precious Cause meant I did not enquire, having no wish to enter into an argument with the good lady which might have become exacerbated. Besides, she would only have parroted Randall. I had never yet detected her in the expression of an original idea.

"Perhaps he has dribbled away too?" I suggested grimly. She was silent. I bent forward. "Wouldn't you like him to dribble into the great flood?"

She lifted her lean shoulders despairingly.

"He's the only son of a widow. Even in France and Germany they're not expected to fight. But if he were different I would let him go gladly--I'm not selfish and unpatriotic, Major," she said with an unaccustomed little catch in her throat--and for the very first time I found in her something sympathetic--"but," she continued, "it seems so foolish to sacrifice all his intellectual brilliance to such crudities as fighting, when it might be employed so much more advantageously elsewhere."

"But, good God, my dear lady!" I cried. "Where are your wits? Where's your education? Where's your intelligent understanding of the daily papers? Where's your commonsense?"--I'm afraid I was brutally rude. "Can't you give a minute's thought to the situation? If there's one institution on earth that's shrieking aloud for intellectual brilliance, it's the British Army! Do you think it's a refuge for fools? Do you think any born imbecile is good enough to outwit the German Headquarters Staff? Do you think the lives of hundreds of his men--and perhaps the fate of thousands--can be entrusted to any brainless ass? An officer can't have too much brains. We're clamouring for brains. It's the healthy, brilliant-brained men like Randall that the Army's yelling for--simply yelling for," I repeated, bringing my hand down on the arm of my chair.

Two little red spots showed on each side of her thin face.

"I've never looked at it in that light before," she admitted.

"Of course I agree with you," I said diplomatically, "that Randall would be more or less wasted as a private soldier. The heroic stuff of which Thomas Atkins is made is, thank God, illimitable. But intellect is rare--especially in the ranks of God's own chosen, the British officer. And Randall is of the kind we want as officers. As for a commission, he could get one any day. I could get one for him myself. I still have a few friends. He's a good-looking chap and would carry off a uniform. Wouldn't you be proud to see him?"

A tear rolled down her cheek. I patted myself on the back for an artful fellow. But I had underrated her wit. To my chagrin she did not fall into my trap.

"It's the uncertainty that's killing me," she said. And then she burst out disconcertingly: "Do you think he has gone off with that dreadful little Gedge girl?"

Phyllis! I was a myriad miles from Phyllis. I was talking about real things. The mother, however, from her point of view, was talking of real things also. But how did she come to know about her son's amours? I thought it useless to enquire. Randall must have advertised his passion pretty widely. I replied:

"It's extremely improbable. In the first place Phyllis Gedge isn't dreadful, but a remarkably sweet and modest young woman, and in the second place she won't have anything to do with him."

"That's nonsense," she said, bridling.

"Why?"

"Because--"

A gesture and a smile completed the sentence. That a common young person should decline to have dealings with her paragon was incredible.

"I can find out in a minute," I smiled, "whether she is still in Wellingsford."

I wheeled myself to the telephone on my writing-table and rang up Betty at the hospital.

"Do you know where Phyllis Gedge is?"

Betty's voice came. "Yes. She's here. I've just left her to come to speak to you. Why do you want to know?"

"Never mind so long as she is safe and sound. There's no likelihood of her running away or eloping?"

Betty's laughter rang over the wires. "What lunacy are you talking? You might as well ask me whether I'm going to elope with you."

"I don't think you're respectful, Betty," I replied. "Good-bye."

I rang off and reported Betty's side of the conversation to my visitor.

"On that score," said I, "you can make your mind quite easy."

"But where can the boy have gone?" she cried.

"Into the world somewhere to learn wisdom," I said, and in order to show that I did not speak ironically, I wheeled myself to her side and touched her hand. "I think his swift brain has realised at last that all his smart knowledge hasn't brought him a little bit of wisdom worth a cent. I shouldn't worry. He's working out his salvation somehow, although he may not know it."

"Do you really think so?"

"I do," said I. "And if he finds that the path of wisdom leads to the German trenches--will you be glad or sorry?"

She grappled with the question in silence for a moment or two. Then she broke down and, to my dismay, began to cry.

"Do you suppose there's a woman in England that, in her heart of hearts, doesn't want her men folk to fight?"

I only allow the earlier part of this chapter to stand in order to show how a man quite well-meaning, although a trifle irascible, may be wanting in Christian charity and ordinary understanding; and of how many tangled knots of human motive, impulse, and emotion this war is a solvent. You see, she defended her son to the last, adopting his own specious line of argument; but at the last came the breaking-point....

The rest of our interview was of no great matter. I did my best to reassure and comfort her; and when I next saw Marigold, I said affably:

"You did quite well to wake me."

"I thought I was acting rightly, sir. Mr. Randall having bolted, so to speak, it seemed only natural that Mrs. Holmes should come to see you."

"You knew that Mr. Randall had bolted and you never told me?"

I glared indignantly. Marigold stiffened himself--the degree of stiffness beyond his ordinary inflexibility of attitude could only have been ascertained by a vernier, but that degree imparted an appreciable dignity to his demeanour.

"I beg pardon, sir, but lately I've noticed that my little bits of local news haven't seemed to be welcome."

"Marigold," said I, "don't be an ass."

"Very good, sir."

"My mind," said I, "is in an awful muddle about all sorts of things that are going on in this town. So I should esteem it a favour if you would tell me at once any odds and ends of gossip you may pick up. They may possibly be important."

"And if I have any inferences to draw from what I hear," said he gravely, fixing me with his clear eye, "may I take the liberty of acquainting you with them?"

"Certainly."

"Very good, sir," said Marigold.

Now what was Marigold going to draw inferences about? That was another puzzle. I felt myself being drawn into a fog-filled labyrinth of intrigue in which already groping were most of the people I knew. What with the mysterious relations between Betty and Boyce and Gedge, what with young Dacre's full exoneration of Boyce, what with young Randall's split with Gedge and his impeccable attitude towards Phyllis, things were complicated enough; Sir Anthony's revelations regarding poor Althea and his dark surmises concerning Randall complicated them still more; and now comes Mrs. Holmes to tell me of Randall's mysterious disappearance.

"A plague on the whole lot!" I exclaimed wrathfully.

I dined that evening with the Fenimores. My dear Betty was there too, the only other guest, looking very proud and radiant. A letter that morning from Willie Connor informed her that the regiment, by holding a trench against an overwhelming German attack, had achieved glorious renown. The Brigadier-General had specially congratulated the Colonel, and the Colonel had specially complimented Willie on the magnificent work of his company. Of course there was a heavy price in casualties--poor young Etherington, whom we all knew, for instance, blown to atoms--but Willie, thank God! was safe.

"I wonder what would happen to me, if Willie were to get the V.C. I think I should go mad with pride!" she exclaimed with flushed cheeks, forgetful of poor young Etherington, a laughter-loving boy of twenty, who had been blown to atoms. It is strange how apparently callous this universal carnage has made the noblest and the tenderest of men and women. We cling passionately to the lives of those near and dear to us. But as to those near and dear to others, who are killed--well--we pay them the passing tribute not even of a tear, but only of a sign. They died gloriously for their country. What can we say more? If we--we survivors, not only invalids and women and other stay-at-homes, but also comrades on the field--were riven to our souls by the piteous tragedy of splendid youth destroyed in its flower, we could not stand the strain, we should weep hysterically, we should be broken folk. But a merciful Providence steps in and steels our hearts. The loyal hearts are there beating truly; and in order that they should beat truly and stoutly, they are given this God-sent armour.

So, when we raised our glasses and drank gladly to the success of Willie Connor the living, and put from our thoughts Frank Etherington the dead, you must not account it to us as lack of human pity. You must be lenient in your judgment of those who are thrown into the furnace of a great war.

Lady Fenimore smiled on Betty. "We should all be proud, my dear, if Captain Connor won the Victoria Cross. But you mustn't set your heart on it. That would be foolish. Hundreds of thousands of men deserve the V.C. ten times a day, and they can't all be rewarded."

Betty laughed gaily at good Lady Fenimore's somewhat didactic reproof. "You know I'm not an absolute idiot. Fancy the poor dear coming home all over bandages and sticking-plaster. 'Where's your V. C?' 'I haven't got it.' 'Then go back at once and get it or I shan't love you.' Poor darling!" Suddenly the laughter in her eyes quickened into something very bright and beautiful. "There's not a woman in England prouder of her husband than I am. No V.C. could possibly reward him for what he has done. But I want it for myself. I'd like my babies to cut their teeth on it."

When I went out to the Boer War, the most wonderful woman on earth said to me on parting:

"Wherever you are, dear, remember that I am always with you in spirit and soul and heart and almost in body."

And God knows she was. And when I returned a helpless cripple she gathered me in her brave arms on the open quay at Southampton, and after a moment or two of foolishness, she said:

"Do you know, when I die, what you'll find engraven on my heart?"

"No," said I.

"Your D.S.O. ribbon."

So when Betty talked about her babies and the little bronze cross, my eyes grew moist and I felt ridiculously sentimental.

Not a word, of course, was spoken before Betty of the new light, or the new darkness, whichsoever you will, that had been cast on the tragedy of Althea. I could not do otherwise than agree with the direct-spoken old lady who had at once correlated the adventure in Carlisle with the plunge into the Wellingsford Canal. And so did Sir Anthony. They were very brave, however, the little man and Edith, in their dinner-talk with Betty. But I saw that the past fortnight had aged them both by a year or more. They had been stabbed in their honour, their trust, and their faith. It was a secret terror that stalked at their side by day and lay stark at their side by night. It was only when the ladies had left us that Sir Anthony referred to the subject.

"I suppose you know that young Randall Holmes has bolted."

"So his mother informed me to-day."

He pricked his ears. "Does she know where he has gone to?"

"No," said I.

"What did I tell you?" said Sir Anthony.

I held up my glass of port to the light and looked through it.

"A lot of damfoolishness, my dear old friend," said I.

He grew angry. A man doesn't like to be coldly called a damfool at his own table. He rose on his spurs, in his little red bantam way. Was I too much of an idiot to see the connection? As soon as the Carlisle business became known, this young scoundrel flies the country. Couldn't I see an inch before my blind nose? Forbearing to question this remarkable figure of speech, I asked him how so confidential a matter could have become known.

"Everything gets known in this infernal little town," he retorted.

"That's where you're mistaken," said I. "Half everything gets known--the unimportant half. The rest is supplied by malicious or prejudiced invention."

We discussed the question after the futile way of men until we went into the drawing-room, where Betty played and sang to us until it was time to go home.

Marigold was about to lift me into the two-seater when Betty, who had been lurking in her car a little way off, ran forward.

"Would it bore you if I came in for a quarter of an hour?"

"Bore me, my dear?" said I. "Of course not."

So a short while afterwards we were comfortably established in my library.

"You rang me up to-day about Phyllis Gedge."

"I did," said I.

She lit a cigarette and seated herself on the fender-stool. She has an unconscious knack of getting into easy, loose-limbed attitudes. I said admiringly:

"Do you know you're a remarkably well-favoured young person?"

And as soon as I said it, I realised what a tremendous factor Betty was in my circumscribed life. What could I do without her sweet intimacy? If Willie Connor's Territorial regiment, like so many others, had been ordered out to India, and she had gone with him, how blank would be the days and weeks and months! I thanked God for granting me her graciousness.

She smiled and blew me a kiss. "That's very gratifying to know," she said. "But it has nothing to do with Phyllis."

"Well, what about Phyllis?"

"I'll tell you," she replied.

And she told me. Her story was not of world-shaking moment, but it interested me. I have since learned its substantial correctness and am able to add some supplementary details.

You see, things were like this.... In order to start I must go back some years.... I have always had a warm corner in my heart for little Phyllis Gedge, ever since she was a blue-eyed child. My wife had a great deal to do with it. She was a woman of dauntless courage and clear vision into the heart of things. I find many a reflection of her in Betty. Perhaps that is why I love Betty so dearly.

Some strange, sweet fool feminine of gentle birth and deplorable upbringing fell in love with a vehemently socialistic young artisan by the name of Gedge and married him. Her casual but proud-minded family wiped her off the proud family slate. She brought Phyllis into the world and five years afterwards found herself be-Gedged out of existence. They were struggling people in those days, and before her death my wife used to employ her, when she could, for household sewing and whatnot. And tiny Phyllis, in a childless home, became a petted darling. When my great loneliness came upon me, it was a solace to have the little dainty prattling thing to spend an occasional hour in my company. Gedge, an excellent workman, set up as a contractor. He took my modest home under his charge. A leaky tap, a broken pane, a new set of bookshelves, a faulty drainpipe--all were matters for Gedge. I abhorred his politics but I admired his work, and I continued, with Mrs. Marigold's motherly aid, to make much of Phyllis.

Gedge, for queer motives of his own, sent her to as good a school as he could afford, as a matter of fact an excellent school, one where she met girls of a superior social class and learned educated speech and graceful manners. Her holidays, poor child, were somewhat dreary, for her father, an anti-social creature, had scarce a friend in the town. Save for here and there an invitation to tea from Betty or myself, she did not cross the threshold of a house in Wellingsford. But to my house, all through her schooldays and afterwards, Phyllis came, and on such occasions Mrs. Marigold prepared teas of the organic lusciousness dear to the heart of a healthy girl.

Now, here comes the point of all this palaver. Young Master Randall used also to come to my house. Now and then by chance they met there. They were good boy and girl friends.

I want to make it absolutely clear that her acquaintance with Randall was not any vulgar picking-up-in-the-street affair.

When she left school, her father made her his book-keeper, secretary, confidential clerk. Anybody turning into the office to summon Gedge to repair a roof or a burst boiler had a preliminary interview with Phyllis. Young Randall, taking over the business of the upkeep of his mother's house, gradually acquired the habit of such preliminary interviews. The whole imbroglio was very simple, very natural. They had first met at my own rich cake and jam-puff bespread tea-table. When Randall went into the office to speak, presumably, about a defective draught in the kitchen range, and really about things quite different, the ethics of the matter depended entirely on Randall's point of view. Their meetings had been contrived by no unmaidenly subterfuge on the part of Phyllis. She knew him to be above her in social station. She kept him off as long as she could. But que voulez-vous? Randall was a very good-looking, brilliant, and fascinating fellow; Phyllis was a dear little human girl. And it is the human way of such girls to fall in love with such fascinating, brilliant fellows. I not only hold a brief for Phyllis, but I am the judge, too, and having heard all the evidence, I deliver a verdict overwhelmingly in her favour. Given the circumstances as I have stated them, she was bound to fall in love with Randall, and in doing so committed not the little tiniest speck of a peccadillo.

My first intimation of tender relations between them came from my sight of them in February in Wellings Park. Since then, of course, I have much which I will tell you as best I may.

So now for Betty's story, confirmed and supplemented by what I have learned later. But before plunging into the matter, I must say that when Betty had ended I took up my little parable and told her of all that Randall had told me concerning his repudiation of Gedge. And Betty listened with a curiously stony face and said nothing.

When Betty puts on that face of granite I am quite unhappy. That is why I have always hated the statues of Egypt. There is something beneath their cold faces that you can't get at.

CHAPTER XI

Gedge bitterly upbraided his daughter, both for her desertion of his business and her criminal folly in abandoning it so as to help mend the shattered bodies of fools and knaves who, by joining the forces of militarism, had betrayed the Sacred Cause of the International Solidarity of Labour. His first ground for complaint was scarcely tenable; with his dwindling business the post of clerk had dwindled into a sinecure. To sit all day at the receipt of imaginary custom is not a part fitted for a sane and healthy young human being. Still, from Gedge's point of view her defection was a grievance; but that she could throw in her lot openly with the powers of darkness was nothing less than an outrage.

I suppose, in a kind of crabbed way, the crabbed fellow was fond of Phyllis. She was pretty. She had dainty tricks of dress. She flitted, an agreeable vision, about his house. He liked to hear her play the piano, not because he had any ear for music, but because it tickled his vanity to reflect that he, the agricultural labourer's son and apprentice to a village carpenter, was the possessor both of a Broadway Grand and of a daughter who, entirely through his efforts, had learned to play on it. Like most of his political type, he wallowed in his own peculiar snobbery. But of anything like companionship between father and daughter there had existed very little. While railing, wherever he found ears into which to rail, against the vicious luxury and sordid shallowness of the upper middle classes, his instinctive desire to shine above his poorer associates had sent Phyllis to an upper middle class school. Now Gedge had a certain amount of bookish and political intelligence. Phyllis inheriting the intellectual equipment of her sentimental fool of a mother, had none, Oh! she had a vast fund of ordinary commonsense. Of that I can assure you. A bit of hard brain fibre from her father had counteracted any over-sentimental folly in the maternal heritage. And she came back from school a very ladylike little person. If pressed, she could reel off all kinds of artificial scraps of knowledge, like a dear little parrot. But she had never heard of Karl Marx and didn't want to hear. She had a vague notion that International Socialism was a movement in favour of throwing bombs at monarchs and of seizing the wealth of the rich in order to divide it among the poor--and she regarded it as abominable. When her father gave her Fabian Society tracts to read, he might just as well, for all her understanding of the argument, set her down to a Treatise on the Infinitesimal Calculus. Her brain stood blank before such abstract disquisitions. She loved easily comprehended poetry and novels that made her laugh or cry and set her mind dancing round the glowing possibilities of life; all disastrous stuff abhorred by the International Socialist, to whom the essential problems of existence are of no interest whatever. So, after a few futile attempts to darken her mind, Gedge put her down as a mere fool woman, and ceased to bother his head about her intellectual development. That came to him quite naturally. There is no Turk more contemptuous of his womankind's political ideas than the Gedges of our enlightened England. But on other counts she was a distinct asset. He regarded her with immense pride, as a more ornamental adjunct to his house than any other county builder and contractor could display, and, recognising that she was possessed of some low feminine cunning in the way of adding up figures and writing letters, made use of her in his office as general clerical factotum.

When the war broke out, he discovered, to his horror, that Phyllis actually had political ideas--unshakable, obstinate ideas opposed to his own--and that he had been nourishing in his bosom a viperous patriot. Phyllis, for her part, realised with equal horror the practical significance of her father's windy theories. When Randall, who had stolen her heart, took to visiting the house, in order, as far as she could make out, to talk treason with her father, the strain of the situation grew more than she could bear. She fled to Betty for advice. Betty promptly stepped in and whisked her off to the hospital.

It was on the morning on which Randall interviewed me in the garden, the morning after he had broken with Gedge that Phyllis, having a little off-time, went home. She found her father in the office making out a few bills. He thrust forward his long chin and aggressive beard and scowled at her.

"Oh, it's you, is it? Come at last where your duty calls you, eh?"

"I always come when I can, father," she replied.

She bent down and kissed his cheek. He caught her roughly round the waist and, leaning back in his chair, looked up at her sourly.

"How long are you going on defying me like this?"

She tried to disengage herself, but his arm was too strong. "Oh, father," she said, rather wearily, "don't let us go over this old argument again."

"But suppose I find some new argument? Suppose I send you packing altogether, refuse to contribute further to your support. What then?"

She started at the threat but replied valiantly: "I should have to earn my own living."

"How are you going to do it?"

"There are heaps of ways."

He laughed. "There ain't; as you'd soon find out. They don't even pay you for being scullery-maid to a lot of common soldiers."

She protested against that view of her avocation. In the perfectly appointed Wellingsford Hospital she had no scullery work. She was a probationer, in training as a nurse. He still gripped her.

"The particular kind of tomfoolery you are up to doesn't matter. We needn't quarrel. I've another proposition to put before you--much more to your fancy, I think. You like this Mr. Randall Holmes, don't you?"

She shivered a little and flushed deep red. Her father had never touched on the matter before. She said, straining away:

"I don't want to talk about Mr. Holmes."

"But I do. Come, my dear. In this life there must be always a certain amount of give and take. I'm not the man to drive a one-sided bargain. I'll make you a fair offer--as between father and daughter. I'll wipe out all that's past. In leaving me like this, when misfortune has come upon me, you've been guilty of unfilial conduct-- no one can deny it But I'll overlook everything, forgive you fully and take you to my heart again and leave you free to do whatever you like without interfering with your opinions, if you'll promise me one thing--"

"I know what you're going to say." She twisted round on him swiftly. "I 'll promise at once. I'll never marry Mr. Holmes. I've already told him I won't marry him."

Surprise relaxed his grip. She took swift advantage and sheered away to the other side of the table. He rose and brought down his hand with a thump.

"You refused him? Why, you silly little baggage, my condition is that you should marry him. You're sweet on him aren't you?"

"I detest him," cried Phyllis. "Why should I marry him?"

Her eyes, young and pure, divined some sordid horror behind eyes crafty and ignoble. Once before she had had such a fleeting, uncomprehended vision into the murky depths of the man's soul. This was some time ago. In the routine of her secretarial duties she had, one morning, opened and read a letter, not marked "Private" or "Personal," whose tenor she could scarcely understand. When she handed it to her father, he smiled, vouchsafed a specious explanation, and looked at her in just the same crafty and ignoble fashion, and she shrank away frightened. The matter kept her awake for a couple of nights. Then, for sheer easing of her heart, she went to her adored Betty Fairfax, her Lady Patroness and Mother Confessor, who, being wise and strong, and possessing the power of making her kind eyes unfathomable, laughed, bade her believe her father's explanation, and sent her away comforted. The incident passed out of her mind. But now memory smote her, as she shrank from her father's gaze and the insincere smile on his thin lips.

"For one thing," he replied after a pause, pulling his straggly beard, "your poor dear mother was a lady, and if she had lived she would have wanted you to marry a gentleman. It's for her sake I've given you an education that fits you to consort with gentlefolk--just for her sake--don't make any mistake about it, for I've always hated the breed. If I've violated my principles in order to meet her wishes, I think you ought to meet them too. You wouldn't like to marry a small tradesman or a working man, would you?"

"I'm not going to marry anybody," cried Phyllis. She was only a pink and white, very ordinary little girl. I have no idealisations or illusions concerning Phyllis. But she had a little fine steel of character running through her. It flashed on Gedge.

"I don't want to marry anybody," she declared. "But I'd sooner marry a bricklayer who was fighting for his country than a fine gentleman like Mr. Holmes who wasn't. I'd sooner die," she cried passionately.

"Then go and die and be damned to you!" snarled Gedge, planting himself noisily in his chair. "I've no use for khaki-struck drivelling idiots. I've no use for patriots. Bah! Damn patriots! The upper classes are out for all they can get, and they befool the poor imbecile working man with all their highfalutin phrases to get it for them at the cost of his blood. I've no use for them, I tell you. And I've no use either for undutiful daughters. I've no use for young women who blow hot and cold. Haven't I seen you with the fellow? Do you think I'm a blind dodderer? Do you think I haven't kept an eye on you? Haven't I seen you blowing as hot as you please? And now because he refuses to be a blinking idiot and have his guts blown out in this war of fools and knaves and capitalists, you blast him like a three-farthing iceberg."

Everything in her that was tender, maidenly, English, shrank lacerated. But the steel held her. She put both her hands on the table and bent over towards him.

"But, father, except that he's a gentleman, you haven't told me why you want me to marry Mr. Holmes."

He fidgeted with his fingers. "Haven't you a spark of affection for me left?"

She said dutifully, "Yes, father."

"I want you to marry him. I've set my heart on it. It has been the one bright hope in my life for months. Can't you marry him because you love me?"

"One generally marries because one loves the man one's going to marry," said Phyllis.

"But you do love him," cried Gedge. "Either you're just a wanton little hussy or you must care for the fellow."

"I don't. I hate him. And I don't want to have anything more to do with him." The tears came. "He's a pro-German and I won't have anything to do with pro-Germans."

She fled precipitately from the office into the street and made a blind course to the hospital; feeling, in dumb misery, that she had committed the unforgivable sin of casting off her father and, at the same time, that she had made stalwart proclamation of her faith. If ever a good, loyal little heart was torn into piteous shreds, that little heart was Phyllis's.

In the bare X-ray room of the hospital, which happened to be vacant, Betty sat on the one straight-backed wooden chair, while a weeping damsel on the uncarpeted floor sobbed in her lap and confessed her sins and sought absolution.

Of course Gedge was a fool. If I, or any wise, diplomatic, tactful person like myself, had found it necessary to tackle a young woman on the subject of a matrimonial alliance, we should have gone about the business in quite a different way. But what could you expect from an anarchical Turk like Gedge?

Phyllis, not knowing whether she were outcast and disinherited or not, found, of course, a champion in Betty, who, in her spacious manner, guaranteed her freedom from pecuniary worries for the rest of her life. But Phyllis was none the less profoundly unhappy, and it took a whole convoy of wounded to restore her to cheerfulness. You can't attend to a poor brave devil grinning with pain, while a surgeon pokes a six-inch probe down a sinus in search of bits of bone or shrapnel, and be acutely conscious of your own two-penny-half-penny little miseries. Many a heartache, in this wise, has been cured in the Houses of Pain.

Now, nothing much would have happened, I suppose, if Phyllis, driven from the hospital by superior decree that she should take fresh air and exercise, had not been walking some days afterwards across the common by the canal. Bordering the latter, Wellingsford has an avenue of secular chestnuts of which it is inordinately proud. Dispersed here and there are wooden benches sanctified by generations of lovers. Carven thereon are the presentments, often interlaced, of hearts that have long since ceased to beat; lonely hearts transfixed by arrows, which in all probability survived the wound and inspired the owner to the parentage of a dozen children; initials once, individually, the record of many a romance, but now, collectively, merely an alphabet run mad.

Phyllis entered the avenue, practically deserted at midday, and rested, a pathetically lonely little grey-uniformed figure on one of the benches. On the common, some distance behind her, stretched the lines of an Army Service train, with mules and waggons, and here and there a tent. In front of her, beyond the row of trees, was the towing-path; an old horse in charge of a boy jogged by, pulling something of which only a moving stove pipe like a periscope was visible above the bank. Overhead the chestnuts rioted in broad leaf and pink and white blossom, showing starry bits of blue sky and admitting arrow shafts of spring sunshine. A dirty white mongrel dog belonging to the barge came up to her, sniffed, and made friends; then, at last obeying a series of whistles from the boy, looked at her apologetically and trotted off. Her gaze followed him wistfully, for he was a very human dear dog, and with a sympathetic understanding of all her difficulties in his deep topaz eyes. After that she had as companions a couple of butterflies and a bumble-bee and a perky, portly robin who hopped within an inch of her feet and looked up at her sideways out of his hard little eye (so different from the dog's) with the expression of one who would say: "The most beauteous and delectable worm I have ever encountered. If I were a bit bigger, say the size of the roc of the Arabian Nights, what a dainty morsel you would make! In the meantime can't you shed something of yourself for my entertainment like others, though grosser, of your species?" She laughed at the cold impudence of the creature, just as she had smiled at the butterflies and the bumble-bee. She surrendered herself to the light happiness of the moment. It was good to escape for an hour from the rigid lines of beds and the pale suffering faces and the eternal faint odour of disinfectants, into all this greenery and the fellowship of birds and beasts unconscious of war. She remembered that once, in the pocket of her cloak, there had been a biscuit or two. Very slowly and carefully, her mind fixed on the robin, she fished for crumbs and very carefully and gently she fed the impudent, stomach-centred fellow. She had attracted him to the end of the seat, when, whizz and clatter, came a motor cycle down the avenue, and off in a terrible scare flew the robin; the idyll of tree and beast and birds suffered instant disruption and Randall Holmes, in his canvas suit, stood before her.

He said:

"Good morning, Phyllis."

She said, with cold politeness: "Good morning." But she asked the spring morning in dumb piteousness, "Oh, why has he come? Why has he come to spoil it all?"

He sat down by her side. "This is the luckiest chance I've ever had--finding you here," he said. "You've had all my letters, haven't you?"

"Yes," she answered, "and I've torn them all up."

"Why?"

"Because I didn't want them," she flashed on him: "I've destroyed them without reading them."

He flushed angrily. Apart from the personal affront, the fact that the literary products of a poet, precious and, in this case, sincere, should have been destroyed, unread, was an anti-social outrage.

"If it didn't please a woman to believe in God," he said, "and God came in Person and stood in front of her, she would run out of the room and call upon somebody to come and shoot Him for a burglar, just to prove she was right."

Phyllis was shocked. Her feminine mind pounced on the gross literalness of his rhetorical figure.

"I've never heard anything more blasphemous and horrible," she exclaimed, moving to her end of the bench. "Putting yourself in the position of the Almighty! Oh!" she flung out her hand. "Don't speak to me."

In spite of the atheistical Gedge, Phyllis believed in God and Jesus Christ and the Ten Commandments. She also believed in a host of other simple things, such as Goodness and Truth, Virtue and Patriotism. The arguments and theories and glosses that her father and Randall wove about them appeared to her candid mind as meaningless arabesques. She could not see how all the complications concerning the elementary canons of faith and conduct could arise. She appreciated Randall's intellectual gifts; his power of weaving magical words into rhyme fascinated her; she was childlike in her wonder at his command of the printed page; when he revealed to her the beauty of things, as the rogue had a pretty knack of doing, her nature thrilled responsive. He gave her a thousand glimpses into a new world, and she loved him for it. But when he talked lightly of sacred matters, such as God and Duty, he ran daggers into her heart. She almost hated him.

He had to expend much eloquence and persuasion to induce her to listen to him. He had no wish to break any of the Commandments, especially the Third. He professed penitence. But didn't she see that her treatment of him was driving him into a desperate unbelief in God and man? When a woman accepted a man's love she accepted many responsibilities.

Phyllis stonily denied acceptance.

"I've refused it. You've asked me to marry you and I told you I wouldn't. And I won't."

"You're mixing up two things," he said, with a smile. "Love and marriage. Many people love and don't marry, just as many marry and don't love. Now once you did tell me that you loved me, and so you accepted my love. There's no getting out of it. I've given you everything I've got, and you can't throw it away. The question is-

-what are you going to do with it? What are you going to do with me?"

His sophistries frightened her; but she cut through them.

"Isn't it rather a question of what you're going to do with yourself?"

"If you give me up I don't care a hang what becomes of me." He came very near and his voice was dangerously soft. "Phyllis dear, I do love you with all my heart. Why won't you marry me?"

But a hateful scene rushed to her memory. She drew herself up.

"Why are my father and you persecuting me to marry you?"

"Your father?" he interrupted, in astonishment. "When?"

She named the day, Wednesday of last week. In desperation she told him what had happened. The poor child was fighting for her soul against great odds.

"It's a conspiracy to get me round to your way of thinking. You want me to be a pro-German like yourselves, and I won't be a pro-German, and I think it wicked even to talk to pro-Germans!"

She rose, all sobs, fluster, and heroism, and walked away. He strode a step or two and stood in front of her with his hands on her shoulders.

"I've never spoken to your father in that way about you. Never. Not a word has passed my lips about my caring for you. On my word of honour. On Tuesday night I left your father's house never to go there again. I told him so."

She writhed out of his grasp and spread the palms of her hands against him. "Please don't," she said, and seeing that she stood her ground, he made no further attempt to touch her. The austerity of her grey nurse's uniform gave a touch of pathos to her childish, blue-eyed comeliness and her pretty attitude of defiance.

"I suppose," she said, "he was too pro-German even for you."

He looked at her for a long time disconcertingly: so disconcertingly and with so much pain and mysterious hesitation in his eyes as to set even Phyllis's simple mind a-wondering and to make her emphasize it, in her report of the matter to Betty, as extraordinary and frightening. It seemed, so she explained, in her innocent way, that he had discovered something horrible about her father which he shrank from telling her. But if they had quarrelled so bitterly, why had her father the very next day urged her to marry him? The answer came in a ghastly flash. She recoiled as though in the presence of defilement. If she married Randall, his lips would be closed against her father. That is what her father had meant. The vague, disquieting suspicions of years that he might not have the same standards of uprightness as other men, attained an awful certainty. She remembered the incident of the private letter and the look in her father's eyes.... Finally she revolted. Her soul grew sick. She took no heed of Randall's protest. She only saw that she was to be the cloak to cover up something unclean between them. At a moment like this no woman pretends to have a sense of justice. Randall had equal share with her father in an unknown baseness. She hated him as he stood there so strong and handsome. And she hated herself for having loved him.

At last he said with a smile:

"Yes, That's just it."

"What?"

She had forgotten the purport of her last remark.

"He was a bit too--well, not too pro-German--but too anti-English for me. You have got hold of the wrong end of the stick all the time, Phyllis dear. I'm no more pro-German than you are. Perhaps I see things more clearly than you do. I've been trained to an intellectual view of human phenomena."

Her little pink and white face hardened until it looked almost ugly. The unpercipient young man continued:

"And so I take my stand on a position that you must accept on trust. I am English to the backbone. You can't possibly dream that I'm not. Come, dear, let me try to explain."

His arm curved as if to encircle her waist. She sprang away.

"Don't touch me. I couldn't bear it. There's something about you I can't understand."

In her attitude, too, he found a touch of the incomprehensible. He said, however, with a sneer:

"If I were swaggering about in a cheap uniform, you'd find me simplicity itself."

She caught at his opening, desperately.

"Yes. At any rate I'd find a man. A man who wasn't afraid to fight for his country."

"Afraid!"

"Yes," she cried, and her blue eyes blazed. "Afraid. That's why I can't marry you. I'd rather die than marry you. I've never told you. I thought you'd guess. I'm an English girl and I can't marry a coward--a coward--a coward--a coward."

Her voice ended on a foolish high note, for Randall, very white, had seized her by the wrist.

"You little fool," he cried. "You'll live to repent what you've said."

He released her, mounted his motor bicycle, and rode away. Phyllis watched him disappear up the avenue; then she walked rather blindly back to the bench and sat down among the ruins of a black and abominable world. After a while the friendly robin, seeing her so still, perched first on the back of the bench and then hopped on the seat by her side, and cocking his head, looked at her enquiringly out of his little hard eye, as though he would say:

"My dear child, what are you making all this fuss about? Isn't it early June? Isn't the sun shining? Aren't the chestnuts in flower? Don't you see that bank of dark blue cloud over there which means a nice softening rain in the night and a jolly good breakfast of worms in the morning? What's wrong with this exquisitely perfect universe?"

And Phyllis--on her own confession--with an angry gesture sent him scattering up among the cool broad leaves and cried:

"Get away, you hateful little beast!"

And having no use for robins and trees and spring and sunshine and such like intolerable ironies, a white little wisp of a nurse left them all to their complacent riot and went back to the hospital.

CHAPTER XII

A few days after this, Mrs. Holmes sent me under cover a telegram which she had received from her son. It was dispatched from Aberdeen and ran: "Perfectly well. Don't worry about me. Love. Randall." And that was all I heard of him for some considerable time. What he was doing in Aberdeen, a city remote from his sphere of intellectual, political, and social activities, Heaven and himself alone knew. I must confess that I cared very little. He was alive, he was well, and his mother had no cause for anxiety. Phyllis had definitely sent him packing. There was no reason for me to allow speculation concerning him to keep me awake of nights.

I had plenty to think about besides Randall. They made me Honorary Treasurer of the local Volunteer Training Corps which had just been formed. The members not in uniform wore a red brassard with "G.R." in black. The facetious all over the country called them "Gorgeous Wrecks." I must confess that on their first few parades they did not look very military. Their composite paunchiness, beardedness, scragginess, spectacledness, impressed me unfavourably when, from my Hosea-carriage, I first beheld them. Marigold, who was one of the first to join and to leap into the grey uniform, tried to swagger about as an instructor. But as the little infantry drill he had ever learned had all been changed since the Boer War, I gathered an unholy joy from seeing him hang like a little child on the lips of the official Sergeant Instructor of the corps. In the evenings he and I mugged up the text-books together; and with the aid of the books I put him through all the new physical exercises. I was a privileged person. I could take my own malicious pleasure out of Marigold's enforced humility, but I would be hanged if anybody else should. Sergeant Marigold should instruct those volunteers as he once instructed the recruits of his own battery. So I worked with him like a nigger until there was nothing in the various drills of a modern platoon that he didn't know, and nothing that he could not do with the mathematical precision of his splendid old training.

One night during the thick of it Betty came in. I waved her into a corner of the library out of the way, and she smoked cigarettes and looked on at the performance. Now I come to think of it, we must have afforded an interesting spectacle. There was the gaunt, one-eyed, preposterously wigged image clad in undervest and shrunken yellow flannel trousers which must have dated from his gym-instructor days in the nineties, violently darting down on his heels, springing up, kicking out his legs, shooting out his arms, like an inspired marionette, all at the words of command shouted in fervent earnest by a shrivelled up little cripple in a wheel-chair.

When it was over--the weather was warm--he passed a curved forefinger over his dripping forehead, cut himself short in an instinctive action and politely dried his hand on the seat of his trousers. Then his one eye gleamed homage at Betty and he drew himself up to attention.

"Do you mind, sir, if I send in Ellen with the drinks?"

I nodded. "You'll do very well with a drink yourself, Marigold."

"It's thirsty work and weather, sir."

He made a queer movement of his hand--it would have been idiotic of him to salute--but he had just been dismissed from military drill, so his hand went up to the level of his breast and--right about turn--he marched out of the room. Betty rose from her corner and threw herself in her usual impetuous way on the ground by my chair.

"Do you know," she cried, "you two dear old things were too funny for words."

But as I saw that her eyes were foolishly moist, I was not as offended as I might have been by her perception of the ludicrous.

When I said that I had plenty to think about besides Randall, I meant to string off a list. My prolixity over the Volunteer Training Corps came upon me unawares. I wanted to show you that my time was fairly well occupied. I was Chairman of our town Belgian Relief Committee. I was a member of our County Territorial Association and took over a good deal of special work connected with one of our battalions that was covering itself with glory and little mounds topped with white crosses at the front. If you think I lived a Tom-tabby, tea-party sort of life, you are quite mistaken, if the War Office could have its way, it would have lashed me in red tape, gagged me with Regulations, and sealing-waxed me up in my bed-room. And there are thousands of us who have shaken our fists under the nose of the War Office and shouted, "All your blighting, Man-with-the-Mudrake officialdom shan't prevent us from serving our country." And it hasn't! The very Government itself, in spite of its monumental efforts, has not been able to shackle us into inertia or drug us into apathy. Such non-combatant francs-tireurs in England have done a power of good work.

And then, of course, there was the hospital which, in one way or another, took up a good deal of my time.

I was reposing in the front garden one late afternoon in mid-June, after a well-filled day, when a car pulled up at the gate, in which were Betty (at the wheel) and a wounded soldier, in khaki, his cap perched on top of a bandaged head. I don't know whether it is usual for young women in nurse's uniform to career about the country driving wounded men in motor cars, but Betty did it. She cared very little for the usual. She came in, leaving the man in the car, and crossed the lawn, flushed and bright-eyed, a refreshing picture for a tired man.

"We're in a fix up at the hospital," she announced as soon as she was in reasonable speaking distance, "and I want you to get us out of it."

Sitting on the grass, she told me the difficulty. A wounded soldier, discharged from some distant hospital, and home now on sick furlough before rejoining his depot, had been brought into the hospital with a broken head. The modern improvements on vinegar and brown paper having been applied, the man was now ready to leave. I interrupted with the obvious question. Why couldn't he go to his own home? It appeared that the prospect terrified him. On his arrival, at midday, after eight months' absence in France, he found that his wife had sold or pawned practically everything in the place, and that the lady herself was in the violent phase of intoxication. His natural remonstrances not being received with due meekness, a quarrel arose from which the lady emerged victorious. She laid her poor husband out with a poker. They could not keep him in hospital. He shied at an immediate renewal of conjugal life. He had no relations or intimate friends in Wellingsford. Where was the poor devil to go?

"I thought I might bring him along here and let the Marigolds look after him for a week or two."

"Indeed," said I. "I admire your airy ways."

"I know you do," she replied, "and that's why I've brought him."

"Is that the fellow?"

She laughed. "You're right first time. How did you guess?" She scrambled to her feet. "I'll fetch him in."

She fetched him in, a haggard, broad-shouldered man with a back like a sloping plank of wood. He wore corporal's stripes. He saluted and stood at rigid attention.

"This is Tufton," said Betty.

I despatched her in search of Marigold. To Tufton I said, regarding him with what, without vanity, I may term an expert eye:

"You're an old soldier."

"Yes, sir."

"Guards?"

His eyes brightened. "Yes, sir. Seven years in the Grenadiers. Then two years out. Rejoined on outbreak of war, sir."

I rubbed my hands together in satisfaction. "I'm an old soldier too," said I.

"So Sister told me, sir."

A delicate shade in the man's tone and manner caught at my heart. Perhaps it was the remotest fraction of a glance at my rug-covered legs, the pleased recognition of my recognition, ... perhaps some queer freemasonry of the old Army.

"You seem to be in trouble, boy," said I. "Tell me all about it and I'll do what I can to help you."

So he told his story. After his discharge from the Army he had looked about for a job and found one at the mills in Wellingsford, where he had met the woman, a mill-hand, older than himself, whom he had married. She had been a bit extravagant and fond of her glass, but when he left her to rejoin the regiment, he had had no anxieties. She did not write often, not being very well educated and finding difficult the composition of letters. A machine gun bullet had gone through his chest, just missing his lung. He had been two months in hospital. He had written to her announcing his arrival. She had not met him at the station. He had tramped home with his kit-bag on his back--and the cracked head was his reception. He supposed she had had a lot of easy money and had given way to temptation--and

"And what's a man to do, sir?"

"I'm sure I don't know, Corporal," said I. "It's damned hard lines on you. But, at any rate, you can look upon this as your home for as long as you like to stay."

"Thank you kindly, sir," said he.

I turned and beckoned to Betty and Marigold, who had been hovering out of earshot by the house door. They approached.

"I want to have a word with Marigold," I said.

Tufton saluted and went off with Betty. Sergeant Marigold stood stiff as a ramrod on the spot which Tufton had occupied.

"I suppose Mrs. Connor," said I, "has told you all about this poor chap?"

"Yes, sir," said Marigold.

"We must put him up comfortably. That's quite simple. The only thing that worries me is this--supposing his wife comes around here raising Cain--?"

Marigold held me with his one glittering eye--an eye glittering with the pride of the gunner and the pride (more chastened) of the husband.

"You can leave all that, sir, to Mrs. Marigold. If she isn't more than a match for any Grenadier Guardsman's wife, then I haven't been married to her for the last twenty years."

Nothing more was to be said. Marigold marched the man off, leaving me alone with Betty.

"I'm going to get in before Mrs. Marigold," she remarked, with a smile. "I'm off now to interview Madam Tufton and bring back her husband's kit."

In some ways it is a pity Betty isn't a man. She would make a splendid soldier. I don't think such a thing as fear, physical, moral, or spiritual, lurks in any recess of Betty's nature. Not every young woman would brave, without trepidation, a virago who had cracked a hard-bitten warrior's head with a poker.

"Marigold and I will come with you," I said.

She protested. It was nonsense. Suppose Mrs. Tufton went for Marigold and spoiled his beauty? No. It was too dangerous. No place for men. We argued. At last I blew the police-whistle which I wear on the end of my watch-chain. Marigold came hurrying out of the house.

"Mrs. Connor is going to take us for a run," said I.

"Very good, sir."

"Your blood be on your own heads," said Betty.

We talked a while of what had happened. Vague stories of the demoralization of wives left alone with a far greater weekly income than they had ever handled before had reached our ears. We had read them in the newspapers. But till now we had never come across an example. The woman in question belonged to a bad type. Various dregs from large cities drift into the mills around little country towns and are the despair of Mayors, curates, and other local authorities. We genteel folk regarded them as a plague-spot in the midst of us.

I remember the scandal when the troops first came in August, 1914, to Wellingsford--a scandal put a summary end to, after a fortnight's grinning amazement at our country morals, by the troops themselves. Tufton had married into an undesirable community.

"We're wasting time," said Betty.

So Marigold put me into the back of the car and mounted into the front seat by Betty, and we started.

Flowery End was the poetic name of the mean little row of red-brick houses inhabited exclusively by Mrs. Tufton and her colleagues at the mills. To get to it you turn off the High Street by the Post Office, turn to the right down Avonmore Avenue, and then to the left. There you find Flowery End, and, fifty yards further on, the main road to Godbury crosses it at right angles. Betty, who lived on the Godbury Road, was quite familiar with Flowery End. Mid-June did its best to justify the name. Here and there, in the tiny patches of front garden, a tenant tried to help mid-June by cultivating wall-flowers and geraniums and snapdragon and a rose or two; but the majority cared as much for the beauty of mid-June as for the cleanliness of their children,--an unsightly brood, with any slovenly rags about their bodies, and the circular crust of last week's treacle on their cheeks. In his abominable speeches before the war Gedge used to point out these children to unsympathetic Wellingsfordians as the Infant Martyrs of an Accursed Capitalism.

Betty pulled up the car at Number Seven. Marigold sprang out, helped her down, and would have walked up the narrow flagged path to knock at the door. But she declined his aid, and he stood sentry by the gap where the wicket gate of the garden should have been. I saw the door open on Betty's summons, and a brawny, tousled, red-faced woman appear--a most horrible and forbidding female, although bearing traces of a once blowsy beauty. As in most cottages hereabouts, you entered straight from garden-plot into the principal livingroom. On each side of the two figures I obtained a glimpse of stark emptiness.

Betty said: "Are you Mrs. Tufton? I've come to talk to you about your husband. Let me come in."

The attack was so debonair, so unquestioning, that the woman withdrew a pace or two and Betty, following up her advantage, entered and shut the door behind her. I could not have done what Betty did if I had had as many legs as a centipede. Marigold turned to me anxiously.

"You do think she's safe, sir?"

I nodded. "Anyway, stand by."

The neighbours came out of adjoining houses; slatternly women with babies, more unwashed children, an elderly, vacant male or two--the young men and maidens had not yet been released from the mills. As far as I could gather, there was amused discussion among the gossips concerning the salient features of Sergeant Marigold's physical appearance. I heard one lady bid another to look at his wicked old eye, and receive the humorous rejoinder: "Which one?" I should have liked to burn them as witches; but Marigold stood his ground, imperturbable.

Presently the door opened, and Betty came sailing down the path with a red spot on each cheek, followed by Mrs. Tufton, vociferous.

"Sergeant Marigold," cried Betty. "Will you kindly go into that house and fetch out Corporal Tufton's kit-bag?"

"Very good, madam," said Marigold.

"Sergeant or no sergeant," cried Mrs. Tufton, squaring her elbows and barring his way, "nobody's coming into my house to touch any of my husband's property...." Really what she said I cannot record. The British Tommy I know upside-down, inside-out. I could talk to you about him for the week together. The ordinary soldier's wife, good, straight, heroic soul, I know as well and and profoundly admire as I do the ordinary wife of a brother-officer, and I could tell you what she thinks and feels in her own language. But the class whence Mrs. Tufton proceeded is out of my social ken. She was stale-drunk; she had, doubtless, a vile headache; probably she felt twinges of remorse and apprehension of possible police interference. As a counter-irritant to this, she had worked herself into an astounding temper. She would give up none of her husband's belongings. She would have the law on them if they tried. Bad enough it was for her husband to come home after a year's desertion, leaving her penniless, and the moment he set eyes on her begin to knock her about; but for sergeants suffering under a blight and characterless females masquerading as hospital nurses to come and ride rough-shod over an honest working woman was past endurance. Thus I paraphrase my memory of the lady's torrential speech. "Lay your hand on me," she cried, "and I'll summons you for assault."

As Marigold could not pass her without laying hands on her, and as the laying of hands on her, no matter how lightly, would indubitably have constituted an assault in the eyes of the law, Marigold stiffly confronted her and tried to argue.

The neighbours listened in sardonic amusement. Betty stood by, with the spots burning on her cheek, clenching her slender capable fingers, furious at defeat. I was condemned to sit in the car a few yards off, an anxious spectator. In a moment's lull of the argument, Betty interposed:

"Every woman here knows what you have done. You ought to be ashamed of yourself."

"And you ought to be ashamed of yourself," Mrs. Tufton retorted--"taking an honest woman's husband away from her."

It was time to interfere. I called out:

"Betty, let us get back. I'll fix the man up with everything he wants."

At the moment of her turning to me a telegraph boy hopped from his bicycle on the off-side of the ear and touched his cap.

"I've a telegram for Mrs. Connor, sir. I recognised the car and I think that's the lady. So instead of going on to the house--"

I cut him short. Yes. That was Mrs. Connor of Telford Lodge. He dodged round the car and, entering the garden path, handed the orange-coloured envelope to Betty. She took it from him absent-mindedly, her heart and soul engaged in the battle with Mrs. Tufton. The boy stood patient for a second or two.

"Any answer, ma'am?"

She turned so that I could see her face in profile, and impatiently opened the envelope and glanced at the message. Then she stiffened, seeming in a curious way to become many inches taller, and grew deadly white. The paper dropped from her hand. Marigold picked it up.

The diversion of the telegraph boy had checked Mrs. Tufton's eloquence and compelled the idle interest of the neighbours. I cried out from the car:

"What's the matter?"

But I don't think Betty heard me. She recovered herself, took the telegram from Marigold, and showed it to the woman.

"Read it," said Betty, in a strange, hard voice. "This is to tell me that my husband was killed yesterday in France. Go on your knees and thank God that you have a brave husband still alive and pray that you may be worthy of him."

She went into the house and in a moment reappeared like a ghost of steel, carrying the disputed canvas kit-bag over her shoulder. The woman stared open-mouthed and said nothing. Marigold came forward to relieve Betty of her burden, but she waved him imperiously away, passed him and, opening the car-door, threw the bag at my feet. Not one of the rough crowd moved a foot or uttered a sound, save a baby in arms two doors off, who cut the silence with a sickly wail and was immediately hushed by its mother. Betty turned to the attendant Marigold.

"You can drive me home."

She sat by my side. Marigold took the wheel in front and drove on. She sought for my hand, held it in an iron grip, and said not a word. It was but a five minutes' run at the pace to which Marigold, time-worn master of crises of life and death, put the car. Betty held herself rigid, staring straight in front of her, and striving in vain to stifle horrible little sounds that would break through her tightly closed lips.

When we pulled up at her door she said queerly: "Forgive me. I'm a damned little coward."

And she bolted from the car into the house.

CHAPTER XIII

Thus over the sequestered vale of Wellingsford, far away from the sound of shells, even off the track of marauding Zeppelins, rode the fiery planet. Mars. There is not a homestead in Great Britain that in one form or another has not caught a reflection of its blood-red ray. No matter how we may seek distraction in work or amusement, the angry glow is ever before our eyes, colouring our vision, colouring our thoughts, colouring our emotions for good or for ill. We cannot escape it. Our personal destinies are inextricably interwoven with the fate directing the death grapple of the thousand miles or so of battle line, and arbitrating on the doom of colossal battleships.

Our local newspaper prints week by week its ever-lengthening Roll of Honour. The shells that burst and slew these brave fellows spread their devastation into our little sheltered town; in a thundering crash tearing off from the very trunk of life here a friend, there a son, there a father, there a husband. And I repeat, at the risk of wearisome insistence, that our sheltered homeland shares the calm, awful fatalism of the battlefield; we have to share it because every rood of our country is, spiritually, as much a battlefield as the narrow, blood-sodden wastes of Flanders and France.

Willie Connor, fine brave gentleman, was dead. My beloved Betty was a widow. No Victoria Cross for Betty. Even if there had been one, no children to be bred from birth on its glorious legend. The German shell left Betty stripped and maimed. With her passionate generosity she had given her all; even as his all had been nobly given by her husband. And then all of both had been swept ruthlessly away down the gory draught of sacrifice.

Poor Betty! "I'm a damned little coward," she said, as she bolted into the house. The brave, foolish words rang in my ears all that night. In the early morning I wondered what I should do. A commonplace message, written or telephoned, would be inept. I shrank from touching her, although I knew she would feel my touch to be gentle. You have seen, I hope, that Betty was dearer to me than anyone else in the world, and I knew that, apart from the stirring emotions in her own young life, Betty held me in the closest affection. When she needed me, she would fly the signal. Of that I felt assured. Still...

While I was in this state of perplexity, Marigold came in to rouse me and get me ready for the day.

"I've taken the liberty, sir," said he, "to telephone to Telford Lodge to enquire after Mrs. Connor. The maid said she had Mrs. Connor's instructions to reply that she was quite well."

The good, admirable fellow! I thanked him. While I was shaving, he said in his usual wooden way:

"Begging your pardon, sir, I thought you might like to send Mrs. Connor a few flowers, so I took upon myself to cut some roses, first thing this morning, with the dew on them."

Of course I cut myself and the blood flowed profusely.

"Why the dickens do you spring things like that on people while they're shaving?" I cried.

"Very sorry, sir," said he, solicitous with sponge and towel.

"All the same, Marigold," said I, "you've solved a puzzle that has kept me awake since early dawn. We'll go out as soon as I'm dressed and we'll send her every rose in the garden."

I have an acre or so of garden behind the house of which I have not yet spoken, save incidentally--for it was there that just a year ago poor Althea Fenimore ate her giant strawberries on the last afternoon of her young life; and a cross-grained old misanthropist, called Timbs, attends to it and lavishes on the flowers the love which, owing, I suspect, to blighted early affection, he denies to mankind. I am very fond of my garden and am especially interested in my roses. Do you know an exquisitely pink rose--the only true pink--named Mrs. George Norwood? ... I bring myself up with a jerk. I am not writing a book on roses. When the war is over perhaps I shall devote my old age to telling you what I feel and know and think about them....

I had a battle with Timbs. Timbs was about sixty. He had shaggy, bushy eye-brows over hard little eyes, a shaggy grey beard, and a long, clean-shaven, obstinate upper lip. Stick him in an ill-fitting frock coat and an antiquated silk hat, and he would be the stage model of a Scottish Elder. As a matter of fact he was Hampshire born and a devout Roman Catholic. But he was as crabbed an old wretch as you can please. He flatly refused to execute my order. I dismissed him on the spot. He countered with the statement that he was an old man who had served me faithfully for many years. I bade him go on serving me faithfully and not be a damned fool. The roses were to be cut. If he didn't cut them, Marigold would.

"He's been a-cutting them already," he growled. "Before I came."

Timbs loathed Marigold--why, I could never discover--and Marigold had the lowest opinion of Timbs. It was an offence for Marigold to desecrate the garden by his mere footsteps; to touch a plant or a flower constituted a damnable outrage. On the other side, Timbs could not approach my person for the purpose of rendering me any necessary physical assistance, without incurring Marigold's violent resentment.

"He'll go on cutting them," said I, "unless you start in at once."

He began. I sent off Marigold in search of a wheelbarrow. Then, having Timbs to myself, I summoned him to my side.

"Do you hold with a man sacrificing his life for his country?"

He looked at me for a moment or two, in his dour, crabbed way.

"I've got a couple of sons in France, trying their best to do it," he replied.

That was the first I had ever heard of it. I had always regarded him as a gnarled old bachelor without human ties. Where he had kept the sons and the necessary mother I had not the remotest notion.

"You're proud of them?"

"I am."

"And if one was killed, would you grudge his grave a few roses? For the sake of him wouldn't you sacrifice a world of roses?"

His manner changed. "I don't understand, sir. Is anybody killed?"

"Didn't I say that all these roses were for Mrs. Connor?"

He dropped his secateur. "Good God, sir! Is it Captain Connor?"

The block-headed idiot of a Marigold had not told him! Marigold is a very fine fellow, but occasionally he manifests human frailties that are truly abominable.

"We are going to sacrifice all our roses, Timbs," said I, "for the sake of a very gallant Englishman. It's about all we can do."

Of course I ought to have entered upon all this explanation when I first came on the scene; but I took it for granted that Timbs knew of the tragedy.

"Need we cut those blooms of the Rayon d'Or?" asked Timbs, alluding to certain roses under conical paper shades which he had been breathlessly tending for our local flower show. "We'll cut them first," said I.

Looking back through the correcting prism of time, I fancy this slaughter of the innocents may have been foolishly sentimental. But I had a great desire to lay all that I could by way of tribute of consolation at Betty's feet, and this little sacrifice of all my roses seemed as symbolical an expression of my feelings as anything that my unimaginative brain could devise.

During the forenoon I superintended the packing of the baskets of roses in Pawling the florist's cart, which I was successful in engaging for the occasion,-- neither wheelbarrow nor donkey carriage nor two-seater, the only vehicles at my disposal, being adequate; and when I saw it start for its destination, I wheeled myself, by way of discipline, through my bereaved garden. It looked mighty desolate. But though all the blooms had gone, there were a myriad buds which next week would burst into happy flower. And the sacrifice seemed trivial, almost ironical; for in Betty's heart there were no buds left.

After lunch I went to the hospital for the weekly committee meeting. To my amazement the first person I met in the corridor was Betty--Betty, white as wax, with black rings round unnaturally shining eyes. She waited for me to wheel myself up to her. I said severely:

"What on earth are you doing here? Go home to bed at once."

She put her hand on the back of my chair and bent down.

"I'm better here. And so are the dear roses. Come and see them."

I followed her into one of the military wards on the ground floor, and the place was a feast of roses. I had no idea so many could have come from my little garden.

And the ward upstairs, she told me, was similarly beflowered. By the side of each man's bed stood bowl or vase, and the tables and the window sills were bright with blooms. It was the ward for serious cases--men with faces livid from gas-poisoning, men with the accursed trench nephritis, men with faces swathed in bandages hiding God knows what distortions, men with cradles over them betokening mangled limbs, men recovering from operations, chiefly the picking of bits of shrapnel and splinters of bone from shattered arms and legs; men with pale faces, patient eyes, and with cheery smiles round their lips when we passed by. A gramophone at the end of the room was grinding out a sentimental tune to which all were listening with rapt enjoyment. I asked one man, among others, how he was faring. He was getting on fine. With the death-rattle in his throat the wounded British soldier invariably tells you that he is getting on fine.

"And ain't these roses lovely? Makes the place look like a garden. And that music--seems appropriate, don't it, sir?"

I asked what the gramophone was playing. He looked respectfully shocked.

"Why, it's 'The Rosary,' sir."

After we had left him, Betty said:

"That's the third time they've asked for it to-day. They've got mixed up with the name, you see. They're beautiful children, aren't they?"

I should have called them sentimental idiots, but Betty saw much clearer than I did. She accompanied me back to the corridor and to the Committee Room door. I was a quarter of an hour late.

"I've kept the precious Rayon d'Ors for myself," she said. "How could you have the heart to cut them?"

"I would have cut out my heart itself, for the matter of that," said I, "if it would have done any good."

She smiled in a forlorn kind of way.

"Don't do that, for I shall want it inside you more than ever now. Tell me, how is Tufton?"

"Tufton--?"

"Yes--Tufton."

I must confess that my mind being so full of Betty, I had clean forgotten Tufton. But Betty remembered.

I smiled. "He's getting on fine," said I. I reached out my hand and held her cold, slim fingers. "Promise me one thing, my dear."

"All right," she said.

"Don't overdo things. There's a limit to the power of bearing strain. As soon as you feel you're likely to go FUT, throw it all up and come and see me and let us lay our heads together."

"I despise people who go FUT," said Betty.

"I don't," said I.

We nodded a mutual farewell. She opened the Committee Room door for me and walked down the corridor with a swinging step, as though she would show me how fully she had made herself mistress of circumstance.

Some evenings later she came in, as usual, unheralded, and established herself by my chair.

The scents of midsummer came in through the open windows, and there was a great full moon staring in at us from a cloudless sky. Letters from the War Office, from brother-officers, from the Colonel, from the Brigadier General himself, had broken her down. She gave me the letters to read. Everyone loved him, admired him, trusted him. "As brave as a lion," wrote one. "Perhaps the most brilliant company officer in my brigade," wrote the General. And his death--the tragic common story. A trench; a high-explosive shell; the fate of young Etherington; and no possible little wooden cross to mark his grave.

And Betty, on the floor by my side, gave way.

The proud will bent. She surrendered herself to a paroxysm of sorrow.

She was not in a fit state to return to the hospital, where, I learned, she shared a bedroom with Phyllis Gedge. I shrank from sending her home to the tactless comforting of her aunts. They were excellent, God-fearing ladies, but they had never understood Betty. All her life they had worried her with genteel admonitions. They had regarded her marriage with disfavour, as an act of foolhardiness--I even think they looked on her attitude as unmaidenly; and now in her frozen widowhood they fretted her past endurance. On the night when the news came they sent for the vicar of their parish--not my good friend who christened Hosea--a very worthy, very serious, very evangelistically religious fellow, to administer spiritual consolation. If Betty had sat devoutly under him on Sundays, there might have been some reason in the summons. But Betty, holding her own religious views, had only once been inside the church--on the occasion of her wedding--and had but the most formal acquaintance with the good man.... No, I could not send Betty home, unexpectedly, to have her wounds mauled about by unskilful fingers. Nothing remained but to telephone to the hospital and put her in Mrs. Marigold's charge for the night. So broken was my dear Betty, that she allowed herself to be carried off without a word.... Once before, years ago, she had behaved with the same piteous docility; and that was when, a short-frocked hoiden, she had fallen from an apple tree and badly hurt herself, and Marigold had carried her into the house and Mrs. Marigold had put her to bed....

In the morning I found her calm and sedate at the breakfast table.

"You've been and gone and done for both of us, Majy dear," she remarked, pouring out tea.

"What do you mean?"

"Our reputations. What a scandal in Wellingsford!"

She looked me clearly in the eyes and smiled, and her hand did not shake as she held my cup. And by these signs I knew that she had taken herself again in grip and forbade reference to the agony through which she had passed.

Quickly she turned the conversation to the Tuftons. What had happened? I told her meagrely. She insisted on fuller details. So, flogged by her, I related what I had gleaned from Marigold's wooden reports. He always conveyed personal information as though he were giving evidence against a defaulter. I had to start all over again. Apparently this had happened: Mrs. Tufton had arrayed herself, not in sackcloth and ashes, for that was apparently her normal attire, but in an equivalent, as far as a symbol of humility was concerned; namely, in decent raiment, and had sought her husband's forgiveness. There had been a touching scene in the scullery which Mrs. Marigold had given up to them for the sake of privacy, in which the lady had made tearful promises of reform and the corporal had magnanimously passed the sponge over the terrible reckoning on her slate. Would he then go home to his penitent wife? But the gallant fellow, with the sturdy common-sense for which the British soldier is renowned, contrasted the clover in which he was living here with the aridness of Flowery End, and declined to budge. High sentiment was one thing, snug lying was another. Next time he came back, if she had re-established the home in its former comfort, he didn't say as how he wouldn't--

"But," she cried--and this bit I didn't tell Betty--"the next time you may come home dead!"

"Then," replied Tufton, "let me see what a nice respectable coffin, with brass handles and lots of slap-up brass nails and a brass plate, you can get ready for me."

Since the first interview, I informed Betty, there had been others daily--most decorous. They were excellent friends. Neither seemed to perceive anything absurd in the situation. Even Marigold looked on it as a matter of course.

"I have an idea," said Betty. "You know we want some help in the servant staff of the hospital?"

I did. The matron had informed the Committee, who had empowered her to act.

"Why not let me tackle Mrs. Tufton while she is in this beautifully chastened and devotional mood? In this way we can get her out of the mills, out of Flowery End, fill her up with noble and patriotic emotions instead of whisky, and when Tufton returns, present her to him as a model wife, sanctified by suffering and en-nobled by the consciousness of duty done. It would be splendid!"

For the first time since the black day there came a gleam of fun into Betty's eyes and a touch of colour into her cheeks.

"It would indeed," said I. "The only question is whether Tufton would really like this Red Cross Saint you'll have provided for him."

"In case he does not," said Betty, "you can provide him with a refuge as you are doing now."

She rose from the table, announcing her intention of going straight to the hospital. I realised with a pang that breakfast was over; that I had enjoyed a delectable meal; that, by some sort of dainty miracle, she had bemused me into eating and drinking twice my ordinary ration; that she had inveigled me into talking--a thing I have never done during breakfast for years--it is as much as Marigold's ugly head is worth to address a remark to me during the unsympathetic duty--why, if my poached egg regards me with too aggressive a pinkiness, I want to slap it--and into talking about those confounded Tuftons with a gusto only provoked by a glass or two of impeccable port after a good dinner. One would have thought, considering the anguished scene of the night before, that it would have been one of the most miserably impossible tete-a-tete breakfasts in the whole range of such notoriously ghastly meals. But here was Betty, serene and smiling, as though she had been accustomed to breakfast with me every morning of her life, off to the hospital, with a hard little idea in her humorous head concerning Mrs. Tufton's conversion.

The only sign she gave of last night's storm was when, by way of good-bye, she bent down and kissed my cheek.

"You know," she said, "I love you too much to thank you."

And she went off with her brave little head in the air.

In the afternoon I went to Wellings Park. Sir Anthony was away, but Lady Fenimore was in. She showed me a letter she had received from Betty in reply to her letter of condolence:

"My dears,

"It is good to realise one has such rocks to lean on. You long to help and comfort me. Well, I'll tell you how to do it. You just forget. Leave it to me to do all the remembering.

"Yours, Betty."

CHAPTER XIV

On the first of July there was forwarded to me from the club a letter in an unknown handwriting. I had to turn to the signature to discover the identity of my correspondent. It was Reggie Dacre, Colonel Dacre, whom I had met in London a couple of months before. As it tells its own little story, I transcribe it.

"Dear Major Meredyth:

"I should like to confirm by the following anecdote, which is going the round of the Brigade, what I recently told you about our friend Boyce. I shouldn't worry you, but I feel that if one has cast an unjustifiable slur on a brother-officer's honour--and I can't tell you how the thing has lain on my conscience--one shouldn't leave a stone unturned to rehabilitate him, even in the eyes of one person.

"There has been a good deal of scrapping around Ypres lately--that given away by the communiques; but for reasons which both the Censor and yourself will appreciate, I can't be more explicit as to locality. Enough to say that somewhere in this region--or sector, as we call it nowadays--there was a certain bit of ground that had been taken and retaken over and over again. B.'s Regiment was in this fighting, and at one particular time we were holding a German front trench section. A short distance further on the enemy held a little farm building, forming a sort of redoubt. They sniped all day long. They also had a machine gun. I can't give you accurate details, for I can only tell you what I've heard; but the essentials are true. Well, we got that farmhouse. We got it single-handed. Boyce put up the most amazing bluff that has ever happened in this war. He crawls out by himself, without anybody knowing--it was a pitch-black night--gets through the barbed wire, heaven knows how, up to the house; lays a sentry out with his life-preserver; gives a few commands to an imaginary company; and summons the occupants--two officers and fifteen men--to surrender. Thinking they are surrounded, they obey like lambs, come out unarmed, with their hands up, officers and all, and are comfortably marched off in the dark, as prisoners into our trenches. They say that when the German officers discovered how they had been done, they foamed so hard that we had to use empty sandbags as strait waistcoats.

"Now, it's picturesque, of course, and being picturesque, it has flown from mouth to mouth. But it's true. Verb. sap.

"Hoping some time or other to see you again,

"Yours sincerely,
  "R. DACRE,
  "Lt. Col."

I quote this letter here for the sake of chronological sequence. It gave me a curious bit of news. No man could have performed such a feat without a cold brain, soundly beating heart, and nerves of steel. It was not an act of red-hot heroism. It was done in cold blood, a deliberate gamble with death on a thousand to one chance. It was staggeringly brave.

I told the story to Mrs. Boyce. Her comment was characteristic:

"But surely they would have to surrender if called upon by a British Officer."

To the Day of Judgment I don't think she will understand what Leonard did. Leonard himself, coming home slightly wounded two or three weeks afterwards, pooh-poohed the story as one of no account and only further confused the dear lady's ill-conceived notions.

In the meanwhile life at Wellingsford flowed uneventfully. Now and again a regiment or a brigade, having finished its training, disappeared in a night, and the next day fresh troops arrived to fill its place. And this great, silent movement of men went on all over the country. Sometimes our hearts sank. A reserve Howitzer Territorial Brigade turned up in Wellings Park with dummy wooden guns. The officers told us that they had been expecting proper guns daily for the past two months. Marigold shook a sad head. But all things, even six-inch howitzers, come to him who waits.

Little more was heard of Randall Holmes. He corresponded with his mother through a firm of London solicitors, and his address and his doings remained a mystery. He was alive, he professed robust health, and in reply to Mrs. Holmes's frantically expressed hope that he was adopting no course that might discredit his father's name, he twitted her with intellectual volte-face to the views of Philistia, but at the same time assured her that he was doing nothing which the most self-righteous bourgeois would consider discreditable.

"But it IS discreditable for him to go away like this and not let his own mother know where he is," cried the poor woman.

And of course I agreed with her. I find it best always to agree with mothers; also with wives.

After her own lapse from what Mrs. Boyce would have called "Spartianism," Betty kept up her brave face. When Willie Connor's kit came home she told me tearlessly about the heartrending consignment. Now and then she spoke of him-- with a proud look in her eyes. She was one of the women of England who had the privilege of being the wife of a hero. In this world one must pay for everything worth having. Her widowhood was the price. All the tears of a lifetime could not bring him back. All the storms of fate could not destroy the glory of those few wonderful months. He was laughing, so she heard, when he met his death. So would she, in honour of him, go on laughing till she met hers.

"And that silly little fool, Phyllis, is still crying her eyes out over Randall," she said. "Don't I think she was wrong in sending him away? If she had married him she might have influenced him, made him get a commission in the army. I've threatened to beat her if she talks such nonsense. Why can't people take a line and stick to it?"

"This isn't a world of Bettys, my dear," said I.

"Rubbish! The outrageous Mrs. Tufton's doing it."

Apparently she was. She followed Betty about as the lamb followed Mary. Tufton, after a week or two at Wellington Barracks, had been given sergeant's stripes and sent off with a draft to the front. Betty's dramatic announcement of her widowhood seemed to have put the fear of death into the woman's soul. As soon as her husband landed in France she went scrupulously through the closely printed casualty lists of non-commissioned officers and men in The Daily Mail, in awful dread lest she should see her husband's name. Betty vainly assured her that, in the first place, she would hear from the War Office weeks before anything could appear in the papers, and that, in the second, his name would occur under the heading "Grenadier Guards," and not under "Royal Field Artillery," "Royal Engineers," "Duke of Cornwall's Light Infantry," "R.A.M.C.," or Australian and Canadian contingents. Mrs. Tufton went through the lot from start to finish. Once, indeed, she came across the name, in big print, and made a bee-line through the wards for Betty--an offence for which the Matron nearly threw her, there and then, into the street. It was that of the gallant Colonel of a New Zealand Regiment at Gallipoli. Betty had to point to the brief biographical note to prove to the distracted woman that the late Colonel Tufton of New Zealand could not be identical with Sergeant Tufton of the Grenadiers. She regarded Mrs. Tufton as a brand she had plucked from the burning and took a great deal of trouble with her. On the other hand, I imagine Mrs. Tufton looked upon herself as a very important person, a sergeant's wife, and the confidential intimate of a leading sister at the Wellingsford Hospital. In fact, Marigold mentioned her notorious vanity.

"What does it matter," cried Betty, when I put this view before her, "how swelled her head may be, so long as it isn't swollen with drink?"

And I could find no adequate reply.

Towards the end of the month comes Boyce to Wellingsford, this time not secretly; for the day after his arrival he drove his mother through the town and incidentally called on me. A neglected bullet graze on the neck had turned septic. An ugly temperature had sent him to hospital. The authorities, as soon as the fever had abated and left him on the high road to recovery, had sent him home. A khaki bandage around his bull-throat alone betokened anything amiss. He would be back, he said, as soon as the Medical Board at the War Office would let him.

On this occasion, for the first time since South African days, I met him without any mistrust. What had passed between Betty and himself, I did not know. Relations between man and woman are so subtle and complicated, that unless you have the full pleadings on both sides in front of you, you cannot arbitrate; and, as often as not, if you deliver the most soul-satisfying of judgments, you are hopelessly wrong, because there are all important, elusive factors of personality, temperament, sex, and what not which all the legal acumen in the world could not set down in black and white. So half unconsciously I ruled out Betty from my contemplation of the man. I had been obsessed by the Vilboek Farm story, and by that alone. Reggie Dacre--to say nothing of personages in high command--had proved it to be a horrible lie. He had Marshal Ney's deserved reputation--le brave des braves--and there is no more coldly critical conferrer of such repute than the British Army in the field. To win it a man not only has to do something heroic once or twice--that is what he is there for--but he has to be doing it all the time. Boyce had piled up for himself an amazing record, one that overwhelmed the possibility of truth in old slanders. When I gripped him by the hand, I felt immeasurable relief at being able to do so without the old haunting suspicion and reservation.

He spoke, like thousands of others of his type--the type of the fine professional English soldier--with diffident modesty of such personal experiences as he deigned to recount. The anecdotes mostly had a humorous side, and were evoked by allusion. Like all of us stay-at-homes, I cursed the censorship for leaving us so much in the dark. He laughed and cursed the censorship for the opposite reason.

"The damned fools--I beg your pardon, Mother, but when a fool is too big a fool even for this world, he must be damned--the damned fools allow all sorts of things to be given away. They were nearly the death of me and were the death of half a dozen of my men."

And he told the story. In a deserted brewery behind the lines the vats were fitted up as baths for men from the trenches, and the furnaces heated ovens in which horrible clothing was baked. This brewery had been immune from attack until an officially sanctioned newspaper article specified its exact position. A few days after the article appeared, in fact, as soon as a copy of the paper reached Germany, a thunderstorm of shells broke on the brewery. Out of it poured a helter-skelter stream of stark-naked men, who ran wherever they could for cover. From one point of view it was vastly comic. In the meanwhile the building containing all their clothes, and all the spare clothing for a brigade, was being scientifically destroyed. That was more comic still. The bather cut off from his garments is a world-wide joke. The German battery, having got the exact range, were having a systematic, Teutonic afternoon's enjoyment. But from another point of view the situation was desperate. There were these poor fellows, hordes of them, in nature's inadequate protection against the weather, shivering in the cold, with the nearest spare rag of clothing some miles away. Boyce got them together, paraded them instantly under the shell fire, and led them at a rush into the blazing building to salve stores. Six never came out alive. Many were burned and wounded. But it had to be done, or the whole crowd would have perished from exposure. Tommy is fairly tough; but he cannot live mother-naked through a March night of driving sleet.

"No," said Boyce, "if you suffered daily from the low cunning of Brother Bosch, you wouldn't cry for things to be published in the newspapers."

At the end of their visit I accompanied my guests to the hall. Marigold escorted Mrs. Boyce to the car. Leonard picked up his cap and cane and turned to shake hands. I noticed that the knob of the cane was neatly cased in wash-leather. Idly I enquired the reason. He smiled grimly as he slipped off the cover and exposed the polished deep vermilion butt of the life-preserver which Reggie Dacre had described.

"It's a sort of fetish I feel I must carry around with me," he explained. "When I've got it in my hand, I don't seem to care a damn what I do. When I haven't, I miss it. Remember the story of Sir Walter Scott's boy with the butter? Something like that, you know. But in its bare state it's not a pretty sight for the mother."

"It ought to have a name," said I. "The poilu calls his bayonet Rosalie."

He looked at it darkly for a moment, before refitting the wash-leather.

"I might call it The Reminder," said he. "Good-bye." And he turned quickly and strode out of the door.

The Reminder of what? He puzzled me. Why, in spite of all my open-heartedness, did he still contrive to leave me with a sense of the enigmatic?

Although he showed himself openly about the town, he held himself aloof from social intercourse with the inhabitants. He called, I know, on Mrs. Holmes, and on one or two others who have no place in this chronicle. But he refused all proposals of entertainment, notably an invitation to dinner from the Fenimores. Sir Anthony met him in the street, upbraided him in his genial manner for neglect of his old friends, and pressingly asked him to dine at Wellings Park. Just a few old friends. The duties of a distinguished soldier, said he, did not begin and end on the field. He must uplift the hearts of those who had to stay at home. Sir Anthony had a nervous trick of rattling off many sentences before his interlocutor could get in a word. When he had finished, Boyce politely declined the invitation.

"And with a damned chilly, stand-offish politeness," cried Sir Anthony furiously, when telling me about it. "Just as if I had been Perkins, the fish-monger, asking him to meet the Prettiloves at high tea. It's swelled head, my dear chap; that's what it is. Just swelled head. None of us are good enough for him and his laurels. He's going to remain the modest mossy violet of a hero blushing unseen. Oh, damn the fellow!"

I did my best to soothe my touchy and choleric friend. No soldier, said I, likes to be made a show of. Why had he suggested a dinner party? A few friends. Anyone in Boyce's position knew what that meant. It meant about thirty gawking, gaping people for whom he didn't care a hang. Why hadn't Anthony asked the Boyces to dine quietly with Edith and himself--with me thrown in, for instance, if they wanted exotic assistance? Let me try, I said, to fix matters up.

So the next day I called on Boyce and told him, with such tact as I have at command, of Sir Anthony's wounded feelings.

"My dear Meredyth," said he. "I can only say to you what I tried to explain to the irascible little man. If I accepted one invitation, I should have to accept all invitations or give terrible offence all over the place. I'm here a sick man and my mother's an invalid. And I merely want to be saved from my friends and have a quiet time with the old lady. Of course if Sir Anthony is offended, I'm only too sorry, and I beg you to assure him that I never intended the slightest discourtesy. The mere idea of it distresses me."

The explanation was reasonable, the apology frank. Sir Anthony received them both grumpily. He had his foibles. He set his invitations to dinner in a separate category from those of the rag-tag and bobtail of Wellingsford society. So for the sake of principle he continued to damn the fellow.

On the other hand, for the sake of principle, reparation for injustice, I continued to like the fellow and found pleasure in his company. For one thing, I hankered after the smoke and smell and din of the front, and Boyce succeeded more than anyone else in satisfying my appetite. While he talked, as he did freely with me alone, I got near to the grim essence of things. Also, with the aid of rough military maps, he made actions and strategical movements of which newspaper accounts had given me but a confused notion, as clear as if I had been a chief of staff. Often he went to considerable trouble in obtaining special information. He appeared to set himself out to win my esteem. Now a cripple is very sensitive to kindness. I could not reject his overtures. What interested motive could he have in seeking out a useless hulk like me? On the first opportunity I told Betty of the new friendship, having a twinge or two of conscience lest it might appear to her disloyal.

"But why in the world shouldn't you see him, dear?" she said, open-eyed. "He brings the breath of battle to you and gives you fresh life. You're looking ever so much better the last few days. The only thing is," she added, turning her head away, "that I don't want to run the risk of meeting him again."

Naturally I took precautions against such an occurrence. The circumstances of their last meeting at my house lingered unpleasantly in my mind. Perhaps, for Betty's sake, I ought to have turned a cold shoulder on Boyce. But when you have done a man a foul injustice for years, you must make him some kind of secret reparation. So, by making him welcome, I did what I could.

Now I don't know whether I ought to set down a trivial incident mentioned in my diary under the date of the 15th August, the day before Boyce left Wellingsford to join his regiment in France. In writing an account of other people's lives it is difficult to know what to put in and what to leave out. If you bring in your own predilections or prejudices or speculations concerning them, you must convey a distorted impression. You lie about them unconsciously. A fact is a fact, and, if it is important, ought to be recorded. But when you are not sure whether it is a fact or not, what are you to do?

Perhaps I had better narrate what happened and tell you afterwards why I hesitate.

Marigold had driven me over to Godbury, where I had business connected with a County Territorial Association, and we were returning home. It was a moist, horrible, depressing August day. A slimy, sticky day. Clouds hung low over the reeking earth. The honest rain had ceased, but wet drops dribbled from the leaves of the trees and the branches and trunks exuded moisture. The thatched roofs of cottages were dank. In front gardens roses and hollyhocks drooped sodden. The very droves of steers coming from market sweated in the muggy air. The good slush of the once dusty road, broken to bits by military traffic, had stiffened into black grease. Round a bend of the road we skidded alarmingly. Marigold has a theory that in summer time a shirt next the skin is the only wear for humans and square-tread tyres the only wear for motor-cars. With some acerbity I pointed out the futility of his proposition. With the blandness of superior wisdom he assured me that we were perfectly safe. You can't knock into the head of an artilleryman who has been trained to hang on to a limber by the friction of his trousers, that there can be any danger in the luxurious seat of a motor-car.

There is a good straight half mile of the Godbury Road which is known in the locality as "The Gut." It is sunken and very narrow, being flanked on one side by the railway embankment, and on the other by the grounds of Godbury Chase. A most desolate bit of road, half overhung by trees and oozing with all the moisture of the country-side. On this day it was the wettest, slimiest bit of road in England. We had almost reached the end of it, when it entered the head of a stray puppy dog to pause in the act of crossing and sit down in the middle and hunt for fleas. To spare the abominable mongrel, Marigold made a sudden swerve. Of course the car skidded. It skidded all over the place, as if it were drunk, and, aided by Marigold, described a series of ghastly half-circles. At last he performed various convulsive feats of jugglery, with the result that the car, which was nosing steadily for the ditch, came to a stand-still. Then Marigold informed me in unemotional tones that the steering gear had gone.

"It's all the fault of that there dog," said he, twisting his head so as to glare at the little beast, who, after a yelp and a bound, had calmly recaptured his position and resumed his interrupted occupation.

"It's all the fault of that there Marigold," I retorted, "who can't see the sense of using studded tyres on a greasy surface. What's to be done now?"

Marigold thrust his hand beneath his wig and scratched his head. He didn't exactly know. He got out and stared intently at the car. If mind could have triumphed over matter, the steering gear would have become disfractured. But the good Marigold's mind was not powerful enough. He gave up the contest and looked at me and the situation. There we were, broadside on to the narrow road, and only manhandling could bring us round to a position of safety by the side. He was for trying it there and then; but I objected, having no desire to be slithered into the ditch.

"I would just as soon," said I, "ride a giraffe shod with roller skates."

He didn't even smile. He turned his one reproachful eye on me. What was to be done? I told him. We must wait for assistance. When I had been transferred into the vehicle of a passing Samaritan, it was time enough for the manhandling.

Fate brought the Samaritan very quickly. A car coming from Godbury tooted violently, then slowed down, stopped, and from it jumped Leonard Boyce. As he was to rescue me from a position of peculiar helplessness, I regarded his great khaki-clad figure as that of a ministering angel. I beamed on him.

"Hallo! What's the matter?" he asked cheerily.

I explained. Being merciful, I spared Marigold and threw the blame on the dog and on the County Council for allowing the roads to get into such a filthy condition.

"That's all right," said Boyce. "We'll soon fix you up. First we'll get you into my car. Then Marigold and I will slue this one round, and then we'll send him a tow."

Marigold nodded and approached to lift me out.

Then, what happened next, happened in the flash of a few breathless seconds. There was the dull thud of hoofs. A scared bay thoroughbred, coming from Godbury, galloping hell for leather, with a dishevelled boy in khaki on his back. The boy had lost his stirrups; he had lost his reins; he had lost his head. He hung half over the saddle and had a death grip on the horse's mane. And the uncontrolled brute was thundering down on us. There was my infernal car barring the narrow road. I remember bracing myself to meet the shock. An end, thought I, of Duncan Meredyth. I saw Boyce leap aside like a flash and appear to stand stock-still. The next second I saw Marigold semaphore a few yards in front of the car and then swing sickeningly at the horse's bit; and then the whole lot of them, Marigold, horse and rider, come down in a convulsive heap on the greasy road. To my intense relief I saw Marigold pick himself up and go to the head of the plunging, prostrate horse. In a moment or two he had got the beast on his feet, where he stood quivering. It was a fine, smart piece of work on the part of the old artilleryman. I was so intent on his danger that I forgot all about Boyce: but as soon as the three crashed down, I saw him run to assist the young subaltern who had rolled himself clear.

"By Jove, that was a narrow shave!" he cried cordially, giving him a hand.

"It was indeed, sir," said the young man, scraping the mud off his face. "That's the second time the brute has done it. He shies and bucks and kicks like a regular devil. This time he shied at a steam lorry and bucked my feet out of the stirrups. Everybody in the squadron has turned him down, and I'm the junior, I've had to take him." He eyed the animal resentfully. "I'd just like to get him on some grass and knock hell out of him!"

"I'm glad to see you're not hurt," said Boyce with a smile.

"Oh, not a bit, sir," said the boy. He turned to Marigold. "I don't know how to thank you. It was a jolly plucky thing to do. You've saved my life and that of the gentleman in the car. If we had busted into it, there would have been pie." He came to the side of the car. "I think you're Major Meredyth, sir. I must have given you an awful fright. I'm so sorry. My name is Brown. I'm in the South Scottish Horse."

He had a courteous charm of manner in spite of his boyish desire to appear unshaken by the accident. A little bravado is an excellent thing. I laughed and held out my hand.

"I'm glad to meet you--although our meeting might have been contrived less precipitously. This is Sergeant Marigold, late R.F.A., who does me the honour of looking after me. And this is Major Boyce."

Observe the little devil of malice that made me put Marigold first.

"Of the Rifles?"

A quick gleam of admiration showed in the boy's eyes as he saluted. No soldier could be stationed at Wellingsford without hearing of the hero of the neighbourhood. A great hay waggon came lumbering down the road and pulled up, there being no room for it to pass. This put an end to social amenities. Brown mounted his detested charger and trotted off. Marigold transferred me to Boyce's car. Several pairs of brawny arms righted the two-seater and Boyce and I drove off, leaving Marigold waiting with his usual stony patience for the promised tow. On the way

Boyce talked gaily of Marigold's gallantry, of the boy's spirit, of the idiotic way in which impossible horses were being foisted on newly formed cavalry units. When we drew up at my front door, it occurred to me that there was no Marigold in attendance.

"How the deuce," said I, "am I going to get out?"

Boyce laughed. "I don't think I'll drop you."

His great arms picked me up with ease. But while he was carrying me I experienced a singular physical revolt. I loathed his grip. I loathed the enforced personal contact. Even after he had deposited me--very skilfully and gently--in my wheelchair in the hall, I hated the lingering sense of his touch. He owed his whisky and soda to the most elementary instinct of hospitality. Besides, he was off the next day, back to the trenches and the hell of battle, and I had to bid him good-bye and Godspeed. But when he went, I felt glad, very glad, as though relieved of some dreadful presence. My old distrust and dislike returned increased a thousandfold.

It was only when he got my frail body in his arms, which I realized were twice as strong as my good Marigold's, that I felt the ghastly and irrational revulsion. The only thing to which I can liken it, although it seems ludicrous, is what I imagine to be the instinctive recoil of a woman who feels on her body the touch of antipathetic hands. I know that my malady has made me a bit supersensitive. But my vanity has prided itself on keeping up a rugged spirit in a fool of a body, so I hated myself for giving way to morbid sensations. All the same, I felt that if I were alone in a burning house, and there were no one but Leonard Boyce to save me, I should prefer incineration to rescue.

And now I will tell you why I have hesitated to give a place in this chronicle to the incident of the broken-down car and the runaway horse.

It all happened so quickly, my mind was so taken up with the sudden peril, that for the life of me I cannot swear to the part played by Leonard Boyce. I saw him leap aside, and had the fragment of an impression of him standing motionless between the radiator of his car and the tail of mine which was at right angles. The next time he thrust himself on my consciousness was when he was lugging young Brown out of reach of the convulsive hoofs. In the meanwhile Marigold, single-handed, had rushed into the jaws of death and stopped the horse. But as it was a matter of seconds, I had no reason for believing that, but for adventitious relative positions on the road, Boyce would not have done the same.... And yet out of the corner of my eye I got an instantaneous photograph of him standing bolt upright between the two cars, while the abominable bay brute, with distended red nostrils and wild eyes, was thundering down on us.

On the other hand, the swift pleasure in the boy's eyes when he realised that he was in the presence of the popular hero, proved him free of doubts such as mine. And when Marigold, having put the car in hospital, came to make his report, and lingered in order to discuss the whole affair, he said, in wooden deprecation of my eulogy:

"If Major Boyce hadn't jumped in, sir, young Mr. Brown's head would have been kicked into pumpkin-squash."

Well, I have known from long experience that there are no more untrustworthy witnesses than a man's own eyes; especially in the lightning dramas of life.

I was kept awake all night, and towards the dawn I came into thorough agreement with Sir Anthony and I heartily damned the fellow.

What had I to do with him that he should rob me of my sleep?

CHAPTER XV

The next morning he strode in while I was at breakfast, handsome, erect, deep-chested, the incarnation of physical strength, with a glad light in his eyes.

"Congratulate me, old man," he cried, gripping my frail shoulder. "I've three days' extra leave. And more than that, I go out in command of the regiment. No temporary business but permanent rank. Gazetted in due course. Bannatyne--that's our colonel--damned good soldier!--has got a staff appointment. I take his place. I promise you the Fourth King's Rifles are going to make history. Either history or manure. History for choice. As I say, Bannatyne's a damned good soldier, and personally as brave as a lion, but when it comes to the regiment, he's too much on the cautious side. The regiment's only longing to make things hum, and I'm going to let 'em do it."

I congratulated him in politely appropriate terms and went on with my bacon and eggs. He sat on the window-seat and tapped his gaiters with his cane life-preserver. He wore his cap.

"I thought you'd like to know," said he. "You've been so good to the old mother while I've been away and been so charitable, listening to my yarns, while I've been here, that I couldn't resist coming round and telling you."

"I suppose your mother's delighted," said I.

He threw back his head and laughed, as though he had never a black thought or memory in the world.

"Dear old mater! She has the impression that I'm going out to take charge of the blessed campaign. So if she talks about 'my dear son's army,' don't let her down, like a good chap--for she'll think either me a fraud or you a liar."

He rose suddenly, with a change of expression.

"You're the only man in the world I could talk to like this about my mother. You know the sterling goodness and loyalty that lies beneath her funny little ways."

He strode to the window which looks out on to the garden, his back turned on me. And there he stood silent for a considerable time. I helped myself to marmalade and poured out a second cup of tea. There was no call for me to speak. I had long realized that, whatever may have been the man's sins and weaknesses, he had a very deep and tender love for the Dresden china old lady that was his mother. There was London of the clubs and the theatres and the restaurants and the night-clubs, a war London full and alive, not dead as in Augusts of far-off tradition, all ready to give him talk and gaiety and the things that matter to the man who escapes for a brief season from the never-ending hell of the battlefield; ready, too, to pour flattery into his ear, to touch his scars with the softest of its lingers. Yet he chose to stay, a recluse, in our dull little town, avoiding even the kindly folk round about, in order to devote himself to one dear but entirely uninteresting old woman. It is not that he despised London, preferring the life of the country gentleman. On the contrary, before the war Leonard Boyce was very much the man about town. He loved the glitter and the chatter of it. From chance words during this spell of leave, I had divined hankering after its various fleshpots. For the sake of one old woman he made reckless and gallant sacrifice. When he was bored to misery he came round to me. I learned later that in visiting Wellingsford he faced more than boredom. All of this you must put to the credit side of his ledger.

There he stood, his great broad shoulders and bull-neck silhouetted against the window. That broad expanse, a bit fleshy, below the base of the skull indicates brutality. Never before, to my eyes, had the sign asserted itself with so much aggression. I had often wondered why, apart from the Vilboek Farm legend, I had always disliked and distrusted him. Now I seemed to know. It was the neck not of a man, but of a brute. The curious repulsion of the previous evening, when he had carried me into the house, came over me again. From junction of arm and body protruded six inches of the steel-covered life-preserver, the washleather that hid its ghastly knob staring at me blankly. I hated the thing. The gallant English officer--and in my time I have known and loved a many of the most gallant--does not go about in private life fondling a trophy reeking with the blood of his enemies. It is the trait of a savage. That truculent knob and that truculent bull-neck correlated themselves most horribly in my mind. And again, with a shiver, I had the haunting flash of a vision of him, out of the tail of my eye, standing rigid and gaping between the two cars, while my rugged old Marigold, in a businesslike, old-soldier sort of way, without thought of danger or death, was swaying at the head of the runaway horse.

Presently he turned, and his brows were set above unfathomable hard eyes. The short-cropped moustache could not hide the curious twitch of the lips which I had seen once before. It was obvious that these few minutes of silence had been spent in deep thought and had resulted in a decision. A different being from the gay, successful soldier who had come in to announce his honours confronted me. He threw down cap and stick and passed his hand over his crisp brown hair.

"I don't know whether you're a friend of mine or not," he said, hands on hips and gaitered legs slightly apart. "I've never been able to make out. All through our intercourse, in spite of your courtesy and hospitality, there has been some sort of reservation on your part."

"If that is so," said I, diplomatically, "it is because of the defects of my national quality."

"That's possibly what I've felt," said he. "But it doesn't matter a damn with regard to what I want to say. It's a question not of your feelings towards me, but my feelings towards you. I don't want to make polite speeches--but you're a man whom I have every reason to honour and trust. And unlike all my other brother-officers, you have no reason to be jealous--"

"My dear fellow," I interrupted, "what's all this about? Why jealousy?"

"You know what a pot-hunter is in athletics? A chap that is simply out for prizes? Well, that's what a lot of them think of me. That I'm just out to get orders and medals and distinctions and so forth."

"That's nonsense," said I. "I happen to know. Your reputation in the brigade is unassailable."

"In the way of my having done what I'm credited with, it is," he answered. "But all the same, they're right."

"What do you mean?" I asked.

"What I say. They're right. I'm out for everything I can get. Now I'm out for a V.C. I see you think it abominable. That's because you don't understand. No one but I myself could understand. I feel I owe it to myself." He looked at me for a second or two and then broke into a sardonic sort of laugh. "I suppose you think me a conceited ass," he continued. "Why should Leonard Boyce be such a vastly important person? It isn't that, I assure you."

I lit a cigarette, having waved an invitation to join me, which with a nod he refused.

"What is it, then?"

"Has it ever struck you that often a man's most merciless creditor is himself?"

Here was a casuistical proposition thrown at my head by the last person I should have suspected of doing so. It was immensely interesting, in view of my long puzzledom. I spoke warily.

"That depends on the man--on the nice balance of his dual nature. On the one side is the power to demand mercilessly; on the other, the instinct to respond. Of course, the criminal--"

"What are you dragging in criminals for?" he said sharply. "I'm talking about honourable men with consciences. Criminals haven't consciences. The devil who has just been hung for murdering three women in their baths hadn't any dual nature, as you call it. Those murders didn't represent to him a mountain of debt to God which his soul was summoned to discharge. He went to his death thinking himself a most unlucky and hardly used fellow."

His fingers went instinctively into the cigarette-box. I passed him the matches.

"Precisely," said I. "That was the point I was about to make."

He puffed at his cigarette and looked rather foolish, as though regretting his outburst.

"We've got away," he said, after a pause, "from what I was meaning to tell you. And I want to tell you because I mayn't have another chance." He turned to the window-seat and picked up his life-preserver. "I'm out for two things. One is to kill Germans--" He patted the covered knob--and there flashed across my mind a boyhood's memory of Martin--wasn't it Martin?--in "Hereward the Wake," who had a deliciously blood-curdling habit of patting his revengeful axe.--"I've done in eighty-five with this and my revolver. That, I consider, is my duty to my country. The other is to get the V.C. That's for payment to my creditor self."

"In full, or on account?" said I.

"There's only one payment in full," he answered grimly, "and that I've been offering for the past twelve months. And it's a thousand chances to one it will be accepted before the end of this year. And that, after all this palaver, is what I've just made up my mind to talk to you about."

"You mean your death?"

"Just that," said he. "A man pot-hunting for Victoria Crosses takes a thousand to one chance." He paused abruptly and shot an eager and curiously wavering glance at me. "Am I boring you with all this?"

"Good Heavens, no." And then as the insistence of his great figure towering over me had begun to fret my nerves--"Sit down, man," said I, with an impatient gesture, "and put that sickening toy away and come to the point."

He tossed the cane on the window-seat and sat near me on a straight-backed chair.

"All right," he said. "I'll come to the point. I shan't see you again. I'm going out in command. Thank God we're in the thick of it. Round about Loos. It's a thousand to one I'll be killed. Life doesn't matter much to me, in spite of what you may think. There are only two people on God's earth I care for. One, of course, is my old mother. The other is Betty Fairfax--I mean Betty Connor. I spoke to you once about her--after I had met her here--and I gave you to understand that I had broken off our engagement from conscientious motives. It was an awkward position and I had to say something. As a matter of fact I acted abominably. But I couldn't help it."

The corners of his lips suddenly worked in the odd little twitch. "Sometimes circumstances, especially if a man's own damn foolishness has contrived them, tie him hand and foot. Sometimes physical instincts that he can't control." He narrowed his eyes and bent forward, looking at me intently, and he repeated the phrase slowly--"Physical instincts that he can't control-"

Was he referring to the incident of yesterday? I thought so. I also believed it was the motive power of this strangely intimate conversation.

He rose again as though restless, and once more went to the window and seemed to seek inspiration or decision from the sight of my roses. After a short while he turned and dragged up from his neck a slim chain at the end of which hung a round object in a talc case. This he unfastened and threw on the table in front of me.

"Do you know what that is?"

"Yes," said I. "Your identification disc."

"Look on the other side."

I took it up and found that the reverse contained the head cut out from some photograph of Betty. After I had handed back the locket, he slipped it on the chain and dropped it beneath his collar.

"I'm not a damned fool," said he.

I nodded understandingly. No one would have accused him of mawkish sentiment. The woman whose portrait he wore night and day next his skin was the woman he loved. He had no other way of proving his sincerity than by exhibiting the token.

"I see," said I. "What do you propose to do?"

"I've told you. The V.C. or--" He snapped his fingers.

"But if it's the V.C. and a Brigade, and perhaps a Division--if it's everything else imaginable except--" I snapped my fingers in imitation--"What then?"

Again the hateful twitch of the lips, which he quickly dissimulated in a smile.

"I'll begin to try to be a brave man." He lit another cigarette. "But all that, my dear Meredyth," he continued, "is away from the point. If I live, I'll ask you to forget this rotten palaver. But I have a feeling that I shan't come back. Something tells me that my particular form of extermination will be a head knocked into slush. I'm absolutely certain that I shall never see you again. Oh, I'm not morbid," he said, as I raised a protesting hand. "You're an old soldier and know what these premonitions are. When I came in--before I had finally made up my mind to pan out to you like this--I felt like a boy who has been made captain of the school. But all the same, I know I shan't see you again. So I want you to promise me two things--quite honourable and easy."

"Of course, my dear fellow," said I rather tartly, for I did not like the wind-up of his sentence. It was unthinkable that an officer and a gentleman should inveigle a brother-officer into a solemn promise to do anything dishonourable. "Of course. Anything you like."

"One is to look after the old mother--"

"That goes without promising," said I.

"The other is to--what shall I say?--to rehabilitate my memory in the eyes of Betty Connor. She may hear all kinds of things about me--some true, others false--I have my enemies. She has heard things already. I didn't know it till our last meeting here. There's no one else on God's earth can do what I want but you. Do you think I'm putting you into an impossible position?"

"I don't think so," said I. "Go on."

"Well--there's not much more to be said. Try to make her realise that, whatever may be my faults--my crimes, if it comes to that--I've done my damndest out there to make reparation. By God! I have," he cried, in a sudden flash of passion. "See that she realises it. And--" he thumped the hidden identification disc, "tell her that she is the only woman that has ever really mattered in the whole of my blasted life."

He threw his half-smoked cigarette into the fire-place and walked over to the sideboard, where stood decanters and syphon.

"May I help myself to a drink?"

"Certainly," said I.

He gulped down half a whisky and soda and turned on me.

"You promise?"

"Of course," said I.

"She may have reasons to think the worst of me. But whatever I am there is some good in me. I'm not altogether a worthless hound. If you promise to make her think the best of me, I'll go away happy. I don't care a damn whether I die or live. That's the truth. As long as I'm alive I can take care of myself. I'm not dreaming of asking you to say a word to win her favour. That would be outrageous impudence. You clearly understand. I don't want you ever to mention my name unless I'm dead. If I feel that I've an advocate in you--advocatus diaboli, if you like--I'll go away happy. You've got your brief. You know my life at home. You know my record."

"My dear fellow," said I, "I promise to do everything in my power to carry out your wishes. But as to your record--are you quite certain that I know it?"

You must realise that there was a curious tension in the situation, at any rate as far as it affected myself. Here was a man with whom, for reasons you know, I had studiously cultivated the most formal social relations, claiming my active participation in the secret motives of his heart. Since his first return from the front a bluff friendliness had been the keynote of our intercourse. Nothing more. Now he came and without warning enmeshed me in this intimate net of love and death. I promised to do his bidding--I could not do otherwise. I was in the position of an executor according to the terms of a last will and testament. Our comradeship in arms--those of our old Army who survive will understand--forbade refusal. Besides, his intensity of purpose won my sympathy and admiration. But I loved him none the more. To my cripple's detested sensitiveness, as he stood over me, he loomed more than ever the hulking brute. His semi-confessions and innuendoes exacerbated my feelings of distrust and repulsion. And yet, at the same tune, I could not--nor did I try to--repress an immense pity for the man; perhaps less for the man than for the soul in pain. At the back of his words some torment burned at red heat, remorselessly. He sought relief. Perhaps he sought it from me because I was as apart as a woman from his physical splendour, a kind of bodiless creature with just a brain and a human heart, the ghost of an old soldier, far away from the sphere of poor passions and little jealousies.

I felt the tentacles of the man's nature blindly and convulsively groping after something within me that eluded them. That is the best way in which I can describe the psychology of these strange moments. The morning sun streamed into my little oak-panelled dining-room and caught the silver and fruit on the breakfast table and made my frieze of old Delft glow blue like the responsive western sky. With his back to the vivid window, Leonard Boyce stood cut out black like a silhouette. That he, too, felt the tension, I know; for a wasp crawled over his face, from cheek-bone, across his temples, to his hair, and he did not notice it.

Instinctively I said the words: "Your record. Are you quite certain that I know it?"

With what intensity, with what significance in my eyes, I may have said them, I know not. I repeat that I had a subconsciousness, almost uncanny, that we were souls rather than men, talking to each other. He sat down once more, drawing the chair to the table and resting his elbow on it.

"My record," said he. "What about it?"

Again please understand that I felt I had the man's soul naked before me. An imponderable hand plucked away my garments of convention.

"Some time ago," said I, "you spoke of my attitude towards you being marked by a certain reserve. That is quite true. It dates back many years. It dates back from the South African War. From an affair at Vilboek's Farm."

Again his lips twitched; but otherwise he did not move.

"I remember," he answered. "My men saw me run away. I came out of it quite clean."

I said: "I saw the man afterwards in hospital at Cape Town. His name was Somers. He told me quite a different story."

His face grew grey. He glanced at me for a fraction of a second. "What did he tell you?" he asked quietly.

In the fewest possible words I repeated what I have set down already in this book. When I had ended, he said in the same toneless way:

"You have believed that all these years?"

"I have done my best not to believe it. The last twelve months have disproved it."

He shook his head. "They haven't. Nothing I can do in this world can disprove it. What that man said was true."

"True?"

I drew a deep breath and stared at him hard. His eyes met mine. They were very sad and behind them lay great pain. Although I expressed astonishment, it proceeded rather from some reflex action than from any realised shock to my consciousness. I say the whole thing was uncanny. I knew, as soon as he sat down by the table, that he would confess to the Vilboek story. And yet, at last, when he did confess and there were no doubts lingering in my mind, I gasped and stared at him.

"I was a bloody coward," he said. "That's frank enough. When they rode away and left me, I tried to shoot myself--and I couldn't. If the man Somers hadn't returned, I think I should have waited until they sent to arrest me. But he did come back and the instinct of self-preservation was too strong. I know my story about the men's desertion and my forcing him to back me up was vile and despicable. But I clung to life and it was my only chance. Afterwards, with the horror of the thing hanging over me, I didn't care so much about life. In the little fighting that was left for me I deliberately tried to throw it away. I ask you to believe that."

"I do," I said. "You were mentioned in dispatches for gallantry in action."

He passed his hand over his eyes. Looking up, he said:

"It is strange that you of all men, my neighbour here, should have heard of this. Not a whisper of its being known has ever reached me. How many people do you think have any idea of it?"

I told him all that I knew and concluded by showing him Reggie Dacre's letter, which I had kept in the letter-case in my pocket. He returned it to me without a word. Presently he broke a spell of silence. All this time he had sat fixed in the one attitude--only shifted once, when Marigold entered to clear away the breakfast things and was dismissed by me with a glance and a gesture.

"Do you remember," he said, "a talk we had about fear, in April, the first time I was over? I described what I knew. The paralysis of fear. Since we are talking as I never thought to talk with a human being, I may as well make my confession. I'm a man of strong animal passions. When I see red, I daresay I'm just a brute beast. But I'm a physical coward. Owing to this paralysis of fear, this ghastly inhibition of muscular or nervous action, I have gone through things even worse than that South-African business. I go about like a man under a curse. Even out there, when I don't care a damn whether I live or die, the blasted thing gets hold of me." He swung himself away from the table and shook his great clenched firsts. "By the grace of God, no one yet has seemed to notice it. I suppose I have a swift brain and as soon as the thing is over I can cover it up. It's my awful terror that one day I shall be found out and everything I've gained shall be stripped away from me."

"But what about a thing like this?" said I, tapping Colonel Dacre's letter.

"That's all right," he answered grimly. "That's when I know what I'm facing.

That's deliberate pot-hunting. It's saving face as the Chinese say. It's doing any damned thing that will put me right with myself."

He got up and swung about the room. I envied him, I would have given a thousand pounds to do the same just for a few moments. But I was stuck in my confounded chair, deprived of physical outlet. Suddenly he came to a halt and stood once more over me.

"Now you know what kind of a fellow I am, what do you think of me?"

It was a brutal question to fling at my head. It gave me no time to co-ordinate my ideas. What was one to make of a man avowedly subject to fits of the most despicable cowardice from the consequences of which he used any unscrupulous craftiness to extricate himself, and yet was notorious in his achievement of deeds of the most reckless courage? It is a problem to which I have devoted all the months occupied in waiting this book. How the dickens could I solve it at a minute's notice? The situation was too blatant, too raw, too near bedrock, too naked and unashamed, for me to take refuge in platitudinous generalities of excuse. The bravest of men know Fear. They know him pretty intimately. But they manage to kick him to Hades by the very reason of their being brave men. I had to take Leonard Boyce as I found him. And I must admit that I found him a tragically miserable man. That is how I answered his question--in so many words.

"You're not far wrong," said he.

He picked up cap and stick.

"When I get up to town I shall make my will. I've never worried about it before. Can I appoint you my executor?"

"Certainly," said I.

"I'm very grateful. I'll assure you a fireworks sort of finish, so that you shan't be ashamed. And--I don't ask impossibilities--I can't hold you to your previous promise--but what about Betty Connor?"

"You may count," said I, "on my acting like an officer and a gentleman, and, if I may say so, like a Christian."

He said: "Thank you, Meredyth. Good-bye." Then he stuck on his cap, brought his fingers to the peak in salute and marched to the door.

"Boyce!" I cried sharply.

He turned. "Yes?"

"Aren't you going to shake hands with me?"

He retraced the few steps to my chair.

"I didn't know whether it would be--" he paused, seeking for a word--"whether it would be agreeable."

Then I broke down. The strain had been too great for my sick man's nerves. I forgot all about the brutality of his bull-neck, for he faced me in all his gallant manhood and there was a damnable expression in his eyes like that of a rated dog. I stretched out my hand.

"My dear good fellow," I cried, "what the hell are you talking about?"

CHAPTER XVI

Boyce left Wellingsford that afternoon, and for many months I heard little about him. His astonishing avowal had once more turned topsy-turvy my conception of his real nature. I had to reconstruct the man, a very complicated task. I had to reconcile in him all kinds of opposites--the lusty brute and the sentimental lover; the physical coward and the baresark hero; the man with hell in his soul and the debonair gentleman. After a vast deal of pondering, I arrived not very much nearer a solution of the problem. The fact remained, however, that I found myself in far closer sympathy with him than ever before. After all that he had said, I should have had a heart of stone if it had not been stirred to profound pity. I had seen an instance both of his spell-bound cowardice and of his almost degrading craft in extrication. That in itself repelled me. But it lost its value in the light that he had cast on the never-ceasing torment that consumed him. At any rate he was at death-grips with himself, strangling the devils of fear and dishonour with a hand relentlessly certain. He appeared to me a tragic figure warring against a doom.

At first I expected every day to receive an agonised message from Mrs. Boyce announcing his death. Then, as is the way of humans, the keenness of my apprehension grew blunted, until, at last, I took his continued existence as a matter of course. I wrote him a few friendly letters, to which he replied in the same strain. And so the months went on.

Looking over my diary I find that these months were singularly uneventful as far as the lives of those dealt with in this chronicle were concerned. In the depths of our souls we felt the long-drawn-out agony of the war, with its bitter humiliations, its heartrending disappointments. In our daily meetings one with another we cried aloud for a great voice to awaken the little folk in Great Britain from their selfish lethargy--the little folk in high office, in smug burgessdom, in seditious factory and shipyard. They were months of sordid bargaining between all sections of our national life, in the murk of which the glow of patriotism seemed to be eclipsed. And in the meantime, the heroic millions from all corners of our far-flung Empire were giving their lives on land and sea, gaily and gallantly, too often in tragic futility, for the ideals to which the damnable little folk at home were blind. The little traitorous folk who gambled for their own hands in politics, the little traitorous folk who put the outworn shibboleths of a party before the war-cry of an Empire, the little traitorous folk who strove with all their power to starve our navy of ships, our ships of coal, our men in the trenches of munitions, our armies of men, our country of honour--all these will one day be mercilessly arraigned at the bar of history. The plains of France, the steeps of Gallipoli, the swamps of Mesopotamia, the Seven Seas will give up their dead as witnesses.

We spoke bitterly of all these things and thought of them with raging impotence; but the even tenor of our life went on. We continued to do our obscure and undistinguished work for the country. It became a habit, part of the day's routine. We almost forgot why we were doing it. The war seemed to make little real difference in our social life. The small town was pitch black at night. Prices rose. Small economies were practised. Labour was scarce. Fewer young men out of uniform were seen in the streets and neighbouring roads and lanes. Groups of wounded from the hospital in their uniform of deep blue jean with red ties and khaki caps gave a note of actuality to the streets. Otherwise, there were few signs of war. Even the troops who hitherto swarmed about the town had gradually been removed from billets to a vast camp of huts some miles away, and appeared only sporadically about the place. I missed them and the stimulus of their presence. They brought me into closer touch with things. Marigold, too, pined for more occupation for his one critical eye than was afforded by the local volunteers. He grew morose, sick of a surfeit of newspapers. If he could have gone to France and got through to the firing-line, I am sure he would have dug a little trench all to himself and defied the Germans on his own account.

In November Colonel Dacre was brought home gravely wounded, to a hospital for officers in London. A nurse gave me the news in a letter in which she said that he had asked to see me before an impending hazardous operation. I went up to town and found him wrecked almost beyond recognition. As we were the merest of acquaintances with nothing between us save our common link with Boyce, I feared lest he should desire to tell me of some shameful discovery. But his gay greeting and the brave smile, pathetically grotesque through the bandages in which his head was wrapped, reassured me. Only his eyes and mouth were visible.

"It's worth while being done in," said he. "It makes one feel like a Sultan. You have just to clap your hands and say 'I want this,' and you've got it. I've a good mind to say to this dear lady, 'Fetch their gracious Majesties from Buckingham Palace,' and I'm sure they'd be here in a tick. It's awfully good of you to come, Meredyth."

I signed to Marigold, who had carried me into the ward and set me down on a chair, and to the Sister, the "dear lady" of Dacre's reference, to withdraw, and after a few sympathetic words I asked him why he had sent for me.

"I'm broken to bits all over," he replied. "The doctors here say they never saw such a blooming mess-up of flesh pretending to be alive. And as for talking, they'd just as soon expect speech from a jellyfish squashed by a steam-roller. If I do get through, I'll be a helpless crock all my days. I funked it till I thought of you. I thought the sight of another fellow who has gone through it and stuck it out might give me courage. I've had my wife here. We're rather fond of one another, you know ... My God! what brave things women are! If she had broken down all over me I could have risen to the occasion. But she didn't, and I felt a cowardly worm."

"I had a brave wife, too," said I, and for a few moments we talked shyly about the women who had played sacred parts in our lives. Whether he was comforted by what I said I don't know. Probably he only listened politely. But I think he found comfort in a sympathetic ear.

Presently he turned on to Boyce, the real motive of his summons. He repented much that he had told and written to me. His long defamation of the character of a brother-officer had lain on his conscience. And lately he had, at last, met Boyce personally, and his generous heart had gone out to the man's soldierly charm.

"I never felt such a slanderous brute in my life as when I shook him by the hand. You know the feeling--how one wants to get behind a hedge and kick one-self. Kick oneself," he repeated faintly. Then he closed his eyes and his lips contracted in pain.

The Sister, who had been watching him from a distance, came up. He had talked enough. It was time to go. But at the announcement he opened his eyes again and with an effort recovered his gaiety.

"The whole gist of the matter lies in the postscript. Like a woman's letter. I must have my postscript."

"Very well. Two more minutes."

"Merciless dragon," said he.

She smiled and left us.

"The dearest angel, bar one, in the world." said he. "What were we talking about?"

"Colonel Boyce."

"Oh, yes. Forgive me. My head goes FUT now and then. It's idiotic not to be able to control one's brain.... The point is this. I may peg out. I know this operation they're going to perform is just touch and go. I want to face things with a clear conscience. I've convinced you, haven't I, that there wasn't a word of truth in that South-African story? If ever it crops up you'll scotch it like a venomous snake?"

The ethics of my answer I leave to the casuist. I am an old-fashioned Church of England person. As I am so mentally constituted that I am unable to believe cheerfully in nothing. I believe in God and Jesus Christ, and accept the details of doctrine as laid down in the Thirty-nine Articles. For liars I have the Apocryphal condemnation. Yet I lied without the faintest rippling qualm of conscience.

"My dear fellow," said I, stoutly, "there's not the remotest speck of truth in it. You haven't a second's occasion to worry."

"That's all right," he said.

The Sister approached again. Instinctively I stretched out my hand. He laughed.

"No good. You must take it as gripped. Goodbye, old chap."

I bade him good-bye and Marigold wheeled me away.

A few days afterwards they told me that this gay, gallant, honourable, sensitive gentleman was dead. Although I had known him so little, it seemed that I knew him very intimately, and I deeply mourned his loss.

I think this episode was the most striking of what I may term personal events during those autumn months.

Of Randall Holmes we continued to hear in the same mysterious manner. His mother visited the firm of solicitors in London through whom his correspondence passed. They pleaded ignorance of his doings and professional secrecy as to the disclosure of his whereabouts. In December he ceased writing altogether, and twice a week Mrs. Holmes received a formal communication from the lawyers to the effect that they had been instructed by her son to inform her that he was in perfect health and sent her his affectionate greetings. Such news of this kind as I received I gave to Betty, who passed it on to Phyllis Gedge.

Of course my intimacy with my dear Betty continued unbroken. If the unmarried Betty had a fault, it was a certain sweet truculence, a pretty self-assertiveness which sometimes betrayed intolerance of human foibles. Her widowhood had, in a subtle way, softened these little angularities of her spiritual contour. And bodily, the curves of her slim figure had become more rounded. She was no longer the young Diana of a year ago. The change into the gracious woman who had passed through the joy and the sorrow of life was obvious even to me, to whom it had been all but imperceptibly gradual. After a while she rarely spoke of her husband. The name of Leonard Boyce was never mentioned between us. With her as with me, the weeks ate up the uneventful days and the months the uneventful weeks. In her humdrum life the falling away of Mrs. Tufton loomed catastrophic.

For four months Mrs. Tufton shone splendid as the wife of the British warrior. The Wellingsford Hospital rang with her praises and glistened with her scrubbing brush. She was the Admirable Crichton of the institution. What with men going off to the war and women going off to make munitions, there were never-ending temporary gaps in the staff. And there was never a gap that Mrs. Tufton did not triumphantly fill. The pride of Betty, who had wrought this reformation, was simply monstrous. If she had created a real live angel, wings and all, out of the dust-bin, she could not have boasted more arrogantly. Being a member of the Hospital Committee, I must confess to a bemused share in the popular enthusiasm. And was I not one of the original discoverers of Mrs. Tufton? When Marigold, inspired doubtless by his wife, from time to time suggested disparagement of the incomparable woman, I rebuked him for an arrant scandal-monger. There had been a case or two of drunkenness at the hospital. Wounded soldiers had returned the worse for liquor, an almost unforgivable offence.... Not that the poor fellows desired to get drunk. A couple of pints of ale or a couple of glasses of whisky will set swimming the head of any man who has not tasted alcohol for months. But to a man with a septic wound or trench nephritis or smashed up skull, alcohol is poison and poison is death, and so it is sternly forbidden to our wounded soldiers. They cannot be served in public houses. Where, then, did the hospital defaulters get their drink?

"If I was you, sir," said Marigold, "I'd keep an eye on that there Mrs. Tufton."

I instantly annihilated him--or should have done so had his expressionless face not been made of non-inflammable timber. He said: "Very good, sir." But there was a damnably ironical and insubordinate look in his one eye.

Gradually the lady lapsed from grace. She got up late and complained of spasms. She left dustpan and brush on a patient's bed. She wrongfully interfered with the cook, insisting, until she was forcibly ejected from the kitchen, on throwing lettuces into the Irish stew. Finally, one Sunday afternoon, a policeman wandering through some waste ground, a deserted brickfield behind Flowery End, came upon an unedifying spectacle. There were madam and an elderly Irish soldier sprawling blissfully comatose with an empty flask of gin and an empty bottle of whisky lying between them. They were taken to the hospital and put to bed. The next morning, the lady, being sober, was summarily dismissed by the matron. Late at night she rang and battered at the door, clamouring for admittance, which was refused. Then she went away, apparently composed herself to slumber in the roadway of the pitch-black High Street, and was killed by a motor-car. And that, bar the funeral, was the end of Mrs. Tufton.

From her bereaved husband, with whom I at once communicated, I received the following reply:

"Dear Sir,

"Yours to hand announcing the accidental death of my wife, which I need not say I deeply regret. You will be interested to hear that I have been offered a commission in the Royal Fusiliers, which I am now able to accept. In view of the same, any expense to which you may be put to give my late wife honourable burial, I shall be most ready to defray.

"With many thanks for your kindness in informing me of this unfortunate circumstance,

"I am,
"Yours faithfully,
    "JOHN P. TUFTON."

"I think he's a horrid, callous, cold-blooded fellow!" cried Betty when I showed her this epistle.

"After all," said I, "she wasn't a model wife. If the fatal motor-car hadn't come along, the probability is that she would have received poor Tufton on his next leave with something even more deadly than a poker. Now and again the Fates have brilliant inspirations. This was one of them. Now, you see the virago-clogged Tufton is a free man, able to accept a commission and start a new life as an officer and a gentleman."

"I think you're perfectly odious. Odious and cynical," she exclaimed wrathfully.

"I think," said I, "that a living warrior is better than a dead-- Disappointment."

"You don't understand," she stormed. "If I didn't love you, I could rend you to pieces."

"It is because I do understand, my dear," said I, enjoying the flashing beauty of her return to Artemisian attitudes, "that I particularly characterised the dear lady as a disappointment."

"I think," she said, in dejected generalisation, "the working out of the whole scheme of the universe is a disappointment."

"The High Originators of the scheme seem to bear it pretty philosophically," I rejoined; "so why shouldn't we?"

"They're gods and we're human," said Betty.

"Precisely," said I. "And oughtn't it to be our ideal to approximate to the divine attitude?"

Again Betty declared that I was odious. From her point of view--No. That is an abuse of language. There are mental states in which a woman has no point of view at all. She wanders over an ill-defined circular area of vision. That is why, in such conditions, you can never pin a woman down with a shaft of logic and compel her surrender, as you can compel that of a mere man. We went on arguing, and after a time I really did not know what I was arguing about. I advanced and tried to support the theory that on the whole the progress of humanity as represented by the British Empire in general and the about-to-be Lieutenant Tufton in particular, was advanced by the opportune demise of an unfortunately balanced lady. From her point--or rather her circular area of vision--perhaps my dear Betty was right in declaring me odious. She hated to be reminded of the intolerable goosiness of her swan. She longed for comforting, corroborative evidence of essential swaniness for her own justification. In a word, the poor dear girl was sore all over with mortification, and wherever one touched her, no matter with how gentle a finger, one hurt.

"I would have trusted that woman," she cried tragically, "with a gold-mine or a distillery."

"We trusted her with something more valuable, my dear," said I. "Our guileless faith in human nature. Anyhow we'll keep the faith undamaged."

She smiled. "That's considerably less odious."

Nothing more could be said. We let the unfortunate subject rest in peace for ever after.

These two episodes, the death of poor Reggie Dacre and the Tufton catastrophe, are the only incidents in my diary that are worth recording here. Christmas came and went and we entered on the new year of 1916. It was only at a date in the middle of February, a year since I had driven to Wellings Park to hear the tragic news of Oswald Fenimore's death, that I find an important entry in my diary.

CHAPTER XVII

Mrs. Boyce was shown into my study, her comely Dresden china face very white and her hands shaking. She held a telegram. I had seen faces like that before. Every day in England there are hundreds thus stricken. I feared the worst. It was a relief to read the telegram and find that Boyce was only wounded. The message said seriously wounded, but gave consolation by adding that his life was not in immediate danger. Mrs. Boyce was for setting out for France forthwith. I dissuaded her from a project so embarrassing to the hospital authorities and so fatiguing to herself. In spite of the chivalry and humanity of our medical staff, old ladies of seventy are not welcome at a busy base hospital. As soon as he was fit to be moved, I assured her, he would be sent home, before she could even obtain her permits and passes and passport and make other general arrangements for her journey. There was nothing for it but her Englishwoman's courage. She held up her hand at that, and went away to live, like many another, patiently through the long hours of suspense.

For two or three days no news came. I spent as much time as I could with my old friend, seeking to comfort her.

On the third morning it was announced in the papers that the King had been graciously pleased to confer the Victoria Cross on Lt. Colonel Leonard Boyce for conspicuous gallantry in action. It did not occur in a list of honours. It had a special paragraph all to itself. Such isolated announcements generally indicate immediate recognition of some splendid feat. I was thrilled by the news. It was a grand achievement to win through death to the greatest of all military rewards deliberately coveted. Here, as I had strange reason for knowing, was no sudden act of sublime valour. The final achievement was the result of months of heroic, almost suicidal daring. And it was repayment of a terrible debt, the whole extent of which I knew not, owed by the man to his tormented soul.

I rang up Mrs. Boyce, who replied tremulously to my congratulations. Would I come over and lunch?

I found a very proud and tearful old lady. She may not have known the difference between a platoon and a howitzer, and have conceived the woolliest notions of the nature of her son's command, but the Victoria Cross was a matter on which her ideas were both definite and correct. She had spent the morning at the telephone receiving calls of congratulation. A great sheaf of telegrams had arrived. Two or three of them were from the High and Mighty of the Military Hierarchy. She was in such a twitter of joy that she almost forgot her anxiety as to his wounds.

"Do you think he knows? I telegraphed to him at once."

"So did I."

She glanced at the ormolu clock on the mantelpiece.

"How long would it take for a telegram to reach him?"

"You may be sure he has it by now," said I, "and it has given him a prodigious appetite for lunch."

Her face clouded over. "That horrid tinned stuff. It's so dangerous. I remember once Mary's aunt--or was it Cook's aunt--one of them any way--nearly died of eating tinned lobster--ptomaine poisoning. I've always told Leonard not to touch it."

"They don't give Colonels and V.C.s tinned lobster at Boulogne," I answered cheerfully. "He's living now on the fat of the land."

"Let us hope so," she sighed dubiously. "It's no use my sending out things for him, as they always go wrong. Some time ago I sent him three brace of grouse and three brace of partridges. He didn't acknowledge them for weeks, and then he said they were most handy things to kill Germans with, but were an expensive form of ammunition. I don't quite know what he meant--but at any rate they were not eatable when they arrived. Poor fellow!" She sighed again. "If only I knew what was the matter with him."

"It can't be much," I reassured her, "or you would have heard again. And this news will act like a sovereign remedy."

She patted the back of my hand with her plump palm. "You're always so sympathetic and comforting."

"I'm an old soldier, like Leonard," said I, "and never meet trouble halfway."

At lunch, the old lady insisted on opening a bottle of champagne, a Veuve Clicquot which Leonard loved, in honour of the glorious occasion. We could not drink to the hero's health in any meaner vintage, although she swore that a teaspoonful meant death to her, and I protested that a confession of champagne to my medical adviser meant a dog's rating. We each, conscience-bound, put up the tips of our fingers to the glasses as soon as Mary had filled them with froth, and solemnly drank the toast in the eighth of an inch residuum. But by some freakish chance or the other, there was nothing left in that quart bottle by the time Mary cleared the table for dessert. And to tell the honest truth, I don't think the health of either my hostess or myself was a penny the worse. Let no man despise generous wine. Treated with due reverence it is a great loosener of human sympathy.

Generous ale similarly treated produces the same effect. Marigold, driving me home, cocked a luminous eye on me and said:

"Begging your pardon, sir, would you mind very much if I broke the neck of that there Gedge?"

"You would be aiding the good cause," said I, "but I should deplore the hanging of an old friend. What has Gedge been doing?"

Marigold sounded his horn and slowed down round a bend, and, as soon as he got into a straight road, he replied.

"I'm not going to say, sir, if I may take the liberty, that I was ever sweet on Colonel Boyce. People affect you in different ways. You either like 'em or you don't like 'em. You can't tell why. And a Sergeant, being, as you may say, a human being, has as much right to his private feelings regarding a Colonel as any officer."

"Undoubtedly," said I.

"Well, sir, I never thought Colonel Boyce was true metal. But I take it all back--every bit of it."

"For God's sake," I cried, stretching out a foolish but instinctive hand to the wheel, "for God's sake, control your emotions, or you'll be landing us in the ditch."

"That's all right, sir," he replied, steering a straight course. "She's a bit skittish at times. I was saying as how I did the Colonel an injustice. I'm very sorry. No man who wasn't steel all through ever got the V.C. They don't chuck it around on blighters."

"That's all very interesting and commendable," said I, "but what has it to do with Gedge?"

"He has been slandering the Colonel something dreadful the last few months, sneering at him, saying nothing definite, but insinuatingly taking away his character."

"In what way?" I asked.

"Well, he tells one man that the Colonel's a drunkard, another that it's women, another that he gambles and doesn't pay, another that he pays the newspapers to put in all these things about him, while all the time in France he's in a blue funk hiding in his dugout."

"That's moonshine," said I. And as regards the drinking, drabbing, and gaming of course it was. But the suggestion of cowardice gave me a sharp stab of surprise and dismay.

"I know it is," said Marigold. "But the people hereabouts are so ignorant, you can make them believe anything." Marigold was a man of Kent and had a poor opinion of those born and bred in other counties. "I met Gedge this morning," he continued, and thereupon gave me the substance of the conversation. I hardly think the adjectives of the report were those that were really used.

"So your precious Colonel has got the V.C.," sneered Gedge.

"He has," said Marigold. "And it's too great an honour for your inconsiderable town."

"If this inconsiderable town knew as much about him as I do, it would give him the order of the precious boot."

"And what do you know?" asked Marigold.

"That's what all you downtrodden slaves of militarism would like to find out," replied Gedge. "The time will come when I, and such as I, will tear the veils away and expose them, and say 'These be thy gods, O Israel.'"

"The time will come," retorted Marigold, "when if you don't hold your precious jaw, I and such as I will smash it into a thousand pieces. For twopence I'd knock your ugly head off this present minute."

Whereupon Gedge apparently wilted before the indignant eye of Sergeant Marigold and faded away down the High Street.

All this in itself seemed very trivial, but for the past year the attitude of Gedge had been mysterious. Could it be possible that Gedge thought himself the sole repository of the secret which Boyce had so desperately confided to me? But when had the life of Gedge and the military life of Leonard Boyce crossed? It was puzzling.

Well, to tell the truth, I thought no more about the matter. The glow of Mrs. Boyce's happiness remained with me all the evening. Rarely had I seen her so animated, so forgetful of her own ailments. She had taken the rosiest view of Leonard's physical condition and sunned herself in the honour conferred on him by the King. I had never spent a pleasanter afternoon at her house. We had comfortably criticised our neighbours, and, laudatores temporis acti, had extolled the days of our youth. I went to bed as well pleased with life as a man can be in this convulsion of the world.

The next morning she sent me a letter to read. It was written at Boyce's dictation. It ran:

"Dear Mother:

"I'm sorry to say I am knocked out pro tem. I was fooling about where a C.O. didn't ought to, and a Bosch bullet got me so that I can't write. But don't worry at all about me. I'm too tough for anything the Bosches can do. To show how little serious it is, they tell me that I'll be conveyed to England in a day or two. So get hot-water bottles and bath salts ready.

"Your ever loving Leonard."

This was good news. Over the telephone wire we agreed that the letter was a justification of our yesterday's little merrymaking. Obviously, I told her, he would live to fight another day. She was of opinion that he had done enough fighting already. If he went on much longer, the poor boy would get quite tired out, to say nothing of the danger of being wounded again. The King ought to let him rest on his laurels and make others who hadn't worked a quarter as hard do the remainder of the war.

"Perhaps," I said light-heartedly, "Leonard will drop the hint when he writes to thank the King for the nice cross."

She said that I was laughing at her, and rang off in the best of spirits.

In the evening came Betty, inviting herself to dinner. She had been on night duty at the hospital, and I had not seen her for some days. The sight of her, bright-eyed and brave, fresh and young, always filled me with happiness. I felt her presence like wine and the sea wind and the sunshine. So greatly did her vitality enrich me, that sometimes I called myself a horrid old vampire.

As soon as she had greeted me, she said in her downright way:

"So Leonard Boyce has got his V.C."

"Yes," said I. "What do you think of it?"

A spot of colour rose to her cheek. "I'm very glad. It's no use, Majy, pretending that I ignore his existence. I don't and I can't. Because I loved and married someone else doesn't alter the fact that I once cared for him, does it?"

"Many people," said I, judicially, "find out that they have been mistaken as to the extent and nature of their own sentiments."

"I wasn't mistaken," she replied, sitting down on the piano stool, her hands on the leathern seat, her neatly shod feet stretched out in front of her, just as she had sat on her wedding eve talking nonsense to Willie Connor. "I wasn't mistaken. I was never addicted to silly school-girl fancies. I know my own mind. I cared a lot for Leonard Boyce."

"Eh bien?" said I.

"Well, don't you see what I'm driving at?"

"I don't a bit."

She sighed. "Oh, dear! How dull some people are! Don't you see that, when an affair like that is over, a woman likes to get some evidence of the man's fine qualities, in order to justify her for having once cared for him?"

"Quite so. Yet--" I felt argumentative. The breach, as you know, between Betty and Boyce was wrapped in exasperating obscurity. "Yet, on the other hand," said I, "she might welcome evidence of his worthlessness, so as to justify her for having thrown him over."

"If a woman isn't a dam-fool already," said Betty, "and I don't think I'm one, she doesn't like to feel that she ever made a dam-fool of herself. She is proud of her instincts and her judgments and the sensitive, emotional intelligence that is hers. When all these seem to have gone wrong, it's pleasing to realise that originally they went right. It soothes one's self-respect, one's pride. I know now that all these blind perceptions in me went straight to certain magnificent essentials--those that make the great, strong, fearless fighting man. That's attractive to a woman, you know. At any rate, to an independent barbarian like myself--"

"My dear Betty," I interrupted with a laugh. "You a barbarian? You whom I regard as the last word, the last charming and delightful word, in modern womanhood?"

"Of course I'm the child of my century," she cried, flushing. "I want votes, freedom, opportunity for expansion, power--everything that can develop Betty Connor into a human product worthy of the God who made her. But how she could fulfil herself without the collaboration of a man, has baffled her ever since she was a girl of sixteen, when she began to awake to the modern movement. On one side I saw women perfectly happy in the mere savage state of wifehood and motherhood, and not caring a hang for anything else, and on the other side women who threw babies back into limbo and preached of nothing but intellectual and political and economic independence. Oh, I worried terribly about it, Majy, when I was a girl. Each side seemed to have such a lot to say for itself. Then it dawned upon me that the only way out of the dilemma was to combine both ideals--that of the savage woman in skins and the lady professor in spectacles. That is what, allowing for the difference of sex, a man does. Why shouldn't a woman? The woman, of course, has to droop a bit more to the savage, because she has to produce the babies and suckle them, and so forth, and a man hasn't. That was my philosophy of life when I entered the world as a young woman. Love came into it, of course. It was a sanctification of the savagery. I've gone on like this," she laughed, "because I don't want you to protest in your dear old-fashioned way against my calling myself an independent barbarian. I am, and I glory in it. That's why, as I was saying, I'm deeply glad that Leonard Boyce has made good. His honour means a good deal to me--to my self-esteem. I hope," she added, rising and coming to me with a caressing touch. "I hope you've got the hang of the thing now."

Within myself I sincerely hoped I had. If her sentiments were just as she analysed them, all was well. If, on the other hand, the little demon of love for Boyce still lurked in her heart, in spite of the marriage and widowhood, there might be trouble ahead. I remembered how once she had called him a devil. I remembered, too, uncomfortably, the scrap of conversation I had overheard between Boyce and herself in the hall. She had lashed him with her scorn, and he had taken his whipping without much show of fight. Still, a woman's love, especially that of a lady barbarian, was a curiously complex affair, and had been known to impel her to trample on a man one minute and the next to fall at his feet. Now the worm she had trampled on had turned; stood erect as a properly authenticated hero. I felt dubious as to the ensuing situation.

"I wrote to old Mrs. Boyce," she added after a while. "I thought it only decent. I wrote yesterday, but only posted the letter to-day, so as to be sure I wasn't acting on impulse."

The latter part of the remark was by way of apology. The breach of the engagement had occasioned a cessation of social relations between Betty and Mrs. Boyce. Betty's aunts had ceased calling on Mrs. Boyce and Mrs. Boyce had ceased calling on Betty's aunts. Whenever the estranged parties met, which now and then was inevitable in a little town, they bowed with distant politeness, but exchanged no words. Everything was conducted with complete propriety. The old lady, knowing how beloved an intimate of mine was Betty, alluded but once to the broken engagement.

That was when Betty got married.

"It has been a great unhappiness to me, Major," she said. "In spite of her daring ways, which an old woman like myself can't quite understand, I was very fond of her. She was just the girl for Leonard. They made such a handsome couple. I have never known why it was broken off. Leonard won't tell me. It's out of the question that it could be his fault, and I can't believe it is all Betty Fairfax's. She's a girl of too much character to be a mere jilt."

I remember that I couldn't help smiling at the application of the old-fashioned word to my Betty.

"You may be quite certain she isn't that," said I.

"Then what was the reason? Do you know?"

I didn't. I was as mystified as herself. I told her so. I didn't mention that a few days before she had implied that Leonard was a devil and she wished that he was dead, thereby proving to me, who knew Betty's uprightness, that Boyce and Boyce only was to blame in the matter. It would have been a breach of confidence, and it would not have made my old friend any the happier. It would have fired her with flaming indignation against Betty.

"Young people," said I, "must arrange their own lives." And we left it at that. Now and then, afterwards, she enquired politely after Betty's health, and when Willie Connor was killed, she spoke to me very feelingly and begged me to convey to Betty the expression of her deep sympathy. In the unhappy circumstances, she explained, she was naturally precluded from writing.

So Betty's letter was the first direct communication that had passed between them for nearly two years. That is why to my meddlesome-minded self it appeared to have some significance.

"You did, did you?" said I. Then I looked at her quickly, with an idea in my head. "What did Mrs. Boyce say in reply?"

"She has had no time to answer. Didn't I tell you I only posted the letter to-day?"

"Then you've heard nothing more about Leonard Boyce except that he has got the V.C.?"

"No. What more is there to hear?"

Even Bettys are sly folk. It behooved me to counter with equal slyness. I wondered whether she had known all along of Boyce's mishap, or had been informed of it by his mother. Knowledge might explain her unwonted outburst. I looked at her fixedly.

"What's the matter?" she asked, bending slightly down to me.

"You haven't heard that he is wounded?"

She straightened herself. "No. When?"

"Five days ago."

"Why didn't you tell me?"

"I haven't seen you."

"I mean--this evening."

I reached for her hand. "Will you forgive me, my dear Betty, for remarking that for the last twenty minutes you have done all the talking?"

"Is he badly hurt?"

She ignored my playful rejoinder. I noted the fact. Usually she was quick to play Beatrice to my Benedick. Had I caught her off her guard?

I told her all that I knew. She seated herself again on the piano-stool.

"I hope Mrs. Boyce did not think me unfeeling for not referring to it," she said calmly. "You will explain, won't you?"

Marigold entered, announcing dinner. We went into the dining-room. All through the meal Bella, my parlour-maid, flitted about with dishes and plates, and Marigold, when he was not solemnly pouring claret, stood grim behind my chair, roasting, as usual, his posterior before a blazing fire, with soldierly devotion to duty. Conversation fell a little flat. The arrival of the evening newspapers, half an hour belated, created a diversion. The war is sometimes subversive of nice table decorum. I read out the cream of the news. Discussion thereon lasted us until coffee and cigarettes were brought in and the servants left us to ourselves.

One of the curious little phenomena of human intercourse is the fact that now and again the outer personality of one with whom you are daily familiar suddenly strikes you afresh, thus printing, as it were, a new portrait on your mind. At varying intervals I had received such portrait impressions of Betty, and I had stored them in my memory. Another I received at this moment, and it is among the most delectable. She was sitting with both elbows on the table, her palms clasped and her cheek resting on the back of the left hand. Her face was turned towards me.

She wore a low-cut black chiffon evening dress--the thing had mere straps over the shoulders--an all but discarded vanity of pre-war days. I had never before noticed what beautiful arms she had. Perhaps in her girlhood, when I had often seen her in such exiguous finery, they had not been so shapely. I have told you already of the softening touch of her womanhood. An exquisite curve from arm to neck faded into the shadow of her hair. She had a single string of pearls round her neck. The fatigue of last week's night duty had cast an added spirituality over her frank, sensitive face.

We had not spoken for a while. She smiled at me.

"What are you thinking of?"

"I wasn't thinking at all," said I. "I was only gratefully admiring you."

"Why gratefully?"

"Oughtn't one to be grateful to God for the beautiful things He gives us?"

She flushed and averted her eyes. "You are very good to me, Majy."

"What made you attire yourself in all this splendour?" I asked, laughing. The wise man does not carry sentiment too far. He keeps it like a little precious nugget of pure gold; the less wise beats it out into a flabby film.

"I don't know," she said, shifting her position and casting a critical glance at her bodice. "All kinds of funny little feminine vanities. Perhaps I wanted to see whether I hadn't gone off. Perhaps I wanted to try to feel good-looking even if I wasn't. Perhaps I thought my dear old Majy was sick to death of the hospital uniform perfumed with disinfectant. Perhaps it was just a catlike longing for comfort. Anyhow, I'm glad you like me."

"My dear Betty," said I, "I adore you."

"And I you," she laughed. "So there's a pair of us."

She lit a cigarette and sipped her coffee. Then, breaking a short silence:

"I hope you quite understand, dear, what I said about Leonard Boyce. I shouldn't like to leave you with the smallest little bit of a wrong impression."

"What wrong impression could I possibly have?" I asked disingenuously.

"You might think that I was still in love with him."

"That would be absurd," said I.

"Utterly absurd. I should feel it to be almost an insult if you thought anything of the kind. Long before my marriage things that had happened had killed all such feelings outright." She paused for a few seconds and her brow darkened, just as it had done when she had spoken of him in the days immediately preceding her marriage with Willie Connor. Presently it cleared. "The whole beginning and end of my present feelings," she continued, "is that I'm glad the man I once cared for has won such high distinction, and I'm sorry that such a brave soldier should be wounded."

I could do nothing else than assure her of my perfect understanding. I upbraided myself as a monster of indelicacy for my touch of doubt before dinner; also for a devilish and malicious suspicion that flitted through my brain while she was cataloguing her possible reasons for putting on the old evening dress. The thought of Betty's beautiful arm and the man's bull-neck was a shivering offence. I craved purification.

"If you've finished your coffee," I said, "let us go into the drawing-room and have some music."

She rose with the impulsiveness of a child told that it can be excused, and responded startlingly to my thought.

"I think we need it," she said.

In the drawing-room I swung my chair so that I could watch her hands on the keys. She was a good musician and had the well-taught executant's certainty and grace of movement. It may be the fancy of an outer Philistine, but I love to forget the existence of the instrument and to feel the music coming from the human finger-tips. She found a volume of Chopin's Nocturnes on the rest. In fact she had left it there a fortnight before, the last time she had played for me. I am very fond of Chopin. I am an uneducated fellow and the lyrical mostly appeals to me both in poetry and in music. Besides, I have understood him better since I have been a crock. And I loved Betty's sympathetic interpretation. So I sat there, listening and watching, and I knew that she was playing for the ease of both our souls. Once more I thanked God for the great gift of Betty to my crippled life. Peace gathered round my heart as Betty played.

The raucous buzz of the telephone in the corner of the room knocked the music to shatters. I cried out impatiently. It was the fault of that giant of ineptitude Marigold and his incompetent satellites, whose duty it was to keep all upstairs extensions turned off and receive calls below. Only two months before I had been the victim of their culpable neglect, when I was forced to have an altercation with a man at Harrod's Stores, who seemed pained because I declined to take an interest in some idiotic remark he was making about fish.

"I'll strangle Marigold with my own hands," I cried.

Betty, unmoved by my ferocity, laughed and rose from the piano.

"Shall I take the call?"

To Betty I was all urbanity. "If you'll be so kind, dear," said I.

She crossed the room and stopped the abominable buzzing.

"Yes. Hold on for a minute. It's the post-office"--she turned to me--"telephoning a telegram that has just come in. Shall I take it down for you?"

More urbanity on my part. She found pencil and paper on an escritoire near by, and went back to the instrument. For a while she listened and wrote. At last she said:

"Are you sure there's no signature?"

She got the reply, waited until the message had been read over, and hung up the receiver. When she came round to me--my back had been half turned to her all the time--I was astonished to see her looking rather shaken. She handed me the paper without a word.

The message ran:

"Thanks yesterday's telegram. Just got home. Queen Victoria Hospital, Belton Square. Must have talk with you before I communicate with my mother. Rely absolutely on your discretion. Come to-morrow. Forgive inconvenience caused, but most urgent."

"It's from Boyce," I said, looking up at her.

"Naturally."

"I suppose he omitted the signature to avoid any possible leakage through the post-office here."

She nodded. "What do you think is the matter?"

"God knows," said I. "Evidently something very serious."

She went back to the piano seat. "It's odd that I should have taken down that message," she said, after a while.

"I'll sack Marigold for putting you in that abominable position," I exclaimed wrathfully.

"No, you won't, dear. What does it signify? I'm not a silly child. I suppose you're going to-morrow?"

"Of course--for Mrs. Boyce's sake alone I should have no alternative."

She turned round and began to take up the thread of the Nocturne from the point where she had left off; but she only played half a page and quitted the piano abruptly.

"The pretty little spell is broken, Majy. No matter how we try to escape from the war, it is always shrieking in upon us. We're up against naked facts all the time. If we can't face them we go under either physically or spiritually. Anyhow--" she smiled with just a little touch of weariness,--"we may as well face them in comfort."

She pushed my chair gently nearer to the fire and sat down by my side. And there we remained in intimate silence until Marigold announced the arrival of her car.

CHAPTER XVIII

I shrink morbidly from visiting strange houses. I shrink from the unknown discomforts and trivial humiliations they may hold for me. I hate, for instance, not to know what kind of a chair may be provided for me to sit on. I hate to be carried up many stairs even by my steel-crane of a Marigold. Just try doing without your legs for a couple of days, and you will see what I mean. Of course I despise myself for such nervous apprehensions, and do not allow them to influence my actions--just as one, under heavy fire, does not satisfy one's simple yearning to run away. I would have given a year's income to be able to refuse Boyce's request with a clear conscience; but I could not. I shrank all the more because my visit in the autumn to Reggie Dacre had shaken me more than I cared to confess. It had been the only occasion for years when I had entered a London building other than my club. To the club, where I was as much at home as in my own house, all those in town with whom I now and then had to transact business were good enough to come. This penetration of strange hospitals was an agitating adventure. Apart, however, from the mere physical nervousness against which, as I say, I fought, there was another element in my feelings with regard to Boyce's summons. If I talk about the Iron Hand of Fate you may think I am using a cliche of melodrama. Perhaps I am. But it expresses what I mean. Something unregenerate in me, some lingering atavistic savage instinct towards freedom, rebelled against this same Iron Hand of Fate that, first clapping me on the shoulder long ago in Cape Town, was now dragging me, against my will, into ever thickening entanglement with the dark and crooked destiny of Leonard Boyce.

I tell you all this because I don't want to pose as a kind of apodal angel of mercy.

I was also deadly anxious as to the nature of the communication Boyce would make to me, before his mother should be informed of his arrival in London. In spite of his frank confession, there was still such a cloud of mystery over the man's soul as to render any revelation possible. Had his hurt declared itself to be a mortal one? Had he summoned me to unburden his conscience while yet there was time? Was it going to be a repetition, with a difference, of my last interview with Reggie Dacre? I worried myself with unnecessary conjecture.

After a miserable drive through February rain and slush, I reached my destination in Belton Square, a large mansion, presumably equipped by its owner as a hospital for officers, and given over to the nation. A telephone message had prepared the authorities for my arrival. Marigold, preceded by the Sister in charge, carried me across a tesselated hall and began to ascend the broad staircase.

I uttered a little gasp and looked around me, for in a flash I realised where I was. Twenty years ago I had danced in this house. I had danced here with my wife before we were married. On the half landing we had sat out together. It was the town house of the late Lord Madelow, with whose wife I shared the acquaintance of a couple of hundred young dancing men inscribed on her party list. Both were dead long since. To whom the house belonged now I did not know. But I recognised pictures and statuary and a conservatory with palms. And the place shimmered with brilliant ghosts and was haunted by hot perfumes and by the echo of human voices and by elfin music. And the cripple forgot that he was being carried up the stairs in the grip of the old soldier. He was mounting them with heart beating high and the presence of a beloved hand on his arm.... You see, it was all so sudden. It took my breath away and sent my mind whirling back over twenty years.

It was like awaking from a dream to find a door flung open in front of me and to hear the Sister announce my name. I was on the threshold not of a ward, but of a well-appointed private room fairly high up and facing the square, for the first thing I saw was the tops of the leafless trees through the windows. Then I was conscious of a cheery fire. The last thing I took in was the bed running at right angles to door and window, and Leonard Boyce lying in it with bandages about his face. For the dazed second or two he seemed to be Reggie Dacre over again. But he had thrown back the bedclothes and his broad chest and great arms were free. His pleasant voice rang out at once.

"Hallo! Hallo! You are a good Samaritan. Is that you, Marigold? There's a comfortable chair by the bedside for Major Meredyth."

He seemed remarkably strong and hearty; far from any danger of death. Stubs of cigarettes were lying in an ash-tray on the bed. In a moment or two they settled me down and left me alone with him.

As soon as he heard the click of the door he said:

"I've done more than I set out to do. You remember our conversation. I said I should either get the V.C. or never see you again. I've managed both."

"What do you mean?" I asked.

"I shall never see you or anybody else again, or a dog or a cat, or a tree or a flower."

Then, for the first time the dreadful truth broke upon me.

"Good Heavens!" I cried. "Your eyes--?"

"Done in. Blind. It's a bit ironical, isn't it?" He laughed bitterly.

What I said by way of sympathy and consolation is neither here nor there. I spoke sincerely from my heart, for I felt overwhelmed by the tragedy of it all. He stretched out his hand and grasped mine.

"I knew you wouldn't fail me. Your sort never does. You understand now why I wanted you to come?--To prepare the old mother for the shock. You've seen for yourself that I'm sound of wind and limb--as fit as a fiddle. You can make it quite clear to her that I'm not going to die yet awhile. And you can let her down easy on the real matter. Tell her I'm as merry as possible and looking forward to going about Wellingsford with a dog and string."

"You're a brave chap, Boyce," I said.

He laughed again. "You're anticipating. Do you remember what I said when you asked me what I should do if I won all the pots I set my heart on and came through alive? I said I should begin to try to be a brave man. God! It's a tough proposition. But it's something to live for, anyway."

I asked him how it happened.

"I got sick," he replied, "of bearing a charmed life and nothing happening. The Bosch shell or bullet that could hit me wasn't made. I could stroll about freely where it was death for anyone else to show the top of his head. I didn't care. Then suddenly one day things went wrong. You know what I mean. I nearly let my regiment down. It was touch and go. And it was touch and go with my career. I just pulled through, however. I'll tell you all about it one of these days--if you'll put up with me."

Again the familiar twitch of the lips which looked ghastly below the bandaged eyes. "No one ever dreamed of the hell I went through. Then I found I was losing the nerve I had built up all these months. I nearly went off my head. At last I thought I would put an end to it. It was a small attack of ours that had failed. The men poured back over the parapet into the trench, leaving heaven knows how many dead and wounded outside. I'm not superstitious and I don't believe in premonitions and warnings, and so forth; but in cases of waiting like mine a man suddenly gets to know that his hour has come.... I got in six wounded. Two men were shot while I was carrying them. How I lived God knows. It was cold hell. My clothes were torn to rags. As I was going for the seventh, the knob of my life-preserver was shot away and my wrist nearly broken. I wore it with a strap, you know. The infernal thing had been a kind of mascot. When I realised it was gone I just stood still and shivered in a sudden, helpless funk. The seventh man was crawling up to me. He had a bloody face and one dragging leg. That's my last picture of God's earth. Before I could do anything--I must have been standing sideways on--a bullet got me across the bridge of the nose and night came down like a black curtain. Then I ran like a hare. Sometimes I tripped over a man, dead or wounded, and fell on my head. I don't remember much about this part of it. They told me afterwards. At last I stumbled on to the parapet and some plucky fellow got me into the trench. It was the regulation V.C. business," he added, "and so they gave it to me."

"Specially," said I.

"Consolation prize, I suppose, for losing my sight. They had just time to get me away behind when the Germans counter attacked. If I hadn't brought the six men in, they wouldn't have had a dog's chance. I did save their lives. That's something to the credit side of the infernal balance."

"There can be no balance now, my dear chap," said I. "God knows you've paid in full."

He lifted his hand and dropped it with a despairing gesture.

"There's only one payment in full. That was denied me. God, or whoever was responsible, had my eyes knocked out, and made it impossible for ever. He or somebody must be enjoying the farce."

"That's all very well," said I. "A man can do no more than his utmost--as you've done. He must be content to leave the rest in the hands of the Almighty."

"The Almighty has got a down on me," he replied. "And I don't blame Him. Of course, from your point of view, you're right. You're a normal, honourable soldier and gentleman. Anything you've got to reproach yourself with is of very little importance. But I'm an accursed freak. I told you all about it when you held me up over the South African affair. There were other affairs after that. Others again in this war. Haven't I just told you I let my regiment down?"

"Don't, my dear man, don't!" I cried, in great pain, for it was horrible to hear a man talk like this. "Can't you see you've wiped out everything?"

"There's one thing at any rate I can't ever wipe out," he said in a low voice. Then he laughed. "I've got to stick it. It may be amusing to see how it all pans out. I suppose the very last passion left us is curiosity."

"There's also the unconquerable soul," said I.

"You're very comforting," said he. "If I were in your place, I'd leave a chap like me to the worms." He drew a long breath. "I suppose I'll pull through all right."

"Of course you will," said I.

"I feel tons better, thanks to you, already."

"That's right," said I.

He fumbled for the box of cigarettes on the bed. Instinctively I tried to help him, but I was tied to my fixed chair. It was a trivial occasion; but I have never been so terrified by the sense of helplessness. Just think of it. Two men of clear brain and, to all intents and purposes, of sound bodily health, unable to reach an object a few feet away. Boyce uttered an impatient exclamation.

"Get hold of that box for me, like a good chap," he said, his fingers groping wide of the mark.

"I can't move," said I.

"Good Lord! I forgot."

He began to laugh. I laughed, too. We laughed like fools and the tears ran down my cheeks. I suppose we were on the verge of hysterics.

I pulled myself together and gave him a cigarette from my case. And then, stretch as I would, I could not reach far enough to apply the match to the end of the cigarette between his lips. He was unable to lift his head. I lit another match and, like an idiot, put it between his fingers. He nearly burned his moustache and his bandage, and would have burned his fingers had not the match--a wooden one--providentially gone out. Then I lit a cigarette myself and handed it to him.

The incident, as I say, was trivial, but it had deep symbolic significance. All symbols in their literal objectivity are trivial. What more trivial than the eating of a bit of bread and the sipping from a cup of wine? This trumpery business with the cigarette revolutionised my whole feelings towards Boyce. It initiated us into a sacred brotherhood. Hitherto, it had been his nature which had reached out towards me tentacles of despair. My inner self, as I have tried to show you, had never responded. It was restrained by all kinds of doubts, suspicions, and repulsions. Now, suddenly, it broke through all those barriers and rushed forth to meet him. My death in life against which I had fought, I hope like a brave man (it takes a bit of fighting) for many years, would henceforth be his death in life, at whose terrors he too would have to snap a disdainful finger. I had felt deep pity for him; but if pity is indeed akin to love, it is a very poor relation. Now I had cast pity and such like superior sentiment aside and accepted him as a sworn brother. The sins, whatever they were, that lay on the man's conscience mattered nothing. He had paid in splendid penance and in terrible penalty.

I should have liked to express to him something of this surge of emotion. But I could find no words. As a race, our emotions are not facile, and therefore we lack the necessary practice in expressing them. When they do come, they come all of a heap and scare us out of our wits and leave us speechless. So the immediate outcome of all this psychological upheaval was that we went on smoking and said nothing more about it. As far as I remember we started talking about the recruiting muddle, as to which our views most vigorously coincided.

We parted cheerily. It was only when I got outside the room that the ghastly irony of the situation again made my heart as lead. We passed by the conservatory and the statuary and down the great staircase, but the ghosts had gone. Yet I cast a wistful glance at the spot--it was just under that Cuyp with the flashing white horse--where we had sat twenty years ago. But the new tragedy had rendered the memory less poignant.

"It's a dreadful thing about the Colonel, sir," said Marigold as we drove off.

"More dreadful than anyone can imagine," said I.

"What he's going to do with himself is what I'm wondering," said Marigold.

What indeed? The question went infinitely deeper than the practical dreams of Marigold's philosophy. My honest fellow saw but the outside--the full-blooded man of action cabined in his lifelong darkness. I, to whom chance had revealed more, trembled at the contemplation of his future. The man, goaded by the Furies, had rushed into the jaws of death. Those jaws, by some divine ordinance, had ruthlessly closed against him. The Furies meanwhile attended him unrelenting. Whither now would they goad him? Into madness? I doubted it. In spite of his contradictory nature, he did not seem to be the sort of man who would go mad. He could exercise over himself too reasoned a control. Yet here were passions and despairs seething without an outlet. What would be the end? It is true that he had achieved glory. To the end of his life, wherever he went, he would command the honour and admiration of men. Greater achievement is granted to few mortals. In our little town he would be the Great Hero. But would all that human sympathy and veneration could contrive keep the Furies at bay and soothe the tormented spirit?

I tried to eat a meal at the club, but the food choked me. I got into the car as soon as possible and reached Wellingsford with head and heart racked with pain. But before I could go home I had to execute Boyce's mission.

If I accomplished it successfully, my heart and not my wearied mind deserves the credit. At first Mrs. Boyce broke down under the shock of the news, for all the preparation in the world can do little to soften a deadly blow; but breed and pride soon asserted themselves, and she faced things bravely. With charming dignity she received Marigold's few respectful words of condolence. And she thanked me for what I had done, beyond my deserts. To show how brave she was, she insisted on accompanying us downstairs and on standing in the bleak evening air while Marigold put me in the car.

"After all, I have my son alive and in good strong health. I must realise how merciful God has been to me." She put her hand into mine. "I shan't see you again till I bring him home with me. I shall go up to London early to-morrow morning and stay with my old friend Lady Fanshawe--I think you have met her here--the widow of the late Admiral Fanshawe. She has a house in Eccleston Street, which is, I think, in the neighbourhood of Belton Square. If I haven't thanked you enough, dear Major Meredyth, it is that, when one's heart is full, one can't do everything all at once."

She waved to me very graciously as the car drove off--a true "Spartian" mother, dear lady, of our modern England.

Oh! the humiliation of possessing a frail body and a lot of disorganized nerves! When I got home Marigold, seeing that I was overtired, was all for putting me to bed then and there. I spurned the insulting proposal in language plain enough even to his wooden understanding. Sometimes his imperturbability exasperated me. I might just as well try to taunt a poker or sting a fire-shovel into resentment of personal abuse.

"I'll see you hanged, drawn, and quartered before I'll go to bed," I declared.

"Very good, sir." The gaunt wretch was carrying me. "But I think you might lie down for half an hour before dinner."

He deposited me ignominiously on the bed and left the room. In about ten minutes Dr. Cliffe, my inveterate adversary who has kept life in me for many a year, came in with his confounded pink smiling face.

"What's this I hear? Been overdoing it?"

"What the deuce are you doing here?" I cried. "Go away. How dare you come when you're not wanted?"

He grinned. "I'm wanted right enough, old man. The good Marigold's never at fault. He rang me up and I slipped round at once."

"One of these days," said I, "I'll murder that fellow."

He replied by gagging me with his beastly thermometer. Then he felt my pulse and listened to my heart and stuck his fingers into the corners of my eyes, so as to look at the whites; and when he was quite satisfied with himself--there is only one animal more self-complacent than your medical man in such circumstances, and that is a dog who has gorged himself with surreptitious meat--he ordained that I should forthwith go properly to bed and stay there and be perfectly quiet until he came again, and in the meanwhile swallow some filthy medicine which he would send round.

"One of these days," said he, rebukingly, "instead of murdering your devoted Sergeant, you'll be murdering yourself, if you go on such lunatic excursions. Of course I'm shocked at hearing about Colonel Boyce, and I'm sorry for the poor lady, but why you should have been made to half kill yourself over the matter is more than I can understand."

"I happen," said I, "to be his only intimate friend in the place."

"You happen," he retorted, "to be a chronic invalid and the most infernal worry of my life."

"You're nothing but an overbearing bully," said I.

He grinned again. That is what I have to put up with. If I curse Marigold, he takes no notice. If I curse Cliffe, he grins. Yet what I should do without them, Heaven only knows.

"God bless 'em both," said I, when my aching body was between the cool sheets.

Although it was none of his duties, Marigold brought me in a light supper, fish and a glass of champagne. Never a parlour-maid would he allow to approach me when I was unwell. I often wondered what would happen if I were really ill and required the attendance of a nurse. I swear no nurse's touch could be so gentle as when he raised me on the pillows. He bent over the tray on the table by the bed and began to dissect out the back-bone of the sole.

"I can do that," said I, fretfully.

He cocked a solitary reproachful eye on me. I burst out laughing. He looked so dear and ridiculous with his preposterous curly wig and his battered face. He went on with his task.

"I wonder, Marigold," said I, "how you put up with me."

He did not reply until he had placed the neatly arranged tray across my body.

"I've never heard, sir," said he, "as how a man couldn't put up with his blessings."

A bit of sole was on my fork and I was about to convey it to my mouth, but there came a sudden lump in my throat and I put the fork down.

"But what about the curses?"

A horrible contortion of the face and a guttural rumble indicated amusement on the part of Marigold. I stared, very serious, having been profoundly touched.

"What are you laughing at?" I asked.

The idiot's merriment increased in vehemence. He said: "You're too funny, sir," and just bolted, in a manner unbecoming not only to a sergeant, but even to a butler.

As I mused on this unprecedented occurrence, I made a discovery,--that of Sergeant Marigold's sense of humour. To that sense of humour my upbraidings, often, I must confess, couched in picturesque and figurative terms so as not too greatly to hurt his feelings, had made constant appeal for the past fifteen years. Hitherto he had hidden all signs of humorous titillation behind his impassive mask. To-night, a spark of sentiment had been the match to explode the mine of his mirth. It was a serious position. Here had I been wasting on him half a lifetime's choicest objurgations. What was I to do in the future to consolidate my authority?

I never enjoyed a fried sole and a glass of champagne more in my life.

He came in later to remove the tray, as wooden as ever.

"Mrs. Connor called a little while ago, sir."

"Why didn't you ask her to come in to see me?"

"Doctor's orders, sir."

After the sole and champagne, I felt much better. I should have welcomed my dear Betty with delight. That, at any rate, was my first impulsive thought.

"Confound the doctor!" I cried. And I was going to confound Marigold, too, but I caught his steady luminous eye. What was the use of any anathema when he would only take it away, as a dog does a bone, and enjoy it in a solitary corner? I recovered myself.

"Well?" said I, with dignity. "Did Mrs. Connor leave any message?"

"I was to give you her compliments, sir, and say she was sorry you were so unwell and she was shocked to hear of Colonel Boyce's sad affliction."

This was sheer orderly room. Such an expression as "sad affliction" never passed

Betty's lips. I, however, had nothing to say. Marigold settled me for the night and left me.

When I was alone and able to consider the point, I felt a cowardly gratitude towards the doctor who had put me to bed like a sick man and forbidden access to my room. I had been spared breaking the news to Betty. How she received it, I did not know. It had been impossible to question Marigold. After all, it was a matter of no essential moment. I consoled myself with the reflection and tried to go to sleep. But I passed a wretched night, my head whirling with the day's happenings.

The morning papers showed me that Boyce, wishing to spare his mother, had been wise to summon me at once. They all published an official paragraph describing the act for which he had received his distinction, and announcing the fact of his blindness. They also gave a brief and flattering sketch of his career. One paper devoted to him a short leading article. The illustrated papers published his photograph. Boyce was on the road to becoming a popular hero.

Cliffe kept me in bed all that day, to my great irritation. I had no converse with the outside world, save vicariously with Betty, who rang up to enquire after my health. On the following morning, when I drove abroad with Hosea, I found the whole town ringing with Boyce. It was a Friday, the day of publication of the local newspaper. It had run to extravagant bills all over the place:

"Wellingsford Hero honoured by the King. Tragic End to Glorious Deeds."

The word--Marigold's, I suppose--had gone round that I had visited the hero in London. I was stopped half a dozen times on my way up the High Street by folks eager for personal details. Outside Prettilove the hairdresser's I held quite a little reception, and instead of moving me on for blocking the traffic, as any of his London colleagues would have done, the local police sergeant sank his authority and by the side of a butcher's boy formed part of the assembly.

When I got to the Market Square, I saw Sir Anthony Fenimore's car standing outside the Town Hall. The chauffeur stopped me.

"Sir Anthony was going to call on you, sir, as soon as he had finished his business inside."

"I'll wait for him," said I. It was one of the few mild days of a wretched month and I enjoyed the air. Springfield, the house agent, passed and engaged me in conversation on the absorbing topic, and then the manager of the gasworks joined us.

Everyone listened so reverently to my utterances that I began to feel as if I had won the Victoria Cross myself.

Presently Sir Anthony bustled out of the Town Hall, pink, brisk, full of business. At the august appearance of the Mayor my less civically distinguished friends departed. His eyes brightened as they fell on me and he shook hands vigorously.

"My dear Duncan, I was just on my way to you. Only heard this morning that you've been seedy. Knocked up, I suppose, by your journey to town. Just heard of that, too. Must have thought me a brute not to enquire. But Edith and I didn't know. I was away all yesterday. These infernal tribunals. With the example of men like Leonard Boyce before their eyes, it makes one sick to look at able-bodied young Englishmen trying to wriggle out of their duty to the country. Well, dear old chap, how are you?"

I assured him that I had recovered from Cliffe and was in my usual state of health. He rubbed his hands.

"That's good. Now give me all the news. What is Boyce's condition? When will he be able to be moved? When do you think he'll come back to Wellingsford?"

At this series of questions I pricked a curious ear.

"Am I speaking to the man or the Mayor?"

"The Mayor," said he. "I wish to goodness I could get you inside, so that you and I and Winterbotham could talk things over."

Winterbotham was the Town Clerk. Sir Anthony cast an instinctive glance at his chauffeur, a little withered elderly man. I laughed and made a sign of dissent. When you have to be carried about, you shy at the prospect of little withered, elderly men as carriers. Besides--

"Unless it would lower Winterbotham's dignity or give him a cold in the head," said I, "why shouldn't he come out here?"

Sir Anthony crossed the pavement briskly, gave a message to the doorkeeper of the Town Hall, and returned to Hosea and myself.

"It's a dreadful thing. Dreadful. I never realised till yesterday, when I read his record, what a distinguished soldier he was. A modern Bayard. For the last year or so he seemed to put my back up. Behaved in rather a curious way, never came near the house where once he was always welcome, and when I asked him to dinner he turned me down flat. But that's all over. Sometimes one has these pettifogging personal vanities. The best thing is to be heartily ashamed of 'em like an honest man, and throw 'em out in the dung-heap where they belong. That's what I told Edith last night, and she agreed with me. Don't you?"

I smiled. Here was another typical English gentleman ridding his conscience of an injustice done to Leonard Boyce.

"Of course I do," said I. "Boyce is a queer fellow. A man with his exceptional qualities has to be judged in an exceptional way."

"And then," said Sir Anthony, "it's that poor dear old lady that I've been thinking of. Edith went to see her yesterday afternoon, but found she had gone up to London. In her frail health it's enough to kill her."

"It won't," said I. "A woman doesn't give birth to a lion without having something of the lion in her nature."

"I've never thought of that," said Sir Anthony.

"Haven't you?"

His face turned grave and he looked far away over the red-brick post-office on the opposite side of the square. Then he sighed, looked at me with a smile, and nodded.

"You're right, Duncan."

"I know I am," said I. "I broke the news to Mrs. Boyce. That's why he asked me to go up and see him."

Winterbotham appeared--a tall, cadaverous man in a fur coat and a soft felt hat. He shook hands with me in a melancholy way. In a humbler walk of life, I am sure he would have been an undertaker.

"Now," said Sir Anthony, "tell us all about your interview with Boyce."

"Before I commit myself," said I, "with the Civic Authorities, will you kindly inform me what this conference coram publico is all about?"

"Why, my dear chap, haven't I told you?" cried Sir Anthony. "We're going to give Colonel Boyce a Civic Reception."

CHAPTER XIX

Thenceforward nothing was talked of but the home-coming of Colonel Boyce.

He touched the public imagination. All kinds of stories, some apocryphal, some having a basis of truth, some authentic, went the round of the little place. It simmered with martial fervour. Elderly laggards enrolled themselves in the Volunteer Training Corps. Young married men who had not attested under the Derby Scheme rushed out to enlist. The Tribunal languished in idleness for lack of claimants for exemption. Exempted men, with the enthusiastic backing of employers, lost the sense of their indispensability and joined the colours. An energetic lady who had met the Serbian Minister in London conceived the happy idea of organising a Serbian Flag Day in Wellingsford, and reaped a prodigious harvest. We were all tremendously patriotic, living under Boyce's reflected glory.

At first I had deprecated the proposal, fearing lest Boyce might not find it acceptable. The reputation he had sought at the cannon's mouth was a bubble of a different kind from that which the good townsfolk were eager to celebrate. Vanity had no part in it. For what the outer world thought of his exploits he did not care a penny. He was past caring. His soul alone, for its own sore needs, had driven him to the search. Before his own soul and not before his fellow countrymen, had he craved to parade as a recipient of the Victoria Cross. His own soul, as I knew, not being satisfied, he would shrink from obtaining popular applause under false pretences. No unhappy man ever took sterner measure of himself. Of all this no one but myself had the faintest idea. In explaining my opinion I had to leave out all essentials. I could only hint that a sensitive man like Colonel Boyce might be averse from exhibiting in public his physical disabilities; that he had always shown himself a modest soldier with a dislike of self-advertisement; that he would prefer to seek immediate refuge in the quietude of his home. But they would not listen to me. Colonel Boyce, they said, would be too patriotic to refuse the town's recognition. It was part of the game which he, as a brave soldier, no matter how modest, could not fail to play. He would recognise that such public honourings of valour had widespread effect among the population. In face of such arguments I had to withdraw my opposition; otherwise it might have appeared that I was actuated by petty personal motives. God knows I only desired to save Boyce from undergoing a difficult ordeal. For the same reasons I could not refuse to serve on the Reception Committee which was immediately formed under the chairmanship of the Mayor.

Preliminaries having been discussed, the Mayor and the Town Clerk waited on Boyce in Belton Square, and returned with the triumphant tidings that they had succeeded in their mission.

"I can't make out what you were running your head against, Duncan," said Sir Anthony. "Of course, as you say, he's a modest chap and dislikes publicity. So do we all. But I quickly talked him out of that objection. I talked him out of all sorts of objections before he could raise them. At last what do you think he said?"

"I should have told you to go to blazes and not worry me."

"He didn't. He said--now I like the chap for it, it was so simple and honest--he said: 'If I were alone in the world I wouldn't have it, for I don't like it. But I'll accept on one condition. My poor old mother has had rather a thin time and she's going to have a thinner. She never gets a look in. Make it as far as possible her show, and I'll do what you like.' What do you think of that?"

"I think it's very characteristic," said I.

And it was. In my mental survey of the situation from Boyce's point of view I had not taken into account the best and finest in the man. His reason rang true against my exceptional knowledge of him. I had worked myself into so sympathetic a comprehension that I KNEW he would be facing something unknown and terrible in the proposed ceremony; I KNEW that for his own sake he would have unequivocably declined. But, ad najorem matris gloriam, he assented.

The main question, at any rate, was settled. The hero would accept the honour. It was for the Committee to make the necessary arrangements. We corresponded far and wide in order to obtain municipal precedents. We had interviews with the military and railway authorities. We were in constant communication with the local Volunteer Training Corps; with the Godbury Volunteers and the Godbury School O.T.C., who both desired to take a part in the great event. In compliance with the conditions imposed, we gave as much publicity as we could to Mrs. Boyce. Lieutenant Colonel Boyce, V.C., and Mrs. Boyce were officially associated in the programme of the reception. How to disentangle them afterwards, when the presentation of the address, engrossed on velluni and enclosed in a casket, should be made to the Colonel, was the subject of heated and confused discussion. Then the feminine elements in town and county desired to rally to the side of Mrs. Boyce. The Red Cross and Volunteer Aid Detachment Nurses claimed representation. So did the munitions workers of Godbury. The Countess of Laleham, the wife of the

Lord Lieutenant of the County, a most imposing and masterful woman, signified (in genteel though incisive language) her intention to take a leading part in the proceedings and to bring along her husband, apparently as an unofficial ornament. This, of course, upset our plans, which had all to be reconsidered from the beginning.

"Who is giving the reception?" cried Lady Fenimore, who could stand upon her dignity as well as anybody. "The County or Wellingsford? I presume it's Wellingsford, and, so long as I am Mayoress, that dreadful Laleham woman will have to take a back seat."

So, you see, we had our hands full.

All this time I found Betty curiously elusive. Now and then I met her for a few fugitive moments at the hospital. Twice she ran in for dinner, in uniform, desperately busy, arriving on the stroke of the dinner hour and rushing away five minutes after her coffee and cigarette, alleging as excuse the epidemic of influenza, consequent on the vile weather, which had woefully reduced the hospital staff. She seemed to be feverish and ill at ease, and tried to cover the symptoms by a reversion to her old offhand manner. As I was so seldom alone with her I could find scant opportunity for intimate conversation. I thought that she might have regretted the frank exposition of her feelings regarding Leonard Boyce. But she showed no sign of it. She spoke in the most detached way of his blindness and the coming ceremony. Never once, even on the first occasion when I met her--in the hospital corridor--after my return from London, did her attitude vary from that of any kind-hearted Englishwoman who deplores the mutilation of a gallant social acquaintance. Sometimes I wanted to shake her, though I could scarcely tell why. I certainly would not have had her weep on my shoulder over Boyce's misfortune; nor would I have cared for her to exhibit a vindictive callousness. She behaved with perfect propriety. Perhaps that is what disturbed me. I was not accustomed to associate perfect propriety with my dear Betty.

The days went on. The reception arrangements were perfected. We only waited for the date of Boyce's arrival to be fixed. That depended on the date of the particular Investiture by the King which Boyce's convalescence should allow him to attend. At last the date was fixed.

A few days before the Investiture I went to London and called at Lady Fanshawe's in Eccleston Street, whither he had been removed after leaving the hospital. I was received in the dining-room on the ground floor by Boyce and his mother. He wore black glasses to hide terrible disfigurement--he lifted them to show me. One eye had been extracted. The other was seared and sightless. He greeted me as heartily as ever, made little jests over his infirmity, treating it lightly for his mother's sake. She, on her side, deemed it her duty to exhibit equal cheerfulness. She boasted of his progress in self-reliance and in the accomplishment of various little blind man's tricks. At her bidding he lit a cigarette for my benefit, by means of a patent fuse. He said, when he had succeeded:

"Better than the last time you saw me, eh, Meredyth?"

"What was that?" asked Mrs. Boyce.

"He nearly burned his fingers," said I, shortly. I had no desire to relate the incident.

We talked of the coming ceremony and I gave them the details of the programme. Boyce had been right in accepting on the score of his mother. Only once had she been the central figure in any public ceremony--on her wedding day, in the years long ago. Here was a new kind of wedding day in her old age. The prospect filled her with a tremulous joy which was to both of them a compensation. She bubbled over with pride and excitement at her inclusion in the homage that was to be paid to the valour of her only son.

"After all," she said, "I did bring him into the world. So I can claim some credit. I only hope I shan't cry and make a fool of myself. They won't expect me to keep on bowing, will they? I once saw Queen Victoria driving through the streets, and I thought how dreadfully her poor old neck must have ached."

On the latter point I reassured her. On the drive from the station Boyce would take the salute of the troops on the line of route. If she smiled charmingly on them, their hearts would be satisfied, and if she just nodded at them occasionally in a motherly sort of way, they would be enchanted. She informed me that she was having a new dress made for the occasion. She had also bought a new hat, which I must see. A servant was summoned and dispatched for it. She tried it on girlishly before the mirror over the mantelpiece, and received my compliments.

"Tell me what it looks like," said Boyce.

You might as well ask a savage in Central Africa to describe the interior of a submarine as the ordinary man to describe a woman's hat. My artless endeavours caused considerable merriment. To hear Boyce's gay laughter one would have thought he had never a care in the world ...

When I took my leave, Mrs. Boyce accompanied Marigold and myself to the front door.

"Did you ever hear of anything so dreadful?" she whispered, and I saw her lips quivering and the tears rolling down her cheeks. "If he weren't so brave and wonderful, I should break my heart."

"What do you suppose you are yourself, my dear old friend," said I over Marigold's shoulder.

I went away greatly comforted. Both of them were as brave as could be. For the first time I took a more cheerful view of Boyce's future.

On the evening before the Reception Betty was shown into the library. It was late, getting on towards my bedtime, and I was nodding in front of the fire.

"I'm just in and out, Majy dear," she said. "I had to come. I didn't want to give you too many shocks." At my expression of alarm, she laughed. "I've only run in to tell you that I've made up my mind to come to the Town Hall tomorrow."

I looked at her, and I suppose my hands moved in a slight gesture.

"By that," she said, "I suppose you mean you can never tell what I'm going to do next."

"You've guessed it, my dear," said I.

"Do you disapprove?"

"I couldn't be so presumptuous."

She bent over me and caught the lapels of my jacket.

"Oh, don't be so dreadfully dignified. I want you to understand. Everybody is going to pay honour to-morrow to a man who has given everything he could to his country. Don't you think it would be petty of me if I stood out? What have the dead things that have passed between us to do with my tribute as an Englishwoman?"

What indeed? I asked her whether she was attending in her private capacity or as one of the representatives of the V.A.D. nurses. I learned for the thousandth time that Betty Connor did not deal in half measures. If she went at all, it was as Betty Connor that she would go. Her aunts would accompany her. It was part of the municipal ordering of things that the Town Clerk should have sent them the special cards of invitation.

"I think it my duty to go," said Betty.

"If you think so, my dear," said I, "then it is your duty. So there's nothing more to be said about it."

Betty kissed the top of my head and went off.

We come now to the morning of the great day. Everything had been finally settled. The Mayor and Aldermen, Lady Fenimore and the Aldermen's wives, the Lord Lieutenant (in unofficial mufti) and Lady Laleham (great though officially obscure lady), the General of the Division quartered in the neighbourhood and officers of his staff, and a few other magnates to meet the three o'clock train by which the Boyces were due to arrive. The station hung with flags and inscriptions. A guard of honour and a band in the station-yard, with a fleet of motor cars in waiting. Troops lining the route from station to Town Hall. More troops in the decorated Market Square, including the Godbury School O.T.C. and the Wellingsford and Godbury Volunteers. I heard that the latter were very anxious to fire off a feu de joie, but were restrained owing to lack of precedent. The local fire-brigade in freshly burnished helmets were to follow the procession of motor cars, and behind them motor omnibuses with the nurses.

Marigold, although his attendance on me precluded him from taking part in the parade of Volunteers, appeared in full grey uniform with all his medals and the black patch of ceremony over his eyeless socket. I must confess to regarding him with some jealousy. I too should have liked to wear my decorations. If a man swears to you that he is free from such little vanities, he is more often than not a mere liar. But a broken-down old soldier, although still drawing pay from the Government, is not allowed to wear uniform (which I think is outrageous), and he can't go and plaster himself with medals when he is wearing on his head a hard felt hat. My envy of the martial looking Marigold is a proof that my mind was not busied with sterner preoccupations. I ate my breakfast with the serene conscience not only of a man who knows he has done his duty, but of an organiser confident in the success of his schemes. The abominable weather of snows and tempests from which we had suffered for weeks had undergone a change. It was a mild morning brightened by a pale convalescent sort of sun, and there was just a little hope of spring in the air. I felt content with everything and everybody.

About eleven o'clock the buzz of the library telephone disturbed my comfortable perusal of the newspaper. I wheeled towards the instrument. Sir Anthony was speaking.

"Can you come round at once? Very urgent. The car is on its way to you."

"What's the matter?" I asked.

He could not tell me over the wires. I was to take it that my presence was urgently needed.

"I'll come along at once," said I.

Some hitch doubtless had occurred. Perhaps the War Office (whose ways were ever weird and unaccountable) had forbidden the General to take part in such a village-pump demonstration. Perhaps Lady Laleham had insisted on her husband coming down like a uniformed Lord Lieutenant on the fold. Perhaps the hero himself was laid up with measles.

With the lightest heart I drove to Wellings Park. Marigold, straight as a ramrod, sitting in front by the chauffeur. As soon as Pardoe, the butler, had brought out my chair and Marigold had settled me in it, Sir Anthony, very red and flustered, appeared and, shaking me nervously by the hand, said without preliminary greeting:

"Come into the library."

He, I think, had come from the morning room on the right of the hall. The library was on the left. He flung open the door. I steered myself into the room; and there, standing on the white bearskin hearthrug, his back to the fire, his hands in his pockets, his six inches of stiff white beard stuck aggressively outward, I saw Daniel Gedge.

While I gaped in astonishment, Sir Anthony shut the door behind him, drew a straight-backed chair from the wall, planted it roughly some distance away from the fire, and, pointing to it, bade Gedge sit down. Gedge obeyed. Sir Anthony took the hearthrug position, his hands behind his back, his legs apart.

"This man," said he, "has come to me with a ridiculous, beastly story. At first I was undecided whether I should listen to him or kick him out. I thought it wiser to listen to him in the presence of a reputable witness. That's why I've sent for you, Duncan. Now you just begin all over again, my man," said he, turning to Gedge, "and remember that anything you say here will be used against you at your trial."

Gedge laughed--I must admit, with some justification.

"You forget, Sir Anthony, I'm not a criminal and you're not a policeman."

"I'm the Mayor to this town, sir," cried Sir Anthony. "I'm also a Justice of the Peace."

"And I'm a law-abiding citizen," retorted Gedge.

"You're an infernal socialistic pro-German," exclaimed Sir Anthony.

"Prove it. I only ask you to prove it. No matter what my private opinions may be, you just try to bring me up under the Defence of the Realm Act, and you'll find you can't touch me."

I held out a hand. "Forgive me for interrupting," said I, "but what is all this discussion about?"

Gedge crossed one leg over the other and drew his beard through his fingers. Sir Anthony was about to burst into speech, but I checked him with a gesture and turned to Gedge.

"It has nothing to do with political opinions," said he. "It has to do with the death, nearly two years ago, of Miss Althea Fenimore, Sir Anthony's only daughter."

Sir Anthony, his face congested, glared at him malevolently. I started, with a gasp of surprise, and stared at the man who, caressing his beard, looked from one to the other of us with an air of satisfaction.

"Get on," said Sir Anthony.

"You are going to give a civic reception to-day to Colonel Boyce, V.C., aren't you?"

"Yes, I am," snapped Sir Anthony.

"Do you think you ought to do it when I tell you that Colonel Boyce, V.C., murdered Miss Althea Fenimore on the night of the 25th June, two years ago?"

"Yes," said Sir Anthony. "And do you know why? Because I know you to be a liar and a scoundrel."

I can never describe the awful horror that numbed me to the heart. For a few moments my body seemed as lifeless as my legs. The charge, astounding almost to grotesqueness in the eyes of Sir Anthony, and rousing him to mere wrath, deprived me of the power of speech. For I knew, in that dreadful instant, that the man's words contained some elements of truth.

All the pieces of the puzzle that had worried me at odd times for months fitted themselves together in a vivid flash. Boyce and Althea! I had never dreamed of associating their names. That association was the key of the puzzle. Out of the darkness disturbing things shone clear. Boyce's abrupt retirement from Wellingsford before the war; his cancellation by default of his engagement; his morbid desire, a year ago, to keep secret his presence in his own house; Gedge's veiled threat to me in the street to use a way "that'll knock all you great people of Wellingsford off your high horses;" his extraordinary interview with Boyce; his generally expressed hatred of Boyce. Was this too the secret which he let out in his cups to Randall Holmes and which drove the young man from his society? And Betty? Boyce was a devil. She wished he were dead. And her words: "You have behaved worse to others. I don't wonder at your shrinking from showing your face here." How much did Betty know? There was the lost week--in Carlisle?--in poor Althea's life. And then there were Boyce's half confessions, the glimpses he had afforded me into the tormented soul. To me he had condemned himself out of his own mouth.

I repeat that, sitting there paralysed by the sudden shock of it, I knew--not that the man was speaking the literal truth--God forbid!--but that Boyce was, in some degree, responsible for Althea's death.

"Calling me names won't alter the facts, Sir Anthony," said Gedge, with a touch of insolence. "I was there at the time. I saw it."

"If that's true," Sir Anthony retorted, "you're an accessory after the fact, and in greater danger of being hanged than ever." He turned to me in his abrupt way. "Now that we've heard this blackguard, shall we hand him over to the police?"

Being directly addressed, I recovered my nerve.

"Before doing that," said I, "perhaps it would be best for us to hear what kind of a story he has to tell us. We should also like to know his motives in not denouncing the supposed murderer at once, and in keeping his knowledge hidden all this time."

"With regard to the last part of your remarks, I dare say you would," said Gedge. "Only I don't know whether I'll go so far as to oblige you. Anyhow you may have discovered that I don't particularly care about your class. I've been preaching against your idleness and vanity and vices, and the strangling grip you have on the throats of the people, ever since I was a young man. If one of your lot chose to do in another of your lot--a common story of seduction and crime--"

At this slur in his daughter's honour Sir Anthony broke out fiercely, and, for a moment, I feared lest he would throw himself on Gedge and wring his neck. I managed to check his outburst and bring him to reason. He resumed his attitude on the hearthrug.

"As I was saying," Gedge continued, rather frightened, "from my sociological point of view I considered the affair no business of mine. I speak of it now, because ever since war broke out your class and the parasitical bourgeoisie have done your best to reduce me to starvation. I thought it would be pleasant to get a bit of my own back. Just a little bit," he added, rubbing his hands.

"If you think you've done it, you'll find yourself mistaken."

Gedge shrugged his shoulders and pulled his beard. I hated the light in his little crafty eyes. I feel sure he had been looking forward for months to this moment of pure happiness.

"Having given us an insight into your motives, which seem consistent with what we know of your character," said I, judicially, "will you now make your statement of facts?"

"What's the good of listening further to his lies?" interrupted Sir Anthony. "I'm a magistrate. I can give the police at once a warrant for his arrest."

Again I pacified him. "Let us hear what the man has to say."

Gedge began. He spoke by the book, like one who repeats a statement carefully prepared.

"It was past ten o'clock on the night of the 25th June, 1914. I had just finished supper when I was rung up by the landlord of The Three Feathers on the Farfield road--it's the inn about a quarter of a mile from the lock gates. He said that the District Secretary of the Red Democratic Federation was staying there--his brother-in-law, if you want to know--and he hadn't received my report. I must explain that I am the local secretary, and as there was to be an important conference of the Federation at Derby the next day, the District Secretary ought to have been in possession of my report on local affairs. I had drawn up the report. My daughter Phyllis had typed it, and she ought to have posted it. On questioning her, I found she had neglected to do so. I explained this over the wires and said I would bring the report at once to The Three Feathers. I only tell you all this, in which you can't be interested, so that you can't say: 'What were you doing on a lonely road at that time of night?' My daughter and the landlord of The Three Feathers can corroborate this part of my story. I set out on my bicycle. It was bright moonlight. You know that for about two hundred yards before the lock gate, and for about twenty after, the towing-path is raised above the level of the main road which runs parallel with it a few yards away. There are strips of market garden between. When I got to this open bit I saw two persons up on the towing-path. One was a girl with a loose kind of cloak and a hat. The other was a man wearing a soft felt hat and a light over-coat. The overcoat was open and I saw that he was wearing it over evening dress. That caught my attention. What was this swell in evening dress doing there with a girl? I slowed down and dismounted. They didn't see me. I got into the shadow of a whitethorn. They turned their faces so that the moon beat full on them. I saw them as plain as I see you. They were Colonel Boyce, V.C.,--Major then--and your daughter, Mr. Mayor, Miss Althea Fenimore."

He paused as though to point the dramatic effect, and twisted round, sticking out his horrible beard at Sir Anthony. Sir Anthony, his hands thrust deep in his trouser-pockets and his bullet head bent forward, glared at him balefully out of his old blue eyes. But he said never a word. Gedge continued.

"They didn't speak very loud, so I could only hear a scrap or two of their con-versation. They seemed to be quarrelling--she wanted him to do something which he wouldn't do. I heard the words 'marriage' and 'disgrace.' They stood still for a moment. Then they turned back. I had overtaken them, you know. I remounted my bicycle and rode to The Three Feathers. I was there about a quarter of an hour or twenty minutes. Then I rode back for home. When I came in sight of the lock, there I saw a man standing alone, sharp in the moonlight. As I came nearer I recognised the same man, Major Boyce. There were no lights in the lock-keeper's cottage. He and his wife had gone to bed long before. I was so interested that I forgot what I was doing and ran into the hedge so that I nearly came down. There was the noise of the scrape and drag of the machine which must have sounded very loud in the stillness. It startled him, for he looked all round, but he didn't see me, for I was under the hedge. Then suddenly he started running. He ran as if the devil was after him. I saw him squash down his Trilby hat so that it was shapeless. Then he disappeared along the path. I thought this a queer proceeding. Why should he have taken to his heels? I thought I should like to see him again. If he kept to the towing-path, his shortest way home, he was bound to go along the Chestnut Avenue, where, as you know, the road and the path again come together. On a bicycle it was easy to get there before him. I sat down on a bench and waited. Presently he comes, walking fast, his hat still squashed in all over his ears. I walked my bicycle slap in front of him.

"'Good-night, Major,' I said.

"He stared at me as if he didn't know me. Then he seemed to pull himself together and said: 'Good-night, Gedge. What are you doing out at this time of night?'

"'If it comes to that, sir,' said I, 'what are you?'

"Then he says, very haughty, as if I was the dirt under his feet--I suppose, Sir Anthony Fenimore and Major Meredyth, you think that me and my class are by divine prescription the dirt beneath your feet, but you're damn well mistaken-- then he says: 'What the devil do you mean?' and catches hold of the front wheel of the bicycle and swings it and me out of his way so that I had a nasty fall, with the machine on top of me, and he marches off. I picked myself up furious with anger. I am an elderly man and not accustomed to that sort of treatment. I yelled out: 'What have you been doing with the Squire's daughter on the towing-path?' It pulled him up short. He made a step or two towards me, and again he asked me what I meant. And this time I told him. He called me a liar, swore he had never been on any tow-path or had seen any squire's daughter, and threatened to murder me. As soon as I could mount my bicycle I left him and made for home. The next afternoon, if you remember, the unfortunate young lady's body was found at the bottom of three fathoms of water by the lock gates."

He had spoken so clearly, so unfalteringly, that Sir Anthony had been surprised into listening without interruption. The bull-dog expression on his face never changed. When Gedge had come to the end, he said:

"Will you again tell me your object in coming to me with this disgusting story?"

Gedge lifted his bushy eyebrows. "Don't you believe it even now?"

"Not a word of it," replied Sir Anthony.

"I ought to remind you of another point." said Gedge. "Was Major Boyce ever seen in Wellingsford after that night? No. He went off by the first train the next morning. Went abroad and stayed there till the outbreak of war."

"I happen to know he had made arrangements to start for Norway that morning," said Sir Anthony. "He had called here a day or two before to say good-bye."

"Did he write you any letter of condolence?" Gedge asked sneeringly.

I saw a sudden spasm pass over Sir Anthony's features. But he said in the same tone as before:

"I am not going to answer insolent questions."

Gedge turned to me with the air of a man giving up argument with a child.

"What do you think of it, Major Meredyth?"

What could I say? I had kept a grim iron face all through the proceedings. I could only reply:

"I agree entirely with Sir Anthony."

Gedge rose and thrust his hand into his jacket pocket. "You gentlemen are hard to convince. If you want proof positive, just read that." And he held a letter out to Sir Anthony.

Sir Anthony glared at him and abruptly plucked the letter out of his hand; for the fraction of a second he stood irresolute; then he threw it behind him into the blazing fire.

"Do you think I'm going to soil my mind with your dirty forgeries?"

Gedge laughed. "You think you've queered my pitch, I suppose. You haven't. I've heaps more incriminating letters. That was only a sample."

"Publish one of them at your peril," said I.

"Pray, Mister Major Meredyth," said he, "what is to prevent me?"

"Penal servitude for malicious slander."

"I should win my case."

"In that event they would get you, on your own showing, for being an accessory after the fact of murder, and for blackmail."

"Suppose I risk it?"

"You won't," said I.

Sir Anthony turned to the bell-push by the side of the mantelpiece.

"What's the good of talking to this double-dyed scoundrel?" He pointed to the door. "You infamous liar, get out. And if I ever catch you prowling round this house, I'll set the dogs on you."

Gedge marched to the door and turned on the threshold and shook his fist.

"You'll repent your folly till your dying day!"

"To Hell with you," cried Sir Anthony.

The door slammed. We were left alone. An avalanche of silence overwhelmed us. Heaven knows how long we remained speechless and motionless--I in my wheelchair, he standing on the hearthrug staring awfully in front of him. At last he drew a deep breath and threw up his arms and flung himself down on a leather-covered couch, where he sat, elbows on knees and his head in his hands. After a while he lifted a drawn face.

"It's true, Duncan," said he, "and you know it."

"I don't know it," I replied stoutly, "any more than you do."

He rose in his nervous way and came swiftly to me and clapped both his hands on my frail shoulders and bent over me--he was a little man, as I have told you--and put his face so close to mine that I could feel his breath on my cheek.

"Upon your soul as a Christian you know that man wasn't lying."

I looked into his eyes--about six inches from mine.

"Boyce never murdered Althea," I said.

"But he is the man--the man I've been looking for."

I pushed him away with both hands, using all my strength. It was too horrible.

"Suppose he is. What then?"

He fell back a pace or two. "Once I remember saying: 'If ever I get hold of that man--God help him!'"

He clenched his fists and started to pace up and down the library, passing and repassing my chair. At last my nerves could stand it no longer and I called on him to halt.

"Gedge's story is curiously incomplete," said I. "We ought to have crossexamined him more closely. Is it likely that Boyce should have gone off leaving behind him a witness of his crime whom he had threatened to murder, and who he must have known would have given information as soon as the death was discovered? And don't you think Gedge's reason for holding his tongue very unconvincing? His fool hatred of our class, instead of keeping him cynically indifferent, would have made him lodge information at once and gloat over our discomfiture."

I could not choose but come to the defence of the unhappy man whom I had learned to call my friend, although, for all my trying, I could conjure up no doubt as to his intimate relation with the tragedy. As Sir Anthony did not speak, I went on.

"You can't judge a man with Leonard Boyce's record on the EX PARTE statement of a malevolent beast like Gedge. Look back. If there had been any affair between Althea and Boyce, the merest foolish flirtation, even, do you think it would have passed unnoticed? You, Edith, Betty--I myself--would have cast an uneasy eye. When we were looking about, some months ago, at the time of your sister-in-law's visit, for a possible man, the thought of Leonard Boyce never entered our heads. The only man you could rush at was young Randall Holmes, and I laughed you out of the idea. Just throw your mind back, Anthony, and try to recall any suspicious incident. You can't."

I paused rhetorically, expecting a reply. None came. He just sat looking at me in a dead way. I continued my special pleading; and the more I said, the more was I baffled by his dead stare and the more unconvincing platitudes did I find myself uttering. Some people may be able to speak vividly to a deaf and dumb creature. On this occasion I tried hard to do so, and failed. After a while my words dribbled out with difficulty and eventually ceased. At last he spoke, in the dull, toneless way of a dead man--presuming that the dead could speak:

"You may talk till you're black in the face, but you know as well as I do that the man told the truth--or practically the truth. What he said he saw, he saw. What motives have been at the back of his miserable mind, I don't know. You say I can't recall suspicious incidents. I can. I'll tell you one. I came across them once--about a month before the thing happened--among the greenhouses. I think we were having one of our tennis parties. I heard her using angry words, and when I appeared her face was flushed and there were tears in her eyes. She was taken aback for a second and then she rushed up to me. 'I think he's perfectly horrid. He says that Jingo--' pointing to the dog; you remember Jingo the Sealingham--she was devoted to him--he died last year--'He says that Jingo is a mongrel--a throw back.' Boyce said he was only teasing her and made pretty apologies. I left it at that. Hit a dog or a horse belonging to Althea, and you hit Althea. That was her way. The incident went out of my mind till this morning. Other incidents, too. One thinks pretty quick at times. Again, this scoundrel hit me on the raw. Boyce never wrote to us. Sent us through his mother a conventional word of condolence. Edith and I were hurt. That was one of the things that made me speak so angrily of him when he wouldn't come and dine with us."

Once more I pleaded. "Your Sealingham incident doesn't impress me. Why not take it at its face value? As for the letter of condolence, that may have twenty explanations."

He passed his hand over his cropped iron-grey head. "What are you driving at, Duncan? You know as well as I do--you know more than I do. I saw it in your face ever since that man opened his mouth."

"If you're so sure of everything," said I foolishly, relaxing grip on my self-control, "why did you hound him out of the place for a liar?"

He leaped to his feet and spread himself into a fighting attitude, for all the world like a half-dead bantam cock springing into a new lease of combative life.

"Do you think I'd let a dunghill beast like that crow over me? Do you think I'd let him imagine for a minute that anything he said could influence me in my public duty? By God, sir, what kind of a worm do you think I am?"

His sudden fury disconcerted me. All this time I had been wondering what kind of catastrophe was going to happen during the next few hours. I am afraid I haven't made clear to you the ghastly racket in my brain. There was the town all beflagged, everyone making holiday, all the pomp and circumstance at our disposal awaiting the signal to be displayed. There was the blind conquering hero almost on his way to local apotheosis. And here were Sir Anthony and I with the revelation of the man Gedge. It was a fantastic, baffling situation. I had been haunted by the dread of discussing it. So in reply to his outburst I simply said:

"What are you going to do?"

He drew himself up, with his obstinate chin in the air, and looked at me straight.

"If God gives me strength, I am going to do what lies before me."

At this moment Lady Fenimore came in.

"Mr. Winterbotham would like to speak to you a minute, Anthony. It's something about the school children."

"All right, my dear. I'll go to him at once," said Sir Anthony. "You'll stay and lunch with us, Duncan?"

I declined on the plea that I should have to nurse myself for a strenuous day.

Sir Anthony might play the Roman father, but it was beyond my power to play the Roman father's guest.

CHAPTER XX

How he passed through the ordeal I don't know. If ever a man stood captain of his soul, it was Anthony Fenimore that day. And his soul was steel-armoured. Perhaps, if proof had come to him from an untainted source, it might have modified his attitude. I cannot tell. Without doubt the knavery of Gedge set aflame his indignation--or rather the fierce pride of the great old Tory gentleman. He would have walked through hell-fire sooner than yielded an inch to Gedge. So much would scornful defiance have done. But behind all this--and I am as certain of it as I am certain that one day I shall die--burned even fiercer, steadier, and clearer the unquenchable fire of patriotic duty. He was dealing not with a man who had sinned terribly towards him, but with a man who had offered his life over and over again to his country, a man who had given to his country the sight of his eyes, a man on whose breast the King himself had pinned the supreme badge of honour in his gift. He was dealing, not with a private individual, but with a national hero. In his small official capacity as Mayor of Wellingsford, he was but the mouthpiece of a national sentiment. And more than that. This ceremony was an appeal to the unimaginative, the sluggish, the faint-hearted. In its little way--and please remember that all tremendous enthusiasms are fit by these little fires--it was a proclamation of the undying glory of England. It was impersonal, it was national, it was Imperial. In its little way it was of vast, far-reaching importance.

I want you to remember these things in order that you should understand the mental processes, or soul processes, or whatever you like, of Sir Anthony Fenimore. Picture him. The most unheroic little man you can imagine. Clean-shaven, bullet-headed, close-cropped, his face ruddy and wrinkled like a withered apple, his eyes a misty blue, his big nose marked like a network of veins, his hands glazed and reddened, like his face, by wind and weather; standing, even under his mayoral robes, like a jockey. Of course he had the undefinable air of breeding; no one could have mistaken his class. But he was an undistinguished, very ordinary looking little man; and indeed he had done nothing for the past half century to distinguish himself above his fellows. There are thousands of his type, masters of English country houses. And of all the thousands, every one brought up against the stern issues of life would have acted like Anthony Fenimore. I say "would have acted," but anyone who has lived in England during the war knows that they have so acted. These incarnations of the commonplace, the object of the disdain, before the war, of the self-styled "intellectuals"--if the war sweeps the insufferable term into oblivion it will have done some good--these honest unassuming gentlemen have responded heroically to the great appeal; and when the intellectuals have thought of their intellects or their skins, they have thought only of their duty. And it was only the heroical sense of duty that sustained Sir Anthony Fenimore that day.

I did not see the reception at the Railway Station or join the triumphal procession; but went early to the Town Hall and took my seat on the platform. I glibly say "took my seat." A wheel-chair, sent there previously, was hoisted, with me inside, on to the platform by Marigold and a porter. After all these years, I still hate to be publicly paraded, like a grizzled baby, in Marigold's arms. For convenience' sake I was posted at the front left-hand corner. The hall soon filled. The first three rows of seats were reserved for the recipients of the municipality's special invitation; the remainder were occupied by the successful applicants for tickets. From my almost solitary perch I watched the fluttering and excited crowd. The town band in the organ gallery at the further end discoursed martial music. From the main door beneath them ran the central gangway to the platform. I recognised many friends. In the front row with her two aunts sat Betty, very demure in her widow's hat relieved by its little white band of frilly stuff beneath the brim. She looked unusually pale. I could not help watching her intently and trying to divine how much she knew of the story of Boyce and Althea. She caught my eye, nodded, and smiled wanly.

My situation was uncanny. In this crowded assemblage in front of me, whispering, talking, laughing beneath the blare of the band, not one, save Betty, had a suspicion of the tragedy. At times they seemed to melt into a shadow-mass of dreamland .... Time crawled on very slowly. Anxious forebodings oppressed me. Had Sir Anthony's valiancy stood the test? Had he been able to shake hands with his daughter's betrayer? Had he broken down during the drive side by side with him, amid the hooraying of the townsfolk? And Gedge? Had he found some madman's means of proclaiming the scandal aloud? Every nerve in my body was strained. Marigold, in his uniform and medals and patch and grey service cap plugged over his black wig, stood sentry by the side of the platform next my chair. All of a sudden he pulled out of his side pocket a phial of red liqueur in a medicine glass. He poured out the dose and handed it to me. I turned on him wrathfully.

"What the dickens is that?"

"Dr. Cliffe's orders, sir."

"When did he order it?"

"When I told him what you looked like after interviewing Mister Daniel Gedge. And he said, if you was to look like that again I was to give you this. So I'm giving it to you, sir."

There was no arguing with Marigold in front of a thousand people. I swallowed the stuff quickly. He put the phial and glass back in his pocket and resumed his wooden sentry attitude by my chair. I must own to feeling better for the draught. But, thought I, if the strain of the situation is so great for me, what must it be for Sir Anthony?

Presently the muffled sounds of outside cheering penetrated the hall. The band stopped abruptly, to begin again with "See the Conquering Hero Comes" when the civic procession appeared through the great doors. There was little Sir Anthony in his robes, grave and imposing, and beside him Mrs. Boyce, flushed, bright-eyed, and tearful. Then came Lady Fenimore with Boyce, black-spectacled, soldierly, bull-necked, his little bronze cross conspicuous among the medals on his breast, his elbow gripped by a weatherbeaten young soldier, one of his captains, as I learned afterwards, home on leave, who had claimed the privilege of guiding his blind foot-steps. And behind came the Aldermen and the Councillors, and the General and his staff, and the Lord Lieutenant and Lady Laleham and the other members of the Reception Committee. The cheering drowned the strains of the "Conquering Hero." Places were taken on the platform. To the right of the Mayor sat Boyce, to the left his mother. On the table in front were set scrolls and caskets. You see, we had arranged that Mrs. Boyce should have an address and a casket all to herself. The gallery soon was picturesquely filled with the nurses, and the fire-brigade, bright-helmeted, was massed in the doorway.

God gave the steel-hearted little man strength to go through the ordeal. He delivered his carefully prepared oration in a voice that never faltered. The passages referring to Boyce's blindness he spoke with an accent of amazing sincerity. When he had ended the responsive audience applauded tumultuously. From my seat by the edge of the platform I watched Betty. Two red spots burned in her cheeks. The addresses were read, the caskets presented. Boyce remained standing, about to respond. He still held the casket in both hands. His FIDUS ACHATES, guessing his difficulty, sprang up, took it from him, and laid it on the table. Boyce turned to him with his charming smile and said: "Thanks, old man." Again the tumult broke out. Men cheered and women wept and waved wet handkerchiefs. And he stood smiling at his unseen audience. When he spoke, his deep, beautifully modulated voice held everyone under its spell, and he spoke modestly and gaily like a brave gentleman. I bent forward, as far as I was able, and scanned his face. Never once, during the whole ceremony, did the tell-tale twitch appear at the corners of his lips. He stood there the incarnation of the modern knights sans fear and sans reproach.

I cannot tell which of the two, he or Sir Anthony, the more moved my wondering admiration. Each exhibited a glorious defiance.

You may say that Boyce, receiving in his debonair fashion the encomiums of the man whom he had wronged, was merely exhibiting the familiar callousness of the criminal. If you do, I throw up my brief. I shall have failed utterly to accomplish my object in writing this book. I want no tears of sensibility shed over Boyce. I want you to judge him by the evidence that I am trying to put before you. If you judge him as a criminal, it is my poor presentation of the evidence that is at fault. I claim for Boyce a certain splendour of character, for all his grievous sins, a splendour which no criminal in the world's history has ever achieved. I beg you therefore to suspend your judgment, until I have finished, as far as my poor powers allow, my unravelling of his tangled skein. And pray remember too that I have sought all through to present you with the facts PARI PASSU with my knowledge of them. I have tried to tell the story through myself. I could think of no other way of creating an essential verisimilitude. Yet, even now, writing in the light of full knowledge, I cannot admit that, when Boyce in that Town Hall faced the world--for, in the deep tragic sense Wellingsford was his world--anyone knowing as much as I did would have been justified in calling his demeanour criminal callousness.

I say that he exhibited a glorious defiance. He defied the concrete Gedge. He defied the more abstract, but none the less real, tormenting Furies. He defied remorse. In accepting Sir Anthony's praise he defied the craven in his own soul.

After a speech or two more, to which I did not listen, the proceedings in the Town Hall ended. I drew a breath of relief. No breakdown by Sir Anthony, no scandalous interruption by Gedge, had marred the impressive ceremony. The band in the gallery played "God Save the King." The crowd in the body of the hall, who had stood for the anthem, sat down again, evidently waiting for Boyce and the notables to pass out. The assemblage on the platform broke up. Several members, among them the General, who paused to shake hands with Boyce and his mother, left the hall by the private side door. The Lord Lieutenant and Lady Laleham followed him soon afterwards. Then the less magnificent crowded round Boyce, each eager for a personal exchange of words with the hero. Sir Anthony remained at his post, keeping on the outskirts of the throng, bidding formal adieux to those who went away. Presently I saw that Boyce was asking for me, for someone pointed me out to his officer attendant, who led him down the steps of the platform and round the edge to my seat.

"Well, it has gone off all right," said he. "Let me introduce Captain Winslow, more than ever my right-hand man--Major Meredyth."

We exchanged bows.

"The old mother's as pleased as Punch. She didn't know she was going to get a little box of her own. I should like to have seen her face. I did hear her give one of her little squeals. Did you?"

"No," said I, "but I saw her face. It was that of a saint in an unexpected beatitude."

He laughed. "Dear old mother," said he. "She has deserved a show." He turned away unconsciously, and, thinking to address me, addressed the first row of spectators. "I suppose there's a lot of folks here that I know."

By chance he seemed to be looking through his black glasses straight at Betty a few feet away. She rose impulsively and, before all Wellingsford, went up to him with hand outstretched.

"There's one at any rate, Colonel Boyce. I'm Betty Connor--"

"No need to tell me that," said he, bowing.

Winslow, at his elbow, most scrupulous of prompters, whispered:

"She wants to shake hands with you."

So their hands met. He kept hers an appreciable second or two in his grasp.

"I hope you will accept my congratulations," said Betty.

"I have already accepted them, very gratefully. My mother conveyed them to me. She was deeply touched by your letter. And may I, too, say how deeply touched I am by your coming here?"

Betty looked swiftly round and her cheeks flushed, for there were many of us within earshot. She laughed off her embarrassment.

"You have developed from a man into a Wellingsford Institution, and I had to come and see you inaugurated. My aunts, too, are here." She beckoned to them. "They are shyer than I am."

The elderly ladies came forward and spoke their pleasant words of congratulation. Mrs. Holmes and others, encouraged, followed their example. Mrs. Boyce suddenly swooped from the platform into the middle of the group and kissed Betty, who emerged from the excited lady's embrace blushing furiously. She shook hands with Betty's aunts and thanked them for their presence; and in the old lady's mind the reconciliation of the two houses was complete. Then, with cheeks of a more delicate natural pink than any living valetudinarian of her age could boast of, and with glistening eyes, she made her way to me, and reaching up and drawing me down, kissed me, too.

While all this was going on, the body of the hall began to empty. The programme had arranged for nothing more by way of ceremonial to take place. But a public gathering always hopes for something unexpected, and, when it does not happen, takes its disappointment philosophically. I think Betty's action must have shown them that the rest of the proceedings were to be purely private and informal.

The platform also gradually thinned, until at last, looking round, I saw that only Sir Anthony and Lady Fenimore and Winterbotham, the Town Clerk, remained. Then Lady Fenimore joined us. We were about a score, myself perched on the edge and corner of the platform, the rest standing on the floor of the hall in a sector round me, Marigold, of course, in the middle of them by my side, like an ill-graven image. As soon as she could Lady Fenimore came up to me.

"Don't you think it splendid of Betty Connor to bury the hatchet so publicly?"

she whispered.

"The war," said I, "is a solvent of many human complications."

"It is indeed." Then she added: "I am going to have a little dinner party some time soon for the Boyces. I sounded him to-day and he practically promised. I'll ask the Lalehams. Of course you'll come. Now that things have shown themselves so topsy-turvy I've been wondering whether I should ask Betty."

"Does Anthony know of this dinner party?" I enquired.

"What does it matter whether he does or not?" she laughed. "Dinner parties come within my province and I'm mistress of it."

Of course Boyce had half promised. What else could he do without discourtesy? But the banquet which, in her unsuspecting innocence she proposed, seemed to me a horrible meal. Doubtless it would seem so to Sir Anthony. At the moment I did not know whether he intended to tell Gedge's story to his wife. At any rate, hitherto, he had not done so.

"All the same, my dear Edith," I replied, "Anthony may have a word to say. I happen to know he has no particular personal friendship for Boyce, who, if you'll forgive my saying so, has treated you rather cavalierly for the past two years. Anthony's welcome to-day was purely public and official. It had nothing to do with his private feelings."

"But they have changed. He was referring to the matter only this morning at breakfast and suggesting things we could do to lighten the poor man's affliction."

"I don't think a dinner party would lighten it," I said. "And if I were you, I wouldn't suggest it to Anthony."

"That's rather mysterious." She looked at me shrewdly. "And there's another mysterious thing. Anthony's like a yapping sphinx over it. What were you two talking to Gedge about this morning?" "Nothing particular."

"That's nonsense, Duncan. Gedge was making himself unpleasant. He never does anything else."

"If you want to know," said I, with a convulsive effort of invention, "we heard that he was preparing some sort of demonstration, going to bring down some of his precious anti-war-league people."

"He wouldn't have the pluck," she exclaimed.

"Anyhow," said I, "we thought we had better have him in and read him the

Riot--or rather the Defence of the Realm--Act. That's all."

"Then why on earth couldn't Anthony tell me?"

"You ought to know the mixture of sugar and pepper in your husband's nature better than I do, my dear Edith," I replied.

Her laugh reassured me. I had turned a difficult corner. No doubt she would go to Sir Anthony with my explanation and either receive his acquiescence or learn the real truth.

She was bidding me farewell when Sir Anthony came along the platform to the chair. I glanced up, but I saw that he did not wish to speak to me. He was looking grim and tired. He called down to his wife:

"It's time to move, dear. The troops are still standing outside."

She bustled about giving the signal for departure, first running to Boyce and taking him by the sleeve. I had not noticed that he had withdrawn with Betty a few feet away from the little group. They were interrupted in an animated conversation. At the sight I felt a keen pang of repulsion. Those two ought not to talk together as old friends. It outraged decencies. It was all very well for Betty to play the magnanimous and patriotic Englishwoman. By her first word of welcome she had fulfilled the part. But this flushed, eager talk lay far beyond the scope of patriotic duty. How could they thus converse over the body of the dead Althea? With both of them was I indignant.

In my inmost heart I felt horribly and vulgarly jealous. I may as well confess it. Deeply as I had sworn blood-brotherhood with Boyce, regardless of the crimes he might or might not have committed, I could not admit him into that inner brotherhood of which Betty and I alone were members. And this is just a roundabout, shame-faced way of saying that, at that moment, I discovered that I was hopelessly, insanely in love with Betty. The knowledge came to me in a great wave of dismay.

"You'll let me see you again, won't you?" he asked.

"If you like."

I don't think I heard the words, but I traced them on their lips. They parted. Sir Anthony descended from the platform and gave his arm to Mrs. Boyce. Lady Fenimore still clung to Boyce. Winterbotham came next, bearing the two caskets, which had been lying neglected on the table. The sparse company followed down the empty hall. Marigold signalled to the porter and they hoisted down my chair.

Betty, who had lingered during the operation, walked by my side. Being able now to propel myself, I dismissed Marigold to a discreet position in the rear. Betty, her face still slightly flushed, said:

"I'm waiting for congratulations which seem to be about as overwhelming as snow in August. Don't you think I've been extraordinarily good?"

"Do you feel good?"

"More than good," she laughed. "Christianlike. Aren't we told in the New Testament to forgive our enemies?"

"'And love those that despitefully use us?'" I misquoted maliciously. A sudden gust of anger often causes us to do worse things than trifle with the text of the Sermon on the Mount.

She turned on me quickly, as though stung. "Why not? Isn't the sight of him maimed like that enough to melt the heart of a stone?"

I replied soberly enough. "It is indeed."

I had already betrayed my foolish jealousy. Further altercation could only result in my betraying Boyce. I did not feel very happy. Conscious of having spoken to me with unwonted sharpness, she sought to make amends by laying her hand on my shoulder.

"I think, dear," she said, "we're all on rather an emotional edge to-day."

We reached the front door of the hall. At the top of the shallow flight of broad stairs the little group that had preceded us stood behind Boyce, who was receiving the cheers of the troops--soldiers and volunteers and the Godbury School Officers' Training Corps--drawn up in the Market Square. When the cheers died away the crowd raised cries for a speech.

Again Boyce spoke.

"The reception you have given my mother and myself," he said, "we refuse to take personally. It is a reception given to the soldiers, and the mothers and wives of soldiers, of the Empire, of whom we just happen to be the lucky representatives. Whole regiments, to say nothing of whole armies, can't all, every jack man, receive Victoria Crosses. But every regiment very jealously counts up its honours. You'll hear men say: 'Our regiment has two V.C.s, five D.S.O.s, and twenty Distinguished Conduct Medals.' and the feeling is that all the honours are lumped together and shared by everybody, from the Colonel to the drummer-boys. And each individual is proud of his share because he knows that he deserves it. And so it happens that those whom chance has set aside for distinction, like the lucky winners in a sweep-stake, are the most embarrassed people you can imagine, because everybody is do-ing everything that they did every day in the week. For instance, if I began to tell you a thousandth part of the dare-devil deeds of my friend here, Captain Winslow of my regiment, he would bolt like a rabbit into the Town Hall and fall on his knees and pray for an earthquake. And whether the earthquake came off or not, I'm sure he would never speak to me again. And they're all like that. But in honouring me you are honouring him, and you're honouring our regiment, and you're honouring the army. And in honouring Mrs. Boyce, you are honouring that wonderful wom-anhood of the Empire that is standing heroically behind their men in the hell upon God's good earth which is known as the front."

It was a soldierlike little speech, delivered with the man's gallant charm. Young Winslow gripped his arm affectionately and I heard him say--"You are a brute, sir, dragging me into it." The little party descended the steps of the Town Hall. The words of command rang out. The Parade stood at the salute, which Boyce acknowl-edged, guided by Winslow and his mother he reached his car, to which he was attended by the Mayor and Mayoress. After formal leave-taking the Boyces and Winslow drove off amid the plaudits of the crowd. Then Sir Anthony and Lady Fenimore. Then Betty and her aunts. Last of all, while the troops were preparing to march away and the crowd was dispersing and all the excitement was over, Mari-gold picked me out of my chair and carried me down to my little grey two-seater.

CHAPTER XXI

Of course, after this (in the words of my young friends) I crocked up. The con-founded shell that had played the fool with my legs had also done something silly to my heart. Hence these collapses after physical and emotional strain. I had to stay in bed for some days. Cliffe told me that as soon as I was fit to travel I must go to Bournemouth, where it would be warm. I told Cliffe to go to a place where it would be warmer. As neither of us would obey the other, we remained where we were.

Cliffe informed me that Lady Fenimore had called him in to see Sir Anthony, whom she described as being on the obstinate edge of a nervous breakdown. I was sorry to hear it.

"I suppose you've tried to send him, too, to Bournemouth?"

"I haven't," Cliffe replied gravely. "He has got something on his mind. I'm sure of it. So is his wife. What's the good of sending him away?"

"What do you think is on his mind?" I asked.

"How do I know? His wife thinks it must be something to do with Boyce's reception. He went home dead-beat, is very irritable, off his food, can't sleep, and swears cantankerously that there's nothing the matter with him,--the usual symptoms. Can you throw any light on it?"

"Certainly not," I replied rather sharply.

Cliffe said "Umph!" in his exasperating professional way and proceeded to feel my pulse.

"I don't quite see how Friday's mild exertion could account for YOUR breakdown, my friend," he remarked.

"I'm so glad you confess, at last, not to seeing everything," said I.

I was fearing this physical reaction in Sir Anthony. It was only the self-assertion of Nature. He had gone splendidly through his ordeal, having braced himself up for it. He had not braced himself up, however, sufficiently to go through the other and far longer ordeal of hiding his secret from his wife. So of course he went to pieces.

After Cliffe had left me, with his desire for information unsatisfied, I rang up Wellings Park. It was the Sunday morning after the reception. To my surprise, Sir Anthony answered me; for he was an old-fashioned country churchgoer and plague, pestilence, famine, battle, murder and sudden death had never been known to keep him out of his accustomed pew on Sunday morning. Edith, he informed me, had gone to church; he himself, being as nervous as a cat, had funked it; he was afraid lest he might get up in the middle of the sermon and curse the Vicar.

"If that's so," said I, "come round here and talk sense. I've something important to say to you."

He agreed and shortly afterwards he arrived. I was shocked to see him. His ruddy face had yellowed and the firm flesh had loosened and sagged. I had never noticed that his stubbly hair was so grey. He could scarcely sit still on the chair by my bedside.

I told him of Cliffe's suspicions. We were a pair of conspirators with unavowable things on our minds which were driving us to nervous catastrophe. Edith, said I, was more suspicious even than Cliffe. I also told him of our talk about the projected dinner party.

"That," he declared, "would drive me stark, staring mad."

"So will continuing to hide the truth from Edith," said I. "How do you suppose you can carry on like this?"

He grew angry. How could he tell Edith? How could he make her understand his reason for welcoming Boyce? How could he prevent her from blazing the truth abroad and crying aloud for vengeance? What kind of a fool's counsel was I giving him?

I let him talk, until, tired with reiteration, he had nothing more to say. Then I made him listen to me while I expounded that which was familiar to his obstinate mind--namely, the heroic qualities of his own wife.

"It comes to this," said I, by way of peroration, "that you're afraid of Edith letting you down, and you ought to be ashamed of yourself."

At that he flared out again. How dared I, he asked, eating his words, suggest that he did not trust the most splendid woman God had ever made? Didn't I see that he was only trying to shield her from knowledge that might kill her? I retorted by pointing out that worry over his insane behaviour--please remember that above our deep unchangeable mutual affection, a violent surface quarrel was raging--would more surely and swiftly kill her than unhappy knowledge. Her quick brain--had already connected Gedge, Boyce, and his present condition as the main factors of some strange problem. "Her quick brain!" I cried. "A half idiot child would have put things together."

Presently he collapsed, sitting hopelessly, nervelessly in his chair. At last he lifted a piteously humble face.

"What would you suggest my doing, Duncan?"

There seemed to me to be only one thing he could do in order to preserve, if not his reason, at any rate his moral equilibrium in the position which he had contrived for himself. To tell him this had been my object in seeking the interview, and the blessed opportunity only came after an hour's hard wrangle--in current metaphor after an hour's artillery preparation for attack. He looked so battered, poor old

Anthony, that I felt almost ashamed of the success of my bombardment.

"It's not a question of suggesting," said I. "It's a question of things that have to be done. You need a holiday. You've been working here at high pressure for nearly a couple of years. Go away. Put yourself in the hands of Cliffe, and go to Bournemouth, or Biarritz, or Bahia, or any beastly place you can fix up with him to go to. Go frankly For three or four months. Go to-morrow. As soon as you're well out of the place, tell Edith the whole story. Then you can take counsel and comfort together."

He was in the state of mind to be impressed by my argument. I followed up my advantage. I undertook to send a ruthless flaming angel of a Cliffe to pronounce the inexorable decree of exile. After a few faint-hearted objections he acquiesced in the scheme. I fancy he revolted against even this apparent surrender to Gedge, although he was too proud to confess it. No man likes running away. Sir Anthony also regarded as pusillanimous the proposal to leave his wife in ignorance until he had led her into the trap of holiday. Why not put her into his confidence before they started?

"That," said I, "is a delicate question which only you yourself can decide. By following my plan you get away at once, which is the most important thing. Once comfortably away, you can choose the opportune moment."

"There's something in that," he replied; and, after thanking me for my advice, he left me.

I do not defend my plan. I admit it was Machiavellian. My one desire was to remove these two dear people from Wellingsford for a season. Just think of the horrible impossibility of their maintaining social relations with the Boyces ....

By publicly honouring Boyce, Sir Anthony had tied his own hands. It was a pledge to Boyce, although the latter did not know it, of condonation. Whatever stories Gedge might spread abroad, whatever proofs he might display, Sir Anthony could take no action. But to carry on a semblance of friendship with the man responsible for his daughter's death--for the two of them, mind you, since Lady Fenimore would sooner or later learn everything--was, as I say, horribly impossible.

Let them go, then, on their nominal holiday, during which the air might clear. Boyce might take his mother away from Wellingsford. She would do far more than uproot herself from her home in order to gratify a wish of her adored and blinded son. He would employ his time of darkness in learning to be brave, he had told me. It took some courage to face the associations of dreadful memories unflinchingly, for his mother's sake. Should he learn, however, that the Fenimores had an inkling of the truth, he would recognise his presence in the place to be an outrage. And such inkling--who would give it him? Perhaps I, myself. The Boyces would go--the Fenimores could return. Anything, anything rather than that the Fenimores and the Boyces should continue to dwell in the same little town.

And there was Betty--with all the inexplicable feminine whirring inside her--socially reconciled with Boyce. Where the deuce was this reconciliation going to lead? I have told you how my lunatic love for Betty had stood revealed to me. Had she chosen to love and marry any ordinary gallant gentleman, God knows I should not have had a word to say. The love that such as I can give a woman can find its only true expression in desiring and contriving her happiness. But that she should sway back to Leonard Boyce--no, no. I could not bear it. All the shuddering pictures of him rose up before me, the last, that of him standing by the lock gates and suddenly running like a frightened rabbit, with his jaunty soft felt hat squashed shapelessly over his ears.

Gedge could not have invented that abominable touch of the squashed hat.

I have said that possibly I myself might give Boyce an inkling of the truth. Thinking over the matter in my restless bed, I shrank from doing so. Should I not be disingenuously serving my own ends? Betty stepped in, whom I wanted for myself. Neither could I go to Boyce and challenge him for a villain and summon him to quit the town and leave those dear to me at peace. I could not condemn him. I had unshaken faith in the man's noble qualities. That he drowned Althea Fenimore I did not, could not, believe. After all that had passed between us, I felt my loyalty to him irrevocably pledged. More than ever was I enmeshed in the net of the man's destiny.

As yet, however, I could not bear to see him. I could not bear to see Betty, who called now and then. For the first time in my life I took refuge in my invalidity, whereby I earned the commendation of Cliffe. Betty sent me flowers. Mrs. Boyce sent me grapes and an infallible prescription for heart attacks which, owing to the hopeless mess she had made in trying to copy the wriggles indicating the quantities of the various drugs, was of no practical use. Phyllis Gedge sent me a few bunches of violets with a shy little note. Lady Fenimore wrote me an affectionate letter bidding me farewell. They were going to Bude in Cornwall, Anthony having put himself under Dr. Cliffe's orders like a wonderful lamb. When she came back, she hoped that her two sick men would be restored to health and able to look more favourably upon her projected dinner party. Marigold also brought into my bedroom a precious old Waterford claret jug which I had loved and secretly coveted for twenty years, with a card attached bearing the inscription "With love from Anthony." That was his dumb, British way of informing me that he was taking my advice.

When my self-respect would allow me no longer to remain in bed, I got up; but I still shrank from publishing the news of my recovery, in which reluctance I met with the hearty encouragement both of Cliffe and Marigold. The doctor then informed me that my attack of illness had been very much more serious than I realised, and that unless I made up my mind to lead the most unruffled of cabbage-like existences, he would not answer for what might befall me. If he could have his way, he would carry me off and put me into solitary confinement for a couple of months on a sunny island, where I should hold no communication with the outside world. Marigold heard this announcement with smug satisfaction. Nothing would please him more than to play gaoler over me.

At last, one morning, I said to him: "I'm not going to submit to tyranny any longer. I resume my normal life. I'm at home to anybody who calls. I'm at home to the devil himself."

"Very good, sir," said Marigold.

An hour or two afterwards the door was thrown open and there stood on the threshold the most amazing apparition that ever sought admittance into a gentleman's library; an apparition, however, very familiar during these days to English eyes. From the shapeless Tam-o'-Shanter to the huge boots it was caked in mud. Over a filthy sheepskin were slung all kinds of paraphernalia, covered with dirty canvas which made it look a thing of mighty bulges among which a rifle was poked away. It wore a kilt covered by a khaki apron. It also had a dirty and unshaven face. A muddy warrior fresh from the trenches, of course. But what was he doing here?

"I see, sir, you don't recognise me," he said with a smile.

"Good Lord!" I cried, with a start, "it's Randall."

"Yes, sir. May I come in?"

"Come in? What infernal nonsense are you talking?" I held out my hand, and, after greeting him, made him sit down.

"Now," said I, "what the deuce are you doing in that kit?"

"That's what I've been asking myself for the last ten months. Anyhow I shan't wear it much longer."

"How's that?"

"Commission, sir," he answered.

"Oh!" said I.

His entrance had been so abrupt and unexpected that I hardly knew as yet what to make of him. Speculation as to his doings had led me to imagine him engaged in some elegant fancy occupation on the fringe of the army, if indeed he were serving his country so creditably. I found it hard to reconcile my conception of Master Randall Holmes with this businesslike Tommy who called me "Sir" every minute.

"I'll tell you about it, sir, if you're interested. But first--how is my mother?"

"Your mother? You haven't seen her yet?"

Here, at least, was a bit of the old casual Randall. He shook his head.

"I've only just this minute arrived. Left the trenches yesterday. Walked from the station. Not a soul recognised me. I thought I had better come here first and report, just as I was, and not wait until I had washed and shaved and put on Christian clothes again. He looked at me and grinned. "Seeing is believing."

"Your mother is quite well," said I. "Haven't you given her any warning of your arrival?"

"Oh, no!" he answered. "I didn't want any brass bands. Besides, as I say, I wanted to see you first. Then to look in at the hospital. I suppose Phyllis Gedge is still at the hospital?"

"She is. But I think, my dear chap, your mother has the first call on you."

"She wouldn't enjoy my present abominable appearance as much as Phyllis," he replied, coolly. "You see, Phyllis is responsible for it. I told you she refused to marry me, didn't I, sir? After that, she called me a coward. I had to show her that I wasn't one. It was an awful nuisance, I admit, for I had intended to do something quite different. Oh! not Gedging or anything of that sort--but--" he dived beneath his sheepskin and brought out a tattered letter case and from a mass of greasy documents (shades of superior Oxford!) selected a dirty, ragged bit of newspaper--"but," said he, handing me the fragment, "I think I've succeeded. I don't suppose this caught your eye, but if you look closely into it, you'll see that 11003 Private R. Holmes, 1st Gordon Highlanders, a couple of months ago was awarded the Distinguished Conduct Medal. I may be any kind of a fool or knave she likes to call me, but she can't call me a coward."

I congratulated him with all my heart, which, after the first shock, was warming towards him rapidly.

"But why," I asked, still somewhat bewildered, "didn't you apply for a commission? A year ago you could have got one easily. Why enlist? And the 1st Gordons-- that's the regular army."

He laughed and asked permission to help himself to a cigarette. "By George, that's good," he exclaimed after a few puffs. "That's good after months of Woodbines. I found I could stand everything except Tommy's cigarettes. Everything about me has got as hard as nails, except my palate for tobacco .... Why didn't I apply for a commission? Any fool could get a commission. It's different now. Men are picked and must have seen active service, and then they're sent off to cadet training corps. But last year I could have got one easily. And I might have been kicking my heels about England now."

"Yet, at the sight of a Sam Browne belt, Phyllis would have surely recanted," said I.

"I didn't want the girl I intended to marry and pass my life with to have her head turned by such trappings as a Sam Browne belt. She has had to be taught that she is going to marry a man. I'm not such a fool as you may have thought me, Major," he said, forgetful of his humble rank. "Suppose I had got a commission and married her. Suppose I had been kept at home and never gone out and never seen a shot fired, like heaps of other fellows, or suppose I had taken the line I had marked out--do you think we should have been assured a happy life? Not a bit of it. We might have been happy for twenty years. And then--women are women and can't help themselves--the old word--by George, sir, she spat it at me from a festering sore in her very soul--the old word would have rankled all the time, and some stupid quarrel having arisen, she would have spat it at me again. I wasn't taking any chances of that kind."

"My dear boy," said I, subridently, "you seem to be very wise." And he did. So far as I knew anything about humans, male and female, his proposition was incontrovertible. "But where did you gather your wisdom?"

"I suppose," he replied seriously, "that my mind is not entirely unaffected by a very expensive education."

I looked at the extraordinary figure in sheepskin, bundles and mud, and laughed out loud. The hands of Esau and the voice of Jacob. The garb of Thomas Atkins and the voice of Balliol. Still, as I say, the fellow was perfectly right. His highly trained intelligence had led him to an exact conclusion. The festering sore demanded drastic treatment,--the surgeon's knife. As we talked I saw how coldly his brain had worked. And side by side with that working I saw, to my amusement, the insistent claims of his vanity. The quickest way to the front, where alone he could re-establish his impugned honour was by enlistment in the regular army. For the first time in his life he took a grip on essentials. He knew that by going straight into the heart of the old army his brains, provided they remained in his head, would enable him to accomplish his purpose. As for his choice of regiment, there his vanity guided. You may remember that after his disappearance we first heard of him at Aberdeen. Now Aberdeen is the depot of the Gordon Highlanders.

"What on earth made you go there?" I asked.

"I wanted to get among a crowd where I wasn't known, and wasn't ever likely to be known," he replied. "And my instinct was right. I was among farmers from Skye and butchers from Inverness and drunken scallywags from the slums of Aberdeen, and a leaven of old soldiers from all over Scotland. I had no idea that such people existed. At first I thought I shouldn't be able to stick it. They gave me a bad time for being an Englishman. But soon, I think, they rather liked me. I set my brains to work and made 'em like me. I knew there was everything to learn about these fellows and I went scientifically to work to learn it. And, by Heaven, sir, when once they accepted me, I found I had never been in such splendid company in my life."

"My dear boy," I cried in a burst of enthusiasm, "have you had breakfast?"

"Of course I have. At the Union Jack Club--the Tommies' place the other side of the river--bacon and eggs and sausages. I thought I'd never stop eating."

"Have some more?"

He laughed. "Couldn't think of it."

"Then," said I, "get yourself a cigar." I pointed to a stack of boxes. "You'll find the Corona--Coronas the best."

As I am not a millionaire I don't offer these Coronas to everybody. I myself can only afford to smoke one or two a week.

When he had lit it he said: "I was led away from what I wanted to tell you,--my going to Aberdeen and plunging into the obscurity of a Scottish regiment. I was absolutely determined that none of my friends, none of you good people, should know what an ass I had made of myself. That's why I kept it from my mother. She would have blabbed it all over the place."

"But, my good fellow," said I, "why the dickens shouldn't we have known?"

"That I was making an ass of myself?"

"No, you young idiot!" I cried. "That you were making a man of yourself."

"I preferred to wait," said he, coolly, "until I had a reasonable certainty that I had achieved that consummation--or, rather, something that might stand for it in the prejudiced eyes of my dear friends. I knew that you all, ultimately, you and mother and Phyllis, would judge by results. Well, here they are. I've lived the life of a Tommy for ten months. I've been five in the thick of it over there. I've refused stripes over and over again. I've got my D.C.M. I've got my commission through the ranks, practically on the field. And of the draft of two hundred who went out with me only one other and myself remain."

"It's a splendid record, my boy," said I.

He rose. "Don't misunderstand me, Major. I'm not bragging. God forbid. I'm only wanting to explain why I kept dark all the time, and why I'm springing smugly and complacently on you now."

"I quite understand," said I.

"In that case," he laughed, "I can proceed on my rounds." But he did not proceed. He lingered. "There's another matter I should like to mention," he said. "In her last letter my mother told me that the Mayor and Town Council were on the point of giving a civic reception to Colonel Boyce. Has it taken place yet?"

"Yes," said I. "And did it go off all right?"

In spite of wisdom learned at Balliol and shell craters, he was still an ingenuous youth.

"Gedge was perfectly quiet," I answered.

He started, as he had for months learned not to start, and into his eyes sprang an alarm that was usually foreign to them.

"Gedge? How do you know anything about Gedge and Colonel Boyce? Good Lord! He hasn't been spreading that poisonous stuff over the town?"

"That's what you were afraid of when you asked about the reception?"

"Of course," said he.

"And you wanted to have your mind clear on the point before interviewing Phyllis."

"You're quite right, sir," he replied, a bit shamefacedly. "But if he hasn't been spreading it, how do you know? And," he looked at me sharply, "what do you know?"

"You gave your word of honour not to repeat what Gedge told you. I think you may be absolved of your promise. Gedge came to Sir Anthony and myself with a lying story about the death of Althea Fenimore."

"Yes," said he. "That was it."

"Sit down for another minute or two," said I, "and let us compare notes."

He obeyed. We compared notes. I found that in most essentials the two stories were identical, although Gedge had been maudlin drunk when he admitted Randall into his confidence.

"But in pitching you his yarn," cried Randall, "he left out the blackmail. He bragged in his beastly way that Colonel Boyce was worth a thousand a year to him. All he had to live upon now that the blood-suckers had ruined his business. Then he began to weep and slobber--he was a disgusting sight--and he said he would give it all up and beg with his daughter in the streets as soon as he had an opportunity of unmasking 'that shocking wicked fellow.'"

"What did you say then?" I asked.

"I told him if ever I heard of him spreading such infernal lies abroad, I'd wring his neck."

"Very good, my boy," said I. "That's practically what Sir Anthony told him."

"Sir Anthony doesn't believe there's any truth in it?"

"Sir Anthony," said I, boldly, "knows there's not a particle of truth in it. The man's malignancy has taken the form of a fixed idea. He's crack-brained. Between us we put the fear of God into him, and I don't think he'll give any more trouble."

Randall got to his feet again. "I'm very much relieved to hear you say so. I must confess I've been horribly uneasy about the whole thing." He drew a deep breath. "Thank goodness I can go to Phyllis, as you say, with a clear mind. The last time I saw her I was half crazy."

He held out his hand, a dirty, knubbly, ragged-nailed hand--the hand that was once so irritatingly manicured.

"Good-bye, Major. You won't shut the door on me now, will you?"

I wrung his hand hard and bade him not be silly, and, looking up at him, said:

"What was the other thing quite different you were intending to do before you, let us say, quarreled with Phyllis?"

He hesitated, his forehead knit in a little web of perplexity.

"Whatever it was," I continued, "let us have it. I'm your oldest friend, a sort of father. Be frank with me and you won't regret it. The splendid work you've done has wiped out everything."

"I'm afraid it has," said he ruefully. "Wiped it out clean." With a hitch of the shoulders he settled his pack more comfortably. "Well, I'll tell you, Major. I thought I had brains. I still think I have. I was on the point of getting a job in the Secret Service--Intelligence Department. I had the whole thing cut and dried--to get at the ramifications of German espionage in socialistic and so-called intellectual circles in neutral and other countries. It would have been ticklish work, for I should have been carrying my life in my hands. I could have done it well. I started out by being a sort of 'intellectual' myself. All along I wanted to put my brains at the service of my country. I took some time to hit upon the real way. I hit upon it. I learned lots of things from Gedge. If he weren't an arrant coward, he might be dangerous. He would be taking German money long ago, but that he's frightened to death of it." He laughed. "It never occurred to you, I suppose, a year ago," he continued, "that I spent most of my days in London working like a horse."

"But," I cried--I felt myself flushing purple--and, when I flush purple, the un-regenerate old soldier in me uses language of a corresponding hue--"But," I cried--and in this language I asked him why he had told me nothing about it.

"The essence of the Secret Service, sir," replied this maddening young man, "is--well--secrecy."

"You had a billet offered to you, of the kind you describe?"

"The offer reached me, very much belated, one day when I was half dead, after having performed some humiliating fatigue duty. I think I had persisted in trying to scratch an itching back on parade. Military discipline, I need not tell you, Major, doesn't take into account the sensitiveness of a recruit's back. It flatly denies such a phenomenon. Now I think I can defy anything in God's quaint universe to make me itch. But that's by the way. I tore the letter up and never answered it. You do these things, sir, when the whole universe seems to be a stumbling-block and an offence. Phyllis was the stumbling-block and the rest of the cosmos was the other thing. That's why I have reason on my side when I say that, all through Phyllis Gedge, I made an ass of myself."

He clutched his rude coat with both hands. "An ass in sheep's clothing."

He drew himself up, saluted, and marched out.

He marched out, the young scoundrel, with all the honours of war.

CHAPTER XXII

So, in drawing a bow at a venture, I had hit the mark. You may remember that I had rapped out the word "blackmail" at Gedge; now Randall justified the charge. Boyce was worth a thousand a year to him. The more I speculated on the danger that might arise from Gedge, the easier I grew in my mind. Your blackmailer is a notorious saver of his skin. Gedge had no desire to bring Boyce to justice and thereby incriminate himself. His visit to Sir Anthony was actuated by sheer malignity. Without doubt, he counted on his story being believed. But he knew enough of the hated and envied aristocracy to feel assured that Sir Anthony would not subject his beloved dead to such ghastly disinterment as a public denunciation of Boyce would necessitate. He desired to throw an asphyxiating bomb into the midst of our private circle. He reckoned on the Mayor taking some action that would stop the reception and thereby put a public affront on Boyce. Sir Anthony's violent indignation and perhaps my appearance of cold incredulity upset his calculations. He went out of the room a defeated man, with the secret load (as I knew now) of blackmail on his shoulders.

I snapped my fingers at Gedge. Randall seemed to do the same, undesirable father-in-law IN PROSPECTU as he was. But that was entirely Randall's affair. The stomach that he had for fighting with Germans would stand him in good stead against Gedge, especially as he had formed so contemptuous an estimate of the latter's valour.

I emerged again into my little world. I saw most of my friends. Phyllis lay in wait for me at the hospital, radiant and blushing, ostensibly to congratulate me on recovery from my illness, really (little baggage!) to hear from my lips a word or two in praise of Randall. Apparently he had come, in his warrior garb, seen, and conquered on the spot. I saw Mrs. Holmes, who, gladdened by the Distinguished Conduct Medallist's return, had wiped from her memory his abominably unfilial behaviour. I saw Betty and I saw Boyce.

Now here I come to a point in this chronicle where I am faced by an appalling difficulty. Hitherto I have striven to tell you no more about myself and my motives and feelings than was demanded by my purpose of unfolding to you the lives of others. Primarily I wanted to explain Leonard Boyce. I could only do it by showing you how he reacted on myself--myself being an unimportant and uninteresting person. It was all very well when I could stand aside and dispassionately analyse such reactions. The same with regard to my dear Betty. But now if I adopted the same method of telling you the story of Betty and the story of Boyce--the method of reaction, so to speak--I should be merely whining into your ears the dolorous tale of Duncan Meredyth, paralytic and idiot.

The deuce of it is that, for a long time, nothing particular or definite happened. So how can I describe to you a very important period in the lives of Betty and Boyce and me?

I had to resume my intimacy with Boyce. The blind and lonely man craved it and claimed it. It would be an unmeaning pretence of modesty to under-estimate the value to him of my friendship. He was a man of intense feelings. Torture had closed his heart to the troops of friends that so distinguished a soldier might have had. He granted admittance but to three, his mother, Betty and--for some unaccountable reason--myself. On us he concentrated all the strength of his affection. Mind you, it was not a case of a maimed creature clinging for support to those who cared for him. In his intercourse with me, he never for a moment suggested that he was seeking help or solace in his affliction. On the contrary, he ruled it out of the conditions of social life. He was as brave as you please. In his laughing scorn of blindness he was the bravest man I have ever known. He learned the confidence of the blind with marvellous facility. His path through darkness was a triumphant march.

Sometimes, when he re-fought old battles and planned new ones, forecast the strategy of the Great Advance, word-painted scenes and places, drew character sketches of great leaders and quaint men, I forgot the tragedy of Althea Fenimore. And when the memory came swiftly back, I wondered whether, after all, Gedge's story from first to last had not been a malevolent invention. The man seemed so happy. Of course you will say it was my duty to give a hint of Gedge's revelation. It was. To my shame, I shirked it. I could not find it in my heart suddenly to dash into his happiness. I awaited an opportunity, a change of mood in him, an allusion to confidences of which I alone of human beings had been the recipient.

Betty visited me as usual. We talked war and hospital and local gossip for a while and then she seemed to take refuge at the piano. We had one red-letter day, when a sailor cousin of hers, fresh from the North Sea, came to luncheon and told us wonders of the Navy which we had barely imagined and did not dare to hope for. His tidings gave subject for many a talk.

I knew that she was seeing Boyce constantly. The former acquaintance of the elders of the two houses flamed into sudden friendship. From a remark artlessly let fall by Mrs. Boyce, I gathered that the old ladies were deliberately contriving such meetings. Boyce and Betty referred to each other rarely and casually, but enough to show me that the old feud was at an end. And of what save one thing could the end of a feud between lovers be the beginning? What did she know? Knowing all, how could she be drawn back under the man's fascination? The question maddened me. I suffered terribly.

At last, one evening, I could bear it no longer. She was playing Chopin. The music grated on me. I called out to her:

"Betty!"

She broke off and turned round, with a smile of surprise. Again she was wearing the old black evening dress, in which I have told you she looked so beautiful.

"No more music, dear. Come and talk to me."

She crossed the room with her free step and sat near my chair.

"What shall I talk about?" she laughed.

"Leonard Boyce."

The laughter left her face and she gave me a swift glance.

"Majy dear, I'd rather not," she said with a little air of finality.

"I know that," said I. "I also know that in your eyes I am committing an unwarrantable impertinence."

"Not at all," she replied politely. "You have the right to talk to me for my good. It's impertinence in me not to wish to hear it."

"Betty dear," said I, "will you tell me what was the cause of your estrangement?"

She stiffened. "No one has the right to ask me that."

"A man who loves you very, very dearly," said I, "will claim it. Was the cause Althea Fenimore?"

She looked at me almost in frightened amazement.

"Is that mere guesswork?"

"No, dear," said I quietly.

"I thought no one knew--except one person. I was not even sure that Leonard Boyce was aware that I knew."

Another bow at a venture. "That one person is Gedge."

"You're right. I suppose he has been talking," she said, greatly agitated. "He has been putting it about all over the place. I've been dreading it." Then she sprang to her feet and drew herself up and snapped her fingers in an heroical way. "And if he has said that Althea Fenimore drowned herself for love of Leonard Boyce, what is there in it? After all, what has Leonard Boyce done that he can't be forgiven? Men are men and women are women. We've tried for tens of thousands of years to lay down hard and fast lines for the sexes to walk upon, and we've failed miserably. Suppose Leonard Boyce did make love to Althea Fenimore--trifle with her affections, in the old-fashioned phrase. What then? I'm greatly to blame. It has only lately been brought home to me. Instead of staying here while we were engaged, I would have my last fling as an emancipated young woman in London. He consoled himself with Althea. When she found he meant nothing, she threw herself into the canal. It was dreadful. It was tragic. He went away and broke with me. I didn't discover the reason till months afterwards. She drowned herself for love of him, it's true. But what was his share in it that he can't be forgiven for? Millions of men have been forgiven by women for passing loves. Why not he? Why not a tremendous man like him? A man who has paid every penalty for wrong, if wrong there was? Blind!"

She walked about and threw up her hands and halted in front of my chair. "I'll own that until lately I accused him of unforgivable sin--deceiving me and making love to another girl and driving her to suicide. I tore him out of my heart and married Willie. We won't speak of that .... But since he has come back, things seem different. His mother has told me that one day when he was asleep she found he was still wearing his identification disc ... there was an old faded photograph of me on the other side ... it had been there all through the war .... You see," she added, after a pause during which her heaving bosom and quivering lip made her maddeningly lovely, "I don't care a brass button for anything that Gedge may say."

And that was all my clean-souled Betty knew about it! She had no idea of deeper faithlessness; no suspicion of Boyce's presence with Althea on the bank of the canal. She stood pathetic in her half knowledge. My heart ached.

From her pure woman's point of view she had been justified in her denunciation of Boyce. He had left her without a word. A wall of silence came between them. Then she learned the reason. He had trifled with a young girl's affections and out of despair she had drowned herself .... But how had she learned? I had to question her. And it was then that she told me the story of Phyllis and her father to which I have made previous allusion: how Phyllis, as her father's secretary, had opened a letter which had frightened her; how her father's crafty face had frightened her still more; how she had run to Betty for the easing of her heart. And this letter was from Leonard Boyce. "I cannot afford one penny more," so the letter ran, according to Betty's recollection of Phyllis's recollection, "but if you remain loyal to our agreement, you will not regret it. If ever I hear of your coupling my name with that of Miss Fenimore, I'll kill you. I am a man of my word." I think Betty crystallised Phyllis's looser statement. But the exact wording was immaterial. Here was Boyce branding himself with complicity in the tragedy of Althea, and paying Gedge to keep it dark. Like Sir Anthony, Betty remembered trivial things that assumed grave significance. There was no room for doubt. Catastrophe following on his villainy had kept Boyce away from Wellingsford, had terrified him out of his engagement. And so her heart had grown bitter against him. You may ask why her knowledge of the world had not led her to suspect blacker wrong; for a man does not pay blackmail because he has led a romantic girl into a wrong notion of the extent of his affection. My only answer is that Betty was Betty, clean-hearted and clean-souled like the young Artemis she resembled.

And now she proclaimed that he had expiated his offence. She proclaimed her renewed and passionate interest in the man. I saw that deep down in her heart she had always loved him.

After telling me about Phyllis, she returned to the point where she had broken off. She supposed that Gedge had been talking all over the place.

"I don't think so, dear," said I. "So far as I know he has only spoken, first to Randall Holmes--that was what made him break away from Gedge, whose society he had been cultivating for other reasons than those I imagined (you remember telling me Phyllis's sorrowful little tale last year?)." She nodded. "And secondly to Sir Anthony and myself, a few hours before the Reception."

She clenched her fists and broke out again. "The devil! The incarnate devil! And Sir Anthony?"

"Pretended to treat Gedge's story as a lie, threw into the fire without reading it an incriminating letter--possibly the letter that Phyllis saw, ordered Gedge out of the house and, like a great gentleman, went through the ceremony."

"Does Leonard know?"

"Not that I'm aware of," said I.

"He must be told. It's terrible to have an enemy waiting to stab you in the dark--and you blind to boot. Why haven't you told him?"

Why? Why? Why?

It was so hard to keep to the lower key of her conception of things. I made a little gesture signifying I know not what: that it was not my business, that I was not on sufficient terms of intimacy with Boyce, that it didn't seem important enough .... My helpless shrug suggested, I suppose, all of these excuses. Why hadn't I warned him? Cowardice, I suppose.

"Either you or I must do it," she went on. "You're his friend. He thinks more of you than of any other man in the world. And he's right, dear--" she flashed me a proud glance, sweet and stabbing--"Don't I know it?"

Then suddenly a new idea seemed to pass through her brain. She bent forward and touched the light shawl covering my knees.

"For the last month or two you've known what he has done. It hasn't made any difference in your friendship. You must think with me that the past is past, that he has purged his sins, or whatever you like to call them; that he is a man greatly to be forgiven."

"Yes, dear," said I, with a show of bravery, though I dreaded lest my voice should break, "I think he is a man to be forgiven."

Her logic was remorseless.

With her frank grace she threw herself, in her old attitude, by the side of my chair.

"I'm so glad we have had this talk, Majy darling. It has made everything between us so clear and beautiful. It is always such a grief to me to think you may not understand. I shall always be the little girl that looked upon you as a wonderful hero and divine dispenser of chocolates. Only now the chocolates stand for love and forbearance and sympathy, and all kinds of spiritual goodies."

I passed my hand over her hair. "Silly child!"

"I got it into my head," she continued, "that you were blaming me for--for my reconciliation with Leonard. But, my dear, my dear, what woman's heart wouldn't be turned to water at the sight of him? It makes me so happy that you understand. I can't tell you how happy."

"Are you going to marry him?" I think my voice was steady and kind enough.

"Possibly. Some day. If he asks me."

I still stroked her hair. "I wouldn't let it be too soon," said I.

Her eyes were downcast. "On account of Willie?" she murmured.

"No, dear. I don't dare touch on that side of things."

Again a whisper. "Why, then?"

How could I tell her why without betrayal of Boyce? I had to turn the question playfully. I said, "What should I do without my Betty?"

"Do you really care about me so much?"

I laughed. There are times when one has to laugh--or overwhelm oneself in dishonour.

"Now you see my nature in all its vile egotism," said I, and the statement led to a pretty quarrel.

But after it was over to our joint satisfaction, she had to return to the distressful main theme of our talk. She harked back to Sir Anthony, touched on his splendid behaviour, recalled, with a little dismay, the hitherto unnoted fact that, after the ceremony he had held himself aloof from those that thronged round Boyce. Then, without hint from me, she perceived the significance of the Fenimores' retirement from Wellingsford.

"Leonard's ignorance," she said, "leaves him in a frightful position. More than ever he ought to know."

"He ought, indeed, my dear," said I. "And I will tell him. I ought to have done so before."

I gave my undertaking. I went to bed upbraiding myself for cowardice and re-solved to go to Boyce the next day. Not only Fate, but honour and decency forced me to the detested task.

Alas! Next morning I was nailed to my bed by my abominable malady. The at-tacks had become more frequent of late. Cliffe administered restoratives and for the first time he lost his smile and looked worried. You see until quite lately I had had a very tranquil life, deeply interested in other folks' joys and sorrows, but moved by very few of my own. And now there had swooped down on me this ravening pack of emotions which were tearing me to pieces. I lay for a couple of days tortured by physical pain, humiliation and mental anguish.

On the evening of the second day, Marigold came into the bedroom with a puzzled look on his face.

"Colonel Boyce is here, sir. I told him you were in bed and seeing nobody, but he says he wants to see you on something important. I asked him whether it couldn't wait till to-morrow, and he said that if I would give you a password, Vil-boek's Farm, you'd be sure to see him."

"Quite right, Marigold," said I. "Show him in."

Vilboek's Farm! Fate had driven him to me, instead of me to him. I would see him though it killed me, and get the horrible business over for ever.

Marigold led him in and drew up a chair for him by the bedside. After pulling on the lights and drawing the curtains, for the warm May evening was drawing to a close.

"Anything more, sir, for the present?" he asked.

"Could I have materials for a whisky and soda to hand?" said Boyce.

"Of course," said I.

Marigold departed. Boyce said:

"If you're too ill to stand me, send me away. But if you can stand me, for God's sake let me talk to you."

"Talk as much as you like," said I. "This is only one of my stupid attacks which a man without legs has to put up with."

"But Marigold--"

"Marigold's an old hen," said I.

"Are you sure you're well enough? That's the curse of not being able to see. Tell me frankly."

"I'm quite sure," said I.

I have never been able to get over the curious embarrassment of talking to a man whose eyes I cannot see. The black spectacles seemed to be like a wall behind which the man hid his thoughts. I watched his lips. Once or twice the odd little twitch had appeared at the corners.

Even with his baffling black spectacles he looked a gallant figure of a man. He was precisely dressed in perfectly fitting dinner jacket and neat black tie; well-groomed from the points of his patent leather shoes to his trim crisp brown hair. And beneath this scrupulousness of attire lay the suggestion of great strength.

Marigold brought in the tray with decanter, siphon and glasses, and put them on a table, together with cigars and cigarettes, by his side. After a few deft touches, so as to identify the objects, Boyce smiled and nodded at Marigold.

"Thanks very much, Sergeant," he said.

If there is one thing Marigold loves, it is to be addressed as "Sergeant." "Marigold" might indicate a butler, but "Sergeant" means a sergeant.

"Perhaps I might fetch the Colonel a more comfortable chair, sir," said he.

But Boyce laughed, "No, no!" and Marigold left us.

Boyce's ear listened for the click of the door. Then he turned to me.

"I was rather mean in sending you in that password. But I felt as if I should go mad if I didn't see you. You're the only man living who really knows about me. You're the only human being who can give me a helping hand. It's strange, old man--the halt leading the blind. But so it is. And Vilboek's Farm is the damned essence of the matter. I've come to you to ask you, for the love of God, to tell me what I am to do."

I guessed what had happened. "Betty Connor has told you something that I was to tell you."

"Yes," said he. "This afternoon. And in her splendid way she offered to marry me."

"What did you say?"

"I said that I would give her my answer to-morrow."

"And what will that answer be?"

"It is for you to tell me," said Boyce.

"In order to undertake such a terrible responsibility," said I, "I must know the whole truth concerning Althea Fenimore."

"I've come here to tell it to you," said he.

CHAPTER XXIII

It was to a priest rather than to a man that he made full confession of his grievous sin. He did not attempt to mitigate it or to throw upon another a share of the blame. From that attitude he did not vary a hair's breadth. Mea culpa; mea maxima culpa. That was the burthen of his avowal.

I, knowing the strange mingling in his nature of brutality and sensitiveness, of animal and spiritual, and knowing something of the unstable character of Althea Fenimore, may more justly, I think, than he, sketch out the miserable prologue of the drama. That she was madly, recklessly in love with him there can be no doubt. Nor can there be doubt that unconsciously she fired the passion in him. The deliberate, cold-blooded seducer of his friend's daughter, such as Boyce, in his confession, made himself out to be, is a rare phenomenon. Almost invariably it is the woman who tempts--tempts innocently and unknowingly, without intent to allure, still less with thought of wrong--but tempts all the same by the attraction which she cannot conceal, by the soft promise which she cannot keep out of her eyes.

That was the beginning of it. Betty, whom he loved, and to whom he was engaged, was away from Wellingsford. In those days she was very much the young Diana, walking in search of chaste adventures, quite contented with the love that lay serenely warm in her heart and thinking little of a passionate man's needs-- perhaps starting away from too violent an expression of them--perhaps prohibiting them altogether. The psychology of the pre-war young girl absorbed, even though intellectually and for curiosity's sake, in the feminist movement, is yet to be studied. Betty, then, was away. Althea, beata possidens, made her artless, innocent appeal for victory. Unconsciously she tempted. The man yielded. A touch of the lips in a moment of folly, the man blazed, the woman helpless was consumed. This happened in January, just before Althea's supposed visit to Scotland. Boyce was due at a Country House party near Carlisle. In the first flush of their madness they agreed upon the wretched plan. She took rooms in the town and he visited her there. Whether he or she conceived it, I do not know. If I could judge coldly I should say that it was of feminine inspiration. A man, particularly one of Boyce's temperament, who was eager for the possession of a passionately loved woman, would have carried her off to a little Eden of their own. A calm consideration of the facts leads to the suggestion of a half-hearted acquiescence on the part of an entangled man in the romantic scheme of an inexperienced girl to whom he had suddenly become all in all.

Such is my plea in extenuation of Boyce's conduct (if plea there can be), seeing that he raised not a shadow of one of his own. You may say that my plea is no excuse for his betrayal; that no man, even if he is tempted, can be pardoned for non-control of his passions. But I am asking for no pardon; I am trying to obtain your understanding. Remember what I have told you about Boyce, his great bull-neck, his blood-sodden life-preserver, the physical repulsion I felt when he carried me in his arms. In such men the animal instinct is stronger at times than the trained will. Whether you give him a measure of your sympathy or not, at any rate do not believe that his short-lived liaison with Althea was a matter of deliberate and dastardly seduction. Nor must you think that I am setting down anything in disparagement of a child whom I once loved. Long ago I touched lightly on the anomaly of Althea's character--her mid-Victorian sentimentality and softness, combined with her modern spirit of independence. A fatal anomaly; a perilous balance of qualities. Once the soft sentimentality was warmed into romantic passion, the modern spirit led it recklessly to a modern conclusion.

The liaison was short-lived. The man was remorseful. He loved another woman. Very quickly did the poor girl awaken from her dream.

"I was cruel," said Boyce, fixing me with those awful black spectacles, "I know it. I ought to have married her. But if I had married her, I should have been more cruel. I should have hated her. It would have been an impossible life for both of us. One day I had to tell her so. Not brutally. In a normal state I think I am as kind-hearted and gentle as most men. And I couldn't be brutal, feeling an unutterable cur and craving her forgiveness. But I wanted Betty and I swore that only one thing should keep me from her."

"One thing?" I asked.

"The thing that didn't happen," said he.

And so it seemed that Althea accepted the inevitable. The placid, fatalistic side of her nature asserted itself. Pride, too, helped her instinctive feminine secretiveness. She lived for months in her father's house without giving those that were dear to her any occasion for suspicion. In order to preserve the secrecy Boyce was bound to continue his visits to Wellings Park. Now and then, when they met alone, she upbraided him bitterly. On the whole, however, he concluded that they had agreed to bury an ugly chapter in their lives.

Yes, it was an ugly chapter. From such you cannot get away, bury it, as you will, never so deep.

"And all the time remember," he said, "that I was mad for Betty. The more shy she was, the madder I grew. I could not rest in Wellingsford without her. When she came here, I came. When she went to town, I went to town. She was as elusive as a dream. Finally I pinned her down to a date for our marriage in August. It was the last time I saw her. She went away to stay with friends. That was the beginning of June. She was to be away two months. I knew, if I had clamoured, she would have made it three. It was the shyness of the exquisite bird in her that fascinated me. I could never touch Betty in those days without dreading lest I might soil her feathers. You may laugh at a hulking brute like me saying such things, but that's the way I saw Betty, that's the way I felt towards her. I could no more have taken her into my bear's hug and kissed her roughly than I could have smashed a child down with my fist. And yet--My God, man! how I ached for her!"

Long as I had loved Betty in a fatherly way, deeply as I loved her now, the man's unexpected picture of her was a revelation. You see it was only after her marriage, when she had softened and grown a woman and come so near me that I felt the great comfort of her presence when she was by, the need of it when she was away. How could I have known anything of the elusiveness in her maidenhood before which he knelt so reverently?

That he so knelt is the keynote of the man's soul untainted by the flesh.

It made clear to me the tenderness that lay beneath that which was brutal; the reason of that personal charm which had captivated me against my will; his defencelessness against the Furies.

So far the narrative has reached the latter part of June. He had spent the month with his mother. As Betty had ordained that July should be blank, a month during which the moon should know no changes but only the crescent of Diana should shine supreme in the heavens, he had made his mundane arrangements for his fishing excursion to Norway. On the afternoon of the 23rd he paid a farewell call at Wellings Park. Althea, in the final settlement of their relations, had laid it down as a definite condition that he should maintain his usual social intercourse with the family. A few young people were playing tennis. Tea was served on the lawn near by the court. Althea gave no sign of agitation. She played her game, laughed with her young men, and took casual leave of Boyce, wishing him good sport. He drew her a pace aside and murmured: "God bless you for forgiving me."

She laughed a reply out loud: "Oh, that's all right."

When he told me that, I recalled vividly the picture of her, in my garden, on the last afternoon of her life, eating the strawberries which she had brought me for tea. I remembered the little slangy tone in her voice when she had asked me whether I didn't think life was rather rotten. That was the tone in which she had said to him, "Oh, that's all right."

During the early afternoon on the 25th, she rang him up on the telephone. Chance willed that he should receive the call at first hand. She must see him before he left Wellingsford. She had something of the utmost importance to tell him. A matter of life and death. With one awful thought in his mind, he placed his time at her disposal. For what romantic, desperate or tragic reason she appointed the night meeting at the end of the chestnut avenue where the towing-path turns into regions of desolate quietude, he could not tell. He agreed without argument, dreading the possible lack of privacy in their talk over the wires.

On that afternoon she came to me, as I have told you, with her strawberries and her declaration of the rottenness of life.

They met and walked along the towing-path. It was bright moonlight, but she could not have chosen a lonelier spot, more free from curious eyes or ears. And then took place a scene which it is beyond my power to describe. I can only picture it to myself from Boyce's broken, self-accusing talk. He was going away. She would never see him again until he returned to marry another woman. She was making her last frantic bid for happiness. She wept and sobbed and cajoled and upbraided--You know what women at the end of their tether can do. He strove to pacify her by the old arguments which hitherto she had accepted. Suddenly she cried: "If you don't marry me I am disgraced for ever." And this brought them to a dead halt.

When he came to this point I remembered the diabolical accuracy of Gedge's story.

Boyce said: "There is one usual reason why a man should marry a woman to save her from disgrace. Is that the reason?"

She said "Yes."

The light went out of the man's life.

"In that case," said he, "there can be no question about it. I will marry you. But why didn't you tell me before?"

She said she did not know. She made the faltering excuses of the driven girl. They walked on together and sat on the great bar of the lock gates.

"Till then," said he, "I had never known what it was to have death in my heart. But I swear to God, Meredyth, I played my part like a man. I had done a dastardly thing. There was nothing left for me but to make reparation. In a few moments I tore my life asunder. The girl I had wronged was to be the mother of my child. I accepted the situation. I was as kind to her as I could be. She laid her head on my shoulder and cried, and I put my arm around her. I felt my heart going out to her in remorse and pity and tenderness. A man must be a devil who could feel otherwise.... Our lives were bound up together.... I kissed her and she clung to me. Then we talked for a while--ways and means.... It was time to go back. We rose. And then--Meredyth--this is what she said:

"'You swear to marry me?'

"'I swear it,' said I.

"'In spite of anything?'

"I gave my promise. She put her arms round my neck.

"'What I've told you is not wholly true. But the moral disgrace is there all the time.'

"I took her wrists and disengaged myself and held her and looked at her.

"'What do you mean--not wholly true?' I asked.

"My God! I shall never forget it." He stuck both his elbows on the bed and clutched his hair and turned his black glasses wide of me. "The child crumpled up. She seemed to shrivel like a leaf in the fire. She said:

"'I've tried to lie to you, but I can't. I can't. Pity me and forgive me.'

"I started back from her in a sudden fury. I could not forgive her. Think of the awful revulsion of feeling. Foolishly tricked! I was mad with anger. I walked away and left her. I must have walked ten or fifteen yards. Then I heard a splash in the water. I turned. She was no longer on the bank. I ran up. I heard a cry. I just saw her sinking. AND I COULDN'T MOVE. As God hears me, it is true. I knew I must dive in and rescue her--I had run up with every impulse to do so; BUT I COULD NOT MOVE. I stood shivering with the paralysis of fear. Fear of the deep black water, the steep brick sides of the canal that seemed to stretch away for ever--fear of death, I suppose that was it. I don't know. Fear irresistible, unconquerable, gripped me as it had gripped me before, as it has gripped me since. And she drowned before my eyes while I stood like a stone."

There was an awful pause. He had told me the end of the tragedy so swiftly and in a voice so keyed to the terror of the scene, that I lay horror-stricken, unable to speak. He buried his face in his hands, and between the fleshy part of the palms I saw the muscles of his lips twitch horribly. I remembered, with a shiver, how I had first seen them twitch, in his mother's house, when he had made his strange, almost passionate apology for fear. And he had all but described this very incident: the reckless, hare-brained devil standing on the bank of a river and letting a wounded comrade drown. I remember how he had defined it: "the sudden thing that hits a man's heart and makes him stand stock-still like a living corpse--unable to move a muscle--all his will-power out of gear--just as a motor is out of gear.... It is as much of a fit as epilepsy."

The span of stillness was unbearable. The watch on the little table by my bedside ticked maddeningly. Marigold put his head in at the door, apparently to warn me that it was getting late. I waved him imperiously away. Boyce did not notice his entrance. Presently he raised his head.

"I don't know how long I stood there. But I know that when I moved she was long since past help. Suddenly there was a sharp crashing noise on the road below. I looked round and saw no one. But it gave me a shock--and I ran. I ran like a madman. And I thought as I ran that, if I were discovered, I should be hanged for murder. For who would believe my story? Who would believe it now?"

"I believe it, Boyce," I said.

"Yes. You. You know something of the hell my life has been. But who else? He had every motive for the crime, the lawyers would say. They could prove it. But, my God! what motive had I for sending all my gallant fellows to their deaths at Vilboek's Farm? ... The two things are on all fours--and many other things with them.... My one sane thought through the horror of it all was to get home and into the house unobserved. Then I came upon the man Gedge, who had spied on me."

"I know about that," said I, wishing to spare him from saying more than was necessary. "He told Fenimore and me about it."

"What was his version?" he asked in a low tone. "I had better hear it."

When I had told him, he shook his head. "He lied. He was saving his skin. I was not such a fool, mad as I was, as to leave him like that. He had seen us together. He had seen me alone. To-morrow there would be discovery. I offered him a thousand pounds to say nothing. He haggled. Oh! the ghastly business! Eventually I suggested that he should come up to London with me by the first train in the morning and discuss the money. I was dreading lest someone should come along the avenue and see me. He agreed. I think I drank a bottle of whisky that night. It kept me alive. We met in my chambers in London. I had sent my man up the day before to do some odds and ends for me. I made a clear breast of it to Gedge. He believed the worst. I don't blame him. I bought his silence for a thousand a year. I made arrangements for payment through my bankers. I went to Norway. But I went alone. I didn't fish. I put off the two men I was to join. I spent over a month all by myself. I don't think I could tell you a thing about the place. I walked and walked all day until I was exhausted, and got sleep that way. I'm sure I was going mad. I should have gone mad if it hadn't been for the war. I suppose I'm the only Englishman living or dead who whooped and danced with exultation when he heard of it. I think my brain must have been a bit touched, for I laughed and cried and jumped about in a pine-wood with a week old newspaper in my hands. I came home. You know the rest."

Yes, I knew the rest. The woman he had left to drown had been ever before his eyes; the avenging Furies in pursuit. This was the torture in his soul that had led him to many a mad challenge of Death, who always scorned his defiance. Yes, I knew all that he could tell me.

But we went on talking. There were a few points I wanted cleared up. Why should he have kept up a correspondence with Gedge?

"I only wrote one foolish angry letter," he replied.

And I told him how Sir Anthony had thrown it unread into the fire. Gedge's nocturnal waylaying of him in my front garden was another unsuccessful attempt to tighten the screw. Like Randall and myself, he had no fear of Gedge.

Of Sir Anthony he could not speak. He seemed to be crushed by the heroic achievement. It was the only phase of our interview during which, by voice and manner and attitude, he appeared to me like a beaten man. His own bravery at the reception had gone for naught. He was overwhelmed by the hideous insolence of it.

"I shall never get that man's voice out of my ears as long as I live," he said hoarsely.

After a while he added: "I wonder whether there is any rest or purification for me this side of the grave."

I said tentatively, for we had never discussed matters of religion: "If you believe in Christ, you must believe in the promise regarding the sins that be as scarlet."

But he turned it aside. "In the olden days, men like me turned monk and found salvation in fasting and penance. The times in which we live have changed and we with them, my friend. Nos mulamur in illis, as the tag goes."

We went on talking--or rather he talked and I listened. Now and again he would help himself to a drink or a cigarette, and I marvelled at the clear assurance with which he performed the various little operations. I, lying in bed, lost all sense of pain, almost of personality. My little ailments, my little selfish love of Betty, my little humdrum life itself dwindled insignificant before the tragic intensity of this strange, curse-ridden being.

And all the tune we had not spoken of Betty--except the Betty of long ago. It was I, finally, who gave him the lead.

"And Betty?" said I.

He held out his hand in a gesture that was almost piteous.

"I could tear her from my life. I had no alternative. In the tearing I hurt her cruelly. To know it was not the least of the burning hell I lit for myself. But I couldn't tear her from my heart. When a brute beast like me does love a woman purely and ideally, it's a desperate business. It means God's Heaven to him, while it means only an earthly paradise to the ordinary man. It clutches hold of the one bit of immortal soul he has left, and nothing in this world can make it let go. That's why I say it's a desperate business."

"Yes, I can understand," said I.

"I schooled myself to the loss of her. It was part of my punishment. But now she has come back into my life. Fate has willed it so. Does it mean that I am forgiven?"

"By whom?" I asked. "By God?"

"By whom else?"

"How dare man," said I, "speak for the Almighty?"

"How is man to know?"

"That's a hard question," said I. "I can only think of answering it by saying that a man knows of God's forgiveness by the measure of the Peace of God in his soul."

"There's none of it in mine, my dear chap, and never will be," said Boyce.

I strove to help him. For what other purpose had he come to me?

"You think then that the sending of Betty is a sign and a promise? Yes. Perhaps it is. What then?"

"I must accept it as such," said he. "If there is a God, He would not give me back the woman I love, only to take her away again. What shall I do?"

"In what way?" I asked.

"She offered to marry me. I am to give her my answer to-morrow. If I were the callous, murdering brute that everyone would have the right to believe I am, I shouldn't have hesitated. If I hadn't been a tortured, damned soul," he cried, bringing his great fist down on the bed, "I shouldn't have come here to ask you what my answer can be. My whole being is infected with horror." He rose and stood over the bed and, with clenched hands, gesticulated to the wall in front of him. "I'm incapable of judging. I only know that I crave her with everything in me. I've got it in my brain that she's my soul's salvation. Is my brain right? I don't know. I come to you--a clean, sweet man who knows everything--I don't think there's a crime on my conscience or a foulness in my nature which I haven't confessed to you. You can judge straight as I can't. What answer shall I give to-morrow?"

Did ever man, in a case of conscience, have a greater responsibility? God forgive me if I solved it wrongly. At any rate, He knows that I was uninfluenced by mean personal considerations. All my life I have tried to have an honourable gentleman and a Christian man. According to my lights I saw only one clear course.

"Sit down, old man," said I. "You're a bit too big for me like that." He felt for his chair, sat down and leaned back. "You've done almost everything," I continued, "that a man can do in expiation of offences. But there is one thing more that you must do in order to find peace. You couldn't find peace if you married Betty and left her in ignorance. You must tell Betty everything--everything that you have told me. Otherwise you would still be hag-ridden. If she learned the horror of the thing afterwards, what would be your position? Acquit your conscience now before God and a splendid woman, and I stake my faith in each that neither will fail you."

After a few minutes, during which the man's face was like a mask, he said:

"That's what I wanted to know. That's what I wanted to be sure of. Do you mind ringing your bell for Marigold to take me away? I've kept you up abominably." He rose and held out his hand and I had to direct him how it could reach mine. When it did, he gripped it firmly.

"It's impossible," said he, "for you to realise what you've done for me to-night. You've made my way absolutely clear to me--for the first time for two years. You're the truest comrade I've ever had, Meredyth. God bless you."

Marigold appeared, answering my summons, and led Boyce away. Presently he returned.

"Do you know what time it is, sir?" he asked serenely.

"No," said I.

"It's half-past one."

He busied himself with my arrangements for the night, and administered what I learned afterwards was a double dose of a sleeping draught which Cliffe had prescribed for special occasions. I just remember surprise at feeling so drowsy after the intense excitement of the evening, and then I fell asleep.

When I awoke in the morning I gathered my wits together and recalled what had taken place. Marigold entered on tiptoe and found me already aroused.

"I'm sorry to tell you, sir," said he, "that an accident happened to Colonel Boyce after he left last night."

"An accident?"

"I suppose so, sir," said Marigold. "That's what his chauffeur says. He got out of the car in order to sit by the side of the canal--by the lock gates. He fell in, sir. He's drowned."

CHAPTER XXIV

It is Christmas morning, 1916, the third Christmas of the war. The tragedy of Boyce's death happened six months ago. Since then I have been very ill. The shock, too great for my silly heart, nearly killed me. By all the rules of the game I ought to have died. But I suppose, like a brother officer long since defunct, also a Major, one Joe Bagstock, I am devilish tough. Cliffe told me this morning that, apart from a direct hit by a 42-centimetre shell, he saw no reason, after what I had gone through, why I should not live for another hundred years. "I wash my hands of you," said he. Which indeed is pleasant hearing.

I don't mind dying a bit, if it is my Maker's pleasure; if it would serve any useful purpose; if it would help my country a myriadth part of a millimetre on towards victory. But if it would not matter to the world any more than the demise of a daddy-long-legs, I prefer to live. In fact, I want to live. I have never wanted to live more in all my life. I want to see this fight out. I want to see the Light that is coming after the Darkness. For, by God! it will come.

And I want to live, too, for personal and private reasons. If I could regard myself merely as a helpless incumbrance, a useless jellyfish, absorbing for my maintenance human effort that should be beneficially exerted elsewhere, I think I should be the first to bid them take me out and bury me. But it is my wonderful privilege to look around and see great and beautiful human souls coming to me for guidance and consolation. Why this should be I do not rightly know. Perhaps my very infirmity has taught me many lessons....

You see, in the years past, my life was not without its lonelinesses. It was so natural for the lusty and joyous to disregard, through mere thoughtlessness, the little weather-beaten cripple in his wheelchair. But when one of these sacrificed an hour's glad life in order to sit by the dull chair in a corner, the cripple did not forget it. He learned in its terrible intensity the meaning of human kindness. And, in his course through the years, or as the years coursed by him, he realised that a pair of gollywog legs was not the worst disability which a human being might suffer. There were gollywog hearts, brains, nerves, temperaments, destinies.

Perhaps, in this way, he came to the knowledge that in every human being lies the spark of immortal beauty, to be fanned into flame by one little rightly directed breath. At any rate, he learned to love his kind.

It is Christmas day. I am as happy as a man has a right to be in these fierce times in England. Love is all around me. I must tell you little by little. Various things have happened during the last six months.

At the inquest on the body of Leonard Boyce, the jury gave a verdict of death by misadventure. The story of the chauffeur, an old soldier servant devoted to Boyce, received implicit belief. He had faithfully carried out his master's orders: to conduct him from the road, across the field, and seat him on the boom of the lock gates, where he wanted to remain alone in order to enjoy the quiet of the night and listen to the lap of the water; to return and fetch him in a quarter of an hour. This he did, dreaming of no danger. When he came back he realised what had happened. His master had got up and fallen into the canal. What had really happened only a few of us knew.

Well, I have told you the man's story. I am not his judge. Whether his act was the supreme amende, the supreme act of courage or the supreme act of cowardice, it is not for me to say. I heard nothing of the matter for many weeks, for they took me off to a nursing home and kept me in the deathly stillness of a sepulchre. When I resumed my life in Wellingsford I found smiling faces to welcome me. My first pub-lic action was to give away Phyllis Gedge in marriage to Randall Holmes--Randall Holmes in the decent kit of an officer and a gentleman. He made this proposition to me on the first evening of my return. "The bride's father," said I, somewhat ironically, "is surely the proper person."

"The bride's father," said he, "is miles away, and, like a wise and hoary villain, is likely to remain there."

This was news. "Gedge has left Wellingsford?" I cried. "How did that come about?"

He stuck his hands on his hips and looked down on me pityingly.

"I'm afraid, sir," said he, "you'll never do adequate justice to my intelligence and my capacity for affairs."

Then he laughed and I guessed what had occurred. My young friend must have paid a stiff price; but Phyllis and peace were worth it; and I have said that Randall is a young man of fortune.

"My dear boy," said I, "if you have exorcised this devil of a father-in-law of yours out of Wellingsford, I'll do any mortal thing you ask."

I was almost ecstatic. For think what it meant to those whom I held dear. The man's evil menace was removed from the midst of us. The man's evil voice was silenced. The tragic secrets of the canal would be kept. I looked up at my young friend. There was a grim humour around the corners of his mouth and in his eyes the quiet masterfulness of those who have looked scornfully at death. I realised that he had reached a splendid manhood. I realised that Gedge had realised it too; woe be to him if he played Randall false. I stuck out my hand.

"Any mortal thing," I repeated.

He regarded me steadily. "Anything? Do you really mean it?"

"You dashed young idiot," I cried, "do you think I'm in the habit of talking through my hat?"

"Well," said he, "will you look after Phyllis when I'm gone?"

"Gone? Gone where? Eternity?"

"No, no! I've only a fortnight's leave. Then I'm off. Wherever they send me. Secret Service. You know. It's no use planking Phyllis in a dug-out of her own"--shades of Oxford and the Albemarle Review!--"she'd die of loneliness. And she'd die of culture in the mater's highbrow establishment. Whereas, if you would take her in--give her a shake-down here--she wouldn't give much trouble--"

He stammered as even the most audacious young warrior must do when making so astounding a proposal. But I bade him not be an ass, but send her along when he had to finish with her; with the result that for some months my pretty little Phyllis has been an inmate of my house. Marigold keeps a sort of non-commissioned parent's eye on her. To him she seems to be still the child whom he fed solicitously but unemotionally with Mrs. Marigold's cakes at tea parties years ago. She gives me a daughter's dainty affection. Thank God for it!

There have been other little changes in Wellingsford. Mrs. Boyce left the town soon after Leonard's death, and lives with her sister in London. I had a letter from her this morning--a brave woman's letter. She has no suspicion of the truth. God still tempereth the wind.... Out of the innocent generosity of her heart she sent me also, as a keepsake, "a little heavy cane, of which Leonard was extraordinarily fond." She will never know that I put it into the fire, and with what strange and solemn thoughts I watched it burn.

It is Christmas Day. Dr. Cliffe, although he has washed his hands of me, tyrannically keeps me indoors of winter nights, so that I cannot, as usual, dine at Wellings Park. To counter the fellow's machinations, however, I have prepared a modest feast to which I have bidden Sir Anthony and Lady Fenimore and my dearest Betty.

As to Betty--

Phyllis comes in radiant, her pretty face pink above an absurd panoply of furs. She has had a long letter from Randall from the Lord knows where. He will be home on leave in the middle of January. In her excitement she drops prayer-books and hymn-books all over me. Then, picking them up, reminds me it is time to go to church. I am an old-fashioned fogey and I go to church on Christmas Day. I hope our admirable and conscientious Vicar won't feel it his duty to tell us to love Germans. I simply can't do it.

New Year's Day, 1917.

I must finish off this jumble of a chronicle.

Before us lies the most eventful year in all the old world's history. Thank God my beloved England is strong, and Great Britain and our great Empire and immortal France. There is exhilaration in the air; a consciousness of high ideals; an unwavering resolution to attain them; a thrilling faith in their ultimate attainment. No one has died or lost sight or limbs in vain. I look around my own little circle. Oswald Fenimore, Willie Connor, Reggie Dacre, Leonard Boyce--how many more could I not add to the list? All those little burial grounds in France--which France, with her exquisite sense of beauty, has assigned as British soil for all time--all those burial grounds, each bearing its modest leaden inscription--some, indeed, heart-rendingly inscribed "Sacred to the memory of six unknown British soldiers killed in action"-- are monuments not to be bedewed with tears of lamentation. From the young lives that have gone there springs imperishable love and strength and wisdom--and the vast determination to use that love and strength and wisdom for the great good of mankind. If there is a God of Battles, guiding, in His inscrutable omniscience, the hosts that fight for the eternal verities--for all that man in his straining towards the Godhead has striven for since the world began--the men who have died will come into their glory, and those who have mourned will share exultant in the victory. From before the beginning of Time Mithra has ever been triumphant and his foot on the throat of Ahriman.

It was in February, 1915, that I began to expand my diary into this narrative,-- nearly two years ago. We have passed through the darkness. The Dawn is breaking. Sursum corda.

I was going to tell you about Betty when Phyllis, with her furs and happiness and hymn-books, interrupted me. I should like to tell you now. But who am I to speak of the mysteries in the soul of a great woman? But I must try. And I can tell you more now than I could on Christmas Day.

Last night she insisted on seeing the New Year in with me. If I had told Mari- gold that I proposed to sit up after midnight, he would have come in at ten o'clock, picked me up with finger and thumb as any Brobdingnagian might have picked up Gulliver, and put me straightway to bed. But Betty made the announcement in her airily imperious way, and Marigold, craven before Betty and Mrs. Marigold, said "Very good, madam," as if Dr. Cliffe and his orders had never existed. At half past ten she packed off the happy and, I must confess, the somewhat sleepy Phyllis, and sat down, in her old attitude by the side of my chair, in front of the fire, and opened her dear heart to me.

I had guessed what her proud soul had suffered during the last six months. One who loved her as I did could see it in her face, in her eyes, in the little hardening of her voice, in odd little betrayals of feverishness in her manner. But the outside world saw nothing. The steel in her nature carried her through. She left no duty unaccomplished. She gave her confidence to no human being. I, to whom she might have come, was carried off to the sepulchre above mentioned. Letters were forbidden. But every day, for all her bleak despair, Betty sent me a box of fresh flowers. They would not tell me it was Betty who sent them; but I knew. My wonderful Betty.

When they took off my cerecloths and sent me back to Wellingsford, Betty was the first to smile her dear welcome. We resumed our old relations. But Betty, treating me as an invalid, forbore to speak of Leonard Boyce. Any approach on my part came up against that iron wall of reserve of which I spoke to you long ago.

But last night she told me all. What she said I cannot repeat. But she had divined the essential secret of the double tragedy of the canal. It had become obvious to her that he had made the final reparation for a wrong far deeper than she had imagined. She was very clear-eyed and clear-souled. During her long companionship with pain and sorrow and death, she had learned many things. She had been purged by the fire of the war of all resentments, jealousies, harsh judgments, and came forth pure gold.... Leonard had been the great love of her life. If you cannot see now why she married Willie Connor, gave him all that her generous heart could give, and after his death was irresistibly drawn back to Boyce, I have written these pages in vain.

A few minutes before midnight Marigold entered with a tray bearing a cake or two, a pint of champagne and a couple of glasses. While he was preparing to uncork the bottle Betty slipped from the room and returned with another glass.

"For Sergeant Marigold," she said.

She opened the French window behind the drawn curtains and listened. It was a still clear night. Presently the clock of the Parish Church struck twelve. She came down to the little table by my side and filled the glasses, and the three of us drank the New Year in. Then Betty kissed me and we both shook hands with Marigold, who stood very stiff and determined and cleared his throat and swallowed something as though he were expected to make a speech. But Betty anticipated him. She put both her hands on his gaunt shoulders and looked up into his ugly face.

"You've just wished me a Happy New Year, Sergeant."

"I have," said he, "and I mean it."

"Then will you let me have great happiness in staying here and helping you to look after the Major?"

He gasped for a moment (as did I) and clutched her arms for an instant in an iron grip.

"Indeed I will, my dear," said he.

Then he stepped back a pace and stood rigid, his one eye staring, his weather-beaten face the colour of beetroot. He was blushing. The beads of perspiration appeared below his awful wig. He stammered out something about "Ma'am" and "Madam." He had never so far forgotten himself in his life.

But Betty sprang forward and gripped his hand.

"It is you who are the dear," she said. "You, the greatest and loyalest friend a man has ever known. And I'll be loyal to you, never fear."

By what process of enchantment she got an emotion-filled Marigold to the door and shut it behind him, I shall never discover. On its slam she laughed--a queer high note. In one swift movement she was by my knees. And she broke into a passion of tears. For me, I was the most mystified man under heaven.

Soon she began to speak, her head bowed.

"I've come to the end of the tether, Majy dear. They've driven me from the hospital--I didn't know how to tell you before--I've been doing all sorts of idiotic things. The doctors say it's a nervous breakdown--I've had rather a bad time--but I thought it contemptible to let one's own wretched little miseries interfere with one's work for the country--so I fought as hard as I could. Indeed I did, Majy dear. But it seems I've been playing the fool without knowing it,--I haven't slept properly for months--and they've sent me away. Oh, they've been all that's kind, of course--I must have at least six months' rest, they say--they talk about nursing homes--I've thought and thought and thought about it until I'm certain. There's only one rest for me, Majy dear." She raised a tear-stained, tense and beautiful face and drew herself up so that one arm leaned on my chair, and the other on my shoulder. "And that is to be with the one human being that is left for me to love--oh, really love--you know what I mean--in the world."

I could only put my hand on her fair young head and say:

"My dear, my dear, you know I love you."

"That is why I'm not afraid to speak. Perfect love casteth out fear--"

I pushed back her hair. "What is it that you want me to do, Betty?" I asked. "My life, such as it is, is at your command."

She looked me full, unflinchingly in the eyes.

"If you would give me the privilege of bearing your name, I should be a proud and happy woman."

We remained there, I don't know how long--she with her hand on my shoulder, I caressing her dear hair. It was a tremendous temptation. To have my beloved Betty in all her exquisite warm loyalty bound to me for the rest of my crippled life. But I found the courage to say:

"My dear, you are young still, with the wonderful future that no one alive can foretell before you, and I am old--"

"You're not fifty."

"Still I am old, I belong to the past--to a sort of affray behind an ant-hill which they called a war. I'm dead, my dear, you are gloriously alive. I'm of the past, as I say. You're of the future. You, my dearest, are the embodiment of the woman of the Great War--" I smiled--"The Woman of the Great War in capital letters. What your destiny is, God knows. But it isn't to be tied to a Prehistoric Man like me."

She rose and stood, with her beautiful bare arms behind her, sweet, magnificent.

"I am a Woman of the Great War. You are quite right. But in a year or so I shall be like other women of the war who have suffered and spent their lives, a woman of the past--not of the future. All sorts of things have been burned up in it." In a quick gesture she stretched out her hands to me. "Oh, can't you understand?"

I cannot set down the rest of the tender argument. If she had loved me less, she could have lived in my house, like Phyllis, without a thought of the conventions. But loving me dearly, she had got it into her feminine head that the sacredness of the marriage tie would crown with dignity and beauty the part she had resolved to play for my happiness.

Well, if I have yielded I pray it may not be set down to me for selfish exploitation of a woman's exhausted hour. When I said something of the sort, she laughed and cried:

"Why, I'm bullying you into it!"

The First of January, 1917--the dawn to me, a broken derelict, of the annus mirabilis. Somehow, foolishly, illogically, I feel that it will be the annus mirabilis for my beloved country.

And come--after all--I am, in spite of my legs, a Man too of the Great War. I have lived in it, and worked in it, and suffered in it--and in it have I won a Great Thing.

So long as one's soul is sound--that is the Great Matter.

Just before we parted last night, I said to Betty:

"The beginning and end of all this business is that you're afraid of Marigold."

She started back indignantly.

"I'm not! I'm not!"

I laughed. "The Lady protests too much," said I.

The clock struck two. Marigold appeared at the door. He approached Betty.

"I think, Madam, we ought to let the Major go to bed."

"I think, Marigold," said Betty serenely, "we ought to be ashamed of ourselves for keeping him up so late."

THE END

The Codes Of Hammurabi And Moses
W. W. Davies

QTY

The discovery of the Hammurabi Code is one of the greatest achievements of archaeology, and is of paramount interest, not only to the student of the Bible, but also to all those interested in ancient history...

Religion   ISBN: *1-59462-338-4*   Pages:132

MSRP $12.95

The Theory of Moral Sentiments
Adam Smith

QTY

This work from 1749. contains original theories of conscience amd moral judgment and it is the foundation for systemof morals.

Philosophy   ISBN: *1-59462-777-0*   Pages:536

MSRP $19.95

Jessica's First Prayer
Hesba Stretton

QTY

In a screened and secluded corner of one of the many railway-bridges which span the streets of London there could be seen a few years ago, from five o'clock every morning until half past eight, a tidily set-out coffee-stall, consisting of a trestle and board, upon which stood two large tin cans, with a small fire of charcoal burning under each so as to keep the coffee boiling during the early hours of the morning when the work-people were thronging into the city on their way to their daily toil...

Pages:84

Childrens   ISBN: *1-59462-373-2*   *MSRP $9.95*

My Life and Work
Henry Ford

QTY

Henry Ford revolutionized the world with his implementation of mass production for the Model T automobile. Gain valuable business insight into his life and work with his own auto-biography... "We have only started on our development of our country we have not as yet, with all our talk of wonderful progress, done more than scratch the surface. The progress has been wonderful enough but..."

Pages:300

Biographies/   ISBN: *1-59462-198-5*   *MSRP $21.95*

www.bookjungle.com *email: sales@bookjungle.com fax: 630-214-0564 mail: Book Jungle PO Box 2226 Champaign, IL 61825*

The Art of Cross-Examination
Francis Wellman

QTY

I presume it is the experience of every author, after his first book is published upon an important subject, to be almost overwhelmed with a wealth of ideas and illustrations which could readily have been included in his book, and which to his own mind, at least, seem to make a second edition inevitable. Such certainly was the case with me; and when the first edition had reached its sixth impression in five months, I rejoiced to learn that it seemed to my publishers that the book had met with a sufficiently favorable reception to justify a second and considerably enlarged edition. ..

Reference   ISBN: *1-59462-647-2*

Pages:412

MSRP $19.95

On the Duty of Civil Disobedience
Henry David Thoreau

QTY

Thoreau wrote his famous essay, On the Duty of Civil Disobedience, as a protest against an unjust but popular war and the immoral but popular institution of slave-owning. He did more than write—he declined to pay his taxes, and was hauled off to gaol in consequence. Who can say how much this refusal of his hastened the end of the war and of slavery ?

Law   ISBN: *1-59462-747-9*

Pages:48

MSRP $7.45

Dream Psychology Psychoanalysis for Beginners
Sigmund Freud

QTY

Sigmund Freud, born Sigismund Schlomo Freud (May 6, 1856 - September 23, 1939), was a Jewish-Austrian neurologist and psychiatrist who co-founded the psychoanalytic school of psychology. Freud is best known for his theories of the unconscious mind, especially involving the mechanism of repression; his redefinition of sexual desire as mobile and directed towards a wide variety of objects; and his therapeutic techniques, especially his understanding of transference in the therapeutic relationship and the presumed value of dreams as sources of insight into unconscious desires.

Psychology   ISBN: *1-59462-905-6*

Pages:196

MSRP $15.45

The Miracle of Right Thought
Orison Swett Marden

QTY

Believe with all of your heart that you will do what you were made to do. When the mind has once formed the habit of holding cheerful, happy, prosperous pictures, it will not be easy to form the opposite habit. It does not matter how improbable or how far away this realization may see, or how dark the prospects may be, if we visualize them as best we can, as vividly as possible, hold tenaciously to them and vigorously struggle to attain them, they will gradually become actualized, realized in the life. But a desire, a longing without endeavor, a yearning abandoned or held indifferently will vanish without realization.

Self Help   ISBN: *1-59462-644-8*

Pages:360

MSRP $25.45

www.bookjungle.com *email: sales@bookjungle.com fax: 630-214-0564 mail: Book Jungle PO Box 2226 Champaign, IL 61825*

QTY

☐ **The Rosicrucian Cosmo-Conception Mystic Christianity** *by Max Heindel* ISBN: *1-59462-188-8* **$38.95**
The Rosicrucian Cosmo-conception is not dogmatic, neither does it appeal to any other authority than the reason of the student. It is: not controversial, but is: sent forth in the, hope that it may help to clear... *New Age/Religion Pages 646*

☐ **Abandonment To Divine Providence** *by Jean-Pierre de Caussade* ISBN: *1-59462-228-0* **$25.95**
"The Rev. Jean Pierre de Caussade was one of the most remarkable spiritual writers of the Society of Jesus in France in the 18th Century. His death took place at Toulouse in 1751. His works have gone through many editions and have been republished... *Inspirational/Religion Pages 400*

☐ **Mental Chemistry** *by Charles Haanel* ISBN: *1-59462-192-6* **$23.95**
Mental Chemistry allows the change of material conditions by combining and appropriately utilizing the power of the mind. Much like applied chemistry creates something new and unique out of careful combinations of chemicals the mastery of mental chemistry... *New Age Pages 354*

☐ **The Letters of Robert Browning and Elizabeth Barret Barrett 1845-1846 vol II** ISBN: *1-59462-193-4* **$35.95**
by Robert Browning and Elizabeth Barrett *Biographies Pages 596*

☐ **Gleanings In Genesis (volume I)** *by Arthur W. Pink* ISBN: *1-59462-130-6* **$27.45**
Appropriately has Genesis been termed "the seed plot of the Bible" for in it we have, in germ form, almost all of the great doctrines which are afterwards fully developed in the books of Scripture which follow... *Religion/Inspirational Pages 420*

☐ **The Master Key** *by L. W. de Laurence* ISBN: *1-59462-001-6* **$30.95**
In no branch of human knowledge has there been a more lively increase of the spirit of research during the past few years than in the study of Psychology, Concentration and Mental Discipline. The requests for authentic lessons in Thought Control, Mental Discipline and... *New Age/Business Pages 422*

☐ **The Lesser Key Of Solomon Goetia** *by L. W. de Laurence* ISBN: *1-59462-092-X* **$9.95**
This translation of the first book of the "Lernegton" which is now for the first time made accessible to students of Talismanic Magic was done, after careful collation and edition, from numerous Ancient Manuscripts in Hebrew, Latin, and French... *New Age/Occult Pages 92*

☐ **Rubaiyat Of Omar Khayyam** *by Edward Fitzgerald* ISBN:*1-59462-332-5* **$13.95**
Edward Fitzgerald, whom the world has already learned, in spite of his own efforts to remain within the shadow of anonymity, to look upon as one of the rarest poets of the century, was born at Bredfield, in Suffolk, on the 31st of March, 1809. He was the third son of John Purcell... *Music Pages 172*

☐ **Ancient Law** *by Henry Maine* ISBN: *1-59462-128-4* **$29.95**
The chief object of the following pages is to indicate some of the earliest ideas of mankind, as they are reflected in Ancient Law, and to point out the relation of those ideas to modern thought. *Religiom/History Pages 452*

☐ **Far-Away Stories** *by William J. Locke* ISBN: *1-59462-129-2* **$19.45**
"Good wine needs no bush, but a collection of mixed vintages does. And this book is just such a collection. Some of the stories I do not want to remain buried for ever in the museum files of dead magazine-numbers an author's not unpardonable vanity..." *Fiction Pages 272*

☐ **Life of David Crockett** *by David Crockett* ISBN: *1-59462-250-7* **$27.45**
"Colonel David Crockett was one of the most remarkable men of the times in which he lived. Born in humble life, but gifted with a strong will, an indomitable courage, and unremitting perseverance... *Biographies/New Age Pages 424*

☐ **Lip-Reading** *by Edward Nitchie* ISBN: *1-59462-206-X* **$25.95**
Edward B. Nitchie, founder of the New York School for the Hard of Hearing, now the Nitchie School of Lip-Reading, Inc, wrote "LIP-READING Principles and Practice". The development and perfecting of this meritorious work on lip-reading was an undertaking... *How-to Pages 400*

☐ **A Handbook of Suggestive Therapeutics, Applied Hypnotism, Psychic Science** ISBN: *1-59462-214-0* **$24.95**
by Henry Munro *Health/New Age/Health/Self-help Pages 376*

☐ **A Doll's House: and Two Other Plays** *by Henrik Ibsen* ISBN: *1-59462-112-8* **$19.95**
Henrik Ibsen created this classic when in revolutionary 1848 Rome. Introducing some striking concepts in playwriting for the realist genre, this play has been studied the world over. *Fiction/Classics/Plays 308*

☐ **The Light of Asia** *by sir Edwin Arnold* ISBN: *1-59462-204-3* **$13.95**
In this poetic masterpiece, Edwin Arnold describes the life and teachings of Buddha. The man who was to become known as Buddha to the world was born as Prince Gautama of India but he rejected the worldly riches and abandoned the reigns of power when... *Religion/History/Biographies Pages 170*

☐ **The Complete Works of Guy de Maupassant** *by Guy de Maupassant* ISBN: *1-59462-157-8* **$16.95**
"For days and days, nights and nights, I had dreamed of that first kiss which was to consecrate our engagement, and I knew not on what spot I should put my lips..." *Fiction/Classics Pages 240*

☐ **The Art of Cross-Examination** *by Francis L. Wellman* ISBN: *1-59462-309-0* **$26.95**
Written by a renowned trial lawyer, Wellman imparts his experience and uses case studies to explain how to use psychology to extract desired information through questioning. *How-to/Science/Reference Pages 408*

☐ **Answered or Unanswered?** *by Louisa Vaughan* ISBN: *1-59462-248-5* **$10.95**
Miracles of Faith in China *Religion Pages 112*

☐ **The Edinburgh Lectures on Mental Science (1909)** *by Thomas* ISBN: *1-59462-008-3* **$11.95**
This book contains the substance of a course of lectures recently given by the writer in the Queen Street Hall, Edinburgh. Its purpose is to indicate the Natural Principles governing the relation between Mental Action and Material Conditions... *New Age/Psychology Pages 148*

☐ **Ayesha** *by H. Rider Haggard* ISBN: *1-59462-301-5* **$24.95**
Verily and indeed it is the unexpected that happens! Probably if there was one person upon the earth from whom the Editor of this, and of a certain previous history, did not expect to hear again... *Classics Pages 380*

☐ **Ayala's Angel** *by Anthony Trollope* ISBN: *1-59462-352-X* **$29.95**
The two girls were both pretty, but Lucy who was twenty-one who supposed to be simple and comparatively unattractive, whereas Ayala was credited, as her Bombwhat romantic name might show, with poetic charm and a taste for romance. Ayala when her father died was nineteen... *Fiction Pages 484*

☐ **The American Commonwealth** *by James Bryce* ISBN: *1-59462-286-8* **$34.45**
An interpretation of American democratic political theory. It examines political mechanics and society from the perspective of Scotsman James Bryce *Politics Pages 572*

☐ **Stories of the Pilgrims** *by Margaret P. Pumphrey* ISBN: *1-59462-116-0* **$17.95**
This book explores pilgrims religious oppression in England as well as their escape to Holland and eventual crossing to America on the Mayflower, and their early days in New England... *History Pages 268*

www.bookjungle.com *email: sales@bookjungle.com fax: 630-214-0564 mail: Book Jungle PO Box 2226 Champaign, IL 61825*

QTY

The Fasting Cure *by Sinclair Upton*
ISBN: *1-59462-222-1* **$13.95**

In the Cosmopolitan Magazine for May, 1910, and in the Contemporary Review (London) for April, 1910, I published an article dealing with my experiences in fasting. I have written a great many magazine articles, but never one which attracted so much attention... New Age/Self Help/Health Pages 164

Hebrew Astrology *by Sepharial*
ISBN: *1-59462-308-2* **$13.45**

In these days of advanced thinking it is a matter of common observation that we have left many of the old landmarks behind and that we are now pressing forward to greater heights and to a wider horizon than that which represented the mind-content of our progenitors... Astrology Pages 144

Thought Vibration or The Law of Attraction in the Thought World
ISBN: *1-59462-127-6* **$12.95**

by William Walker Atkinson
Psychology/Religion Pages 144

Optimism *by Helen Keller*
ISBN: *1-59462-108-X* **$15.95**

Helen Keller was blind, deaf, and mute since 19 months old, yet famously learned how to overcome these handicaps, communicate with the world, and spread her lectures promoting optimism. An inspiring read for everyone... Biographies/Inspirational Pages 84

Sara Crewe *by Frances Burnett*
ISBN: *1-59462-360-0* **$9.45**

In the first place, Miss Minchin lived in London. Her home was a large, dull, tall one, in a large, dull square, where all the houses were alike, and all the sparrows were alike, and where all the door-knockers made the same heavy sound... Childrens/Classic Pages 88

The Autobiography of Benjamin Franklin *by Benjamin Franklin*
ISBN: *1-59462-135-7* **$24.95**

The Autobiography of Benjamin Franklin has probably been more extensively read than any other American historical work, and no other book of its kind has had such ups and downs of fortune. Franklin lived for many years in England, where he was agent... Biographies/History Pages 332

Name	
Email	
Telephone	
Address	
City, State ZIP	

☐ **Credit Card**   ☐ **Check / Money Order**

Credit Card Number	
Expiration Date	
Signature	

Please Mail to: Book Jungle
PO Box 2226
Champaign, IL 61825
or Fax to: 630-214-0564

ORDERING INFORMATION

web: *www.bookjungle.com*
email: *sales@bookjungle.com*
fax: *630-214-0564*
mail: *Book Jungle PO Box 2226 Champaign, IL 61825*
or PayPal *to sales@bookjungle.com*

Please contact us for bulk discounts

DIRECT-ORDER TERMS

**20% Discount if You Order
Two or More Books**
Free Domestic Shipping!
Accepted: Master Card, Visa,
Discover, American Express

www.ingramcontent.com/pod-product-compliance
Lightning Source LLC
Chambersburg PA
CBHW080012040726
47505CB00016B/2219